Far from Bliss

Other Books by Lexi Blake

ROMANTIC SUSPENSE

Masters and Mercenaries
The Dom Who Loved Me
The Men With The Golden Cuffs
A Dom is Forever
On Her Master's Secret Service
Sanctum: A Masters and Mercenaries Novella
Love and Let Die
Unconditional: A Masters and Mercenaries Novella
Dungeon Royale
Dungeon Games: A Masters and Mercenaries Novella
A View to a Thrill
Cherished: A Masters and Mercenaries Novella
You Only Love Twice
Luscious: Masters and Mercenaries~Topped
Adored: A Masters and Mercenaries Novella
Master No
Just One Taste: Masters and Mercenaries~Topped 2
From Sanctum with Love
Devoted: A Masters and Mercenaries Novella
Dominance Never Dies
Submission is Not Enough
Master Bits and Mercenary Bites~The Secret Recipes of Topped
Perfectly Paired: Masters and Mercenaries~Topped 3
For His Eyes Only
Arranged: A Masters and Mercenaries Novella
Love Another Day
At Your Service: Masters and Mercenaries~Topped 4
Master Bits and Mercenary Bites~Girls Night
Nobody Does It Better
Close Cover
Protected: A Masters and Mercenaries Novella
Enchanted: A Masters and Mercenaries Novella
Charmed: A Masters and Mercenaries Novella
Taggart Family Values
Treasured: A Masters and Mercenaries Novella
Delighted: A Masters and Mercenaries Novella, Coming June 7, 2022

Smoke and Sin
At the Pleasure of the President

URBAN FANTASY

Thieves
Steal the Light
Steal the Day
Steal the Moon
Steal the Sun
Steal the Night
Ripper
Addict
Sleeper
Outcast
Stealing Summer
The Rebel Queen

LEXI BLAKE WRITING AS SOPHIE OAK

Texas Sirens
Small Town Siren
Siren in the City
Siren Enslaved
Siren Beloved
Siren in Waiting
Siren in Bloom
Siren Unleashed
Siren Reborn

Nights in Bliss, Colorado
Three to Ride
Two to Love
One to Keep
Lost in Bliss
Found in Bliss
Pure Bliss
Chasing Bliss
Once Upon a Time in Bliss
Back in Bliss
Sirens in Bliss

Happily Ever After in Bliss
Far from Bliss
Unexpected Bliss, Coming 2022

A Faery Story
Bound
Beast
Beauty

Standalone
Away From Me
Snowed In

Far from Bliss

Nights in Bliss, Colorado Book 12

Lexi Blake
writing as
Sophie Oak

Far from Bliss
Nights in Bliss, Colorado Book 12

Published by DLZ Entertainment LLC

Copyright 2021 DLZ Entertainment LLC
Edited by Chloe Vale
ISBN: 978-1-942297-63-5

Sign up for Lexi Blake's newsletter
and be entered to win a $25 gift certificate
to the bookseller of your choice.

Join us for news, fun, and exclusive content
including free Thieves short stories.

There's a new contest every month!

Go to www.LexiBlake.net to subscribe

Acknowledgments

I'm so happy to be back in Bliss. *Far from Bliss* marks the first real original Bliss novel since 2013. Yes, *Happily Ever After in Bliss* came out last year, but it was the continuation of a well-established couple. Lucy, Ty, and Michael are my first new love to bloom in Bliss, and my heart is full to be able to continue stories set in this small town of mine. I've often thought that Texas Sirens' small towns hold all my fears of what living in a small town might mean. But Bliss…oh, Bliss is my small-town heaven. Bliss is a place where no one judges, where everyone is welcome, where we can all find and be our true selves. It is not without pain or heartache. I've learned in the last several years that loss does not have to define us. It is in how we deal with loss, how we absorb the pain and allow it to make us kinder, more thoughtful humans that forms the core of who we are. One thing makes it easier—not to feel the pain, but to work through it—and that is family. Friends. Those we love and who love us back, who open their hearts and share their lives with us often make the difference when heartbreak seems too much to handle. That is what each character finds in Bliss, what I hope each of you finds in your lives.

   To those who loved
   To those who lost
   To those who find the strength to love again
   I wish you Bliss

Prologue

Bliss, CO

Michael Novack woke at the sound of the gun going off. Even through the murky fog that had overtaken his brain, he knew that sound.

Something had gone horribly wrong.

Where the hell was he? Why was it so hard to think?

There was another gunshot and then shouting. Fear sparked through him, wrestling with the confusion that came from the dull pounding in his head.

He forced himself to sit up, his muscles moving like he was trapped in thick mud.

He was in Colorado. He was a US marshal on a job to protect an important witness. Alexei Markov. The information was all there in his brain. If he concentrated enough, he could get it.

Alexei was former Russian mob. He was testifying against some of his syndicate's American partners. Including a couple of dirty politicians.

He had to get to Alexei, had to do his job. He'd been eating dinner and having a beer with Jessie.

Jessie. God, where was Jessie?

Jessie was his partner. Jessie was his lover. If someone had slipped him a roofie, had they done the same to Jessie?

A vague image of Jessie handing him the beer crossed through his brain even as he looked around the tiny room they'd been sharing at the Movie Motel. Jessie had been his partner for years. She'd become his everything. His friend. His lover. One day she was going to be his wife, though she kept putting it off. She wasn't the girliest of girls. She wasn't the one who sat around and planned a big, gorgeous wedding. He would have to tempt her with Vegas and beers.

Yes. She'd been the one to hand him the beer.

Pain flashed through him, and he realized he'd hit his knees and was on the floor. Why wouldn't his legs work right?

A scream sounded out but he couldn't do anything to stop it. His muscles were useless things, and his eyes weren't working right either. He thought he was calling out Jessie's name but he couldn't be sure. Where was Jessie? She was smaller than him. If she'd gotten the same dose…

Jessie had given him the beer. He could see her standing there popping the top off and smiling at him.

Hadn't he known something had been off the last few months? Hadn't he worried something was wrong with the woman he loved?

Darkness took him, and when he opened his eyes again, an eerie blue and red light pulsed through the room in a thin line. He'd shut the heavy curtains earlier but there was a small gap. No. Jessie had done that. He liked watching the movie while they ate. It was a quirky place they were staying at, but he enjoyed it. Jessie hadn't wanted to watch the Doris Day movie playing on the big screen this evening. She'd promised him something far more R rated than the film.

She'd shut him off from the outside world and then handed him that beer. Why couldn't he remember anything else?

He groaned as he pushed off from the floor. He had to talk to her, had to find out what had gone wrong. There had to be an explanation. Maybe he was mistaken about the whole thing.

"Jessie." Her name cracked from his lips.

He forced himself to move for the door. The lights. He knew those lights. Those lights meant trouble.

Those lights meant he hadn't done his job.

His head was starting to clear. What was he thinking? Jessie wouldn't have drugged him. That was a ridiculous thought, and it came from all of his fucking insecurities. She wasn't in the room therefore she was out there. Out there doing the job.

He glanced over and the shoulder holster she'd placed on the dresser earlier was gone. Panic started to thrum through him. How long had he been out? He'd heard screams and gunshots and then he'd passed out again.

He moved for the door, not even considering grabbing his own weapon. He wasn't in his right head. He could just as likely shoot Jessie or Alexei as save them with the damn thing at this point. Besides, those lights told him the worst was probably over.

He stumbled and managed to get the door open and walked into his nightmare.

Four hours later he sat in the Bliss County Sheriff's Office. He'd been through an exam by the very doctor who'd nearly been murdered by Jessie and then taken here to the station house to give his statement. Oh, they'd offered to do all of this in the morning, but Michael wanted to get it over with.

Nate Wright was talking but Michael barely understood what the sheriff was saying.

"According to Holly, Jessie told her she was being paid one hundred thousand dollars by a man named DiStefano to facilitate things for the professional he hired to kill Markov."

Jessie was dead. He'd seen her body himself. He'd known it was her the minute he'd seen the body bag. He'd known she'd done all the things his lizard brain had accused her of. She'd drugged his drink. She'd popped the top off and then turned, ostensibly grabbing the rest of their dinner. But it would have been easy to slip a little pill in there while her back was to him.

Nate stopped, obviously waiting for some kind of a reply.

He didn't have one.

"Michael, I have to ask…" Nate seemed determined to tiptoe around the real subject.

Michael simply waited. He wanted to hear Sheriff Wright say it.

Needed to hear the words so they could sink in.

"Michael, did you know your partner was working for DiStefano?"

Yes, there it was. There was the question every single person he knew, had ever known, would ever know, would ask. The question that would sum up the rest of his fucking life.

"If I did, then I'm as much a criminal as she was. If I didn't, then I'm not much of a marshal."

Nate's head shook. "That's not true."

But it was. "And she wasn't merely my partner. She was my fiancée. I was planning to marry her. I thought I was in love with her. We spent most nights together, so I should have known."

"She told Holly and Caleb that you didn't know, but I had to ask the question."

"Of course." He felt like he was outside his body. Like he was saying words but they didn't make sense because he was standing back and unable to feel anything. Shock. This was what shock felt like.

He'd seen it before. He'd seen it on the faces of survivors. It was the same expression on the faces of people who couldn't believe someone they loved had done something criminal.

He'd known something was wrong with Jessie.

Or was he fooling himself again.

"Mike, you do understand that this wasn't your fault, right?" Nate asked the question in a soothing tone, like the man was used to dealing with powder kegs and didn't want the one sitting in front of him to go off.

What Nate didn't understand was that he had nothing left. When he'd seen Jessie's body, he'd howled his pain. He'd felt his body overcome with a wave of grief, and he'd let it all out.

Now he was numb. Blissfully so, in a way. It was good to stand outside of himself and feel nothing, to look at things logically.

He couldn't go back home. He didn't have anything to go home to. Jessie's family had become his, and he couldn't think about seeing them again. Not now. Oh, he would have to at some point. There would be a million questions he would have to answer, but he couldn't go back to that house where he'd been the dumbass who let a criminal lead him around by the dick.

Half the shit in their house she'd picked out because she'd told him he had no taste at all. He'd been happy to let her do it. He'd given over so much of his life to her, and now he couldn't go back to it. He'd been at his job for six years, and that was down the tubes.

"Hey, do you need a place to stay for the night?" Nate asked.

"Do you need anything else from me or can I go?" He wasn't about to take charity from anyone, much less a man who could only look at him with pity.

That was what would happen if he went back to Florida. His teammates would look at him with pity. Or suspicion.

Nate studied him for a moment. "You're going to be a hard one, aren't you?"

He wasn't sure what Nate meant. "Not at all. I'm willing to comply with any investigation you or the marshals require. If I'm found to be negligent, I'm willing to deal with those consequences. I allowed myself to be used to harm the person I was supposed to protect. I failed at my primary job."

Nate pointed his way. "Yes, that's the key word there. Used. You didn't participate."

Oh, but he had. He'd participated as often as she'd asked him. He'd given her cover even though he hadn't realized he was doing it. "I should have known. I should have seen that something was going on. I certainly shouldn't have trusted her."

"You asked the woman to marry you," Nate pointed out with a sigh. "Of course you trusted her. You loved her."

That was his crime. He should have known what she was doing. He shouldn't have trusted her in the first place. He'd known she wasn't nice and often wasn't kind, but he'd thought he was different. He'd thought he could smooth out her rough edges, thought he could change her.

He was a moron, and he'd almost cost Alexei Markov, Holly Lang, and Caleb Burke their lives.

Michael stood. "Well, that will teach me, won't it, Sheriff. I'll be around town if you need me."

"You're staying? I thought you would go back to your office."

"I don't think that's a good idea. They might not fire me, but they won't be able to trust me again. And I damn sure won't trust myself." He would find a place to stay around here. He had some

17

money. Not a ton, but some. He could hide away and figure out what to do with the rest of his life.

"Hey, maybe we should call a friend," Nate offered.

"Don't have any." He'd given them all up because Jessie had been jealous.

He was alone and it was no one's fault but his own.

Chapter One

Two years later

"So Alexei told me I should hang out even if I'm done because you don't like being alone." Sylvan Dean leaned against the doorjamb, his dark hair slightly curly and the tiniest bit too long. "Is that because you're a cautious lass or is there a story behind it? I ask because this is a weird town and you've lived here for a while."

Lucy Carson picked up the pink grapefruit scented cleaner she used on the tables. Trio was Bliss's tavern, and she'd worked there for a while now. The whole time she'd been a waitress here, she'd worked with either Alexei Markov or Zane Hollister. Van had recently hired on as a part-time bartender, and he was already a favorite with the ladies. He seemed like a genuinely nice guy and took all the crazy Bliss stuff in stride. "You don't have to stay. I can close up. I've got keys and everything."

Sometimes she also had an escort. The past few weeks Michael Novack had hung out until closing time and escorted her to her car. He was quiet and awkward at first, and he deeply confused her since he'd never made a single move on her, but she'd liked the fact that he made sure she got to her car all right.

Now she wondered if someone had asked him to.

Van moved his lean body, allowing her to walk out of the supply closet. "No way. First of all, I wouldn't leave anyone to close by themselves. Not at this time of night. I was just wondering. I've heard weird rumors and I'm not sure if they're true or all crazy or a mix of both. See, the whole wolf pack on the prowl thing sounds like it might be true. The pack of rabid possums seems like a stretch."

She had to stop and turn his way. "Who told you that one?"

"The lady at the Trading Post. The kind of mean one."

Ah. Marie was hard at work trying to scare off anyone she considered a tourist. "Possums rarely get rabies. They have a lower base body temperature than other mammals. Marie's screwing with you. And the wolves only come down when they're really hungry, though they will usually run from humans. Do you have a pet?"

"No. I was raised in a family where all animals should be free." Van followed her into the dining room. "Seriously. My parents were beyond hippies. When ants got into our RV, we were told to learn to live in harmony with them. My oldest brother went into the Army and they disowned him. Sometimes I think I should have followed him there."

"They disowned him?" That seemed extreme.

Van shrugged. "They kind of freaked out. I'm pretty sure they thought they could convince him not to do it. Big brother is stubborn. Mom and Dad are eccentric, but they realized they made a mistake. It took them years to correct it. You should have seen my parents pull up in my brother's bougie neighborhood in that ratty RV. It was funny. So why did you ask about a pet?"

"If you don't have a pet, then you're probably safe." Lucy started in on the tables and was happy to see Van pick up a dish towel and help. "The wolves will eat your dog or cat if they're hungry enough. The good news is Maurice will only try to steal your candy bars."

His lips kicked up in a grin. "Ah, yes. I've been told to watch out for the moose and for aliens."

"Then you've met Mel." Mel Hughes was a legend around Bliss. He was known for his whiskey making and more importantly, as a fount of information about the various ways aliens were threatening to take over Earth.

"So you're just cautious," he concluded.

That wasn't the whole story. "I would say nervous due to a prior encounter with a man who tried to use me as bait to get revenge on his ex-wife."

Van stopped, his brows rising. "Revenge? Like he wanted to make her jealous?"

"Like he was a cult leader who got angry that his underaged bride had managed to get away and he wanted to kidnap or kill her. Maybe both. I don't know. I didn't ask him which it was. His reasoning didn't matter when I helped my friend Hope kill him," she explained in a practical way she likely wouldn't have been able to had she not spent some time in therapy. "I know he's gone, but I still get nervous at night. Alexei and Zane are nice men who treat me like a little sister."

Van stared at her for a moment. "Wow. I've heard a lot of crazy stuff happens here, but like I said I didn't quite believe it. Do they really have an *I Shot a Son of a Bitch* club?"

"Oh, yes. They're serious about actually shooting your personal son of a bitch. I'm an ancillary member because I took mine out with a chair." She'd been in Bliss long enough to have developed a slightly mean sense of humor. "I'm always looking to move up."

Van grinned. "I've been isolated at the resort. I thought it was crazy up there with the occasional BDSM party. This place is way cooler."

At least he was open to the experience. She cleaned off a booth and glanced out the windows. Trio was located in Bliss's downtown area, as the mayor liked to call it. Of course the downtown area consisted of three blocks of one road, though they'd recently put in a second light. She was fairly certain that Nate Wright had talked the town council into it because he wanted a new desk. "It has its advantages. Do you like the resort?"

"I do." Van started wiping down the laminated menus. "It's well run, and the owner is pretty cool. Some of the guests are total assholes, but they're mostly the ones who stay in the villas. The hotel guests tend to be okay. I actually prefer it when Mr. Roberts has his private parties. I thought it was weird at first, but those kink people are nice and polite and don't act like massive asses when you mistakenly give them a lime instead of a lemon in their drink."

The Elk Creek Lodge was just outside of Bliss proper. It was a ski resort and housed a good portion of the tourists who poured into the area for skiing during the winter. Van worked there as a bartender in addition to his duties at Trio. "Is it really bad?"

Van stopped and stared for a moment. "Ah, now I know who they offered the job."

Lucy looked around as though worried someone might overhear. She didn't want to hurt Zane's feelings. He'd given her a job when no one else would. "It's nothing more than a test drive. I'm coming in for the party this weekend. No one knows I might take the supervisor position, and you have to keep that quiet."

"My lips are sealed," Van promised. "And I should be good at keeping secrets. My brother is pretty much a spy. Well, he was at one point. Now he mostly complains about the unholy amount of poop his kids can make. He's the reason I have the job out at the resort. He knows the owner and when I needed a job, he came through. I was kind of hoping he'd bring me on at his company, but I suppose we haven't been close in a long time."

She heard a note of wistfulness in his tone. "Are you close to any of your family?"

"I wouldn't say close, but I also don't have ill will for any of them," he replied, paying close attention to every menu. "My parents are 'live in the moment' kind of people. They ramble through life. I wanted some roots."

"And your siblings? Do you have more than your brother?" She was also interested in how other families worked. It was probably because her own had been so deeply dysfunctional.

"I have a bunch of siblings. Most are like my mom and dad. They travel a lot, take odd jobs. I wanted something different. I'm not actually close to my brother, but he's a good guy and when I needed help, he was there for me. The only person I'm close to is Hale. He's pretty much my brother."

And he was also the reason why Sylvan might fit in perfectly here in Bliss because she'd been told they liked to share. "I've got friends like that. River and Ty. We grew up together."

"I've heard you talk about River. She's been gone for a while?" Van seemed perfectly happy to steer talk away from his family.

The mere thought of River Lee returning home brought a smile to her face. "Yes, she's been on the…" She'd been about to say on the run, but she didn't know how much River wanted the world to know about what had happened to her and her husband. "She's been in Europe with her husband for a little over a year. Long honeymoon."

"Wow, that's sounds spectacular." Van settled the menus onto the hostess stand. "Although I'm going to admit I drifted a lot of my childhood. I like staying in one place, and I like the resort. I was worried we would be stuffed into dorms, but on-site staff has apartments. It's probably the nicest place I've ever lived in."

"What does Hale do?" She was curious about the latest duo in town. Mostly they'd stayed at the resort, but apparently Van and Alexei had been in a couple of classes together at the community college, and the big Russian had coaxed him down the mountain to help out until they found a permanent extra bartender.

"He's the handyman. He can fix anything. Cars, plumbing, heaters. He can do it all, and I can fix him a martini afterward," Van said with a grin. "Now tell me about Ty because I do know him and I don't think he considers himself your brother."

Ty worked at the resort during the tourist season. He was a certified EMT and was used to providing backup to the nurse on site. During the summers when he wasn't on call with Bliss's only ambulance, he guided nature tours with River's company. He'd been her friend since that first day their moms had put them on a bus to kindergarten. It had been the three of them. River and Ty and Lucy. They'd stuck together because they'd always been those weird kids. "Cousin, then. The three of us all grew up together. Technically we're from Creede, which is north of here, but we didn't live in town. We were all on larger tracts of land. Well, River and Ty were. My dad inherited his dad's whole two acres, and we lived there in a couple of trailers. River's house was nicer. Ty's was the nicest though because Ty's mom loved to cook, and she never thought twice about feeding the grubby kids who came home with her son."

"That's cool, but you have to know that dude is totally into you."

Everyone got confused by that. She and Ty hung out a lot, but there had never been anything between them. Oh, there had been that time in high school that she'd asked him out and made a complete idiot of herself because she'd thought it was a date and he hadn't liked her that way. But he'd been super nice about it. He'd gone away to college, and she'd found a boyfriend. That had been a truly heartbreaking relationship, and Ty and River had helped her through it. "Like I said, we were childhood friends, and now we've been around each other so long, we can't imagine life without the other. That's why we're so happy to have River coming home. It was a rough year. I worried about her."

Van's raised brows told her he didn't buy what she was selling. "Okay. Maybe I'm reading that all wrong. I'm still getting the lay of the land down here in town. So is it the crazy mountain guy you're into?"

"He's not crazy." She hated it when people said Michael was crazy.

"He lives in a cabin without indoor plumbing and he's got the cra...uhm, he has a strange look to his eyes that can make one think he's perhaps attempting to intimidate those around him." Van proved he could be tactful. Sort of.

Michael didn't have crazy eyes. He had perfectly lovely eyes, and the fact that they'd seen some pain didn't mean they were a reflection of insanity. "He's been through a lot. I'm not sure how much you know, but it's a long story."

"His fiancée tried to kill the person they were supposed to protect. She drugged him and Holly Lang shot her in the parking lot of the Movie Motel," Van surmised.

Okay, maybe it wasn't such a long story. "Yes, and that traumatized him."

"I could be really fucking traumatized and still want a functional toilet."

She frowned his way. She wasn't about to let the man know she actually agreed with him. Michael had seemingly gotten something from living in that ramshackle cabin on the mountain. "He's getting better. Earlier this year, he did that job taking care of Nell and he didn't even shoot anyone."

Van held up his hands, obviously ceding the fight. "I'm sure that means he's all healed and ready to date."

Lucy sighed. "No. He's not. At least he's not ready to date me. A while back he spent time with me at the Fall Festival and I asked him if he wanted to go to the town hall meeting with me and he said no."

"You asked the man on a date to the town hall meeting?" Van asked.

"Oh, yes. It's actually a very popular date night activity here in Bliss," Lucy explained. "He would have had fun if he'd gone with me. That particular town hall featured a debate between Nell and Mel on who is more at fault for climate change—humans or aliens. It included Nell's interpretive dance and Mel's PowerPoint presentation on alien mating seasons coinciding with increased methane production."

Van grinned. "Oh, I will definitely be attending the next one. So you couldn't tempt that guy to go?"

She'd wanted to shut herself away after he'd turned her down. "No. He doesn't do a lot of town activities. He's shown up a couple of times here at Trio."

"I heard Zane talking about how he's been here most nights when you work but he doesn't drink much. He eats dinner and waits until close and then walks you to your car."

Yes, he was very good at playing the big brother, too. She seemed to find a lot of those. It was her lot in life to always end up in the friend zone. "It's habit. For a while there Henry Flanders was worried some bad guys from his past might come to town, and Nate instituted the 'no one walks alone' code. He claims it's in the town charter, but we all know that the town charter was written on a napkin from Stella's back in the sixties and Hiram used it to blow his nose in the eighties. It was a bad cold, so he tossed it out. Now Nate and Rafe seem to think they can make stuff up."

Rafe Kincaid was the mayor of Bliss. He'd taken over after Hiram Jones had passed. When Henry had trouble, the whole town had come together to protect their own. It was one of the reasons she loved living here. People cared about each other.

There was a knock on the windowpane. In the low light she could see Ty standing outside, his coat zipped up to his neck. He was heartbreakingly gorgeous, with golden blond hair and baby blue eyes that always made her breath catch. He waved at her.

"So he's like a cousin who comes by after work to make sure you get home all right?" Van watched as she made her way across the dining room.

"Hush," she admonished his way. "You should be happy he's here. It means you can get back to the resort before it gets too late." It was a weeknight, so Trio closed up at eleven. If Van hustled, he could make it back before midnight. She unlocked the deadbolt and a blast of chilly air hit her. "Hey, Ty."

He gave her the sweetest smile as he walked in. "Hey. I happened to be in the neighborhood, and I thought I'd come by and give you a ride. Did you not get my text?"

She closed the door behind him and turned with a grimace because she was about to get a lecture. She locked the door again. "I forgot my phone. It's on the charger back at my place."

"Hey, Ty. You don't have to wait. I can totally give her a ride," Van offered. "I know you're busy."

"Nah." Ty shook his head. "I can do it. We need to talk about what we're going to do when River and Jazz get back into town. I was thinking surprise party."

Lucy frowned his way. "His name is Jax, and he is her husband."

Ty's lips curled up. "Yeah, but it's fun to tease her. He doesn't even remember his real name, so I figure I'm not really teasing him."

He was terrible. Lucy gave him the stink eye and let her voice go low. "We'll see how you feel when some crazy doctor lady erases your memory."

Jax had an interesting history and one Ty shouldn't make fun of.

"Well, my life would be easier if she erased yours. Then we could start all over again," Ty said under his breath. "The first thing I would do is train you not to leave your phone at home."

Yep. Terrible. "I've got to mop and check the back rooms. If you want to talk, you can do it while I work."

"I'll mop the front," Van offered. "You handle the back rooms."

He was a nice guy. Cleaning wasn't his job. He was supposed to close up the bar and then he was done for the night. "Are you sure? I can get it."

He shook his head and started for the kitchen. "I can help. The cook had to run because of a family emergency, so I know you already finished his close-out duties. Besides, if I can get in good with the new head of hospitality, I'll do it."

He winked her way and she wished she could get Michael out of her head long enough to think seriously about Van Dean. He was a cutie, and he came with a hot best friend who could fix her sink and liked to share. He seemed like he might be interested in her.

Of course she'd thought Michael might want to date her, too. It proved she had terrible instincts about men. She needed to go on a sabbatical from desire. Or simply embrace the idea that she could have an amazing relationship with a vibrator.

She started to make her way toward the back rooms, rounding around the bar. "And I don't need a ride. My car worked fine today."

"You mean it started up earlier." Ty was right behind her. "I know that rattrap. It has a mind of its own, and it's lazy as the day is long. Did you get the battery changed?"

"No. I don't have the cash right now." She needed to head this off at the pass. "And before you grill me about where it all went, the girls needed winter coats, and you know my dad isn't going to pay for that. He told them to suck it up for another year or wear the old ones. I do not have Dolly Parton's momma's skills, so I can't make them a coat of many colors. I had to make due with Walmart, but Walmart wanted money so I dipped into my savings."

Ty groaned. "You don't have savings because you send it all to your sisters."

She turned. "What am I supposed to do, Ty? I'm the oldest. My brothers send back everything they can to me and I buy things for the girls. If I send it to my dad…"

"He'll buy whatever will get him the highest," Ty finished.

"The girls have two years of high school left," she explained. She'd thought a lot about this. Her sisters were fraternal twins and the last of her siblings. Her dad wasn't known for being responsible, but at least his girlfriend the last several years hadn't gotten pregnant and didn't hurt the girls. Mandy wasn't the nicest of women, but she made sure the girls had dinner at night and got to school on time.

"And then you'll worry about how to pay for college." Ty's jaw clenched. "You didn't get to go to college, Luce."

She wasn't sure what his point was. "So they shouldn't go either?" She stopped because she wasn't sure why they were having this fight. "Look, hopefully this job at the resort works out. It's a supervisor role and a lot more money."

"And you can live on property," Ty pointed out.

She wasn't sure about that. Ty lived on property. He had one of the single units that housed part of the resort's staff. Though calling it a single unit didn't mean only Ty was there. She'd heard he had lots of visitors. Women. Women he slept with. Yeah, she wasn't sure she was ready to see that. It was screwed up because she'd given up on Ty romantically long ago, but she worried it would still hurt to see him with all those women. "We'll see."

"Okay. I'm sorry. I worry about you." Ty unzipped his jacket and set it on the counter next to the deep freeze. "I don't want to fight. I hate fighting with you. Please let me know if your sisters need anything. I want to help. And you know my mom stops by out there. She dropped off a casserole the other day."

Because his mom was one of the wonderful people in the world. "I'll thank her when I see her next. So you want to surprise River and Jax with a welcome home party? I think that might be fun. But I'm not letting you order the cake or you'll spell his name *J-e-x* or *J-u-x*."

"Or *S-u-x*." Ty's grin lit up the room. "I'm joking. I like him. He's a good guy. I'm happy he's coming back and we can get Mountain Adventures up and running again. I missed having a third job. But I was kind of hoping the idea was my main contribution. You know I really would screw up ordering the cake. This is one of those things I was hoping you would run with. I am very good at following your instructions."

She'd been joking about the cake. Ty had many skills. Party planning wasn't one of them. "I can do that. You deal with making a great playlist and helping me make sure the cabin's ready for them when they finally get home."

She'd been staying in River's cabin the whole time River had been gone, making sure everything was maintained properly. It had been a godsend since it happened around the time her old roommate had upped her rent and her sisters had wanted to join the marching band. She'd saved a lot of money by staying at River's. Ty had come over to help with maintenance more than once. He'd helped her make sure the place was ready for winter and often brought by one of his mom's casseroles since he couldn't eat it all by himself. He had no idea how those shared meals often were the only dinner or lunch she had.

Had she sat with him and pretended they were in their own cabin? That would be ridiculous.

Only once or twice.

Ty nodded. "Will do." He glanced back toward the dining room. "Are you sure you should be alone with that guy? What do we know about him?"

He was so careful when it came to her. Sometimes she wondered if he thought she couldn't take care of herself. Of course she'd been the one to go out with the crazy cult leader, so he might have a point. "Van is cool. You haven't worked with him? He's got a job at the lodge, too."

"I don't hang out in the bar much," he admitted. "He's only been around for six weeks. I was surprised Zane hired him. He's usually more careful."

"I think he's got ties to Henry's old friends, and that means he's been thoroughly vetted." Henry's old friends had turned out to be ex-CIA, so they ranked high on the paranoid scale. They also had resources by which to vet people that didn't involve beets, so she thought she could trust them.

"Ah, that makes sense."

Lucy opened the storeroom and took out the checklist. It wouldn't take long for her to close since Van was mopping down the dining room. She had to make sure everything was ready for lunch tomorrow and then she could be on her way.

God, she hoped her car worked.

"So he can give me a ride if I need one." It looked like the cook had already done all tomorrow's prep work. She checked off the list and signed it. "If he chooses to murder me, you'll know who to look for."

"Don't fucking joke about that."

The hoarse quality of his voice made her stop and step out of the pantry. "Joke about murders in Bliss? I thought we were supposed to do that to throw the tourists off."

His shoulders were straight, a serious look in his eyes. "Stop it. I still think about it."

She put down the clipboard and walked up to him, putting her hands on those tight shoulders. "I'm sorry. I'm okay. He's dead, and the saddest part was that he was really after Hope. I mean if I'm going to get murdered, I want it to be about me. I don't want to be the side character who dies so the heroine finds the will to fight."

"You're still joking about it."

"Well, it's been two years and I've had some therapy. Maybe we should get you some." She turned again, getting back to work. "You

29

don't have to stop by to make sure I can get home. I'm a big girl now. If something happens to my car, I can always call someone."

"Me. You can call me." His voice had softened. "Unless you only want to call Michael now."

Sometimes he sounded like a jealous little boy. It was left over from their childhood, and she simply rolled her eyes at this point. "I didn't call Michael in the first place. He showed up. I think Nate talked to him after Henry got back and everyone was still worried someone would rush into town guns ablazing and looking for revenge."

"I don't think so. I think Michael knows exactly what he's doing. That's why I want to talk to you." He took a long breath as though he was steeling himself for something. "Are you interested in him?"

The last thing she needed was a lecture on how bad some other man would be for her. "I don't see how that's your business, Ty. You know I don't ask about your girlfriends."

"I don't have girlfriends and you know it."

She huffed. "Okay, I'll be clearer. I don't talk to you about your one-night stands."

"Yes, you do. Do you know the amount of times you've lectured me on venereal diseases? Because I do. It's fifty-nine. Fifty-nine times since I got back from Virginia six years ago. That's once every thirty-seven days, Luce. And that doesn't include all the jokes about it. These are verifiable lectures."

He'd done the math? "What makes it verifiable?"

"I count it as a lecture if it lasts more than four minutes. Otherwise it's just a dig."

Damn. She hadn't realized how often she'd talked to him about his sex life. "I wasn't trying to hurt you, Ty. I was joking."

"Maybe the first couple of times, but after the thousandth or so a man has to think. I know I'm the joke of this town."

He was missing the point. He was considered a stud. "You're not. I don't think you being able to get sex whenever you like is exactly something people feel pity for you about."

"Oh, you'd be surprised," he said with an unamused laugh. "We live in a place filled with happy relationships. I assure you they think my life is sad."

She didn't understand what he was complaining about. She was the one with the pitiable reputation. She was the one who couldn't find a date. "Because you can get any woman you want?"

His head shook. "Because I can't get the only one I do want. Because the only one I want thinks I'm some kind of manwhore who she wouldn't even consider looking at in a different light. Because the woman I want doesn't think I'm pure enough."

She felt her eyes widen because she'd never heard Ty so passionate. How stupid was this woman? Was she up at the lodge? "Holy shit. Who is she? What is she thinking? You're not good enough? I would like to punch her in the face."

He stared at her for a moment, a tension in his body she couldn't quite describe. She only knew it was like the air around him had changed, been charged with some unnamed emotion.

"Luce, it's you. I'm talking about you."

It was her turn to stop. She couldn't have heard that right. "What?"

A stubborn gleam hit his eyes. "I love you. I've always loved you. It's time for us to stop fucking around and get down to business."

He moved in and then his arms were drawing her in, head swooping down.

Yeah, not how she'd thought she would end her day.

* * * *

He knew it was a mistake, but he couldn't stop himself. He'd come here to talk to her, to gently start opening the subject of why they should consider moving their friendship into a more romantic place.

Romance. He hated that word. He didn't understand the word. His parents hadn't been overly demonstrative people. They were practical. His dad once bought his mom a vacuum cleaner for their anniversary, and she'd cried tears of joy because she'd wanted it so badly. Of course, she'd bought him a new tool kit, so no romance there either.

Sometimes he wished it had been River he'd fallen for all those years ago. River was the kind of woman who told it like it was and appreciated practicality. Lucy needed a softer hand.

Soft. She was so fucking soft. He kissed her, half expecting her

31

to shove him away and laugh in his face. Instead, her hands went to his waist and she sighed, a sexy sound that made his dick jump.

How long had he waited for this? He hadn't been ready in high school, hadn't been willing to take the chance that they wouldn't work out in a long-distance relationship, hadn't been willing to potentially lose her. He'd been so dumb, and if he could go back he would kick his high school ass and they would have had all these years together and he wouldn't have this aching regret inside him.

He shoved the thoughts away. All that mattered was the fact that she was in his arms now. She was responding to him, and that was the important thing. The past didn't matter. The future was bright as long as he had Lucy.

He dragged her closer, feeling the way her breasts crushed against his chest. She fit perfectly in his arms, the way he'd always known she would. He locked her against him with one hand and found her hair with the other. She always kept it up when she was working, tying it back with a scrunchy which he pushed away, freeing all that soft, glorious hair. He dreamed about it at night, about getting caught in it and waking up with it tickling his skin, reminding him he wasn't alone.

Lucy. Luce. His friend. His love. His everything.

She pulled away. Well, as much as he would let her, she pulled away. "Ty."

He shook his head. "No. Don't talk. That was my mistake. We don't need to talk."

He kissed her again, and this time her mouth opened, allowing his tongue to slide against hers. Pure desire raced through his veins. All he had to do was push her back against the wall and he'd press himself against her and find the relief he'd needed for years. It didn't matter who he slept with. He found no real comfort in the act because his lovers hadn't been Lucy.

He forced himself to slow down.

He wasn't taking Lucy in the back room of the bar she worked at. Damn it. She wasn't some quick hookup where both parties were only interested in a moment of pleasure. He'd been grateful to them all, but none of those women had been the right one. None of them had been her.

She was Lucy. He wanted so much more from her. She was the

one.

He pulled back. This was precisely why he'd decided to go the slow route. He hadn't meant to push her so hard and fast. "I'm sorry, baby. I meant to make sure you got home okay and maybe come in for a drink. I didn't mean to go this fast. I skipped about five steps."

She was breathless when she stepped away from him, a high flush to her cheeks. "Steps?"

He hadn't meant to mention that either, though maybe she would take him more seriously if she knew how carefully he'd planned things. "Steps to make you see me in a different light, to make you see we're meant to be together."

She smoothed back her hair. "We are together, Ty. We're together all the time."

He needed to make himself plain. He couldn't let her think for a second that he'd gotten horny and she was handy. "Not like that. Together together."

He was slightly offended by the look of horror that washed over her pretty face.

"Don't be ridiculous, Ty." She laughed but it was her nervous laugh, not the full-throated one that he loved to hear. "You don't get together with anyone for more than a night or two."

Yes, at least she understood that much. "No, I don't date. I don't date because I'm in love with you. I've loved you since we were kids. I think I loved you since that day in the fourth grade when you shared your lunch with me because I forgot mine and you made sure I got a little more of the sandwich because you were worried I would be hungry with only half."

It had been a boy's love, but it had been there. That feeling had been something he couldn't stand the thought of losing.

One brow cocked over her eyes. "You loved me then? You should have mentioned it. I mean you've had roughly twenty years to say something. Also, what about everyone else you loved between then and now? It's a lot of people, Ty."

He wanted to tell her the truth, but he couldn't quite make himself tell her what his life had been like before he'd come back home. He might never tell her. "I haven't loved anyone but you. No one else."

"No, you just slept with them."

He felt his fists ball up in pure frustration. Would she even believe him? "We weren't together. When I got back from college, you had a boyfriend. You seemed very serious about him, and so I tried to move on."

"And then I didn't," she replied, her lips a flat line. "I haven't dated in a couple of years. I didn't see you asking me out."

"I asked you out all the time." Was she forgetting how often they were each other's plus one?

"That was two friends hanging out," Lucy countered. "I assure you, I didn't feel like a girlfriend. What is this about, Ty?"

"This is about not wasting more time." This was why he'd had a plan—to avoid a misunderstanding. He needed to calm down because he understood why she might be confused. "Luce, you have to know we belong together. I meant to do this when I got home but you had a boyfriend. Then when you broke up, I wanted to give you a little time. Then my dad got sick and my mom needed me and all the stuff with River went down. I've been stupid. I've let a lot of things get in the way."

"You let a lot of women get in the way," she accused. "Don't use your dad as an excuse. I was there with you all the way. I went to the hospital and helped your mom at home. You didn't look at me because you were having too much fun playing around with any woman who would let you."

"That's not true." At least he hoped it wasn't. He'd had a time in there when sex had been his drug of choice, something that let him forget that he'd made a hash of his life. "I will admit that I was depressed when I got home, and I thought I'd missed my chance with you. I let myself run wild for a while. I got a reputation, but I haven't slept with a single woman since I realized I needed to try again with you. Not one."

Her eyes rolled. "Sure you haven't. And when did you decide this?"

"A year ago."

She snorted. "You haven't slept with a woman in a year? That's not what I heard."

Yes, this was why he wasn't going to tell her that he'd come home from college a virgin. She wouldn't believe him. "I don't care what you've heard. I wouldn't lie to you. You're too important to me."

Her mouth came open slightly, and it was like a lightbulb went off over her head. "A year ago was when Michael came down the mountain and started hanging out here at Trio. A year ago was when the rumors about me and Michael started."

He didn't like the accusation in her tone. He also didn't like that she was right about the timing. "Sometimes a man needs a little kick in the pants."

Her eyes narrowed in pure suspicion. "So you didn't decide you wanted me until he wanted me."

"That isn't true. I always wanted you." A little panic started to thrum through his system because this wasn't going the way he'd hoped it would.

"Not enough to come after me. Not until someone else did. You're a dog with two bones, Ty."

"But I only want one bone. I never really wanted the other one."

She growled, a deeply frustrated sound. "Go away. I'm not doing this with you tonight. The truth of the matter is you have nothing to worry about. Michael Novack doesn't want me. Not that way. He's just a nice guy who looks out for the women around him. He doesn't want me any more than you truly do. I won't be dating him so you can happily go back to your ski bunnies."

"I don't want to go back to ski bunnies." He obviously wasn't any good at talking. He'd been right the first time. Well, the first time he'd planned to talk to her, so he'd been right the second time. He moved into her space, looming over her. She'd responded to him when he'd kissed her. "I want you."

Her eyes had widened, head tilting up. "You want to sleep with me?"

"I want to sleep with you but only after I fuck you so long and so hard you can't think of any other man except me." Going at her soft hadn't worked. Maybe it was time to show her what he'd learned over the years. He might have gotten a terrible reputation, but he'd also learned how to be excellent in bed.

"Don't be silly, Ty." The words were said with a breathless awe even as she frowned up at him.

"It's not silly. Nothing about this is, and I'm going to show you," he vowed. "I'm going to make sure you don't even remember

Michael Novack's name."

"If your kiss can wipe out her memory, we should probably talk to someone about that."

Lucy gasped and pushed against Ty's chest at the sound of that deep voice. "Michael."

Sure enough there was the cranky asshole who'd waltzed in and screwed up his whole life. He wouldn't have fumbled this had it not been for Michael Novack. He would have been able to play it cool and avoided this fiasco.

He wore his normal uniform of a black T-shirt, jeans, and boots that had seen far better days. His dark hair was in need of a cut, but it was easy to see why some women might be attracted to him. He had that broody, fix-me-up vibe women tended to go for.

"Sorry to interrupt," Michael said in a tone that let him know he wasn't sorry at all. "The new guy let me in. I stopped by to see if you needed a ride or a walk to your car. Now I can see that I'm not needed here at all."

"No, you're not." It was time to start staking his real claim. Michael needed to understand that Lucy wasn't without options. He'd been protecting her for a long time, and he didn't need some fly-by-night guy around. Except he knew that wasn't the proper way to describe Michael. He was more like a cautious wolf stalking his prey, and if he ever got his hands on Lucy, Ty was worried he wouldn't let her go. "Luce and I are fine on our own."

"Are you? Because I haven't seen you here every night making sure she's safe." Michael's body straightened, puffing up to show his full height.

"I've called her every day," he countered. "Unlike some people I have to work for a living. I've been on call saving lives."

"Yeah, I heard you had an emergency call with Mel. Was it about aliens?" Michael asked in that deeply sarcastic tone of his.

"Hey, he fell out of a tree and twisted his ankle." Though that wasn't what Mel had said happened. Mel claimed he'd fallen out of an alien light that was trying to pull him up into the spaceship. It had been odd since there hadn't been a ladder around, so he wasn't sure how the old guy had managed to get up in that tree, but that wasn't the point. It had been an actual emergency.

"Both of you stop it." Lucy moved to get in between them.

She was small compared to them. She would be swallowed up if she got in between them.

"I'll stop if that little shit does," Michael vowed.

"Hey, I'm not exactly little." He wasn't taking crap from this guy. "Just because you're a giant doesn't mean I can't take you."

Michael snorted, an inelegant sound. "Sure you can, buddy."

"I mean it. Stop." Lucy put a hand on each of their chests. "Stop right now. You are both acting like children."

Michael's face went a stony blank, and he stepped back. "Sorry. I didn't mean to offend. I can see plainly that you don't need any help."

"I didn't…" Lucy stopped, a frown coming over her face. She backed off, going as cold as Michael had. "No, I don't."

Michael merely tipped his head, turned, and walked out.

Well, at least that was one problem solved. If Michael wanted to be an asshole, he was fine with that. He turned back to Lucy. "I'm sorry about that. Why don't we head to your place and I'll make us something to eat and we can talk about this. I've got a bottle of wine in my truck."

Lucy turned away from him, walking the few steps to where a broom was hanging neatly on the wall. She picked it up and when she faced him again, he knew he was in trouble.

"No, Luce," he began.

"Out. Get out. I can't talk to you right now." She swung the broom his way.

He barely managed to get out of the way. He backed up, finding himself stumbling into the bar again. "Luce, this is ridiculous."

She waved the broom his way again, getting way too close to his head for comfort. "No, what's ridiculous is expecting me to think this play of yours is anything but the actions of a jealous little boy."

"You didn't kiss me like I was a little boy." He had to duck to avoid that one. He moved into the dining room.

"I didn't kiss you at all. You kissed me and you did it so he couldn't have me." She waved the broom toward the door.

That was when he realized Van was standing there, holding the damn thing open, and he had Ty's coat in one big hand.

"And Michael doesn't want me, so the joke's on you." Lucy pressed the broom to his chest, forcing him out the door. "Go away,

Ty. I can take care of myself. I'm a grown-ass woman."

She turned and walked away.

Van gave him a shake of his head and handed him his coat. "Don't worry. I'll make sure she gets home okay."

He slammed the door in his face, the lock clicking into place.

And he was left on the outside looking in.

He should have stuck with the plan. He stared at that locked door and heard a deep chuckle coming from the shadows to his left.

"Guess Lucy knows how to take out the trash," Michael said.

"Why the hell are you still here?" He forced his arms into his coat and zipped up.

He watched as Michael's shadowy figure shrugged. "Her car doesn't work half the time, and I don't know that kid in there enough to trust him to take care of her."

Asshole. Still, it was exactly what a man who cared about a woman would say. He knew he'd been right.

And Lucy was interested in Michael. She didn't take Ty seriously, but he couldn't deny that she'd responded to him sexually.

"I don't think I would like what's going on in that head of yours, would I?" Michael asked.

Lucy wanted Michael. Ty wanted Lucy. But Lucy was only a moth to Michael's cranky, crabby flame, and if she could see how much better Ty could take care of her, she would come around.

What to do about that?

If he was back in Virginia, it would be a quandary.

But he was in Bliss.

"No. I don't think you'll like it at all." It was a plan. A bad plan. A Bliss plan.

Chapter Two

Michael pulled his SUV into the parking lot of Hell on Wheels and thought about not going in. It had been a shitty night, and the better choice would be to go home and drink alone.

But then he might not be able to punch someone, and he really felt like punching someone.

I'm going to make sure you don't even remember Michael Novack's name.

Little shit.

He probably should have let them know he was standing in the doorway. He hated the fact that he'd stood there and listened in and when he'd realized Ty was kissing her, he hadn't walked away. He'd moved closer so he could watch.

He'd been in Bliss too long.

He slammed out of the SUV and his boots were hitting the gravel when he realized someone was pulling up next to him.

Just his fucking luck. There was nearly no one in the parking lot but this asshole decided to park right beside his SUV.

His mood dipped even further as he realized he recognized that Jeep.

"Are you following me?" He might be able to start a fight right here and now. Cracking that pretty boy's face might make him feel better, might make him forget the way Lucy had looked when he'd been such an ass to her.

I can see plainly that you don't need any help.

The words themselves hadn't been particularly nasty, but he'd meant them to hurt. He'd meant to lash out at both of them because they were younger and less fucking damaged and they probably belonged together in their happy Bliss world. He didn't have a place with her, and that was exactly why he'd held back. He wanted her. He burned for her.

He'd been around Nell too much. He was starting to sound like one of her heroines. Nell Flanders wrote books where one character burned for another and longed and wished.

"I thought we should talk." Ty's jaw squared like he was ready to take a coming punch.

When had he become the old man who yelled at kids playing too close to his yard? Lucy wasn't even his yard, and she never would be. He should have taken this evening as another reminder that he was too old for her, too hard for her. He needed a drink or five. He turned toward the worst bar in the county and started for the front door. "Nothing to talk about. Lucy got home all right. The new guy followed her all the way and then waited to make sure she got in the door. You saw that as well as I did."

Because they'd formed a caravan that would have worried most women. Lucy had a line of vehicles following her tiny piece of crap, wouldn't-even-call-that-thing a car. She'd waved the new guy's way and disappeared into River's cabin.

And then he'd driven to the other side of the mountain to drink his cares away, except one of those cares had fucking followed him.

"I know that, but I still need to talk to you," Ty insisted.

He slammed through the red metal door that led inside the den of regret and bad choices known as Hell on Wheels. He was immediately hit with the smell of beer and possible criminal activity. Crime in Colorado, Michael had learned, smelled a little like beer but held unmistakable notes of tobacco and freshly mown grass.

But he wasn't paying attention to that. He didn't care. He wasn't a lawman anymore. He was the dude who sat at a booth because he didn't want to talk to anyone or see anyone or be around anyone unless there was a fight and he was in a fighting mood.

"She's yours. I'll keep my paws off her. You made yourself plain a couple of months ago. Got it." Maybe that would get him the peace he needed.

Ty had shown up shortly before he'd taken the assignment to watch over Nell Flanders while her husband, Henry, had been out of town doing whatever ex-CIA agents did. He was fairly certain being around Nell was where he'd gone wrong. She was optimistic and creative and so positive it sometimes hurt. He'd also liked having a comfy bed and hot showers and food that didn't taste like crap.

For the first time since Jessie had betrayed him, he'd asked how long he would keep punishing himself.

It was Nell's fault he'd started to think that maybe, just maybe, he could hang out with Lucy and see where it went.

"Yeah, well that's not working." Ty followed him in. "I have to admit that my plans thus far have been a bust. So it's time for a new plan."

The jukebox was on, playing "November Rain" by Guns N' Roses, which was odd because that juke usually played southern fried rock or country songs about drinking beer and crying over women and dogs.

Though, granted, "November Rain" kind of fit that latter motif.

Sawyer looked up and nodded his way. Sawyer's family owned the bar. He tended to work the later shifts, so he was the bartender Michael was most familiar with. The place was usually filled with bikers, some casual and some one percenters Michael usually would have watched carefully.

He didn't care now.

Sawyer's eyes widened as he took in Tyler. He crossed his arms over his massive chest and frowned. "Hey, no murders. Not tonight. I'm tired and I don't want to clean up the blood, man."

"Whiskey, and I promise nothing," Michael replied on his way to the booth in the back he thought of as his second home. "You could bounce him, you know."

When he slid onto the side of the booth that let him look out over the whole bar, including the front door, Ty eased in across from him.

Perfect.

"I'm not being bounced," Ty swore. "I only want a couple of minutes of your time. Maybe half an hour."

It was obvious he wasn't getting rid of the kid. "To talk about what?"

Ty's face went mulishly stubborn, like he was about to say something he didn't want to say.

He was saved by Sawyer, who placed a double whiskey in front of Michael. "I'm serious about the murders. It's been a week. Fucking Texas tourists going to kill me. What do you want, Ty?"

Ty looked up at him. "Piña colada."

Sawyer stared. "You're fucking with me, right? Do I look like I have a blender and a bunch of umbrellas behind that bar? Do you think this is girls night?"

"You know you used to be more tolerant. I happen to remember when you used to drink wine coolers, the sweeter the better. Piña coladas are delightful, and I don't care what you think, Sawyer. You liked Cosmopolitans that night in Denver," Ty pointed out.

There was the slightest uptick of Sawyer's lips. "I was trying to get into a woman's panties that night." He sighed and rolled his dark eyes. "I don't have any freaking cream of coconut, Ty. The best I can do is rum and coke, or I might have enough lime for a margarita."

Now he was curious. Sawyer didn't exactly bend for anyone Michael had seen. He was a hardass who might be slightly criminal.

Ty brightened. "Margarita, please. No umbrella. And what's with the hair metal?"

"November Rain" had given way to "Mr. Brownstone."

Sawyer's frown seemed to encompass his whole body. "Some asshole who bought Hiram's old place in town came in. Gorgeous wife, but he didn't like my choice in music. I'm fairly certain he had someone hack my digital juke and now it only plays Guns N' Roses. All day. Every day. I might shoot myself."

He turned and walked away.

"So you know Sawyer." It was the only reason the man hadn't simply told Ty to fuck off.

"We went to high school together." Ty sat back, seemingly more comfortable now that he had a fruity drink on the way. "He's not a bad guy. Just cranky. Kind of like you."

Well, cranky did sum him up. He took a drink of the whiskey and bit back a groan. It was shit whiskey, but then if he wanted the good stuff he should have gone to Trio. Which was closed for the night and might be forever closed to him from now on. "If you don't like the company, the door's that way."

"Do you care about Lucy?" Ty asked.

"That's none of your business." So this was another *stay away from Lucy* talk. "And like I said before, she made herself plain tonight. I won't bother her again."

"You didn't even let her talk," Ty pointed out. "You looked around, decided the world was shit, and walked out. She didn't make herself plain. You didn't give her a chance to make a choice. From what I can tell she didn't know there was a choice to be made at all."

He was confused. "Choice?"

"Between you and me."

"I thought you didn't want her to make a choice. I thought she was yours and you were some caveman asshole who intended to club her over the head and run away with her."

"No, I intended to turn our friendship into something more," Ty explained. "We've always been close. We've always been end game, if you know what I mean."

"So you thought she would wait around while you sowed your wild oats," Michael surmised.

Ty huffed. "No. That's not how it was."

"Oh, I've heard. It was a whole lot of oats. There's rumors that you sowed all the oats of Southern Colorado, and all the tourist oats, too." He liked the way Ty's face had gone slightly pink.

Ty frowned, a stubborn expression. "This is not what I came here to talk about."

Michael stopped baiting him. He wanted to get this over with. "All right, then tell me why you're here so you can go."

Ty looked back like he was waiting for something. Or trying to make sure Sawyer wasn't listening. "I screwed up tonight. I pushed her too hard."

"Give her a couple of days. Take her some flowers. I'm sure you'll be back in her good graces soon." Lucy wouldn't stay alone for long. She was too sweet, and he'd seen how she lit up when Ty came in a room. She relied on Ty. He himself was nothing more than a flirtation. She was sweet, and she thought she could save him.

He was worried she might be right.

"I don't think so."

43

Sawyer was back, putting a glass in front of Ty. "We're closing in an hour. There's a pitcher of this shit behind the bar, and you know where the whiskey is. I've got paperwork to do. Let me know if anyone else comes in."

He stalked away.

So Sawyer trusted Ty. That was interesting.

He glanced around. They were the only ones in the bar. It would have been perfect if only Ty wasn't here. He could quietly drink himself into a stupor. Sawyer had a cot in the back for just such an occasion. It was sad he knew that. Even sadder he'd slept there more than once.

Ty took a sip of his margarita and winced slightly. "He's heavy-handed with the tequila. Anyway, like I was saying, I don't think my plans were going to work no matter how soft I went in, and you're the reason why."

He wasn't sure when he'd become Tyler Davis's relationship sounding board. "I told you, she's all yours."

"But she can't be while she's got a crush on you."

He hated that word. "Crush? That seems like a juvenile word to use."

"She likes you. She's attracted to you. Fascinated. What word do you want me to use? Lucy's always had a thing for strays." Ty winced again. "Damn it. I didn't mean to say that. You're not a stray."

He didn't take offense. He was a practical man, and Ty had merely used a word that correctly described him. "I wouldn't say that. I was part of what I thought was a family and then I wasn't. That's kind of the definition of a stray." He was starting to get tired of being alone. The whiskey wasn't working the way it used to. "I like her, too, but I don't think I'm good for her."

He expected Ty to agree with him, to point his way and nod. "Why?"

Michael decided to be very clear with the other man. "I don't even have a house here. I know I defend that piece of crap I live in, but it doesn't have a toilet. I have an outhouse. I don't have a job. I've been living like this for two years now."

Ty shrugged. "She has all those things. She doesn't need them from you."

Now the kid was being naïve. "She obviously could use some help."

One shoulder shrugged. "And I'll give it to her. Next objection."

What was going on here? "Fine. I'm too old for her."

"She's twenty-seven. You're what? Fifty?"

Michael felt a growl in the back of his throat. He was surprised he could still be offended. He'd thought he'd gotten past all that. "I'm thirty-five, asshole."

If he'd intimidated Ty, the other man didn't show it. "So not exactly a dinosaur. You're eight years older than us."

It was about far more than a number. "I wasn't really talking about age. I was talking about experience. I've seen a lot of crap in my days."

"And she grew up taking care of all her siblings in poverty I would bet you can't truly understand," Ty pointed out. "You aren't living in squalor because you have to. You still own a house in Florida and have a decent-sized savings account. That place you live in isn't the best you can do. It's your choice. It's your prison."

He downed the rest of the whiskey and shoved out of the booth. "Good for you, kid. There's your answer. I'm fucking messed up beyond all repair, and that's why I can't touch the princess."

Ty followed him. It seemed to be the theme of the night. "That's my point. She's not a princess, man. She's a woman who's seen some shit, too. She doesn't need a hero to come in and save her. I'm not saying she doesn't need help every now and then. I hope that once I get her in bed, she'll let me buy her a new car. It won't be easy, but I can manage the payments when Mountain Adventures gets going again."

He couldn't say the kid didn't work hard. He reached for the bottle. It was a blended whiskey he'd never heard of. God, he hoped it wasn't one of Mel's tonics. Still, he poured far too much of it into his glass. "I offered to loan her some money to fix her car."

He'd done it the night of the Fall Festival. He'd helped her pack up the Trio stall and walked her back to that steaming pile of crap she drove. The battery had been dead. He'd given her a jump. She needed a new battery, but she said it would have to wait until next month.

She'd turned him down on the loan offer.

"There's no fixing that car. I think it's cursed," Ty offered as he poured himself another margarita. He grabbed a can of lemon-lime soda and cut the drink with it. "And she's real proud. She doesn't want anyone to think she can't handle things. That comes from being the oldest of five kids in a family that got a lot of visits from child services."

His gut twisted at the thought. It pointed out that he knew very little about Lucy's past. He knew quite a bit about her current life, but she didn't talk about her parents at all. "Her childhood was that bad?"

"Like I said, there wasn't a lot of money. Her dad was in and out of prison and her mom ditched her early on. Her dad kind of collected women who walked out. She had to hold things together or they would have been split up. She still behaves like everyone's looking at her and if she's not strong enough she'll lose everything."

"I didn't know about that." It explained a lot about how Lucy behaved.

"She doesn't talk about it." Ty slapped at the bar as though trying to make a point. "That's why you need me."

"I appreciate the info, but I meant what I said. I'm not good for her. She needs someone… I don't know…shinier. If you stay close to her, I think she'll turn to you eventually." Ty was just about the shiniest person he knew. There was a sunniness to the man that sometimes made Michael want to punch him in the face. It was like the universe loved Tyler Davis and blessed him with warmth.

Michael got the darkness.

He would bet Tyler Davis wouldn't have gotten tricked by a woman. He wouldn't have lost his whole life because he loved the wrong person. No, Ty was going to end up with Lucy, and that made his gut curl with envy. It was time to give serious consideration to the offer he'd recently gotten. At first he'd blown it off, but the thought of watching as Lucy and Ty became a couple made him want to walk away. It might be time to start over again someplace new. If he stayed here in Bliss, he didn't trust himself to not become the villain. The temptation Lucy offered might be too much to turn away. Keeping them apart would be wrong, especially when he knew damn well he couldn't give her what Ty could.

"Or we can go after her together, give her everything she needs, and when you decide to go back to your life, I'll be there to take care of her."

Of all the things he'd thought he might hear this evening, that was the last. "What?"

There was a challenge in Ty's blue eyes as he turned Michael's way. "Tell me you aren't thinking about going back to your old job."

He'd allowed that Ty might know about his place in Florida. A couple of people knew he hadn't sold his house there. But no one knew he'd met his boss in Alamosa last week. Susan Conners had somehow gotten his new number and asked him to join her for lunch. He'd thought about saying no, but he had to admit the thought of breaking up his everyday routine had been too tempting to avoid. The days had become a never-ending cycle. Again he blamed Nell. Until he'd followed her around, he hadn't realized how much he'd missed work. "You have someone following me?"

"No. I just know everyone in Southern Colorado, and some of them I didn't even sleep with," Ty replied with a smirk. "So I know you met with your old supervisor from the US marshals. She wants you to come back, right?"

His former boss had offered him any number of ways to come back. Not all of them involved leaving Colorado. "I'm mulling over my options."

"Then mull this one over, big guy." There was nothing about Ty's manner that told him he was anything but serious. "I'm offering to share Lucy with you until you leave town."

The words went through him like a shot, leaving him damn near speechless. He sat there for a moment and then forced the question out of his mouth. "Why the hell would you do that?"

Ty leaned forward, his voice going low. "Because everyone gets what they need. Lucy gets to satisfy her curiosity about you. You get to have her. I get to keep her. I don't care about the sex. I mean I do care about the sex. I want the sex, but I'm not going to be some jealous asshole who freaks out when my woman even looks at another man."

"She would be doing more than looking." He didn't like the way his whole body had tightened at the hint of a possibility of getting in Lucy's bed. He definitely didn't like the voice that had opened up at Ty's words. The one that told him this was what he'd been waiting for, that he should go for it, that Ty was offering him the best of all worlds.

"My love for Lucy goes beyond the idea that I'm the only man who'll ever touch her. Besides, after we're married there won't be any more sharing," Ty said, that American-hero jaw of his going straight. "She can get you out of her system, and you can do the same with her. You can both move on."

"And if she falls for me?" He knew it wouldn't happen, but he found he couldn't quite hold back the words. Ty was standing there challenging him, and he needed to do the same.

Ty huffed. "She won't."

"What if she does?" Michael pushed him a little more. It was an insane plan, and he wasn't about to do it.

Was he?

"Then I'll be there for her when you leave. You won't take her with you. You know that wouldn't be good for her. Her whole life is here."

"And what if I decide to live my life here?" He was being perverse, but he couldn't stand the fact that Ty was so fucking confident. He'd never intended to stay in Bliss for so long. He'd gotten stuck in a routine, and now he had a potential exit plan.

Ty shrugged that concern off. "It's Bliss. We learn to share."

No one would think twice about them sharing Lucy here in Bliss. They would be accepted, and their kids wouldn't be judged for their parents' lifestyle.

He hadn't just thought about having kids, hadn't considered this insane plan. "Just like that? You know from what I can tell, we don't exactly get along."

"That's because I haven't tried with you. I get along with everyone. I'm a goddamn delight, and you would be lucky to have me for a partner. Hey, is it so terrible an idea to have someone around who can trade off mowing the lawn? Split the chores with? It works for a lot of people," Ty replied.

Michael slammed the rest of his whiskey down and reached for his wallet. He slapped a twenty on the counter. "It won't work for me. My answer is no."

Because it couldn't possibly be yes.

He started for the door.

"Think about it," Ty yelled.

Think about having the only woman he'd wanted in years? Think about the fact that if he fucked up, Ty would be there to take care of Lucy? Think about how he could be warm for a while?

Yeah, he was pretty sure he wouldn't think about anything else.

* * * *

Ty watched the door slam shut and sighed. Nothing was going the way he wanted tonight, but then what should he have expected? Michael was right. They didn't get along. Michael had never taken to his sunny personality. Of course he hadn't exactly tried.

Axl Rose was wailing again.

And then he wasn't. The place went quiet, and he turned to see Sawyer standing there, the plug to the jukebox in his hand. "Fucker hasn't figured out how to hack electricity yet."

Sawyer met some interesting people here at Hell on Wheels. And by interesting Ty meant crazy and often deadly. "You know Cam Briggs has a background with this kind of thing. He could probably fix it for you. I'm sure you miss your daily dose of Skynyrd."

Sawyer snorted and moved to the bar. "Gotta keep the assholes happy, man. If I don't, they tend to try to stab me. Sometimes I wish my granddad had dreamed about opening an ice cream parlor or something." He glanced down at the twenty. "Novack thinks a lot of this whiskey. I can buy two bottles for this. And somehow I don't think the deputy is going to be racing over here to solve my GNR problem."

Sawyer had issues with the Bliss County Sheriff's Department. Hell on Wheels was technically on unincorporated land, but that didn't mean the sheriff didn't care about what happened here. Sawyer and Nate Wright had gotten off on the wrong foot, and Sawyer hadn't done much to fix the problem. The fact that Sawyer had once been in an MC didn't help Nate's opinion. "You know you could tell him why you fell in with the Horde."

At one point Sawyer had prospected for the motorcycle club that called themselves The Colorado Horde. He'd left when he'd done the job he'd needed to do. Sawyer glanced down at his left arm. Once it had been decorated with Horde tats. Now there was nothing but black ink. He often wondered if Sawyer had covered those tats instead of having them removed as a reminder of what he'd had to do.

"I don't like to talk about it, and I don't care what the sheriff thinks," Sawyer said, picking up the whiskey bottle and putting it back on the shelf.

Stubborn man. "Well, then I suppose you get to listen to a whole lot of 'Welcome to the Jungle.' Hey, at least the place won't sound like you pulled up a *Supernatural* playlist. The man brought you into the early nineties."

That got a smirk from Sawyer. "Don't hate on the Winchesters."

It was something few people knew about Sawyer. He was a geek when it came to his entertainment choices. But then Ty had introduced him to sci-fi/fantasy a very long time ago. "Never. And I'll ask around and see if I can get your jukebox back under your own control."

"Thanks, man." Sawyer picked up the pitcher of margaritas and poured himself one. It must be closing time because Sawyer rarely drank, and never on the job. "So I heard a little bit of what you and Novack talked about. You insane?"

He should have known he couldn't hide this from Sawyer. "Aren't you a little big and scary to be hiding in hallways eavesdropping on your friends."

"Friend. I was only listening in on one friend and one dude I haven't made my mind up about yet," Sawyer corrected, taking a sip of the margarita and grimacing. "You should have told me it needed more tequila. And I was eavesdropping precisely because you are my friend. Also, I don't call it eavesdropping. It's called information gathering, and I gathered that you're playing a dangerous game with Novack. Do you honestly think sharing Luce with him is going to work out? I thought we decided you were going to play it slow for a while."

This was why he hadn't particularly wanted Sawyer listening in. "That plan went to hell tonight."

Sawyer frowned. "What happened?"

"I kind of lost it and kissed her."

Sawyer nodded as though considering the problem. "Okay. Well, that was bound to happen. How did she respond?"

She'd melted in his arms. "It was perfect."

Sawyer's face screwed into a disgusted expression. "Ty, dude, can you pretend to be a little more manly? I'm getting a stomachache."

"It's not unmanly to have enjoyed the embrace of the woman I love," he shot back. "Also, I want to point out to this whole damn town that I can't be both some unmanly child in love and an overused manwhore at the same time. Everyone needs to pick their evil when it comes to me."

"Already made my pick. Unmanly child in love. You've been that for damn near twenty years," Sawyer replied. "The manwhore stuff was because you came home and Luce was firmly in my brother's arms. Probably be married to him if he hadn't been a stupid asshole and gotten himself thrown in jail."

Which was precisely why Sawyer had gone into the Horde. He'd gone in to make sure his brother survived jail. "How's Wes doing?"

"He's got a job in Denver. He's good. I'm pretty sure he doesn't like to think about any of us. He wants his fresh start." Though his face remained stoic, there was a softness to the words that let him know Sawyer ached from the loss of his brother.

He had a lot of problems with the way Wes had treated the people who'd loved him. "He never called Luce. She wouldn't have known he was out if you hadn't told her."

"He's got a new woman, one who doesn't know his sad history. I haven't even met her."

"I could punch him for you." After everything Sawyer had done to help his brother, Wes didn't even call him?

"It's water under the bridge. Best to keep moving forward. And it was best that Luce didn't end up with Wes," Sawyer said, brushing his family issues aside. "She's always loved you. I think she took up with Wes because she was sure she couldn't have you. But Novack could be dangerous."

"Why?" He didn't understand the appeal. The man was attractive, but he was dour and grumpy and obviously unhappy. Maybe that was the key—the unhappy part.

"Because I've seen the way she looks at him. She's got it bad," Sawyer explained.

"She doesn't know him. She sees all the crap he went through, and that makes her want to help him. You know how she is. She can't see a person in pain without feeling for them." Unless it was him. She could perfectly well sweep him out when he was hurting.

"It's more than that." Sawyer leaned back against the bar.

They could argue all night, but Ty knew something Sawyer didn't. "It doesn't matter because I happen to know that he's planning on leaving."

"He told you that?"

"Not in so many words, but I know he met with his old boss last week."

"How do you know that?" Sawyer asked.

"Polly's daughter Kelly recently took a job at the Alamosa Chili's." Polly ran Polly's Cut and Curl, Bliss's one and only salon. "You know Polly runs on information. So Kelly listened in while she was serving them some boneless wings. She reported back to her momma, who told Marie that she should get ready to sell that property Michael's living on, and Marie told me because she's got twenty bucks on me in the betting book."

Sawyer's brows rose. "Do they really have a betting book at the Trading Post?"

"Oh, they do. Some of those bets have been going on for years. Let's just say if there is ever real proof that aliens exist, Mel's going to make a shit ton of cash off this town."

"What does that betting book say about Novack?"

He didn't want to think about the bets that Michael would end up with Lucy. "It doesn't matter."

A light hit Sawyer's eyes. "The town thinks she'll end up with him, don't they?"

The town, in this case, was wrong. "Like I said. It doesn't matter because she won't. I know I've been an idiot the last couple of years, but it's time to stop sitting on my ass. It's time to get my girl, and if that means getting nasty with another dude in the room, then that's how it has to be."

"You know all of this is weird, right?"

"I don't know. I've been around it so long it seems normal. Though I have to admit I'm probably not going to mention it to my parents. They don't come into Bliss much." They were closer to Creede, and his parents had friends there so they rarely made it into Bliss.

Sawyer pointed his way. "The fact that you're not telling them means you know this is a bad idea."

"It means I know that it's temporary, and I don't want to worry them." He didn't want a lecture on how he'd screwed up. It would be a nice lecture and would come with cookies, but it would still be a lecture. His mom had always told him he should go after Lucy before it was too late. His dad would shake his head and tell him he'd always known it would end poorly.

"Sure," Sawyer said in that way that told Ty he didn't believe him at all.

"Okay, what do you think I should do?" He was always open to suggestions.

Sawyer seemed to think for a moment. "Tell me why you would share her with Michael."

He wasn't about to tell Sawyer that it had been an impulsive decision. "Because she wants him, and I want her happy."

Sawyer hesitated for a moment. "Even if she picks him in the end?"

The thought made his gut twist, but there was only one answer. "Yeah. Even if she picks him."

"And if she doesn't want to pick? She's been here long enough that she might view this as her right. Not many men tell a Bliss woman she has to choose."

He'd told Michael he wouldn't care, but he wasn't sure he could share her long term. It was blatantly obvious that Michael didn't like him, and despite his previous statements, he wasn't sure he could turn that around.

"I don't know." He'd known Sawyer most of his life. They'd been odd friends over many years, the big, intimidating guy and the one with the constant smile.

"Well, I'm glad at least you're honest with yourself." Sawyer leaned against the bar. "I think it's probably for the best that he said no. Especially if he's leaving anyway. You'll see. River will be home soon, and Luce will go straight to her for advice and she'll back you up. She's always been in your corner. You have to be patient."

"I hope so. I thought this might work." He was still a bit surprised it hadn't. "He seems to care about her. As much as he annoys me, he's a good man."

That questioning brow rose over Sawyer's dark eyes. "How do you know that?"

"He was a US marshal."

"That doesn't make him good. I've known lots of bad cops."

"Not Michael Novack. I've studied his record. I did it because I didn't like the way he was looking at Lucy," Ty admitted. "I talked to Alexei about him. When Alexei came back to Bliss from testifying against his old cohorts, it was Michael who protected him. Alexei thinks the world of him. He says he hasn't always been this way."

"Yeah, I've heard that story," Sawyer said with a long sigh. "I never met the guy Alexei talks about. I've only met the surly bastard who can't stop punishing himself."

"Why would he punish himself?"

Sawyer sent him the special look he always used when he thought Ty was a moron. "Seriously?"

He knew the story. He didn't understand all of it though. "I know his partner betrayed him. Why would he punish himself for that? I don't get it."

"He blames himself. He should have seen what she was doing."

"Not if she was good at her job." He'd thought a lot about this. "I mean when you really think about it, she was a spy. A good spy tricks everyone around her."

"Sometimes I wonder why we're friends, man. All right, I'll try to explain it to you. What if you found out Luce was tricking you all these years and using you?" Sawyer asked.

It was a ridiculous thought. "That would never happen."

"But it happened to him," Sawyer countered. "I assure you he thought that woman loved him. He thought he knew her. He thought he knew what his world was made of, thought he controlled it. And then he woke up and didn't recognize a single thing about it. He discovered not only was he not in control, but he'd been controlled. That is why he punishes himself by living in a rattrap. That awful cabin of his is a prison, and I don't know if he breaks out of it. I don't know if that man has what it takes to do the hardest thing in the world."

He didn't like thinking about Michael in some prison. "What's that?"

"Fucking forgive yourself," Sawyer said in that low growl of his. "That's what you can't understand. You've never done something so bad you can't figure out how to come back from it. For Novack it wasn't something he did, but something he allowed to happen, and he can't trust himself again. That's precisely why I think he's stayed away from Lucy. You're giving him the chance to get close to her without having the responsibility of being the only one to take care of her."

"Yes. That's why it could work."

"Or why it could go wrong, and you could end up being left behind. If he relaxes and lets his guard down, Lucy is going to get inside, and that girl is pure sunshine. She might be able to do what he can't do on his own—get him to forgive himself. Once he does that, he'll want to keep her."

Sawyer could be a pessimist. "Or he could get better and go on with his life. Everyone wins."

Sawyer patted his arm. "And that is why we're friends. Because I cannot even think like that. You know if it all goes to hell, I'll be there for you, right?"

"It doesn't matter. He said no." He would have to think this through. Maybe it was better this way. Maybe he should listen to Sawyer and try to be a little more patient.

The door slammed open and suddenly Sawyer had a massive gun in his hand, pointing it at the entryway.

Michael stood there, and if he was worried a six-and-a-half-foot dude was pointing a gun at him, he didn't show it. He simply frowned Ty's way.

"It won't work, but I'll try."

Had he heard that right? "You're in?"

Michael nodded, grunted, and then turned and walked out.

Ty sat there for a moment. "Should I go after him? Doesn't he think we should talk? Plan a little?"

Sawyer slid the gun back into the holster he wore at the small of his back. He could be touchy, but then at one time he'd had a whole MC after him. "Absolutely not. That man has had enough stimulation for one night. I'm locking the door. Pour us another drink and I'll tell you again how dumb this idea is."

He might be right, but he also might be wrong. Sawyer knew a lot but he didn't know everything, and he often took a pessimistic view of life.

This could work. And hey, if Michael Novack got a new lease on life, then he and Lucy would have done something good and they would remember the man fondly.

"You're not going to listen to a word I say, are you?" Sawyer locked the door this time.

"Of course I am." He would listen. Sort of.

But he knew this could work.

It had to because he worried this might be his very last shot.

Chapter Three

"So are we asking the new chick in? I've heard she's shot more sons of bitches than all of us combined." Callie had a big mug of coffee in front of her.

Lucy sat in Stella's Café the following morning, her brain still working on what had happened the night before. She'd gotten very little sleep and still felt like she was strapped onto an emotional roller coaster. Why had Michael followed her home? She'd known his SUV had been the one behind Van's Subaru. She'd also recognized Ty's Jeep, but she knew why he'd followed her. Habit.

Rachel frowned her friend's way. "Yes, she did that on a professional basis. She didn't shoot her sons of bitches out of self-preservation."

"No, but she did blow up someone who was trying to kill her," Jen pointed out. "At least that's what I heard. I don't know. I like her. She seems fun."

"Then why did your husband tell her husband he couldn't put in a shower?" Hope Glen-Bennet sat to Lucy's left. Stella had shoved three tables together close to the back of the restaurant for this midmorning meeting of the Winter Festival committee.

It was a meeting of some of the most powerful people in Bliss, and like all things that required intricate planning, long hours, and free labor, it was entirely made up of women.

A brilliant smile came over Jennifer Talbot's face. She was married to Stef Talbot, known all around as the King of Bliss. Mostly because he was the richest man in town and had his fingers in all of Bliss's pies, including the fact that he was the town's chief engineer. He'd also been on the committee that declared Hiram Jones's rundown cabin a historical landmark shortly before it sold to a friend of Henry Flanders. The Taggarts were a robust family of five who came up for vacations and loaned out the place to their friends. They were good tippers, and while the husband seemed like a dude who could kill everyone in the world, the wife was super nice.

The scary dude was also attractive. Like stare-at-him hot.

Like Michael. She had a type. Dark. Brooding. Dangerous.

Sweet. Kind. Sunny.

No. That last one was just Ty, and he actually ran against her type. It was only habit to be attracted to Ty. He'd been her first love, and she was over him.

Of course it hadn't felt over the night before. She could still feel Ty's lips on hers, feel him pulling her close. She'd placed her hands on his chest and felt the muscle there. For a moment she hadn't thought of anything but being in his arms.

And then Michael had been there.

"Stef is only fucking with him. He likes how Big Tag gets completely red in the face and then threatens to do all sorts of terrible things like taking his insides out," Jen replied. "Stef thinks it's funny. But he always gives in. The latest renovation was to the bathroom. Hi didn't believe in showers. He always said if he wanted a shower, he would wait for it to rain. So he only had that tiny bathtub. Stef explained that the tub itself was a historical landmark since several baptisms had happened there before the Feed Store Church put in running water."

Marie Warner raised her hand. "I was baptized right in that tub. Taggart wants to take it out he can go through me."

Teeny Warner shook a finger her wife's way. "Absolutely not. I am talking to Stef about that. Charlotte stopped bathing the kids because that tub is rusty, and now when they're in town they stink to high heaven about three days in, and she sends them into the store and they run off all the other customers."

"He's already approved the plans," Jen promised. "They're adding on another bathroom with a shower. Henry's going to oversee the work since they're back in Dallas until Christmas break."

"Well, I don't think we should have members who aren't actual full-time residents," Rachel Harper said. "Though we should absolutely invite her to give a lecture on how to blow up a son of a bitch. We never know when that skill might come in handy."

"I thought we were supposed to be talking about Winter Festival," Callie gently reminded everyone.

Lucy picked up her pen. She was the notetaker. She also might end up being the liaison with the resort. She prayed this weekend went well. She was taking a couple of shifts to see if she fit in. The way Cole Roberts had put it, those shifts should help her decide if she wanted the job. She rather thought it was to decide if Cole wanted her there.

If she got the position at the resort, she wouldn't need to work doubles every day. She could work a single job and have some time for herself. If she lived out at the resort, she would save money.

Of course if she lived out at the resort, she would get to see Ty work his magic on all the gorgeous women who came through for a vacation and spent a night with Ty as a souvenir.

She realized the women had all gone quiet. And they were all staring at her.

"Lucy, honey, I was wondering what you want for breakfast." Stella stood at the head of the table, her notepad in her hands. The owner of Stella's wore a bright yellow western shirt, jeans, and red boots.

She hadn't even looked over the menu, though she didn't need to. Everything on the menu cost cash, and she had very little. "Oh, I ate before I came. I'll just have the coffee."

She could leave behind a couple of dollars for her part of the coffee and the tip. And then she would hope she had a granola bar in her purse because otherwise she would have to wait until her late shift at Trio. Zane had made one meal per shift part of her compensation package when he'd first hired her. Probably because she'd sat in his office during the interview and her stomach had growled so loud the man had noticed.

She blamed Zane Hollister for her hips. She'd been somewhat

skinny before she'd started eating meals that weren't the cheapest ramen she could find.

Of course Ty showed up at least once a week with a casserole dish in his hands. His mom made them for him, and he always shared because there was so much, and he usually ate at the resort anyway.

Her stomach growled at the thought of Ty's mom's cheesy enchilada casserole.

Rachel frowned her way as Stella started for the kitchen to put the order in. "Really? You're not hungry?"

Damn her stomach. "I'm good." She needed a distraction because of all the women at the table, Rachel was the one who would sniff a problem and then bloodhound her way to the root, and she didn't want to talk about how sad her bank account was right now. The good news was she had something that would interest all of them far more than why she hadn't ordered the pancakes with chocolate chips she adored. "Actually, I'm not good. I'm confused, and I need to call on the matriarchal counsel of Bliss."

Every head at the table turned. It was a fancy way of saying *I've got a problem and I want the wisest women in Bliss to help me.*

"Honey, did you get taken?" Cassidy Meyer sat at the end of the table, her steel-colored hair in its normal bun. She was a slender woman on the higher side of sixty. She'd very likely ordered her pancakes with beets. She would have done that because beets, as everyone who had come through Bliss knew, were a preventative against all sorts of alien incursions. This was what she got for living close to what alien hunters called the Alien Highway. "It's mating season for the reptilians, and I know that there are those romance novels about women and their gentle velociraptor lovers, but that's nothing but alien propaganda."

Cassidy and her de facto husband, Mel Hughes, were very invested in the alien fighter community. She was on the board to ensure that the Winter Festival remained strictly for humans.

"Some of those monster romances are quite beautiful. You have to view them as a metaphor. Some of those stories are just a way to say that all beings of goodwill can get along." Nell Flanders was around to ensure the Winter Festival didn't harm the earth. So when she thought about it, Earth and space were both represented here. "It doesn't matter if your genitals are barbed. It's what's in your heart that's important."

Cassidy frowned Nell's way. "Says the woman who has never been penetrated by a barbed penis."

Rachel's eyes were suddenly bright with glee. "Does a piercing count?"

Nell gasped.

This was the other reason she'd agreed to be the group's secretary. There was always good gossip.

Rachel shrugged. "Henry whined about it a lot. Told Rye he might never ride a horse again. Girl, I just said we should all high five you for getting your man to do that."

"How about we get back to the problem at hand?" Hope turned Lucy's way. "What's going on? I'm sorry we haven't talked recently. I've been working on getting the ranch ready for winter, and it's been a lot."

Hope was a sweet woman and they were friends, but Hope had Beth. That was her bestie. They were both out at the Circle G and shared a life that orbited around ranching. Their husbands were partners.

She hoped River got home sooner than she estimated. It hit Lucy hard how much she'd missed her. Phone calls weren't the same as sitting with her closest friend and sharing their troubles and a bottle of cheap wine. She could use River's sound judgment on what to do about Ty.

There was nothing at all to do about Michael. He'd made himself clear. But she still didn't understand.

"Why would a man be nice to you, like really, really nice to you and then not…" She struggled for how to put this in a ladylike fashion. "Not want to spend the time with you that a man would normally get for being so nice to you. I mean, not that anyone owes someone for being nice. That came out wrong."

"I'm sorry." Rachel sat back in her chair, leaning toward Callie. "I don't speak tact. What is she asking?"

"She's asking why Michael Novack acts like he wants to sleep with her and then doesn't sleep with her." Callie totally spoke tact.

"Oh." Rachel turned her way. She was a lovely woman with reddish blonde hair, and she'd recently given birth to her second child, a boy they'd named Ethan Harper. "That's because he's not very smart."

"He's smart," Jen argued. "He's still processing what happened to him."

"Yes, that kind of betrayal can wound a person." Nell took Jen's side. "He needs time to heal."

Rachel rolled her eyes. "He's had two damn years. He needs to pull his big boy shorts up and get right back on the saddle. The saddle, in this case, is Lucy. He needs to ride her until he can't see straight and he'll feel so much better."

"Rachel, that's insensitive," Nell whispered as though no one else could hear her.

"Rachel is pretty much the definition of insensitive," Jen said with a practical air. "She's been around Max far too long. And she's right about how long Michael's been in this awful routine of his."

"I think we should give Michael as much time as he needs," Nell returned. "I've worked with the man recently, and I believe he has a deeply sensitive soul. That sweet soul bears some deep wounds."

"That sweet soul needs to stop growling at everyone or I might have to take him out." Marie was also on Rachel's side.

The table split, half the women supporting the Michael is Wounded theory and the other half backing a Michael Should Start Having Healing Sex agenda. Though Marie merely wanted him to stop growling, and Cassidy mentioned that the Reticulan Greys might be at work and Michael could benefit from taking the beet.

She was definitely not getting the answers she wanted. "So I should give up on him?"

"Absolutely not," Nell advised. "You have to be patient with him. Perhaps you should start by making certain you're looking deeply into his eyes so he knows you see his soul."

"Or he figures out you got some crazy in there and he runs," Rachel replied.

"Some men like a little crazy," Callie countered. "And are we forgetting that Tyler is also in love with Lucy?"

"What?" That was so news to her. It wasn't, but it was. He'd said the same thing the night before, but she'd had no idea that people around town had heard the rumor, too. "We've never been anything but friends. I asked him out in high school, but he turned me down."

"I don't know what he did then, but he eats you up with his eyes now," Callie replied.

"He eats other women up with his mouth." Probably not the most tactful way to put it, but it was true.

"Not lately he hasn't," Hope offered. "At least that's what Gemma says. Ty spends some time with Jesse and Cade, and according to them he hasn't fallen into any vaginas lately and he whines a lot."

He'd said he hadn't slept with anyone in a long time. Could he possibly be telling her the truth? Would it matter if he was? He'd turned her down before and she'd moved on.

Did she want another chance? In a lot of ways she understood why he'd turned her down all those years ago. "Ty's friendship is way too important to risk."

"Well, then you should tell him you aren't interested in him that way." Callie smiled as though those words solved all her problems.

"I did. That's what I told him last night."

Nell reached across the table and patted her hand. "Good. You got it all out and hopefully now you two can move on as friends. Give Michael some time and perhaps the two of you can try dating."

It was probably sound advice.

So why didn't she like it? "Why would Ty suddenly be interested in me?"

"I don't think it's a sudden thing, hon." Teeny sipped her coffee. "You know I did a bit of substitute teaching back in the day, and I remember he was always looking your way when he was a kid. And when the two of you were real young, you would stand outside the store waiting for the school bus and he would reach out and hold your hand."

The bus didn't come far enough out to pick any of them up, so they'd formed a carpool. Ty's mom, River's dad, and Sawyer's granddad would pick them each up and cart them to and from the Trading Post all the school year. Rain or shine they would stand out there waiting for the bus that would take them into Del Norte, and often Teeny would be there with some kind of treat she claimed she'd just baked and oh, wouldn't you kids like some?

There had been days when Teeny's sweets were the only treats she and her siblings would get. Her younger sisters went to a closer school in Creede that had opened up after Lucy had graduated.

She felt tears threaten at the sweetness of the memory. "Yes, I remember how nice it would be to see your face when you would come to school. I never felt like we belonged, but when you were there it was better. But Ty...I think that taking care of me was a habit for him."

"That sounds like a good habit to me," Rachel said. "I wish like hell I could get my men in that habit. Don't get me wrong. They get the job done when it comes to my physical needs, but sometimes a girl wants to wake up to the sound of a vacuum cleaner being used."

"Don't listen to her," Callie said with a shake of her head. "Though she's right about the habit thing. I'm not sure how that's bad. It kind of is the definition of marriage. You take care of each other. Does he still take care of you?"

"Sure," Lucy replied. "His mom sends home food with him almost every weekend. He always shares with me. He's there when I need him."

"But you're not interested in him?" Hope asked. "Not in more than a friendship way?"

"Nah, she's interested, but she's scared because that boy has a bad reputation," Rachel replied. "But Hope's right about the fact that he's slowed way down lately. You believe Gemma's men?"

Hope nodded. "They said they haven't seen him with a ski bunny in forever. I think he figured out that Michael liked Lucy and decided to get his head out of his butt and secure his girl."

"But Michael doesn't want me so if he's trying to one up Michael, then he's going to be disappointed, and then where would we be?" It was the conundrum that had gone through her head all night long. If this was really about making sure the other man didn't have her, how long could they last even if she was willing to take the shot? How long would it be before Ty missed his freedom?

"What if they got together and decided to play nice and share you?" Cassidy asked.

"I would say they'd gone insane," Lucy shot back. Those two didn't like each other. "They're complete opposites."

Cassidy had been hitting the beet juice a little too often.

The doors to the kitchen swung open and Stella swept in, her niece Shannon walking behind her. Both women balanced plates on their arms as they started doling out the breakfast orders.

Lucy's stomach growled but she ignored it. She had notes to take, after all.

"Here you go, hon. Chocolate chip pancakes and crispy bacon," Stella said, putting the plate in front of her.

The heavenly scent hit her nostrils, and she kind of wanted to cry. "Stella, I didn't order this. I'm sorry. I appreciate the kindness, but I can't let you feed me for free."

"Oh, I didn't," Stella replied. "Someone in the café ordered for you and asked to be anonymous. I've been told to tell you to pay it forward when you can."

"That always happens to you," Hope said with a frown. "The last three times we've been out with Lucy someone anonymously pays for her meal. It's weird."

"I bet it was them." Cassidy had a grin on her face as she pointed to a spot behind Lucy's head.

Lucy turned and felt her jaw drop because sitting right there across the café was Ty. That wasn't so surprising. He often came to Stella's, but he never came here with Michael Novack. The big, gorgeous former marshal was sitting across from Ty, and they seemed to be in deep conversation.

"Teeny, I would like to change my bet," Rachel said firmly.

Lucy stood, picking up the plate. She was getting to the bottom of this.

* * * *

Michael watched as Lucy walked into the café, greeting her friends. It looked like there was some big gathering for breakfast this morning. "Any idea what's going on over there?"

Shannon was fairly new in town. From what he'd heard, she was Stella's niece, and like many people in Bliss had come with a shit ton of baggage. The dark-haired woman refilled his coffee. He pegged her right around twenty-five, though there was a grimness to the woman that made her seem older. She wasn't the partying type. "My aunt said it was something to do with the festival."

Ah, that made sense. Bliss loved festivals. The year was marked with celebrations of all kinds. Spring Festival, Big Game Dinner, Founder's Day, Woo Woo Fest—which had another name but that one truly encompassed what it was like to be surrounded by people who believed in ley lines. There was a Groundhog Day party that did not in any way involve a groundhog after Nell protested. Now they all simply watched the movie at the Movie Motel and drank beer. If Max passed out before midnight, Bliss was doomed to six more weeks of winter.

Not that Michael went. He'd avoided all festivals until he'd been forced to follow Nell to one. Lucy had been there, and he'd spent much of the night following her around and helping her out.

It had been one of the best nights he'd had in a long time. And then Henry had come home and Michael had gone back to his corner.

"Do you want the usual?" Shannon asked.

He grunted his assent, and she turned to walk away.

"Ooo, Shannon, I'll take a Denver omelet, some home fries, and bacon," a familiar voice said. "Oh, and are there cinnamon rolls left?"

Shannon shook her head. "Sheriff's already been in. He said Gemma's got her monthly, and he needs to feed the beast. I would say that's sexist but Gemma's got anger issues on a regular basis, much less when her uterus is cramping. Chocolate doesn't do it for her. It's cinnamon and sugar. If you want breakfast dessert, you're going to have to settle for an apple fritter."

"That works." Ty gave her a smile that showed off brilliantly white teeth. "Oh, and Lucy is taking notes for the Winter Festival committee but they're not actually paying for her breakfast, so she's going to tell you she's not hungry. She is. She'll take a short stack of chocolate chip pancakes and some crispy bacon. Send the check to me but tell her it's one of those pay it forward things. Unless the big guy here wants to take it. Are we going to split the bill for feeding her? You should think about it. She can eat more than you think."

Why had he said yes? He felt like a dumbass sitting there with Shannon watching him like it was a completely normal question between two men. Who was feeding their almost shared girlfriend today? "Uh, yeah. I'll take care of it."

Ty shrugged out of his big coat and hung it on the hook on his side of the booth. Michael had taken the one at the very back where he could look out over the rest of the café.

"Excellent." Ty slid in across from him. "See, this is money saving, too. Go team. I've decided to call us Tychael. I think that's better than Myler."

"No." He was a little horrified. He'd thought Ty would be some bubble-brained idiot who only thought about sex and parties. It was so much worse.

"You want to go with Myler?" Ty asked with a frown.

"We are not some celebrity couple. We're two guys who have very little in common except we both want the same woman. We're leaving it there. There's no mystical connection here."

"Okay. We can play this cool, but I had a night to think about it and the pros of this whole partnership thing outweigh the cons. Like the money thing. She really can eat, and she won't if she doesn't have the cash, so we have to be sneaky."

"She works a lot. Where is the money going?" One part of this partnership that would work in his favor was the fact that Ty could answer some questions about Lucy. He happened to know Trio paid its staff well, and Lucy raked in the tips. She also did short-term jobs. She was always hustling.

Always looking for cash. Like Jessie.

"Her siblings. She stayed at home as long as she could, but she and her dad's girlfriend at the time didn't get along. So she moved here to the valley. She stayed in a rental for a while and then moved into River's when she left. I'm not sure what she's planning if the job at the lodge doesn't work out. I hope she doesn't go back to that dingy rental. I happen to know her former roommate hasn't found a replacement yet. She runs the quilt shop during the day and at night she mostly prays. She prays for Lucy a lot. The only person she prays for more is me, and I find it quite insulting. I'm not that bad."

The thought of Lucy's roommate praying God forgave Ty for his multitudinous sins was kind of funny. But he didn't like the thought of Lucy feeling shamed by anyone. "Why would she need to pray for Lucy?"

"Oh, Susie Jean prays for everyone. I mean that girl has to have a direct line to the All Mighty. She prays for Lucy because she works in a den of iniquity. I think that's Trio, and it's because of the quantity of beer served there and the chipotle wings. Beer makes men crazy and chipotle wings give them heartburn. Both are looked down on by the lord. I try not to tell her that I've seen our local pastor at Trio indulging in both. But Susie Jean also prays that Lucy's car works, so she's an all-encompassing prayer person. You ever need thoughts and prayers, she will give them to you by the bucketful. And as for your other question, Lucy pays for all kinds of things for her sisters. I'm worried when they graduate, she's going to work herself to death to try to put them through college. One of her brothers got a football scholarship that paid for most of his four years. The other went to trade school and is deep into an apprenticeship. They help her out as much as they can, but they have classes."

"Lucy didn't get to go to school."

"No." Ty's eyes went soft. "There wasn't anyone willing to pay her way. She didn't have the best grades because she worked two jobs all the way through high school. She doesn't like to feel like a charity case, so you have to be a little sneaky. I do the pay it forward thing on her a lot. I also make her casseroles and pretend they come from my mom and I'm trying not to waste them."

"You make her casseroles?"

Ty nodded. "I'm not a great cook, but I can casserole the shit out of meat and cheese."

The lengths the other man went to for Lucy hit Michael hard. This wasn't about wanting to get into her panties. This was years' worth of longing. "You really care about her."

"I told you. I love her."

He wasn't sure how Ty so easily said the words. There wasn't a hint of vulnerability in the announcement, merely truth. "Then this is a mistake."

Ty sat back, a weary look on his face. "I should have known you would be a wishy-washy bastard."

"I'm not wishy-washy." He was smart. He'd been impulsive the night before, but now he had to look at the reality of the situation. The idea of getting to have her had caused him to sit in his SUV until he finally had to say yes. But this morning he was worried he'd leapt way before bothering to look.

Damn. He was wishy-washy. He'd never been wishy-washy. He was the man who made decisions.

"You said you were in, and now you're talking like you're out," Ty complained.

He wasn't sure he wanted to be out, but there were problems Ty wasn't considering. "I guess I thought you weren't in love with her."

"Well, you thought wrong. I don't know how that changes things."

"I'm not in love with her." He needed to make that plain.

A muscle in Ty's jaw twitched slightly, but he obviously tried to look like that statement hadn't bothered him. "Good, because then when you leave you won't try to take her with you."

Ty didn't have a great poker face. He wasn't sure why, but he didn't like the thought of Ty thinking he was an asshole. Which was weird because for the last several years he hadn't cared what anyone thought. "It's not that I don't care about her. It's just…I can't do that again. I can't be in love with someone again. Why are we having this conversation?"

Ty shrugged. "I have no idea, man, but as long as we're having it, you should know that I call bullshit."

"Bullshit?"

Ty nodded sagely. "Bullshit."

"What is that supposed to mean? You can't just call bullshit. You have no idea what I've been through and what I'm capable of."

"I know you're real damn capable of being a jerk, but you're not with Lucy. You grumble and growl your way through everything, but when she walks in a room you're suddenly a big old ball of jelly."

He did not like the thought of that. "I am not."

"Are, too." Ty sounded like a kid on a playground. Rubber and glue.

There was a laugh from the group of women across the café, and Michael turned to glance over. Lucy was sitting in the middle of the women, and she was so pretty it hurt. Dark hair and big eyes that kicked him in the gut every time he saw her. He wasn't quite sure why she did it for him. He worried that it was about the fact that she was the polar opposite of Jessie.

"There. That look on your face is precisely why this could work," Ty said.

It was time to stop being a wishy-washy prick. He needed to be in or out, and having the conversation with himself wasn't fixing the problem. His brain told him this was a bad idea and it would end up hurting someone. His dick thought it was a perfect idea. So he needed to put it out there and make a logical decision. He could still make those. "I don't see what I bring to the table. Even in the short term."

His dick saw exactly what he brought, but then his dick might have an overinflated sense of importance.

Ty considered the statement for a moment. "Lucy wants you. You coming in for the short term means Luce gets to satisfy her curiosity, and she won't wonder if it could have worked. Because according to you, it won't."

It was perverse since he'd literally said the words about fifty times now, but he wanted to argue. "So I'm just the second dick."

"Do you want to be more?"

That was the question. It was the idea that he wouldn't have any responsibility that made him say yes in the first place. But then morning had come, and he'd started to wonder what the hell he was doing. "I don't know."

"Here you go." Shannon slid a plate in front of him. Eggs, bacon, toast. His usual.

"Thank you, ma'am." Ty's eyes had a sparkle in them as he looked down at his plate.

When was the last time he'd been so enthusiastic about something simple? About anything at all? The last few years had been misery and self-punishment. But still the idea of being nothing more than a curiosity rankled.

"You want half?" Ty gestured to his apple fritter. "It's delicious but Doc says I should watch my cholesterol. I thought maybe half of it could go into you."

He was a dork. "You should stop eating like a five-year-old. You're a medical professional. You shouldn't walk around eating fried dough for breakfast."

"It isn't breakfast," Ty countered. "The omelet is for breakfast. The fritter is my breakfast dessert."

"There's no such thing."

Ty chuckled as if he'd said the stupidest thing ever. "Of course there is. There's dessert for lunch and dinner. There's one for breakfast, too."

"First of all, there isn't a lunch dessert. Second, how do you not weigh five hundred pounds?" Michael suddenly feared for Ty's arteries.

"I run a lot. The whole EMT thing keeps a man on his toes. People don't think you're serious about saving them if you don't run.

Then there's picking up people. That helps with the upper body work." Ty's smile faded. "Damn. Cassidy is pointing our way. Have you done anything that might indicate alien possession?"

He turned slightly and sure enough, Cassidy was pointing their way, and she wasn't the only one to notice them. The whole table had turned, and he decided he didn't particularly like having all that attention from the women of Bliss.

Lucy stood, picking up the plate of food that had been placed in front of her. Her shoulders squared and she started walking toward them.

"Damn. Okay, so I'm going to need you to back me up, brother," Ty said.

What the hell had put that glint in Lucy's eyes? That stare of hers promised retribution. What exactly did she think was about to happen?

She ignored him completely and put the plate down on the table in front of Ty. It landed with a smack but nothing fell off. "Did you do this?"

Ty's hands came up in the universal gesture of surrender. "I did not make any pancakes this morning. None. I've been sitting right here with my friend, Mike. Haven't been in the kitchen at all, have I?"

She frowned. "That's not what I meant and you know it, Ty. I don't know what you're up to, but I'm not playing around. You don't get to do all this sneaky stuff to get me to...what? What are you trying to do?"

Ty muttered something but Michael was stuck on what a brat she was being. Ty had to play those games because she wouldn't allow him to help her and why?

She was saying something to Ty about keeping his nose out of her business, and he'd had about enough of that.

"Lucy, pick up that damn plate, go back to your table, and eat your breakfast. He sent it to you anonymously because he can't stand the thought of you going hungry." Michael eased out of the booth, standing over her. "And you're acting like a woman who doesn't care about anything but her own feelings, and I don't think that's who you want to be."

Lucy's big eyes had widened, and for a moment he thought she was going to walk away without saying a thing. "What are you two doing together?"

"Baby, we're only talking," Ty said, watching them both. "He doesn't believe in breakfast dessert."

Her gaze shifted between the two of them. "I don't understand."

He did have something to add to this. Discipline. Control. She obviously needed a little, responded to a lot. Tyler kind of did, too. He would have sat there and taken her emotional outburst without confronting her about the problem. "We're negotiating."

"About what?" The question was a little puff coming out of her mouth. Like she was deathly afraid of the answer.

"Go out with us tonight and find out." Had he meant that air of challenge to the question?

Hell, yeah he had. Now that he was standing in front of her, his blood thrummed through his system. All of their encounters before this had been polite, stilted in the way that two awkward people could be. They'd tiptoed around each other, but the insertion of Ty had given her a confidence she hadn't had before. He liked it. But she needed that sassiness only when it was deserved.

"Go out? I...I..." She seemed to stumble with her reply.

"You wanted me to make sure the flue in the fireplace is working before it gets too cold," Ty reminded her. "I can do that tonight. I'll pick us up some dinner and beer, and maybe we can watch a movie."

"I..." She didn't seem to be able to get past that one word.

He could take care of it for her. "We'll pick you up after work. I would ask what time your shift is, but I bet Ty has that written down somewhere."

Ty gave him a grin and a thumbs-up.

Ty might be insane.

Lucy stood there looking cute and confused.

"You can take your breakfast back to your friends or you are free to join us. But unless you're truly not hungry, you'll eat the food Ty provided for you," he said.

"Uh, I thought we decided you were picking up this one," Ty reminded him. "We're sharing all of the things."

Lucy gasped slightly. "Do I have a say in this?"

"Sure. You can always say no." He didn't think she would though.

She picked up her plate and walked back to her table.

That felt a little like victory. Yeah, he did have something to offer.

"Dude, that was awesome." That ridiculous grin was back on Ty's face as Michael eased into the booth. "Usually she yells at me and I say how sorry I am even when I don't know exactly what I'm apologizing for."

They were going to have to work on that. It seemed like Lucy had been running that relationship for far too long.

Ty started to pick up the apple fritter.

"Hey, half of that is mine." He was probably paying for Ty's breakfast, too, after all.

Ty frowned. "But you don't believe in breakfast dessert."

He didn't believe in a lot of things. It didn't make them less true. "Get used to sharing, buddy."

After all, they would be doing a lot of that.

Chapter Four

"Do you need to get ready?" Callie Hollister-Wright pulled the Trio apron over her head and tied it around her waist. Her chestnut brown hair was in a high ponytail, and she was brimming with enthusiasm. She only worked a few shifts a week at the bar her family owned, but she always seemed to enjoy it.

"I've got one last table. I think they're almost ready to leave." She gestured over where the group of the biggest douchebags the world had ever seen sat. "They look familiar. At least a couple of them do. Have they been here before?"

Callie glanced at the table, and her nose wrinkled. "They're Bob Foster's kids. He owns Foster's Sports and Recreation in addition to about a hundred other companies. I think it's called Foster Corp now and they're one of those massive multinational companies Nell always protests, but around here they're best known for sporting equipment."

"The big box stores?" Lucy had certainly heard of them. She'd heard River and Ty talk about how crappy their products were and how they made it hard to order the truly good equipment. They came into a market, shoved all the mom and pop shops out, and then jacked up the prices when they had gotten rid of all the competition.

"Yes," Callie replied. "He's worth a couple of billion dollars. I heard they're staying at their villa this week. I will never forgive Cole Roberts for coming up with the idea of the villas."

"Don't blame the buildings. They're gorgeous," Lucy said with a sigh of appreciation. "One day I want to stay in one."

The villas were twelve elegantly decorated ski chalets located close to the lodge but with enough privacy that the people who stayed there could feel like they were a part of nature.

"Well, I wish he vetted the guests better. That group over there has been coming here a couple of years now, and while the dad is perfectly nice, the kids are assholes when he isn't around," Callie said with a frown. "I don't know. I guess one of the daughters is all right. At least she tips. How long have they been here?"

"They're three drinks in." There were four people sitting at the table across the dining room. They were the perfect picture of overindulged twenty-somethings. Two women, two men, all dripping in designer wear that would feed and clothe her sisters for at least a year.

"They'll still be here for a while then." Callie leaned against the bar while Alexei Markov poured out beer, getting the perfect amount of foam on each. "So, I saw how you distracted me from my real job of getting information out of you. Are you going out with Tychael tonight?"

"What?"

Callie grinned, the expression lighting up her whole face. "Shannon overheard Ty saying that all duos need a name. He's apparently trying to start a trend. Like instead of Rye and Max, Rachel should be able to call them Rax. I've taken to it." She turned to the little window that looked through to the kitchen. "I love Nane. Or should I call you Zate?"

Zane Hollister's handsome face was framed by the window. The man had a bunch of scars, but they did nothing to take away from how attractive he was. "Don't even start that, baby. Although I like the idea of Calexei."

"Do not to be doing this." Alexei frowned their way. "I only start to properly be pronouncing the names. We do not need new ones. Also, shouldn't they be thruple names? Calholexei?"

Callie shook her head. "No, that sounds like we're trying to summon demons or weird alien creatures, and you know how that will go with Mel. I think we're going to have to tell Ty this just won't work out for him. But it could work for Lucy."

She felt herself blush. "I wish Michael hadn't asked me out in front of the whole dining room at Stella's."

"I didn't think he asked you so much as challenged you," Zane said. "At least that's what I heard."

She frowned Callie's way. "I wonder who you heard that from?"

Although everyone had seen her being taken down by Michael, Callie was the world's worst gossip.

It was Callie's turn to blush. "It's my only flaw."

She grimaced and went to take the tray of beers over to table five. The tourists were out in droves this week, and the ski season didn't truly start until this weekend when the Elk Creek Lodge had its opening party.

"Hey, I heard a rumor about you that has nothing to do with Ty or the crazy dude on the mountain." Zane walked around from the kitchen. He had a dark apron wrapped around his waist that he wiped his hands on.

"He isn't crazy." He'd been very much in control of himself this morning. The way he'd stared down at her and called her out on her crap had actually done something for her. She had been acting like a brat. Deep down she'd always known someone was paying her breakfast bills, and it wasn't some random stranger who wanted her to pay it forward. She'd known it was Ty. Forcing herself to acknowledge that had made her mad, lit some small anger in her about the fact that he was trying to change things now. He'd said no to her a long time ago, and she'd had to recognize that she might not be over that yet.

"Jury's still out on that one. We all thought he would mourn for a little while and then get on with his life. Here we are years later and he's still living like a hobo," Zane countered. "But that's neither here nor there. I want you to know if you take that job at the resort, you have my full support."

He'd heard about that, too? She thought she'd kept that quiet. "I don't know what to say. I was going to tell you."

"You wanted to make sure you got the job first," Zane replied. "I understand. It's a big step up, but you have to know that you're ready for it."

"I don't have it yet. Mr. Roberts wants me to work the opening weekend welcome party to see how I do." Her anxiety about that party was sky high, not to mention she had some work to do for the festival coming up in a few weeks. And she intended to keep up some shifts here at Trio. "I'm not quitting. Are you firing me?"

"Not at all. And I think you've got the job in the bag. You know Cole uses me to vet the locals he hires, right?"

She hadn't thought about that at all. Cole Roberts spent more than half the year at his home in Dallas. His partner, Mason, worked for a law firm, so he didn't spend as much time here as he had once. Their wife was a lovely woman who ran a charity for victims of sexual abuse. They had busy, vibrant lives, and that meant outsourcing some of their work here in Bliss. Normally the Roberts family would be at the lodge for the opening, but this year they were staying close to Dallas. This year Kate Roberts was pregnant and close to giving birth. It made sense that Cole would rely on Nate. "He had you run a background check on me?"

"I think the background check went something like me telling him he would be a fool to not give you a shot," Zane said softly. "Lucy, you have grown so much since you started here. Waitressing is the kind of job you do on the way to your future. Unless you own the place like Callie does, and then it's good business."

"There's nothing wrong with waitressing."

"Not at all, but it's time for you to see what else you can do. Take Cole up on his tuition assistance program."

She wasn't even close to thinking about that. "That's for upper-level employees to get their master's."

"Says who? I don't think that's written down anywhere. Walk in and tell him you want to go as far as you can in his operation and you need your degree for that. Adams State offers a business degree with an emphasis on management."

"I don't know. I don't... I never saw myself in college. That was more Ty and River's thing."

"Because they had the money to go," Zane prompted. "Because they didn't have family obligations that held them back. At some point it's going to be your turn, Lucy. Don't be afraid of it. I know that sounds dumb, but change can be unnerving. You can do a thing for so long you don't remember how to not do it. You're almost there, but it's going to take something you haven't had to do up until now. Something that's hard as hell to do."

"What's that?"

"Believe in yourself. Believe in your value, and don't be afraid to ask for what you deserve," Zane replied. "You followed the rules because they kept your family safe. You did your job. Now break a few and make a real life for yourself. Don't view this new job as the be-all, end-all of existence."

"But it's a great job. I would be in charge of all the serving staff," she countered.

"Yeah, and then you learn how to be in charge of all of hospitality, and then you learn how to run the whole damn thing," Zane said. "You can do it all if you want to. And you can handle those men if you want them. I've watched those two dumbasses cry in their beers over you for years now. Well, Michael drank beer. Ty drank whatever was the sweetest. I worry about him."

She laughed, relief flooding her. Zane had been good to her. She'd worried about possibly telling him she was taking another job. She hated the thought of leaving him short-staffed. "I can still work some shifts here."

"Absolutely not. If you get that job, the only time I want to see you in here is when you're on a date with your weirdos." Zane had the sweetest smile. "See, you tried to change the subject, but I came back to it. And don't worry about me finding a new waitress. It's been a while since I stole someone from Stella's. I think Shannon might need a change of scenery."

He was the worst. "She's Stella's niece."

Zane pointed her way as though he'd made her point. "Yeah, and imagine how awful that would be." He glanced toward the dining room. "Hey, can you take care of that table? Callie looks like she's taking a big order, and they look impatient. Cook's coming in soon, and then I'll hop on tables with my wife."

"Of course. You know if you need me, I could stay late," she offered.

Zane backed away. "And miss your date? Never. Be brave, Lucy. And run if things get weird."

She wasn't sure how he thought things wouldn't get weird. She was going on a date with two guys who up until the previous day had refused to talk to each other. One was her best friend in the world and the other was her crush. She started for the table filled with young people who could buy and sell the world.

Was she being ridiculous? If she got the job, she would be working at the same place as Ty. Well, she would be there full time and he would be around on certain shifts, but they might be living in close proximity since her job would be year round and an apartment at the resort was one of the perks. She shouldn't jeopardize their relationship this way.

"Thank god. I thought you were never going to get over here." The blondest of the women huffed and pushed an empty wine glass Lucy's way. "I need another Pinot if I'm going to sit here and listen to my brothers talking about their portfolios one second more."

"Well, you should listen because if you don't you're going to have to sell that Maserati Dad bought you to pay for your fillers." A man who looked to be in his mid-twenties sat next to the woman who had spoken and sneered her way.

Yep, they were lovely.

"Please forgive my siblings," the other blonde said. Her hair was a honey color and looked far warmer than the platinum of her sister. "They get obnoxious when they drink, but then they're obnoxious when they're sober, too. It's kind of a different level of irritating. I'm Sonya, by the way."

"You don't have to introduce yourself to the help," the youngest of the men said.

"I don't know. She's kind of pretty," the first man replied, looking her up and down. "I'm Brock. Brock Foster. These are my brothers and sisters. Don't mind Sonya. She's the boring one. This is Chet. He's barely old enough to drink, but don't let that fool you, and Kendall is the pretty one. I'm the smart one, by the way."

He was the smarmy one, that was for sure. "I'm Lucy and my shift is almost over, so Zane will be taking over your table. I'll bring you all another round. Can I put in a food order for you?"

"Do you have a charcuterie board?" Kendall asked. "But only with organic meats and cheeses."

Chet snorted. "Like you eat."

Sonya gave her an apologetic smile. "I think we'll skip the food. Just another round of drinks. And don't worry about us driving.

Someone's picking us up in thirty minutes."

That was good to know. "I'll be right back with your drinks."

She turned and walked to the bar, putting the order in. She was used to serving jerks. They always came from out of town because Zane had dealt with anyone who lived around here very quickly. The truth was she enjoyed working during the off season most of all. Things were quiet, and the tavern took on a family feel, with the locals bringing their kids in and turning Trio into a communal meeting spot.

But tourists tended to pay her bills, and she was about to go into a place where tourists were kings.

"What are your plans for the night?" Callie asked while they both waited as Alexei worked on their orders. "I mean I know you're supposed to go out with…"

"Don't say it." If she let this go, she would forever be known as Luty or Mucy or even worse Miluyer.

Callie grinned. "Michael and Ty. Where are you going? I could set up a table for you."

And have her giving all of Bliss a blow by blow of what might be her only date of the year? "We're picking up some pizza and going back to River's to watch a movie."

"What are you going to do once she's back permanently?"

"Cheer. Thank the universe she's safe." It didn't matter that she would have to find a place to stay. She just wanted her friend back. "I'll look around once she's settled in."

"If you need help, you know where to go," Callie said. "I'll keep a lookout for any cabins that open up in the valley."

She wouldn't be able to afford a whole cabin. "Let me know if you hear about anyone needing a roommate."

"I will, but I don't think that will be necessary. If you get that job you'll get your own place, right? From what I understand the waitstaff who live out there share rooms, but management get their own apartments."

Her own place. Actually she didn't mind having roommates, but she was always the one struggling to make rent. She wanted a place she could decorate and feel comfortable in, a place she wasn't worried she would lose. It wouldn't be so hard to live in that place with someone she cared about. A friend.

Or two.

It was way too soon to even think about that.

Except she couldn't get that kiss out of her head. When Ty had dragged her against him, she'd forgotten about everything except how good it felt to be in his arms. How right.

It had also felt right to look up at Michael.

I don't think that's who you want to be.

He'd been right about that. She didn't want to be the person who couldn't accept a little help from someone who cared about her. She didn't want to be the woman who wasn't brave enough to try for what she wanted.

"Yes," she replied. "But I could also live in the valley if I wanted to. It's close enough that I could get to work even if I had to take a snowmobile. Lots of people ski in. I don't know. I'll have to see how I feel if I get the job."

She liked Bliss. She worried living at the resort would put her in a bubble. She wanted to be surrounded by happy families and the kookiness that came with living in this amazing, weird town.

"Good for you," Callie said. "Now go on and get changed. I'll take your drinks out. I saw that pretty dress hanging in the supply closet. It's definitely what I would wear to hang out."

She flashed Callie a frown but knew she was right. This was supposed to be nothing more than a hangout. Except Michael had called it a date, and a date felt like something she should dress for even if it was nothing more than pizza and a movie that hopefully worked because sometimes the Internet was spotty out at River's, and she was pretty sure their choices would be extremely limited if they had to use River's DVD collection. It was mostly romcoms from their teen years and her dad's plethora of war films.

She was pretty sure those romcoms hadn't covered what to do if she was approached by two completely opposite men who wanted to share her. Nope. She hadn't ever seen one of those.

She thanked Callie for giving her time to get ready. Michael had texted her earlier that he and Ty would pick her up around seven. That only left her fifteen minutes to change. She hurried to the supply closet to grab her dress and bag before going into the women's bathroom. There was a roomy stall that everyone used when they needed to change. It happened more often than she would have thought. She changed into the dress that she'd been told made her eyes shine.

Ty had told her. She'd needed a dress for a friend's wedding, and he'd driven her into Alamosa because he didn't trust her piece of crap car to make it that far. They'd had lunch at a burger joint, and he'd watched as she'd tried on at least twenty different dresses before declaring this one to be perfect.

Was he telling her the truth? She stared at herself in the mirror and tried to be the person she wanted to be. Brave. Confident. Willing to take a risk.

But if she lost Ty, she would be devastated.

She cared about Michael, could even see herself really trying with the man, but that was because she didn't have anything to lose with him. She didn't remember a time when Ty wasn't around to hold her hand, to tell her everything would be okay. To buy her breakfast when she couldn't afford it.

She needed to talk to him. Tonight was nothing more than a friendly hangout.

Which was why she was wearing her pushuppiest bra and the Chanel lip gloss Georgia Warner-Stark had given her for Secret Santa last year that she hoarded like it was gold.

She looked good. Definitely good enough to hang around her best friend's place, eat pizza, and watch some Netflix.

She took a deep breath and stepped out of the bathroom and into the tiny hallway that would lead her back out past the bar, where she would catch hell from Callie for how dressed up she was for a hangout.

She walked right into a big body.

Lucy gasped and stepped back. "I'm so sorry. I wasn't watching where I was going."

"No problem, sweetheart," a deep voice said.

She tilted her head and realized she'd bumped into the douchiest of the Foster siblings. Brock stood there, blocking her way out. She moved back again, trying to let him get past her to the men's room. "Well, I hope you have a good night."

His hand came out, effectively cutting off that escape route. "I hope I have a good night, too. I wanted to find you before you snuck off."

She got serious creep vibes off the dude. Before he'd been mildly annoying, but now she worried he was about to get nasty. "I'm not sneaking off. It's the end of my shift, and now Zane or Callie will be helping. In fact, I'm sure it's Zane. I'll introduce you."

If this man was going to get aggressive with staff, then six-foot-five Zane could handle his needs. Including the need to get punched and tossed out into the snow.

His lips curled up in a smirk that she was pretty sure he thought was charming. "But I don't want some guy to serve me. Not when I could have you."

He probably had seen her smile and read weakness. "You can't have me. I'm off work."

He moved in, crowding her and forcing her against the wall. "Good, then come back to my place. We're going to have a party. You would be very welcome. What do you say?"

She was going to give him one more out. "No, thank you. I have plans for the evening."

His jaw went tight, and he leaned in. "I can make it worthwhile for you. You live in this hick town. You probably haven't been around real men who can take care of you."

She sometimes hated the fact that she didn't look like a woman who could take care of herself. "Step back. I need to leave now."

He moved in closer. So close she could smell the bourbon on his breath. "That's what I'm telling you. You don't have to leave. You don't have to go back to your sad little world. You can spend the night in mine. I'll take care of you."

He reached out, his hand starting for her chest.

And she was done being polite. She thought she heard a growl come from her left but she ignored it because she had something to deal with. She had to shove down her fear. It was there because he was bigger than she was. It was there because all the times that she'd been physically vulnerable came rushing back in that instant. But she'd learned that fear could freeze her or it could be fuel.

She took a breath and let her body do what it had been trained to do. She pushed out to gain space, using the wall behind her as leverage. When she had space, she brought her knee up as hard as she could. When he moved to cup himself as any wounded man would, she brought her fist up in an uppercut that caught his chin. Pain flared in her hand, but she would bet it was nothing compared to what Brock was feeling.

"I don't need anyone to take care of me." She stepped around him, and when she turned there was a massive dark shadow at the end of the hallway.

"You okay?" Michael stood there looking big and strong and safe.

She nodded. "I am. I think Mr. Foster understands that I already have plans for the evening."

"Bitch," Brock hissed. "You have no idea who you're fucking with."

Michael took a step forward.

Brock ran for the men's room. Well, *ran* was giving him too much credit. He kind of stumbled and moaned.

She put a hand on Michael's chest. "I would like to go now."

She would learn a lot about the man by what he did next. Everyone talked about how angry he was, but she thought he was mostly sad. If he was as angry as they said, he might take this moment to indulge himself. He could make the excuse that she needed to be avenged or some masculine crap. She believed she'd made her point clear, and she hadn't even had to go for her pepper spray.

His jaw tightened and she could see the impulse there in his eyes. He wanted to follow Brock into that bathroom and teach him a lesson. His choice would make hers easier.

He reached out a hand. "All right. But we're telling Zane what happened. Okay?"

Of course. It was Zane's place of business, and he needed to make sure Callie didn't come anywhere near that man. "Agreed."

She followed him out, liking the way he held her hand.

* * * *

That had been a close thing.

Michael still felt the adrenaline thudding through him as Lucy unlocked the door to River Lee's place on the Rio Grande. He wanted to murder that guy. When he'd walked into Trio and Callie had told him Lucy was getting ready in the back, he'd gone behind the bar to wait for her. He'd been talking to Alexei when he'd noticed the lanky guy make his way to the back. He hadn't thought much of it until he'd heard Lucy talking.

Then the fucker had tried to touch her, and he'd almost launched himself at the guy. But then Lucy had surprised him.

"So where did you learn self-defense? Did Zane teach you?" He followed her. She'd left a light on inside, giving the cabin a friendly glow. As though everything good and warm was inside that house.

It was the opposite of what he could offer her. His place was nothing but cold, and he wasn't merely thinking of the rickety cabin he stayed in now. His place in Florida might be neatly kept, but it was cold compared to this cabin.

She shrugged out of her coat and hung it on the row of pegs just inside, then reached out for his. "No. I mean, he offered. All the guys always offer to teach the ladies, but I've found I prefer a woman instructor. So Laura teaches a class, and I'm in a group who meets regularly to practice."

That was odd coming from her. "Seriously? You don't want a man to teach you? I assure you Nate and Zane know what they're doing."

Nate and Zane had once been federal law enforcement. It would be the same as telling him that he didn't know what he was doing and had nothing to teach her.

"Of course they do. They know exactly how a large, muscular guy takes down another guy," she replied. "They could teach me all their moves, and they could even teach me the philosophies and mechanics behind a small person taking down a larger opponent. But they don't know what it means to be a woman."

She was missing the point. He'd taught plenty of women how to defend themselves, including Jessie. They'd sparred often to keep their skills up, though now he had to wonder if she hadn't done it because she genuinely liked hitting him. She would often "slip" and end up landing a hard punch and then apologize with a smirk on her face. Yet another red flag he'd overlooked. Maybe he was missing them with Lucy, too. "They know what it means to be human, and I assure you they understand fear. Just because I'm bigger than you doesn't mean I've never been afraid in a fight."

"Yes, I'm sure you were scared in a fight, but do you worry

when you walk down a street at night? When you jog on your own?" Lucy asked the question with a practicality that made him wonder if she was holding back her emotions, if she'd perhaps placed a polite wall between them. "Bliss is mostly safe, but I still feel vulnerable in certain situations. Even smaller men are going to be physically stronger than me. I should know. The man who nearly killed me was pretty much my weight. He had a little height on me, but when I had to fight, I had no shot. So when I wanted to learn, I went to a woman who understood what it meant to be powerless before a man."

Laura. Laura had been FBI until she'd been stalked and kidnapped by a serial killer. She'd barely made it out, and now she was strong and offering women like Lucy her expertise. And he was arguing with her choices because he didn't like feeling butt hurt.

Shit. He'd been an asshole. He hadn't liked the idea of her dismissing men and forgot entirely why she should fear them. She'd been assaulted, and he was questioning her choice of who could make her feel safe. It was selfish, and he was falling into the habit of being selfish because he'd spent two years concentrating on nothing but his own misery.

He handed her his coat and then held out his hand when she turned back to him. "Forgive me. I'm glad you had Laura. I'm glad you have a place where you can feel safe. I was feeling dismissed, and that wasn't what you were trying to do. I'll be less of an asshole if you give me a second chance."

Her smile lit up the room, and she took his hand. "Of course."

She let him bring her close, allowed him to wrap his arms around her, and the tension he'd felt eased. He could fucking breathe, and it made him wonder how long he'd been so wound up.

She rested her head against his chest, the affection coming off her soothing to his whole damn soul. "Thank you for not beating the crap out of that guy."

He chuckled. "I thought about it, but you handled it well." He didn't like to think about the time she almost hadn't gotten herself to safety. "I wish I'd been around when Hope's ex-husband tried to hurt you." That was wrong. He had been around. "I wish I'd known you better then."

"You didn't come off the mountain much in the beginning. You needed some time," she replied. "I wish I'd been less naïve. I was lonely, and I let myself get into a bad position because of it. I won't let that happen again. I didn't even like him, but I wanted something of my own."

"And now?"

"Now, I only go out with men I really connect to, as evidenced by what happened in that hallway," she said, her head tilting up to look at him. "You should know there haven't been many. Any in the last year or so. You see I like this guy but he's a weirdo and I have to be patient with him."

Oh, she made him smile. "I'm glad to hear that." But he needed to be honest with her. "I still wanted to smash that guy's face."

"I can see that was hard for you. Thanks." She squeezed him and then backed away. "So you said Ty had an emergency?"

He didn't want to talk about Ty. He wanted to kiss her. He wanted to indulge himself for as long as he could, but that wasn't their bargain. "Yes, and I think it was an actual emergency and not him trying to get out of anything."

She moved into the kitchen, glancing back his way. "Well, he did have a shift scheduled for today, and he's an actual emergency medical tech, so I believe him. I also believe that he snuck in here before his shift because he knows I didn't have any…" She opened the fridge and leaned in, coming back with a bottle. "…wine. Or beer. I think that's for you because Ty will drink this Moscato with me."

Ty's taste in liquor left something to be desired, but Michael couldn't argue with the fact that the other man was thoughtful. He wasn't sure he would have remembered what Lucy liked to drink. "He said it wouldn't take too long and he's close to the pizza place, so he'll bring it with him."

Ty had sounded incredibly peppy for a man who was transporting a guy who'd taken on a hive of bees to the hospital. He'd sounded excited to get the evening going, and he didn't seem worried at all that he would be sharing his date with a guy who wasn't known for being nice.

He was known for growling at everyone, for frowning and being generally unpleasant.

He hadn't always been. He'd been quite charming once.

You're too nice, Novack. It's going to bite you in the ass one of these days.

He tried to shake off that voice in his head. Jessie's voice, the one that reminded him she'd shown him exactly who she was and he'd fooled himself into thinking he could be the one to change her.

Lucy popped the top off his beer and offered it to him. The cabin had a bar that separated the kitchen from the dining area and living space. He sat down on one of the barstools and took the longneck.

Naturally the little bastard had bought his preferred beer.

He didn't like to think about the fact that it had been a long time since someone gave a damn about what he wanted, made an effort to figure out what he preferred. It was weird that the person being so thoughtful was another man.

A man who was willing to share the woman he wanted but only because he believed Michael would walk away in the end.

While Lucy started to open her wine bottle, Michael glanced around the neatly appointed kitchen. There was a big basket of apples at the end of the bar.

"Did Ty bring you the apples, too?" It was quite a few. At least twenty of them.

"Nope, they're for a project I'm working on. I'm experimenting. It takes a lot of apples to make the perfect pie, you know," Lucy replied. "Ty would never just eat an apple. It has to be covered in sugar or fried to an inch of its fruity life for Ty to be interested in it. But he does know his pizza. The pizza place usually gives Ty a big discount so he gets two pizzas because I love mushrooms and he can't stand them. He won't even split a pizza with me because he says mushrooms anywhere ruins the thing. If you'd gone you would have been charged full price, but that waitress will give it all to him for half off."

That didn't sound right. "So Ty buys two pizzas but only pays for one and one of those pizzas is entirely for you but you don't have to pay because it's buy one, get one free?"

"No, I would pay my half, of course" she began and then went silent.

He stared at her for a moment, waiting for her to reach the proper conclusion.

"There's no buy one, get one free that's only for Ty, is there?" She poured wine into her glass. "He told me it was because the waitress is sweet on him, but she couldn't possibly be there every single time we order pizza."

He had more news for her. "I eat a lot of pizza since I don't have a working kitchen. They haven't had a waitress for six months. The owner's sons took over running the whole place. So unless one of them has a big crush on Ty…"

She growled, a sound he found utterly enchanting. He had to admit, he was more attracted to her because she could protect herself. He'd watched her, and she'd given that shit every opportunity to make the right choice and when he hadn't she'd taken care of him.

"Why would Ty do that? Why would he lie to me?"

It occurred to Michael that he could undermine Ty if he wanted to. Lucy was looking at this as a deception. All it would take was for him to agree with her and maybe he could turn this into a night just for the two of them. She was already wary of how Ty felt about her. All she needed was a little push.

He glanced down at the beer and realized even as far gone as he was, he couldn't fuck over Ty. He wouldn't be sitting here with her if it wasn't for Ty.

"He worries about you having enough to eat." She had to get over this pride thing when it came to food. "I believe you do the same with your siblings. It's food, Lucy. He's not making sure you have fifteen pairs of designer shoes. He wants to make sure you don't go hungry."

"He's the one who pays it forward by buying me breakfast at Stella's." She seemed to be putting all the pieces together. Her mouth firmed in a stubborn line. "And that also explains why his mom looked at me so weird when I told her how delicious all her casseroles are. He's making them. I knew I recognized that dish from his place. I just thought he never sent it back to her."

"Yes." He knew it was Ty's story to tell, but he wasn't going to lie to her. "He works hard to make sure you have the food you need. I'm with him on this."

She frowned and stared down at her drink. "Of course you are. You don't understand."

He eased off the barstool because she needed to know how he felt about this. "I don't understand what?"

She bit her bottom lip as he rounded the bar and got into her space. But she didn't back up the way she had with that douchebag.

She stood her ground, her eyes coming up to meet his. "Don't understand what it means to be an object of pity."

He barely managed to not roll his eyes. "Really?"

She gasped as though realizing her mistake. "Michael, you did nothing wrong. You didn't know she was going to hurt Alexei."

"Yes, and that's why they all pitied me. That's why I couldn't go back. I was a marshal. I was literally supposed to catch the bad guys, not ask one to marry me, so when I talk to you about pride, I know what I'm talking about. Pride has kept me in a prison for two damn years. Don't let pride keep you hungry. Don't let it cost you a lifelong friend. Ask yourself what you would do if he was hungry. If I was hungry."

He was suddenly awfully hungry, and not for food. She was so pretty standing there in the soft glow of the lights from the kitchen.

She moved a little closer to him, close enough that her body brushed against his. Her eyes were clear as she looked up at him and let her hands find his waist. "If you were hungry, I would make sure you were fed. I wouldn't let your pride stand in the way of giving you what you need, Michael."

She was the sweetest thing he'd seen in forever, and he knew he was moving too fast.

Or was he? They'd been circling each other for a year and a half. He reached for the nape of her neck, finding soft, warm skin there. He didn't care if it was too soon. It might technically be their first date, but he had spent time with her. And he wanted her so badly, wanted this kiss more than he wanted his next breath.

Besides, Ty already got to kiss her. He remembered the jealousy that had burned through him while he'd watched her respond to Ty's kiss. He hadn't been able to do what Ty would be able to do. Ty would be able to walk in, toss the pizza aside, and demand equal time.

"Then let me do the same. Let me give you what you need, baby." It had been so long since he'd felt necessary to someone. He could be important to Lucy. He could be important to Ty. Even if it was only for a little while.

"I think I might need you," she whispered.

And then nothing would have stopped him from lowering his mouth to hers. He took her lips in a kiss that should show her exactly how hungry he was. He was starved. For her.

He started slow, not wanting to scare her off. He explored her lips with gentle brushes of his own while one arm wound around her waist, hugging her tight to his body.

She groaned quietly as she rubbed against him and opened her mouth, offering him more.

He took it. He surged inside her mouth, the heat between them ramping up and taking over all his best intentions. His tongue slid against hers and the hand around her waist went lower, finding her ass and cupping her there.

Her hands moved, too, mimicking his. She cupped his ass and gave him a squeeze, rubbing her body against his lengthening cock.

Fuck. "Baby, you're playing with fire."

"Am I? Will you think less of me if what I need is for you to strip me and take me to the bedroom? I've thought about this for months and months."

The impulse to do exactly that was right there, begging to be acted on. But if he did that he would have her naked, spread out, and penetrated in minutes. He wanted this to last far longer. Instead, he moved her so her back was against the wall. He wasn't thinking about anything but making sure she was satisfied. He would consider it an appetizer or a way to let off some of the steam between them. If he didn't do it, he would be grumpy and frustrated all through dinner and the movie.

Yeah, that was why he should do it. Then he and Ty could take her to bed together.

That thought didn't make his dick deflate. Not one bit. In fact, the image of Lucy in between the two of them made him growl and kiss her again. Or he could watch. He wouldn't have told anyone he was a kinky guy, but since Ty offered him this bargain, he couldn't stop thinking about how pretty they would be together. He could watch and stroke his own cock or he could order Ty to get her on her knees so she could suck him while Ty fucked her from behind.

Lucy's legs parted, allowing him to move between them. Her skirt shoved up, revealing pretty legs. She was caught on his thigh, pressed between him and the wall, and her breath went ragged.

He kissed her for the longest time, easing her up and taking her weight on his leg. She wrapped her arms around his neck and rubbed

Lexi Blake

against him until the skirt of her dress was up around her waist and there was nothing but thin cotton between him and her pussy.

He moved against her, his cock stroking the denim of his jeans. He was well aware that he was acting like a teenager, grabbing whatever pleasure he could, but he couldn't stop himself.

"Please, Michael." Lucy's face was gorgeously flush and the tie to her wrap dress had come undone while she'd been riding his leg like a rodeo queen.

He could please her. He could please her all night. Maybe they didn't need the movie at all. When Ty got here, they would take her straight to bed.

Her breasts were barely encased by the white cotton bra she wore. She was so fucking gorgeous, and he couldn't wait until she was naked and he was deep inside her.

Her arms tightened around him, and her body stiffened and then went limp.

Fuck. She was so sexy when she came. In that brief moment the weight he'd been carrying slid off and he felt good, really fucking good for the first time in years. A few more strokes against her and he would need to change.

He lowered Lucy down to the floor, and that was the moment he realized they weren't alone because there was a big fluffy marshmallow with eyes and a tail staring up at them.

Lucy gasped. "Buster?"

"Uhm, we should probably give you a minute," a feminine voice said.

Michael stepped in front of Lucy and saw a petite woman, her dark hair up in a ponytail and a backpack still on her back standing next to a tall man with broad shoulders and golden hair that was slightly too long.

River and Jax were home, and a little earlier than expected. He'd never met them formally, but he knew what they looked like. The puppy they'd left town with was now a massive fluff ball of a dog.

If only they'd been alone. Ty stood right behind them, his eyes wide, and Michael could see the pain there before Ty's face went blank.

Lucy gasped and retied her dress at the waist, but there was zero question she was a woman who'd just had an orgasm. It was there in

92

how mussed her hair was and the pink flush to her skin.

"I can see I'm not needed here. Guess now I know how it feels, right, Mike?" Ty dumped the pizza on the table.

Lucy started after him.

"Did we interrupt a twosome that was supposed to be a threesome?" Jax was the only one in the place with a smile on his face.

River slapped at her husband's arm, but he was wasn't exactly wrong.

Michael started after Lucy, hoping he could make this right.

Chapter Five

Ty stormed out, slamming the door, anger thrumming through him.

He'd offered to get the pizza, set everything up, planned it all out, and Michael had gone straight for sex. Not that Lucy had looked like she didn't want it. She'd been so hot he'd stood there for a moment and thought seriously about dropping the food and joining them. Of course he hadn't been able to do that since when he'd driven up, River and Jax had been getting out of a big black SUV. He'd been so happy to see them that he'd completely forgotten it was supposed to be date night for a moment. He'd decided they could make it a small welcome home dinner, and then he'd walked in and found Lucy and Michael.

That was when it hit him that they hadn't even realized he was in the room or that two other people were there along with a massive ball of fur. Buster had walked right up to them, and they hadn't stopped. They'd kept right on, and they probably would have ended up fucking on the counter had Lucy not finally noticed they weren't alone.

He wasn't needed. Not at all.

"Ty!"

He kept walking toward his Jeep.

"Ty! Tyler Davis, you stop."

He glanced back and Lucy was stepping off the front porch. She was wearing the dress they'd shopped for last year, the one that made her skin glow and clung to her every curve.

It struck suddenly and forcibly that she hadn't dressed for him. If it had been the two of them, she'd have changed into pj pants and a T-shirt. She wouldn't have carefully put on makeup and done her hair. She'd dressed for Michael.

She wanted Michael. She'd gone along with this date thing so she could be close to another man. Michael had been worried about being the second dick, but it appeared Ty was the one in that particular position.

He'd wanted her for so long, loved her for as long as he could remember, and she wanted someone else.

Humiliation swirled through him. Why had he thought Lucy might want him as anything more than a friend? She'd made herself plain. He'd thought giving her time would change things, but it hadn't. "You don't have to say anything, Luce. I know when I'm not wanted."

Her eyes narrowed. "Don't you play that way with me. You are the one who started this. You're the one who said you wanted to be more than friends, and you're the one who invited Michael in."

"Well, I wouldn't have if I'd known the only reason you would agree to it was because you wanted him," Ty shot back.

"That isn't the only reason." Lucy's hands were fists at her sides. "I wanted to try with you, too, but I can't lie and say I don't feel something for him."

"Yeah, I saw exactly what you felt for him."

"Don't you try to make me feel bad about kissing him."

"You weren't just kissing him."

"No. I wasn't. I got carried away." She seemed to deflate. "How did you think this was going to work, Ty? Did you think I would watch a couple of movies with him and decide I didn't really want to be with him? Did you think I wouldn't kiss him or touch him?"

"He thought he could handle it, but it seems like he can't," a deep voice said.

Oh, great. Michael had followed her. He stood on the porch, leaning against one of the posts and looking like a man who was about to get everything he wanted.

95

"I thought we had an agreement," Ty corrected. "I thought we were going after her together, not that you would jump on her the first moment you had a chance. I thought Lucy cared about me enough to not fuck you behind my back."

"We have two different definitions of fucking." Michael sighed and stepped off the porch. "Come on. Let's go to Trio and the three of us can sit down and have a beer and talk this out. What you saw wasn't what you think you saw."

"I have two eyes." He wasn't about to let Michael turn this thing around on him. "I know exactly what I saw. The minute Lucy had a chance to let you in her panties, she took it, and I didn't matter at all."

"Are you kidding me?" Lucy crossed her arms over her chest, a sure sign that she was pissed and defensive. "This is not the way the whole threesome thing works, and now I'm pretty sure you never wanted it to work at all. This was all some kind of joke to you."

How could she possibly think that way? "You are never a joke to me."

Lucy sighed, a weary sound. "Good night, Ty. Michael, I'm sorry, but I think I need some time and space. I'll see y'all around."

She turned and started to walk back inside.

Michael frowned his way. "Well, that didn't go well."

"It seems like it went real well for you," he shot back. He knew he should run after her and try to fix this situation, but there was an ache in his chest he wasn't sure he could work around. "I'm the one who takes care of her. I'm the one who's loved her for all of our lives."

A brow rose over Michael's eyes. "So she owes you what? The first kiss? The first fuck? Do you think you earned it from her? Do you have a punch card? Every time you do something nice for her, you're one step closer to fucking her? Because that's not how this whole thing works. You don't get to have her simply because you think you worked for her. She's a person, not some trophy."

"That's not what I meant." He didn't like how that accusation made him feel. He didn't treat Lucy like that. Hell, most of the time Lucy didn't even realize he'd helped her because he didn't want to make her feel awkward about it.

"But it's how you sound right now." Michael crossed his arms over his chest, shivering a bit as he approached. "You sound like a little boy who thought he'd earned his toy only to find out someone else already took it out of the box and played with it."

"Yeah, I get it." How had he ever thought this could work? It had been another stupid idea in a long line of stupid ideas he'd had over the last several years. He needed to wrap his head around the fact that he'd had his chance with Luce and he'd blown it, and she wouldn't give him another one no matter how hard he tried to take care of her. "I'm some dipshit little boy who doesn't deserve the time of day from you."

A low growl came from Michael. "You are going to make me wish I'd never come off my mountain."

Ty turned because he got it. Michael thought he was a little shit. He'd told him time and time again, but Ty never learned. Well, he would learn this time. He strode toward his Jeep, opening the driver's side door. He had barely welcomed River back and now she would likely take Lucy's side and he would be out. He would lose the best friends he'd ever had. It was everything he'd feared all those years before. It was precisely why he'd turned Lucy down when she'd asked him out in high school.

He was about to back the Jeep up and drive away when the passenger door opened and Michael hopped in.

"Hey, what the hell are you doing?" Ty wanted to leave. He would go back to his place at the resort and he would stay there for at least a week. Maybe two. He had no delusion that Lucy wouldn't go back to Michael and finish what they started. He didn't want to watch them as they started their happy coupledom.

"I'm doing exactly what you did to me, asshole." Michael settled his big body on the seat, slamming the door. "You pulled me into this situation. I didn't want to be here. I didn't want the damn responsibility, which is precisely why I stayed away from her. But now I'm here and I have to be the reasonable adult, and that means getting into this Jeep to talk some sense into you, and I don't like it at all. In fact, I'm pretty pissed about it."

"Then feel free to get the fuck out." He was pretty pissed about everything.

"I can't, you asshole," Michael replied with the huff Ty had started to understand meant he was resigned to something. "You brought me into this, and now I realize why you and Lucy haven't gotten together."

"I'm sure it's because I'm not half the man you are."

"No, it's because the two of you don't fucking communicate for shit. I thought it was fine, Ty. I thought it would be fine to kiss her. I didn't realize you had some rule against how she and I should act when you aren't around. I needed clear guidelines because I thought my relationship with Lucy was controlled by me and not by you."

Ty sat back because put like that he did sound like a petulant child. "I didn't mean to try to control anything."

Michael was quiet for a moment as though he was trying to figure something out. "I don't know if you're lying to me or yourself."

That was a good question, and one he should be honest about. He was good at one, not so great with the other. "Probably both."

Michael pointed a finger his way. "And now we're somehow both in trouble with Lucy and my coat is in that cabin and I'm fucking cold and it's fucking your fault."

A sense of dread was starting to replace the righteous anger he'd felt. Had he been wrong? He'd seen what was going on and hadn't bothered to ask why they'd been doing what they were doing. What would he have done if he'd been the one alone with Lucy and he'd had the chance to kiss her? Would he have stopped and said hell no, honey, we have to wait for Michael? We have to make sure we each get equal time with you. If I touch your boobs, you have to let Michael touch them, too.

How had he thought this would work?

"I'm sorry. I didn't realize how it would feel when I saw you with her. I thought I could handle it," Ty said quietly.

Michael groaned, and his head fell back against the seat. He did that huffing thing that made Ty wonder if he was thinking about punching someone—usually him.

"I could go and knock on the door and ask for your coat," Ty offered.

All he got for the offer was a grunt.

"Man, I don't speak your language yet. I'm going to need more than a huff or a grunt because all I pretty much get from those sounds are that you're pissed at me."

"Good. Then you're learning. And you can turn on the heater

because I'm still freezing."

There was a knock on the window and Ty damn near jumped out of his skin. He turned and Jax was standing there, Michael's coat in his hand. At least that solved one problem. He rolled the window down and held a hand out.

"Lucy wanted me to bring this out here," Jax explained.

He gripped Michael's coat and passed it over. Now the other man could leave him alone to his misery. He could get in that SUV of his and head back to his shitty place on the mountain and he and Lucy could start over without him tomorrow. "Thanks. Sorry for wrecking the homecoming."

Jax grinned. "Hell, no. It was a very Bliss way to come home. And now I've got pizza."

It was okay since he wasn't hungry anymore. Why wasn't Michael moving? He kept his attention on Jax because there were still some problems he hadn't considered at all. "Are you going to let Lucy stay in the guest room tonight? She doesn't have anywhere to go." He looked Michael's way. "Unless you were planning to take her back to your place."

"Ty, I don't want to go back to my place," Michael shot back. He'd covered his torso with his coat like it was a blanket. "I told you it's fucking cold and now I'm hungry and that dude's going to eat my dinner."

Jax gave him a thumbs-up. "I am. It smells delicious, and aren't you the survivalist guy? Shouldn't you forage or find something to kill and eat?"

"He's not a survivalist." Apparently Jax hadn't spent a lot of time with Michael during his brief stay here.

"Then why would he live in that rattrap?" Jax asked. "It's cold as hell and that place doesn't have heat, from what I heard. I thought he was probably writing about how to survive or maybe he was trying to stay off the grid for some reason. You know you can be off the grid and still have heat."

"I had my rage to keep me warm," Michael growled back. "And honestly, I'm not much of a hunter. I've been living off MREs and canned chili. I was looking forward to the pizza."

He was going to ignore Michael for now since he didn't seem to be going away. "Can you let Lucy stay?"

"Oh, I don't think River would let her leave at this point," Jax replied. "They are doing that thing that women do where they way overshare. This could take all night. Lucy can stay in the guest room for as long as she needs to. So don't worry about her. Worry about her ever talking to you again and the way the whole town is going to react to this scandal."

"Scandal?" He wasn't sure why anyone had to know that he'd gotten shut out.

"Yeah, it's a fucking scandal because you acted like an ass and made Lucy feel bad for being with one of the men who is trying to date her," Michael said, his jaw tight. "It's like you slut shamed her for kissing her boyfriend, which is stupid because I'm not a boy."

"Yes, whole-ass-grown-man friend is better," Jax replied. "We should call you that."

"It's not a scandal because no one knows about it." Now that he really considered it, Michael had a point. He should have communicated better. He should have been calm and asked them if they'd meant to leave him out and explained how it made him feel.

There was a dinging on his cell phone that let him know a text was coming through. Maybe it was Lucy. Maybe she knew he was out here and wanted to explain what had happened now that they had calmed down. There was another ding from Michael's cell which made Ty wonder how the man charged his phone at his rage-heated home.

They both pulled their phones, and Michael started growling again.

Gentlemen, it has come to our attention that you're struggling. I invite you to come out to the estate tomorrow for breakfast to talk about this problem.

"Why is Stef Talbot texting me?" Stef was kind of a big deal in Bliss. "What problem is he talking about?"

Before Michael could reply, there was another ding. Ty glanced down. This one was from Max Harper.

Dude, you fucked around and Stef found out and now I have to get my ass up early in the morning. Fuck you, Ty.

Max made it clear how he felt with a series of poop emojis. A cold chill that had nothing to do with the fact that it had started snowing went through Ty. "Does this mean what I think it means?"

"It means we're getting called to Stef's so the men of Bliss can drag us over hot coals because you're a jealous little shit," Michael said. "There better be bacon, and if it's not a buffet, I'm eating yours."

"How do they know?" Ty whispered the question because now he was a bit worried Stef had the whole town wired for sound.

Michael sent him a look that let him know it was a dumb question. "I would say your friend there is a meddling asshole."

Ty turned to Jax, who gave him a thumbs-up. "Stef sent his personal plane to pick us up from Dallas but he told me I had to monitor the situation with Lucy for him. Apparently the Men's Council on Bliss Relations is worried you two won't be good at sharing and will give the whole town a bad reputation."

"With who?" Michael asked. "Is there a Zagat rating system for towns filled with freaking threesomes?"

Jax shrugged. "It's a bigger community than you would think. I was just doing my job. Have fun, you two. I've got pizza to eat and a whole lot of naps to take. I've spent years on the run waiting for someone to kill me or to get arrested and thrown in some European jail. I'm going to enjoy every minute of the rest of my life."

He turned and jogged back into his cabin.

Ty sat back, the whole of what he'd done hitting him squarely in the chest.

He'd fucked everything up.

"Roll up the damn window, Ty. You might be used to this kind of cold, but I'm from Florida and my rage doesn't warm me like it used to," Michael complained.

Ty rolled the window up. "I'm sorry. I...I saw the two of you together and I overreacted."

Michael was quiet for a moment. "Did you hate seeing me with her that much?"

"I don't know. I didn't think I would. I've kind of had a couple of fantasies about it over the last few weeks. I might have been thinking about it longer than I admitted."

"And I didn't think about it at all, and when I was kissing her tonight, I thought about the fact that you might walk in and demand equal attention." Michael sighed. "And I didn't have a problem with it. I thought about how hot it might be to watch you with her."

"Seriously?"

Michael looked straight ahead, watching the snow drift around outside, swirling in white waves. "Yeah."

"You weren't trying to cut me out?" This is what they should have done.

"No. I wasn't. I got caught up in a moment, and I honestly can't promise you it won't happen again. I don't expect you to not touch her if I'm not around."

"Of course you don't. I don't either. I'm sorry, Michael."

"Yeah, I am, too. I'm especially sorry about the pizza and not getting to finish what I started and not getting to sleep in a nice bed tonight," Michael admitted.

"I thought you didn't like nice things." He was known for shunning the things everyone else wanted, but maybe Sawyer was right and Michael was going through more than a minimalist stage.

"Like I said, my rage doesn't keep me warm the way it used to. And my spinal column doesn't give a crap that I want to punish myself in an endless guilt cycle. It wants a nice bed."

Well, at least the man was willing to admit what he was doing to himself. It was a good start. "No one's using my second bedroom for now."

Michael relaxed again, his eyes closing. "Good. Then we can tell those nosy assholes we sat up all night talking about our feelings when what we really did was drink a couple of beers, watch the game, and go to bed. But I was serious about the bacon. I'm going to eat yours tomorrow. It's your punishment."

How had he gone from walking away from the whole relationship to ending up with Michael as a houseguest? And he was being called in before the King of Bliss to account for his actions. And he'd lost his bacon rights.

It had been a weird, shitty night.

"Shouldn't you take your own car?"

Michael didn't even open his eyes. "The keys are inside the cabin. It's lost to me now. Just go. Hope you have food at your place."

"Well, it is a resort. We can go to the kitchens." Was he really going to hang with Michael tonight? Maybe they should have done more of that, too.

"Good."

He glanced back at the cabin, thinking about Lucy in there. She'd been so beautiful tonight, and he'd made her feel bad. "Maybe we should try to talk to her."

"Oh, hell no. I promise you she's cursing your name. Better to let her yell about you to her girlfriend than get in the line of fire right now," Michael advised. "You can send her a groveling text later on tonight. You can talk about how crappy our night was without her."

He was probably right. He started the Jeep. "Are you sure you shouldn't take your car?"

"Just drive, Ty. You wanted a partner. Well, you've got one, and that means we have to stick together. I assure you once she finds out I went back to your place, she'll have a million questions, and she'll have to deal with us if she wants them answered," Michael murmured.

Actually, that wasn't a terrible plan. He could text her a sincere apology and ask her if they could talk when she felt comfortable talking. To both of them.

Ty pulled away feeling slightly more positive than he'd been before.

* * * *

"I am so sorry, River. I didn't realize you were coming home tonight. I apologize for you walking in on something you shouldn't have had to see." Lucy's heart was still pounding in her chest as she walked back into the cabin.

Ty was such an asshole. How could he have done that to her?

River walked up to her, opening her arms. "Don't you apologize. I missed you. I missed you and Ty, and I missed this place so much while we were gone. I'm sorry I didn't call you to warn you we'd managed to find a ride home this evening. I wanted to surprise you."

She hugged her friend, breathing her in. She'd missed River on a level she hadn't thought possible. Tears sprang to her eyes, and she held her tight. "I'm so happy you're home. Phone calls don't cut it."

River squeezed her, too. "They do not, and as much as I came to love the people we were with, they weren't you."

Had she worried about this? Deep down, had she worried that River would go out into the big world and find more interesting friends and leave her behind? Yes. She had. That fear of being left behind by someone important to her had been simmering underneath everything. It might be why she'd reacted the way she had to Ty. "I spend a lot of time with Hope and Beth, but they aren't you."

River stepped back, looking her over. "You have a lot to tell me. When did you start dating Ty? And Michael?"

"Tonight." It hadn't taken long for that experiment to fail.

River looked over where her husband was moving the pizza boxes Ty left behind. Her eyes narrowed. "Tell me you didn't text Stef."

"Of course I did," Jax replied. "Hey, what festivals did I miss? And protests. I'm excited about joining all the protests."

"The Winter Festival is coming up, and Nell and Henry always have a protest going on. Why would Jax text Stef?" Suspicion crept over her. "Tell me the town isn't talking about us. It was our first date. I know they know, but they can't possibly be this nosy."

"Okay, I know you're not technically from Bliss," River began, "but I need you to hear those words coming out of your mouth."

"Everyone's up in everyone else's business," Jax agreed and sighed, a happy sound. "It makes me miss my old team. They were a bunch of dudes who pretend to be all tough but really live for gossip. So relationship meddling feels like home."

Lucy felt herself flush. "And you are one of those, Jax?"

"One of the dudes who spent a lot of time in the military and now lives to watch other people fuck up?" Jax asked. "Yes. That is who I am. Not that you fucked up. You seemed to be doing real well there."

She'd probably gone past pink and into ruby red.

"Jax," River hissed. "We talked about this. I'm sorry, Lucy. I'm still teaching him how to act in the real world. Between the whole losing his memory and being tortured thing, and then spending years with Big Tag's group, he is not ready for polite society."

Lucy had to laugh at that thought. "It sounds like he'll fit in quite well in Bliss. Not a lot of polite society here."

Jax held up his phone. "Exactly. I'm getting in good with the king."

Meaning Stef. "So you texted Stef and told him what?"

"That you and Michael understood the whole threesome thing, but Ty needs a refresher course," Jax replied.

"He's going to get called before the men." River put a hand to her mouth, stopping a laugh.

He really was, and it wouldn't be fun for Ty. Michael would likely tell them all to fuck off and go back to his mountain, but Ty would show up. It served him right to have to deal with Max Harper telling him what a fuck-up he was and Stef lecturing him about thruples when he wasn't even in one.

Michael. She'd felt so good when she was in his arms. And then she'd seen Ty and felt guilty.

She caught sight of another reason to feel guilty. She'd left them both out there, but Michael didn't even have a coat. "Jax, could you take Michael his coat?"

"Sure." He grabbed it and nodded his wife's way and then looked down at Buster. "You coming with me, buddy?"

Buster jumped on the couch and settled in.

Jax sighed. "That dog's soft. Be right back."

The minute the door closed, River walked over to the TV and turned it on, quickly finding a sports channel. "Come with me. He's been traveling for days. Between the pizza and the game, he won't even notice we're gone."

"You're trying to ditch your husband?" Lucy grabbed the wine and a couple of glasses. She would need the alcohol because she suspected River had questions.

"We've been together twenty-four seven for eighteen months worried that he was going to be killed or taken into custody. Except for the brief but terrifying period of time when he was actually taken into custody, but that's another story. Yes. I'm happily ditching him, and come tomorrow he's looking for a job and we're going to be normal and take breaks from each other." River walked down the hallway to the main bedroom. It was closed, the guest room open and light on. "You didn't sleep in the big bedroom?"

Lucy shrugged. "I kept it ready for you. I changed the sheets last week and kept it all clean. I made sure everything in the bathroom works." That wasn't exactly true. "I mean Ty did."

River opened the door and walked in, looking around, and the happiness in her heart was easy to see. "Of course he did, and you made sure it was all perfect and warm for me to come home to." There were tears in River's eyes as she turned back to Lucy. "I'm home."

Lucy poured out two glasses of Moscato and handed her one. "To homecomings."

River held the glass up and clinked it with Lucy's. "To homecomings." She sat on the bed and patted the place beside her. "Now tell me what happened with Ty. Or rather let me guess. You finally started to get close to Michael, and Ty realized he couldn't sit back and wait anymore or he was going to lose you."

"Lose me? This is what I don't understand. He shows up at Trio the other night and kisses me and tells me he's always wanted me."

River nodded. "Yes. I suspected he would do that someday."

It would have been good if River had told her. "But I tried to get him to date me in high school and he said no."

A frown crossed River's face. "Luce, that was years and years ago. You didn't exactly tell him you wanted to date him. You asked him to prom, and he suggested the three of us go together as friends. Are you still angry with him for that?"

"No. Of course not." It had been a little more complex than that, but she understood that's what River believed. "I tried to kiss him. I kind of threw myself at him, and he turned me down. I almost understand why he did it now. We're too important to risk it."

"Risk your friendship?" River asked.

"Yes." She'd missed him so much while he'd been in college. She'd been sore about his rejection for a while, but Ty had worked his way back into her life, and when he'd left for college, the world had seemed a bit dimmer. "What if it didn't work out?"

"That is what you say when you don't really want a guy."

Lucy huffed. "Well, that's what he said to me back in high school."

River nodded at her like she'd just made her point. "So you are still mad about it. Come on. You know Ty. Have you asked him why he really turned you down? You asked him to prom. You asked him a

106

couple of months before he was leaving. Up until that moment you didn't show any interest in him at all."

It had been hard to be close to him but to never be with him. It was funny, though, because for all Ty's golden good looks, he hadn't had a high school girlfriend. He'd seemed happy to be around her and River and Sawyer. "I've loved him since I was a kid, but I didn't want a boyfriend for a long time."

"Because of your dad," River said with obvious sympathy.

So many things went back to how she'd been raised. "It was a lot of things, but yeah. I watched my dad go through woman after woman, and it seemed like friends were a better thing to be. Not that Dad had female friends."

"No, but he did have a bunch of drinking buddies who would show up and harass you when we were teens," River pointed out. "I always wondered if one of them ever tried anything he shouldn't."

"A couple of times," Lucy admitted. Sometimes her dad had parties that went late into the night, and more than once one of his friends had thought it would be funny to hit on his teenaged daughter. "But I got away and I told my dad. To his credit he believed me and took care of it. They didn't come around again. And yes, I think that was part of it. I was scared of intimacy for a long time. Dad doesn't party that way anymore. That's why I was able to leave. Now he's just lazy, but I don't worry about anything bad happening to the girls. Back in high school, I finally realized I wasn't going to get what I wanted if I never tried, and Ty said no."

"He knew he was going to college and that he wouldn't be home for more than holidays and summers for four years. He asked you to come with him."

"He was joking about that." It had been an absurd idea. She'd thought he was afraid of going alone.

"No, he wasn't," River countered. "He had it planned out. I remember vividly. He had the applications for that community college that was close to his. He was going to apply for all kinds of scholarships and loans for you, but you told him no."

"I couldn't leave my brothers and sisters." She hadn't gone to college for a lot of reasons, money being the simplest one. Family was much more complex. "They needed me. Dad won't hurt them, but he thinks they should be able to do everything for themselves, and that included feeding themselves when they were just kids. I couldn't go with Ty. Do you think I didn't want to?"

"Did you ask him to stay?" River asked, though she knew the answer. They'd had this conversation before, so Lucy took it as a reminder of what the real history was. Sometimes she needed that.

"He had a scholarship. I couldn't ask him to stay." Even if she'd wanted to, which she hadn't at the time because he'd turned her down. "And he didn't offer to stay." A bitterness she hadn't felt in forever hit her, and she realized River was right. "I'm punishing him for not staying with me. For leaving me behind."

"And there it is. You even got into a relationship right before he came back so you wouldn't have to face him without a man on your arm." River sat back against the headboard. "Honey, you and Ty have been fucked up forever. He was afraid the two of you would fall apart if you tried doing it long distance, and you asked him at the last possible moment because you thought if you were together, he wouldn't leave you like your mom did. Like all of them did."

"You could have pointed that out to me."

"I was a kid, too. I've gotten way better at analyzing since I married Jax. I spent a lot of time with a woman therapist who helped him. And that got me to thinking about my friends who were obviously in love and never managed to make it work," River said. "I also have my theories about our wild man in the woods, but I'm willing to wait and see on that one because the two of you looked hot together tonight. Super hot."

There went the blush again. "It got out of hand, but I wouldn't take it back. Honestly, it's better to know that it won't work."

"Well, it can't if you have that attitude." River set her glass down. "What do you like about Michael?"

"I like how I feel when I'm around him." She'd thought a lot about this. "It's different than Ty. There's a comfort level with Ty, an easy-going affection that I sometimes think is so engrained in my life I don't know how I would live without it. Even when I'm mad at him, I know I'll see him tomorrow and it will be okay. But with Michael, I get to be a slightly different version of me. Sexier. He's exciting on a physical level, but there's more to it. I feel like he might need me in a way Ty doesn't."

"Oh, I think Ty would say he needs you."

"Not like Michael does. And not like Michael might need Ty, too." Lucy finally said the real reason she'd agreed to this crazy plan. "Michael went through something awful, and he needs to learn it's okay to care about people again, to trust people again, and Ty's impossible to ignore. He's that guy who walks in a room and brings sunshine with him."

Was that what she'd always feared? That if she made the wrong decision she would be left in the dark? That the essential light that had filled her life for so long would be taken from her?

"Then it sounds like you need to talk to them," River prodded.

"I think Ty made himself very plain tonight. It's over." Even if she wanted to try again, he'd slammed that door closed. "Michael is like a wounded animal. He won't try again. I wouldn't be surprised if he doesn't head back up to his place and we don't see him again for a long time."

"Then I should go tell Jax to take him his keys." River stood up.

"I thought they would be in his coat pocket." Was the man standing outside in the cold? She started for the living room. The idea of seeing Michael again hurt her heart, but she couldn't leave him out there.

Jax was sitting on his sofa, feet propped up on the ottoman and a piece of pizza in one hand. He was watching a soccer game. Apparently he and River had gotten very British during their time abroad. He grinned up at her. "Hey, they're replaying the Manchester match on satellite."

"I thought you would like that, babe." River took a sip of her wine. "I'm going to take Michael his keys. Is he on the porch?"

"Nah," Jax replied. Buster sat by him, watching that piece of pizza like it was his life's work. "He and Ty took off. Last I heard they were bitching at each other about bacon or something. I mean Ty wasn't bitching. Michael was. Carnivores are serious about their bacon. By the way, there's a mushroom and peppers in the other box. I'm giving the sausage on this one to Buster."

The vegetarians were in the house. "Where did they go? Michael left his car here?"

"Yep." Jax went back to watching a bunch of dudes running around kicking a ball. "I think they were going to Ty's place. Apparently Michael's rage is no longer white hot enough to heat his cabin, and he's done with it. That guy should see a therapist."

Her cell phone buzzed. Lucy walked to the bar and saw what she'd missed before. Michael's key ring was sitting there. It had a whole bunch of keys on it. More than she would have thought he would carry. There was even one that stood out from the others. It was a custom one with white Js all over a black background.

Jessie. He was still carrying around her keys?

Her cell buzzed again, and she turned it over to see the screen. Michael had sent a text.

On our way back to Ty's. Don't worry. He's already sorry. Thanks for tonight. No matter how short it was. Hope he doesn't snore. Good night, baby.

He hadn't left. He'd left her, but he hadn't left them. He was with Ty.

He'd practically told her he would take care of Ty.

She stared at the words for the longest time.

Chapter Six

Michael looked around the elegantly appointed dining room and thought about how he'd aspired to this level of wealth once. Maybe not this level, exactly. Stefan Talbot's kind of wealth tended to be generational, but at least he'd aspired to having a dining room where he could sit down with friends and family and celebrate holidays and birthdays.

He had a folding table, and he only had that because Nell had brought it to his cabin and unfolded a plain tablecloth and set up two chairs.

He'd ignored it, preferring to eat his shitty dinners in the rocking chair that was going to fall apart at any moment.

"I do smell bacon, Mike." Ty looked nervous and had ever since they'd driven up to the circular drive.

They'd been shown to this dining room and told the rest of the party would be in soon. Mr. Talbot, the housekeeper had explained, was dealing with a minor domestic emergency and they should help themselves to coffee.

Ty was a weirdo.

Fuck. He needed to stop thinking that way. He was complex. Ty was naïve about so many things, and then he had insights that kind of set Michael back. He was the single kindest human being Michael had met in a long time, and he couldn't trust it because he'd been burned before. He didn't think he could believe in Ty's goodness because he hadn't seen Jessie's badness.

But hadn't he? He'd mistaken narcissism for self-centeredness. He'd looked for the good in her sea of red flags because he'd wanted her.

"I feel like I'm about to get fired. Can Stef fire me from Bliss?" Ty started pacing. "Like I won't be able to go to Trio or hang out at Stella's? I know I don't buy a ton of groceries, but I get them at the Trading Post."

"Stef isn't going to kick you out of Bliss." Michael grabbed a cup and poured some of the rich-smelling coffee in. "Do you want coffee? Maybe you shouldn't have caffeine."

Ty had seemed jumpy all morning as it was.

Ty frowned and poured his own coffee as though in protest. But then Michael wasn't worried about the caffeine intake at all since Ty put an unholy amount of milk and sugar in the mug. "I don't know. A couple of guys started a coffee shop on the edge of town two years back and they were rude to Stella, and they disappeared. If Stef wants me gone, I'll be gone, and I might not be like in another town. I might be fertilizer. Have you seen how nice the plants are around here?"

"That's because my gardener is excellent at his job," a deep voice said. Stef Talbot walked in dressed in khaki slacks and a collared shirt, boots on his feet. He had dark hair and piercing eyes that let a man know Stef was in charge of most of the world around him. "Though you should know I did get rid of those men who thought they could come into my town and ignore our town ordinances."

"We have ordinances?" Ty asked. "Because I was unaware we believed in those."

"We do." Stef stepped up to the coffee urn. "Including not insulting the women of the town or making fun of our more eccentric citizenry. However, I assure you those enterprising young men aren't buried in the rose beds. I simply bought the building they were housed in and kicked them out. I believe they tried to move their shop to Pagosa Springs before they found all their bank loan prospects had dried up. So sad."

Ty had gone a little pale.

"He's not kicking you out, Ty." One of the things he'd started to suspect was that Ty was an overgrown Golden Retriever. Handsome. Athletic. Looked like he could take down the world if he wanted to, but he almost never wanted to. Sometimes that dumbass loyal Golden needed a Rottweiler best friend. "If he tries, I'll kick his ass. I assure you I still know how to do that. I'm much better since Henry taught me a few things. Stop intimidating him, Stef."

Ty stepped up as though he'd been given the go-ahead to have some confidence. "Yeah. Mike's the only one who gets to intimidate me."

A smile curled Stef's lips up. "Then half my work is done here." He moved to the table as a chime sounded through the house. "That should be Max and Rye. I also invited Jamie and Noah along."

Max Harper strode into the dining room, a baby strapped to his chest. The little guy was facing in and curled against his dad's body. "This better be good because Rach found out she's pregnant, and she is pissed. I'm pretty sure we're never allowed in the house again, much less back in bed. I thought we should stay in the house so she can't lock us out, but Rye insisted on giving her space."

"She's not going to lock us out," Rye said with a sigh. "She's just surprised, and we're both going to have to man up and get deballed."

Max put a hand on his baby's back. "No, we don't. That's why I stole Ethan. She's got to let Ethan back in so she can feed him. We'll slip inside and then never leave again."

"Yes, I believe you're making the point," Stef said with a shake of his head. "Your wife managed to get pregnant before the last baby is off the breast. If she asks me for help, I'll have you kidnapped and get the job done before you know it."

"But I wore a condom and everything." Max gritted his teeth. "Damn my strong sperm."

"Hey, I can do it for you for free." Noah Bennet walked in beside his brother. "I'm a doctor."

James Glen had on jeans and a T-shirt, and his hair was still slightly damp as though he'd come here straight from a shower. He'd very likely been up since the crack of dawn working at the ranch he owned, and he'd had to clean up before coming here. "He's excellent, Max. He can have that problem solved for you in no time at all."

"He castrates bulls." Max moved away from the newcomers. "Rye, we should run."

Noah snorted and poured himself a glass of juice as the housekeeper walked in and began setting up the warm portion of the buffet. "Calm down, man. Your balls are safe."

"Not from Rachel, they aren't," Rye said with a frown.

"Are you three okay?" Stef looked concerned again.

Max held up his free hand. "We're fine. Financially fine. Emotionally fine. Like Rye said. We're surprised is all, and yes, I'll be getting my balls scooped and taking care of everything. We talked about having one more, though we didn't think it would happen so soon."

Michael had thought he would have a couple of kids by now. He'd thought he would be married and moving on with his life.

Lately he'd started to wonder whether or not Lucy wanted kids.

Ty snorted as he drank his milk and sugar with a hint of coffee. "Max is getting his balls scooped out. That's pretty funny."

Of course, Lucy already had a kid. He stared at Ty until Ty sobered.

Michael turned to Stef. He needed to set some ground rules. He got that there was a way to do things in Bliss, but he wasn't simply going to roll over. He might not be here all that much longer. No more than a month or two. Six at the most. "All right. We're here. You have until I'm finished with breakfast to say what you want to say and then Ty and I are leaving."

"We are?" Ty asked.

"Well, I'm leaving and I have the keys to your Jeep, so if you want access to your vehicle, you're leaving, too."

Ty frowned. "That doesn't sound fair, but I do need the Jeep, so I'll go with you. Stef, you should talk fast. He eats like he's in prison, and I think he should be full because he ate everything in my apartment this morning, but he might be able to handle more."

"Well, you didn't have all that much." Ty's place might be neater than his, but it was pretty spartan. Still, that second bed had been comfortable and warm, and despite the fact that he'd lain in it and stared at the ceiling for the longest time trying to decide what he wanted, it hadn't been the worst night of his life.

He'd kind of enjoyed sitting with Ty and watching the late football game while they ate turkey sandwiches they'd made down in the lodge's kitchens. It had been nice. It had been comfortable.

It had felt like they were...friends? He wouldn't not call them that, but there had oddly been something more.

He didn't trust the feeling but he also couldn't shove it away, so he was making a few changes. That's what he'd decided the night before. It wasn't going to be forever, but he could make sure Ty and Lucy would be okay.

He moved to the now set up buffet and filled a plate with bacon and eggs and some delicious-smelling hash browns.

"I thought he didn't eat a lot." Rye Harper was watching him, murmuring to Stef. "I've watched him walk into Stella's, order a burger, and barely touch it."

"It's probably because Hal doesn't like to actually cook beef." Max didn't seem at all worried that he had a sleeping baby on his chest. He just moved in behind Michael and started heaping on the food.

"I wasn't hungry then." It was as simple as that. "I'm hungry now, and I'll stop at the Trading Post and get Ty some food. All he's got is a bunch of canned soup and tinned chicken and cheese."

"And some pasta," Ty corrected. "I'm making cheesy chicken pasta casserole next week. I mean, my mom's making it."

"She figured out you make the casseroles." He should have told him last night.

Ty stopped. "She figured it out or you told her?"

"She figured it out." But he should probably be honest. "Though I might have led her along a little."

"Hah. I call a violation," Noah said, holding a hand up.

"Yeah, that's pretty shitty," James agreed.

"A violation?" Michael moved to the table, wondering how fast he could eat. It was a lot of food, but he could still maybe manage it in five minutes, six tops if he let them talk and didn't defend himself.

"We got a code, man," Max replied. He took the chair across from Michael while Ty settled in beside him. "You have to protect your brother."

"He's not my brother," Michael pointed out between bites.

"You should treat him like he's your brother and you have to protect him," James said. "Unless he's doing something dangerous. You gotta stick together."

"Against your wife?" There were a couple of problems he saw with this whole code thing.

"Not against her," Rye replied. "That's not what we're saying. We are saying you need to present a united front from time to time."

"Against your wife." Maybe he wouldn't storm out. This could be fun because they were under the mistaken impression that he was going to toe some line the other threesomes in town did.

"It isn't like that," James insisted. "All we're saying is you two can't be at each other's throats if you're going to go after the same woman. A threesome can't function if you don't work together. You have to take her down together. That's the mistake you made last night."

He felt the growl in the back of his throat before he heard it. He really wished people would keep their noses out of his business. He wasn't even sure where they were going with this, but he felt the need to defend himself and their privacy. "The mistake was Jax getting in the middle of everything. Stay out of it. Stef, you might be the dude with the most money here, but don't think you can buy me out like you did those assholes. If I want to stay, I'll stay. If I want Lucy and Ty, I'll take Lucy and Ty."

"We're only trying to give you tips on how to make this work," Rye explained.

Stef had taken a place at the head of the table. "I believe what Michael is trying to say is that he's not like the rest of you. He and Ty aren't brothers and likely won't have a brotherly relationship."

"What does that mean?" Noah asked.

It was good to know one person seemed to understand. "It means you four are brothers and have a long history. Your relationship with each other was solidly in place before you met the woman you wanted. In our case, the relationship that was already in place was between Lucy and Ty."

Ty held a hand up. "I have never once thought of Lucy as a sister, so don't make that comparison. I pretty much started to want that girl once I understood what my dick was for."

"All I'm saying is that Lucy, Ty, and I have options," Michael explained. "It means that this whole boys against the girl thing isn't going to work for me. Your wives run your households. Good for you. I'm very likely going to need to run mine, so if you're going to have this conversation, you should have it with Lucy and Ty about how to handle me."

"Are you sure you're not a Dom?" Stef asked.

He sat back. "All I know is I need to be somewhat in control, and Lucy and Ty need me to be."

Ty held up a hand. "Wait. Does this make me the sub?"

He barely managed to not roll his eyes. "I'm not spanking you, Ty. But we are going to talk about how you deal with Lucy because you're fucking up. Of course she is, too."

"Okay, because for a second there it sounded like you were opening the door to..." Ty nodded like everyone knew what he was saying.

"To sex. Between you and him." Max smiled like he was the smartest thing in the world.

Michael shrugged. "If it happens it happens. I'm interested in having sex with Lucy, but if this went anywhere, I don't see why we would shut the door on experimenting if we all three wanted to. That's what I was talking about. The brotherly thing isn't going to work for me. And fuck all of you for forcing us to have this conversation in public. Though you should understand if it happened, I wouldn't give a shit who knew."

"Good for you." Stef picked up his fork. "Ty, I was worried he was going to steamroll over you. Now I know he will, but I approve because I don't believe he's doing it to cut you off from Lucy."

"No, he's doing it because he likes me, too." Ty's lips kicked up.

Again, he'd thought that was all part of the deal. "I don't hate you so much I would give up the chance to be with her, and I'm honest about what could happen and not worried about it."

"So you're saying something could happen, and if it did you wouldn't like freak out and worry about your sexuality and go into some weird shame spiral that would ruin all our lives," Ty prompted.

Michael grunted his assent because that summed up the situation. Max and Rye seemed to have some freaky twin thing going on where they would practically read each other's minds. It probably served them well when in bed with their wife, but he and Ty weren't ever going to have that. It would be awkward and weird, and their dicks would probably brush up against each other at some point because they didn't have a million years of practice. Michael had plugged that scenario into his decision making and decided it wouldn't be the end of the world.

Ty gave him a thumbs-up. "Cool. I wouldn't be worried about it either if it did happen. But if Lucy thinks I'm the one cooking for her, she won't eat it. She'll be real stubborn."

"Then we'll spank her together," he replied. "You're going to learn how to take charge sometimes, and she's going to learn that there are some things she shouldn't be stubborn about. And some things she should. She's going to learn it's okay to lean on you and that you can lean right back. She's also going to let us help out with her siblings."

"Why are we here?" James asked. "Because it sounds like Michael knows what he's doing."

Stef sighed. "Well, he's such a secretive bastard I wouldn't have imagined he was so open with his sexuality and smart about how a relationship like this should work. He seems to understand Ty and Lucy. So I approve."

Michael sent Stef his happy middle finger.

Ty winced. "Sorry about that. He speaks a language of grunts and curse words. The rude hand gestures are new. I'm sorry. I get that you're looking out for Lucy."

Ty needed to stop apologizing. He grunted Ty's way.

Ty huffed and shook his head, but there was a gleam in his eyes when he turned to Stef again. "And now you know our intentions are pure and you can stay out of our relationship with Lucy."

That was better.

"Excellent." Stef speared a potato. "I'll leave it all in your hands, but you should know that if you do need advice, the men of Bliss are willing to help. Have you thought about how you're going to approach Lucy again?"

"I thought we would show her we can work together tonight." He'd had enough of Stef. "If things go well, we'll take her back to our place. Now unless we're going to discuss Max's upcoming vasectomy, we're done talking."

"He's worse than Doc was in the beginning," James whispered to his brother.

"Don't talk about Doc." Max had paled, and he put his fork down. "Does it have to be Caleb? He's awful with the prostate exam. I can't imagine what he'll do to my balls."

"We have a place?" Ty asked.

"We have your place." At least the food was excellent. He'd forgotten what good food tasted like. For a long time everything had tasted like ash in his mouth, but he was starting to remember what a good breakfast could do for a man. "It'll have to do."

"And we might have to be sneaky about getting her there," Ty said with a nod.

"Nope." He wasn't going to spend his time playing games, no matter how well intentioned they were. It was time to strip down to the basics and see if they could work.

"What does that mean?" Ty asked.

"Eat your breakfast. You've got the mid shift and then we'll pick Lucy up. She's working a late shift tonight. I'll handle everything. Just be ready to follow my lead."

"I'm kind of afraid not to," Ty admitted.

Then things would work out. For the first time in a long time, he felt a wave of positivity.

He went back for seconds.

* * * *

It had been almost a whole day and no text.

Somehow she'd thought there would be a text. Or a call. Or Michael might drop by to pick up his SUV.

After telling her he'd gone back to Ty's place, she'd expected that they would show up for breakfast. She'd thought she would wake up and both men would be on the porch waiting to apologize and ask her what she was doing this evening.

Working. That was what she was doing. She was working, and it looked like she would stay working.

"Hey, order up." Van had joined her again. They'd spent much of the shift talking about the party they would both be supervising this weekend. Van would run the bar and she would manage the servers.

Would that be when she saw Ty and Michael? When she was at the lodge?

She picked up the tray that held two glasses of white wine and a glass of red and sighed. The jerk siblings were back, though at least the worst of them wasn't around today. She hadn't taken the order, but Zane was on the phone in the back, and it wasn't worth interrupting him.

"Thanks," Van said, already moving to pour out beers.

Trio was rocking this evening. It had been snowing for a couple of days, good white powder that would bring all the skiers out this weekend. Tourists were starting to outnumber the locals, and she realized that lull they got between seasons was over.

Maybe that was a good thing. That lovely lull meant slower business, and now she could concentrate on work and getting the job at the lodge, and she would be so busy it wouldn't matter that Michael and Ty weren't interested in her anymore. She worked her way around the tables toward the booth at the front of the bar.

They'd likely talked and come to the conclusion that it wouldn't work, and that was all right.

It didn't make her heart hurt. It didn't make her ache with what could have been because she'd never believed they'd had a shot in the first place.

The door came open, cold air whooshing in as two big figures moved into the entryway. One of the new hires stood at the hostess stand. She wore a thick sweater over her jeans and Trio T-shirt in deference to that wind that swooped in every time the door opened. Pilar Gomez was a student at Adams State and lived with her parents in Del Norte. She'd hired on to work a few nights a week. Zane always hired more staff for ski season, and this year that meant a lot of college kids. He'd tried to put the Farley twins to work in the kitchen this summer, but they'd blown up one of the dishwashers trying to make it work faster. So it was Pilar, Holly's oldest kiddo Micky Lang, and Van who were helping part time now.

Pilar smiled at the two newcomers and shivered slightly from the cold.

But Lucy suddenly didn't feel cold at all because it wasn't tourists waiting to be seated. Michael and Ty stood there, side by side. They were big and gorgeous and they were here.

Why were they here?

Michael looked up and his eyes locked with hers and—yup—nothing cold there. She could practically feel his hands on her, moving over her hips and dragging her closer to him. She'd felt his cock against her leg, and she hadn't cared about anything but rubbing herself against him and riding him to pleasure.

Michael nodded her way and then followed Pilar.

Ty gave her a bright smile and waved.

He'd kissed her with those ridiculously sensual lips of his and she'd dreamed about it last night, dreamed about those lips moving lower and lower until he had his mouth on her pussy.

"Uh, you need some help there?" Micky Lang had a beer in one hand and a basket of hot wings in the other. He was a lanky twenty-year-old with dark hair and green eyes. He had an apartment on campus but spent a lot of time with his mom and stepdads and baby sister.

She shook herself out of her very not-safe-for-work thoughts. "No. I'm good. Is that for table five? Because they wanted ranch instead of blue cheese. I'm pretty sure I wrote that down, but it must have gotten mixed up."

Micky winced. "While it goes against all my sensibilities, I shall fix the problem."

She ignored the impulse to look back to where Michael and Ty were and proceeded with the job at hand. She made her way to table twelve, where the Foster siblings were seated.

They were all on their phones, but the one named Sonya looked up and smiled. "Hey. Nice to see you again. How are you?"

Chet set his phone down and slid her a sly smile as he took his glass of wine. "She's been talking about you nonstop, Lila."

"Her name is Lucy," Kendall chimed in, her fingers moving across the screen. She glanced up. "You should wear a name tag. He would remember your name if it was written close to your boobs."

"Kendall," Sonya hissed her sister's way.

Kendall went right back to her phone. "They're nice boobs, and Chet rarely looks at a woman's face. If you want him to retain knowledge, you have to put it on liquor or boobs."

Chet gave her a completely uncharming smile. "Well at least my sister knows me. And I expect credit for even remembering she has a name. I was close. Lucy, dear, I'm so glad you came over because I wanted to thank you for taking my brother down a peg. It's the biggest thing to happen to this family in forever."

Lucy felt herself flush. She'd thought for sure Brock Foster would act like nothing happened. "He talked to you about that? He was…"

Sonya held up a hand to stop her. "You do not have to tell me what my asshole brother was doing. I'm sure he hit on you and when you turned him down, he got aggressive."

Chet chuckled. "Of course that wasn't his story. He said you tried to roll him for cash."

"He doesn't carry cash. He probably wouldn't even know how to pay for something he couldn't use his smart wallet on," Kendall said.

"I didn't…" She hadn't thought she would have to defend herself. "It was what Sonya said."

Sonya reached out and patted her arm. "I knew exactly what happened. Don't worry about it. It's sadly not the first time my brother's harassed a woman, and it won't be the last, but I should warn you to watch out for him because he was really mad about it."

Kendall's lips curved up in a Cheshire cat grin. "He made us call a doctor and everything. Apparently the cute EMT was off that night so he got this super-grumpy hottie. He was not impressed with Brock, and I'm fairly certain the doc meant to handle his junk roughly."

"He was trying to make sure Brock was okay," Sonya countered. "Brock was drunk and being obnoxious. I just wish Dad had been around. Brock always acts like an angel when our dad's around."

"Yeah, well, when the old man dies, Brock will get to be a god," Chet muttered.

She wasn't sure what that meant, but the fact that they'd called Caleb out to the lodge worried her. She wasn't surprised Caleb hadn't talked to her about it. Brock likely wouldn't have remembered her name, and Caleb wouldn't have cared enough to call the police and report an assault. He would have told Brock he'd deserved it and to stay away from the women of Bliss if he wanted to keep his balls.

But that didn't mean she wasn't in trouble. "Is he all right?"

She didn't really care, but she might like to know if she was going to be sued. Nate wouldn't arrest her, but the Foster family had power outside of Bliss.

Kendall shrugged. "He's already screwing some chick he met on the ski lift. He's fine."

"But he didn't want to come here with us." There was a wealth of satisfaction in Sonya's voice. "He dropped us off but wouldn't come in."

"And now we have a safe space," Kendall announced.

Chet lifted his glass. "So cheers to Lucy. I proclaim you Lucy of the hard knee, vanquisher of Brock."

She glanced at her watch. Only another couple of minutes and she could run away. She would hop in her piece of crap car and hide at River's. "Is there anything else I can get you?"

"Nah, we've got to leave in a couple of minutes," Sonya said. "We're heading back to LA after the weekend, but thanks for putting big brother in his place."

At least they would be gone, and even if she got the job at the lodge, she wouldn't be the one personally taking care of the villas. There was a fleet of butlers and housekeepers to deal with the wealthiest of the lodge's clients. She would stick to the main lodge and be happy to do it. "I hope you have a good trip back."

She turned and started to walk toward the kitchen. At least Michael and Ty were on the other side of the building. She could barely see Ty's golden hair over the booth. Hopefully they wouldn't even notice that she was sneaking out the back.

Of course they might not care at all.

It was perverse. She should be brave and march right over there and yell at both of them.

Instead she managed to run into Zane instead.

"Hey, you okay?" Zane glanced over at the booth she'd come from. "They give you trouble? I told the asshole who cornered you not to come back. I assumed they would all stay away."

He'd told Brock not to come back? That wasn't a surprise. Zane wouldn't want that man around any of his employees. "They're fine. Not any worse than other tourists."

"Ah, so that look on your face is about the knuckleheads in the back," Zane surmised. "You know they were called to Stef's this morning, right? I'm surprised they're still hanging out together. I would have given them two days before Michael killed Ty, so I've already lost that bet."

"Yeah, they're together and not with me," she pointed out. She needed to get away. "Can I knock off a couple of minutes early?"

"You know you could go over and talk to them," Zane chided.

"So that's a no?" She wasn't sure she was ready. Obviously this morning and last night had been more than enough trouble for Michael. She'd always known he would be easy to scare off.

Zane sighed. "Nah, you can go. Can you take the trash out before you leave? The kitchen got a big order in and I need to check on a couple of tables."

"Sure." She would happily empty all the trash if it meant getting her out of yet another humiliating position. She would take it out and run like the coward she was.

She grabbed her coat and emptied the trash. The kitchen was bustling and warm, the smell of the day's special scenting the air. It was Zane's beef stew, which he served with cornbread and a side salad. How many times had she been grateful for that winter treat? She was going to miss this place if she got the job.

But sometimes that was what happened. She'd thought about turning Cole Roberts down because she would miss this little family she'd formed here at Trio, but she had to trust that she could come back, that they wouldn't forget her entirely.

Like her mom had.

She shoved through the back door and stomped down the stairs that led to the dumpsters. Was River right and she had deep-seated reasons for holding back from Ty? Did she still believe at her core that she wasn't loveable and no one would stay with her, so why bother trying?

The snow was starting to accumulate. It would be gone as soon as the sun came out tomorrow, but up in the mountains it would stick and add to the winter paradise that was the lodge. In a few weeks even the valley would be blanketed.

Would she and Ty even be talking by then? Or would they pass each other in the hall and nod politely while he went on with his life, went back to his partying ways? As for Michael, she might not see him at all. He would be alone and cold in that cabin of his.

She made her way to the big dumpster and tossed in the bag.

"Hello. I should have known you would be hanging around the trash," a masculine voice said.

She turned and felt her eyes narrow. Brock stood there in the moonlight wearing an expensive-looking coat, jeans, and sneakers that probably cost more than her car. She started to move back to the building when he cut her off.

Fear made her spine straighten. "What do you want?"

"I think you know what I wanted, but you're too much of a bitch to give it to me." He held up his hands as though trying to prove he wasn't dangerous. "But hey, I know when I'm not wanted. I figure you probably don't even like men, and that was my mistake. But *your* mistake was humiliating me."

"I was defending myself," she countered. Luckily there was a security camera looking her way. No one would be monitoring it right now, but at least they would know what happened. "Do I need to do that again?"

Brock chuckled, an unamused sound. "Not at all. You're a violent little thing. No. I won't play your games again. I think you should play some of mine though. The sheriff refused to arrest you for assaulting me, but I think I can do better than putting you in jail. Or we can come to another arrangement."

"I thought I was a lesbian."

He shrugged. "All I care about is my siblings seeing that I get what I want, and nothing stops me. You put me in a position where they think I'm pathetic, and I can't have that. Go out with me and maybe I won't feel the need for revenge. If they think I had you and cut you loose, I might not care what you do with the rest of your small-town shitty life."

"Fuck you." She wasn't about to play his games. She was so sick of assholes who thought they owned the world. "Maybe you should be afraid of me. Maybe I'll sneak into your room one night and you won't wake up in the morning. At least not whole. You like your dick where it is, Brock? Then you better leave me alone."

She moved around him and started up the steps. If he wanted to attack her at least up here the kitchen staff would hear her scream.

She opened the door and ran straight into a mass of muscle.

The door slammed shut behind her and she found herself looking up into Michael's eyes.

"What are you doing here?" The question came out on a little gasp.

Then a great big one because he leaned over and picked her up, tossing her over his broad shoulder like she was a bag of flour. "Asking you to join us for dinner."

Before she could protest, he started for the dining room.

Well, at least she was going to get to eat that stew.

Chapter Seven

Ty looked up when half the dining room started to cheer.

Then he winced because they were cheering on Michael, who had something over his...damn. He knew that backside. He'd dreamed of that curvy, glorious ass about a million times. Lucy. He'd tossed Luce over his shoulder, and that really should make him mad. It should have him longing to take out the man who dared to treat the woman he loved like some furniture to be moved around.

All he could think about was she looked hot like that. The caveman thing was real, and while he considered himself a modern man and something of an ally to all the women in his life, there was still a little Neanderthal in him that wanted to take his woman somewhere quiet and show her who the boss was.

The modern man part of him wondered exactly what had happened that made Michael grab her and run.

"Uh, is there something I should know?" Zane watched as they made their way around the bar. "Because while I understand the impulse, I also have to protect my employee."

"She's not kicking or anything. If Luce was pissed, she would be fighting him." It was the one thing that gave him hope.

"Actually, she looks really relaxed." Zane pulled his order book. "Y'all staying for dinner or taking this show on the road?"

"Oh, I need them both fed. When Michael is hungry he stops using words. Lucy gets real cantankerous, and I need them both communicating on a polite level since our first date didn't go so well." He was starting to worry that his do-over wasn't going to go well either. Had she tried to run? What had Michael said?

Michael made it to the table and stared down at him for a moment as though he'd done all the hard caveman work and wasn't sure what to do now that he'd clubbed his intended over the head and dragged her back to the cave and had to face the consequences of his actions.

"You think she'll escape if you put her down, don't you?" Ty asked.

"I will admit I was running on instinct," Michael replied.

Ty slipped out of the booth and took a knee in front of Lucy, who was calmly hanging off Michael's back. "Hey, you doing okay there?"

Her head turned slightly. Her hair had come out of its ponytail and hung in waves around her face. There was a pretty flush to her skin, and her lips curled up. "I'm not sure. He came to the kitchen and he said he was asking me to dinner, but he didn't actually ask me to dinner."

"Of course I did," Michael insisted.

"No, you told me you were going to but you never did," Lucy shot back.

"He didn't get around to it because he was too busy kidnapping you." Ty was starting to get a handle on how things had gone.

"I didn't kidnap her." Michael made the declaration but he didn't let Lucy go.

Michael—big, manly, cared-about-nothing Michael—was worried she would say no. "He's worried you would leave and not give us another chance. We screwed up."

"I didn't," Michael said with a huff.

Lucy reached out, and Ty sighed as her hand brushed across his face. "We all did. Yes. I would like very much to have dinner with you. Both of you. But Ty, you should understand that I've spent the last couple of minutes staring at Michael's backside, and it's really nice. I need you to be okay with that."

He smiled her way because he'd moved past jealousy. He was

also very comfortable with the state of his own ass. He worked those glutes hard. Lucy would think his butt was nice, too. "Oh, it's all right. Mike and I decided there's no room for jealousy, and that includes you in case in the middle of everything your men decide we're curious and go at it hard with each other."

Lucy was suddenly on her feet, and Michael was frowning his way. "That is not how I put it."

Lucy smoothed back her hair, and her face was lit with amusement. "How did you put it?"

"So you're staying?" Zane interrupted as Ty stood up and slid into the booth, making room for Michael. "Do you want dinner? They ordered drinks and appetizers but wanted to wait on dinner. I'm pretty sure one of these two is paying, so you should know we've got some excellent filets in and the fish of the night is…"

"Trout," Lucy finished, sliding in across from Ty but taking up the whole middle of the booth. "I do work here, and I want the stew and cornbread, and I'll take a glass of your finest white zinfandel."

Ty gave him his order, and Michael did the same. It looked like they might actually have dinner with her this evening.

"Done," Zane said. He nodded toward Michael and put a hand on his shoulder. "Good to know you're an open-minded dude. I say go for it."

Michael growled as Zane moved past.

Ty leaned over the table. "That's his way of saying fuck you without saying fuck you. You're over here with me, buddy. This way we can both talk to her and look at how pretty she is."

The corner of Michael's mouth curled up—an almost smile—and he moved in next to Ty. "She is pretty."

"So pretty you had to toss her over your shoulder and drag her out to dinner." It wasn't a question. It was hopefully an explanation.

"I panicked." Michael's expression was stony. "She was standing there and she looked a little horrified to see me, so I panicked and picked her up and carried her out here, and now I can see where that might have been an overreaction on my part. Did everyone really have to cheer?"

"It's that kind of town," Ty replied. He had his very lovely piña colada in front of him because unlike Sawyer, Zane believed in blenders.

"I wasn't horrified to see you." Lucy reached out and stole his piña colada like she almost always did and took a little drag off the straw. "I was surprised you were there. Not surprised you were here at Trio. Surprised you were behind the door when I opened it and I'd just had…"

She took another drink. He was going to have to order another one.

"Just had what?" Michael was suddenly tense again. "What happened?"

"Nothing." Lucy shook her head and passed Ty's drink back. "I was taking out the trash and I thought I heard something. It freaked me out a little. Too many horror movies. That's all."

That brought up so many good memories. "We used to watch horror movies while we were in college."

"You were in college," she reminded him.

"I was," he said. "We would find a movie on cable and then call each other and watch and talk the whole way through, and I would inevitably get a phone call around two a.m. that night that she heard something."

"You liked that part," she accused.

There it was. That invisible tether that had connected them for as long as he could remember.

Michael reached out a hand, and Lucy took it. "I'm sorry for being overbearing. I didn't want to screw this up a second time. Not that I screwed up the first time."

It was Ty's turn to groan. "Fine. It was all my fault."

Lucy reached for his hand, too. "I should have talked to both of you. I should have taken Michael up on his offer to go have a drink and sort it out. Ty, I've come to realize that I'm scared of losing you. So scared that I would almost rather push you away than try, and that's foolish of me. Michael, in some ways the same goes for you. I'm invested in this relationship even though it's not much of one yet. There's a part of me that would rather hold on to the possibility of what could happen between us than actually attempt to make it happen. Does that make sense?"

"It sounds stupid," Michael replied, his voice hoarse. "But yes, I do know what you mean."

Progress. It was a beautiful thing. "I do, too. It's why I turned you down back in high school. I knew I was going away, and I didn't think I could keep you. Funny thing is we stayed close for the most part. I missed you all those years, and then when I came back you had a boyfriend and I decided it was time to see if there was someone else out there for me."

"Tell her." Michael sat back.

Lucy did the same, breaking their contact, but not in a harsh way. They were still somehow together, the little booth they sat at enclosing them. "Tell me what?"

He glared Michael's way. They'd talked more than sports the night before. Mostly Ty talking because Michael was a closed-up asshole. But he was a pretty good listener.

Michael took a sip of his beer and put it back down again. "This is why you two didn't get together then and wouldn't work today if you didn't have me. You have to talk to each other. And the fact that I have to be the one to say that is sad because I'm not a talker. At least not anymore."

Well, not talking hadn't worked for them. The question was would she actually believe him. He'd admitted this particular secret to Michael last night. He'd expected the man to snort and laugh at him. Instead, Michael had turned his way and given him what Ty now thought of as his understanding grunt.

"I came back from college a virgin." Ty said the words directly and clearly because he didn't want to repeat them. "Like I said, I meant to come home and start a relationship with you because I could give you what you deserved."

"What did I deserve?" Lucy asked, her eyes soft and concerned.

"You deserved to be married. You deserved to have a man with a good job who could support you while you got your education." He'd gotten through college as fast as he could because he'd wanted to come home to Bliss. And then she'd had a boyfriend, one of his best friend's brothers.

"I only wanted you, Ty."

"I should have stayed." That seemed to be where he'd really gone wrong. He'd asked her to come with him, but he'd also known she had to take care of her family.

She reached for his hand again. "No. You needed that time. And you had a full ride. You couldn't turn it down. I'm surprised you came back. You could have gotten a job anywhere."

"But you were here." He needed to make her understand. "My whole life was here. I missed you every second I was gone."

Zane placed a glass of wine in front of her, and the heavenly scent of fried mozzarella hit him. He'd been nervous walking in here but now he was hungry.

Hungry for a lot of things.

"Your food should be out in about ten minutes." Zane gave them a nod before walking back to the kitchen.

"So now you two understand each other?" Michael asked.

Lucy gave him a smile. "We do."

"And you understand that Tyler's long line of very brief sexual relationships was because he couldn't have the woman he wanted," Michael said.

He didn't like the sound of that. "I wouldn't say they were all that brief. I've got stamina."

Michael shot him a frown. "I was talking about the fact that you didn't have real relationships with those women."

"No, he had relationships with their vaginas," Lucy quipped.

He wished he'd chosen a different way to try to get over her. "But none in the last year."

"So your stamina might not be what it used to," Michael said with a snort.

That got Lucy laughing, and when her eyes shone like that Ty would take all the ribbing in the world.

Michael sat up, his shoulders squaring. "We need to talk about something else now that we've gotten that out of the way."

He looked so serious, any hint of amusement fleeing. It made Ty nervous. "What do we need to talk about? Because we seem to be doing a whole lot of talking."

"I think what Michael meant was that we didn't talk about the important stuff," Lucy explained. "I suspect he also thinks we talk too much."

"This is something we definitely have to talk about," Michael insisted. "You need to think about this. Do you still want me here? The two of you love each other. I care about you, Lucy. I even care about Ty, but you both need to understand that I'm not capable of loving anyone. There's nothing soft and sweet about me anymore. So

I'm going to give you a chance to get out of this. If we go back to Ty's tonight and do what will likely feel awkward as hell at first, I'll be involved, and that means I'll be bossy and probably obnoxious about the both of you."

This was his chance. He could get rid of Michael, and Lucy would be all his.

And he hadn't been great at being on his own with her. They wouldn't have had the talk they'd just had without Michael here with them. Lucy would still be keeping him at a distance, and that wasn't what he wanted. He liked the friendship he was finding. He liked having someone to back him up. This was what the other threesomes had. They had a camaraderie he wouldn't have if he was on his own.

He glanced over, and Lucy was obviously waiting for him to reply. "I don't want you to go away. I'm starting to think we might not work without you, and I want us to work."

"I do, too," Lucy said quietly. She reached out to Michael so she had a hand on both of them again. "I want to try with both of you."

Michael stared down at her hand before flipping it over and threading their fingers together. "Well, you were warned."

He kissed her hand and held it for a moment more.

Somehow Ty thought the soft part of Michael was still there. It needed affection. That was all.

And maybe some serious sex.

Ty reached for the appetizer. He had the feeling he was going to need his energy tonight.

* * * *

Michael watched as Ty opened the door to his apartment and thought seriously about how nice it would be to have a cabin in the valley. One close to the town square so they could walk to Trio when the weather was good. Ty's place was simple and comfortable, but there were four other units exactly like it on this floor, and that was too many people for Michael.

Three was a good number of people.

"Hey, do you want a beer?" Ty moved into his tiny kitchen.

Michael wanted something so much more intoxicating than beer. He wanted to stop overthinking every second of his life and live for

133

one night. "No. I want to watch you kiss her and then I want to watch as you undress her, and we'll see where it goes from there."

Lucy stopped, her eyes wide. "You want Ty to undress me?"

How had she thought this was going to go? He'd warned her he could be bossy. He might not be the Dom Stef was, but he liked to be in control in the bedroom. It was the one place he had been in control with…

No. She wasn't going to ruin this night for him.

"Yes. I do. I want to sit here and watch as Ty takes off your clothes." He shrugged out of his jacket and hung it on the peg by the door. The night had been cold, but he hadn't felt the chill the way he normally did. He'd sat in the back of Ty's Jeep and watched the two of them. There was a connection between them he would never truly understand, and yet they needed him. He'd had to ask, had to give them a way out, but he'd been surprised at how much he hadn't wanted them to take it.

He wanted Lucy, and he liked having Ty around. They were almost too good to be true.

He'd learned it was dangerous to want things.

"Okay." Lucy looked from Ty and back to Michael. "I'm nervous but I want this. I just think we should talk about it."

"Talk about the sex?" Michael asked.

"I guess talk about what the sex means," Lucy explained.

Ty moved in behind her, putting his hands on her shoulders. "It means everything to me."

She turned slightly and gave Ty a smile. "I know. It means the same to me. But what if…what if it isn't good?"

He knew exactly what she was saying and what she wasn't saying. *What if I'm not good? What if I'm not enough?* Ty was behind her so Michael moved in front of her. "It will be good, Lucy. And when we do it again, it'll be better. It is meaningful to me, but I meant what I said before."

She looked up at him, those eyes big and guileless. "You can't love me."

"It's not because you're not loveable." His heart actually hurt at the thought that she might misunderstand him. "You are worthy of every bit of love you get. Ty can love you. I can worship you. I can protect you."

"But you'll never tell me you love me."

He couldn't. He couldn't even think the words. "No."

Lucy put her hands on the sides of his face. "All right. You've told me what I need to hear. I'm going into this with my eyes open. You won't love me and you won't stay with us."

"I didn't say that." The words were out before he could think to hold them in. They were true. He wasn't sure how to make her understand that the part of him that could love had been burned away. "I don't know if I'm staying but as long as I'm here, as long as this works, I'd like to be a part of it."

"Okay." Her hand stroked along his cheek, tracing the line of his jaw.

His heart clenched in his chest. He didn't want to hurt her. She was so beautiful, and he'd seen how kind she was. She didn't deserve the heartache he could bring her. "Maybe you should think about this a little more."

She shook her head. "I don't need to. I think too much, and Ty sometimes doesn't think at all."

"I think," Ty countered.

"No. You react. You came home and things weren't perfect, and after saving yourself for me, you decided if you couldn't have me, you would drown yourself in most of Southern Colorado," she replied, not unkindly. "And then when I was available again, you were too ashamed because you'd gotten a bad reputation. Not once did you think *I'll sit down with Lucy and tell her how I feel and we'll figure this thing out together.* Yesterday when you walked in on us, did you think or react?"

"I thought about how mad I was," Ty said with a chuckle, his hand moving Lucy's long hair to the side so he could kiss her neck. "And then I reacted like a butthead."

Sometimes it was easy to remember these two had known each other since they were little kids. It was easy to feel like he was the outsider, but one they needed. He wasn't sure what Ty would have done if he wasn't around. Perhaps he would have tried to move their relationship forward or he might have stayed back in the shadows, worried he would lose her.

Ty would take care of Lucy if Michael needed to leave. That had to be enough. She was accepting him as he was, and he couldn't ask for more.

"Besides, I wouldn't send you away for anything in the world now that I know the two of you throwing down is on the table," Lucy said, a hint of a smile on her generous lips.

"I was really more talking about how I wouldn't be all freaked out if our dicks touched in the middle of fucking you," Michael pointed out. "I don't know. We were there with Max and Rye and James and Noah and they were all sanctimonious about stuff, and I thought I should point out how we would be different."

"He's comfortable enough with his sexuality that he's okay acknowledging that I'm extremely handsome and my appeal goes across all genders," Ty said, his lips moving over Lucy's neck and down the curve of her shoulder.

That was something he definitely hadn't said, but Ty amused him. "I meant that if we're going kinky, I'm not going to feel awkward about anything that happens between the three of us. And that means anything. Including what I'm about to ask. Ty, when was your last checkup?"

"Six months ago," he replied. "And I haven't had sex since, but I do have condoms."

"Of course you do," Lucy murmured.

"No, these are new condoms," Ty vowed. "I bought them a week ago at the Trading Post, and Teeny even commented on how I was buying the brand name ones and that the person I was buying them for must be special."

Lucy flushed a pretty pink. "Ty, she's going to know they're for me."

"Well, yeah, because I told her," Ty admitted.

"Everyone knows." Michael thought Lucy should understand that by now. "Trust me. They know what we're doing right now because everyone saw us walk out of Trio with you. We don't have anything to be ashamed or feel weird about. Any ribbing we'll get will be good natured or I'll deal with it. I mean that for both of you."

He wasn't worried about their friends. Stef had been overbearing and obnoxious today, but he would back off now that he knew Michael was willing to work with Ty, willing to take care of both of them.

How can you take care of them if you aren't willing to be open to them?

He stiffened because that hadn't been his voice he'd heard.

Fuck. He wasn't going to think about her. Jessie had no place here between them.

"Hey." Lucy went on her toes and brushed her lips against his. "Don't go."

"Go?"

"Yeah, sometimes you go somewhere else, and I don't think it's a good place." She smoothed back his hair. "I think too much and Ty reacts too much, and you do both. So stop thinking about the past. Stop worrying about the future. Be here in the moment with the two of us."

"I wasn't…" He wasn't going to lie to her. "I was thinking of the past. It flared up on me. I'm fine."

"No, you're not, but that's okay, too," Lucy promised. "You don't have to be fine with me. You get to be Michael with me. Whoever you are in this moment."

Could he find a new version of himself? One who didn't wallow in guilt and rage? One who could live a life and find some semblance of contentment? If he was going to, it would be with this woman. She calmed him down.

It was weird, but Ty did the same. Once they'd stopped fighting, he'd discovered that Ty's presence was soothing to him, amusing. He liked them both.

Do you like them because they aren't Jessie? Because they're as far from Jessie as possible?

He had the choice to make, to retreat and do exactly what Lucy accused him of. Or he could take that first step back into the real world.

He lowered his mouth down to hers, reveling in the warmth that flooded his system the minute he touched her.

He kissed her, letting their tongues tangle, feeling the rush of arousal hit him.

He didn't have to go to bed alone. He didn't have to be cold. He could wrap himself around Lucy and know that he was welcome in her life, that even if he somehow fucked up, Ty would be there to catch her.

He let his hands play over her curves, and sure enough, his hands bumped against Ty's. They were both touching her, and he'd been right. It didn't bother him at all. He simply skimmed over Ty's callused hands and kept exploring.

Lucy moved in between them, her breasts brushing Michael's chest while she rubbed her backside against Ty.

He moved back and loved the way Lucy's gaze had gone soft, like she was intoxicated by the intimacy.

He could definitely get addicted to that look. Ty's hands came up, cupping Lucy's breasts even as her eyes remained on Michael.

Oh, he might never pick up a paddle or a flogger, but he was definitely going to be in charge of this.

He settled back onto the sofa, watching them both. He'd been right. They were gorgeous together, and his cock did not have a problem watching Ty at all.

Ty, however, had stopped. He'd stepped back from Lucy and seemed awkward, as though trying to figure out what to do next.

Because for all his experience he'd never made love to a woman who mattered to him. It was a harsh way to put it, but true. There was nothing wrong with mutually satisfying sex, but when real emotion was in the mix, there was nothing better.

Ty was as worried as Lucy was.

This was precisely why they needed him. "Have you ever kissed her before the other night?"

Lucy turned to Ty, putting her hands on his chest and looking into his eyes. "He kissed me at a party once. He was trying to prove to this jerk that I had a boyfriend so he would leave me alone."

"I would have kicked his ass, but I already had a sprained wrist from football, and she wouldn't let me fight," Ty revealed. The awkwardness fled and there was nothing but warmth in his tone. "So I kissed her. I figured a guy who was that tied up in his own masculinity would respect dibs."

Lucy's nose wrinkled. "Dibs?"

Ty winced. "You know what I mean. But you should also know that I kissed you for a long time after he walked away. I pretended he was still watching us because I didn't want to stop kissing you."

"I didn't want you to stop either," she whispered.

"But you two dumbasses didn't get together then?" He wasn't going to pull his punches.

"It was the last day of sophomore year and I went to visit my cousins the next day," Ty admitted. "I was gone for six weeks, and when I came home we pretended like nothing happened."

"I was scared to talk to you about it." Lucy's hands found the nape of Ty's neck. "And then we fell back into our habits and we let it go. I don't want to let this go now."

Ty let his head drop gently against hers. "I don't want to either, baby."

"Then kiss her." Michael sat back and let all his other cares go. They were right about being in the moment. He'd spent the last two years living in the past. He wanted the here and now. Lucy and Ty had wasted far too many years. They only had today, and he wanted to make it count.

Which meant not hating himself for a night. Which meant letting them in even if it was only for a little while.

"Kiss her," he repeated. "And take her clothes off so we can show her how good it can be to have two men worship her. So we can show her exactly how we both feel about her."

He was ready to be with her, ready to share this moment with Ty.

For the first time in forever, it felt right to simply be.

Chapter Eight

Lucy watched as Michael sat back. He was so big and gorgeous she couldn't take her eyes off of him, and then there was Ty. They were polar opposites, one dark and brooding and the other pure masculine sunshine.

She wanted them both. It hit her then and there that not only did she want the pleasure she could get out of this encounter, she wanted them. Wanted their emotion and their trust, wanted to be able to believe in what she felt for them.

Wanted a future with them.

And that was probably a bad thing because Michael had promised that he couldn't love her.

He'd told her, but she was willing to take that chance. He'd been through something awful with the last woman who'd held his heart. He was afraid. She'd considered a relationship with him from every angle, including one where he was interested in her for the simple fact that she was as far from Jessie as possible.

This could all end in heartbreak, but she'd let that fear steal years from her and Ty, and she couldn't do the same now.

Or perhaps she and Ty couldn't work without Michael here. They were too similar and needed his commanding presence to bring them out of their shells.

Of course now Ty was starting to try to get her out of her actual shell, and that was a little scary.

His hands tugged at the T-shirt she wore, the one with the Trio logo. She wasn't ready for this. She hadn't prepared the way she had the night before. "I'm wearing terrible underwear."

"It's okay," Michael assured her. "You won't be for long."

"I'm saying I was wearing the nice stuff the other day. I put on my laciest bra and undies for our date," she argued. "And now I'm wearing the plain stuff because I didn't expect either of you to show up today. You didn't call or text or anything."

"That's because we were plotting," Ty explained. "We had to plan all of tonight out because I might have screwed up last night."

"We all did," Michael insisted. "I should have waited for Ty. Ty shouldn't have acted like a jealous ass, and Lucy shouldn't have walked away so quickly. That was yesterday. Today we're not making the same mistakes. Lucy, I'm going to tell you a secret about men that big lingerie doesn't want you to know. We don't care what you're wearing before we get you naked. The minute we see skin our brain goes on the fritz and nothing else matters. So let Ty take off your shirt."

She could argue but why? They wanted to see her naked and she wanted to be naked with them. She liked her body. It was curvy and round. Hours of waiting tables had toned her legs, and the rest of her was all right. She wasn't as perfect as Ty or Michael, but she wasn't ashamed of her body. She'd spent some time at the naturist community, and body shame had no place there. She lifted her arms and let Ty drag the T-shirt over her head. She expected him to undo her bra, but he moved around in front of her and there he was, the boy she'd loved as a girl, the man she'd thought she would never have, the one who was like a star in the sky—gorgeous and shining and unobtainable to a mere mortal.

She looked up at him, not moving when he came into her space. It felt right to be here with Ty, but she still was scared. How could she ever live without him? The years he'd been gone had felt empty, and she hadn't been able to fill them with work or friends or other men.

But she wanted Michael, too. It was perverse. Everything she wanted was standing right in front of her and she had the feeling it wouldn't be enough, wouldn't be complete without Michael. It felt like their stumbling and fumbling had been because the time wasn't

141

right. Because Michael hadn't been with them.

"I forgot about the bossy guy's first order." Ty's eyes gleamed in the low light. "I was supposed to kiss you. For real this time."

"I think it was real the first time. We just didn't know it." That first kiss all those years ago with Ty had damn near killed her. It had been everything to her and she'd stood there, breathless with longing, and Ty had looked around before telling her it was okay, the guy was gone. She'd been crushed.

His expression went serious. "Forever this time."

And just like that the crushed girl she'd been was smiling again, was vindicated because she'd always known he was the one. She hadn't known there would be more than one. "Are you sure?"

He stared down at her and smoothed back her hair like she was something precious. "This is the only thing I've ever been sure of in my life. I know it's weird, but this time it's right. Being here...it's right, Luce. It's everything we need."

Michael. He was talking about Michael. He knew they needed him, too. He was going to kiss her and present her to Michael, and they would start something important. Tonight. "This is everything I need."

She went up on her toes, offering him her lips.

Ty swooped in and covered her mouth with his own, his fingers finding her hair and using it to move her to his liking. His free hand wrapped around her waist, pulling her close as he kissed her. Softly at first, and then with growing hunger that fed her own. His tongue surged in, finding hers and stroking even as he settled her firmly against him, letting her feel the erection against her belly, a promise of what was to come.

"You want me," she managed to whisper between kisses.

"Tell her what you want to do to her," Michael commanded.

"I'd rather show her." Ty's voice had gone deeper than usual, and his hand twisted slightly in her hair, bringing her up on her toes. The tiny bite of pain sent a shock of arousal through her system.

"She needs to hear the words," Michael insisted. "Let me give you an example. I would like to eat your pussy, Lucy. I'm going to have Ty get behind you and hold your legs open with his own. He'll spread you wide and I'll crawl in between them. I'll breathe you in, and the smell of all that cream is going to make my dick so hard I'll think I could die, but it won't stop me. Nothing will stop me from getting a taste of you. Nothing will stop me from parting your pussy and shoving my tongue inside, getting my whole face wet with your juice, baby."

She felt like all the air had left the room. She was certain most of the moisture in her body was now in her pussy, waiting for Michael to do exactly what he'd said he would do. She'd had sex before. She'd had oral sex, but it had been a hurried thing, something her partner wanted to get through because it was something he needed to check off his list before he got to his part.

Michael sounded like he truly wanted to spend time there, to lavish her with affection.

Ty's hand tugged on her hair, forcing her to look his way. "Don't you think I'll sit back and let Mike be the only one to have you. Or to make all the decisions when it comes to this. I know I seem soft, but I won't always be soft in bed. And by bed I mean anywhere I want to fuck you. Baby, I'll pretty much follow you wherever you want to go. I'll always be right beside you. I'll support you in anything you want to do. But I'm going to make you trust me in bed."

"I trust you." She should have always trusted him. It was the world she hadn't had faith in, her own personal history

"Not the way you're going to." Desire was stamped all over Ty's handsome face. "Not the way you will after I've fucked you in every way I can. I mean it. Your body is going to be my playground, and I'll never get sick of it. I'm never going to touch another woman after tonight. You're the be-all, end-all of my existence, and I'll worship your body as often as I can."

"How, Ty?" Michael asked in that deep tone that went straight to her pussy. "How will you worship her?"

"With my hands and mouth and cock." Ty never took his eyes off her. "I'll worship every part of her. And do you know why I'm excited about our ménage?"

Michael chuckled. "I can only imagine."

"Because this way I don't have to ease her into anal sex," Ty confessed. "Because this way I'll see and touch and play with that pretty ass tonight because we have to prepare her to take both of us."

Oh, that thought should scare her more than it did, but the truth was she lived in Bliss and that meant imagining what it meant to be in the middle of two men. She couldn't not think about it. She watched happy threesomes all the time, and it was hard not to fantasize about it for herself. "Tonight?"

"One of the things Mike and I did today was buy a plug and lube. We're going to start getting that pretty asshole ready for our cocks," Ty admitted. "So I'm going to take off these clothes of yours and show you off to Michael, and then he's going to taste that pussy while I have some fun with your ass."

She was going to be between them tonight. Not fully the way they eventually would be, but they would both touch her. They would both be with her.

She let Ty turn her toward Michael, allowed him to slip his hands around and cup her breasts before going lower and undoing the fly of her jeans. She'd slipped out of her shoes and socks when they'd walked in the door, so it was easy for Ty to drag the jeans down her body, leaving her in her bra and underwear.

"These aren't so bad," Ty whispered, his fingertips brushing the cups of her bra. "But they definitely aren't as pretty as what's underneath. Do you know how long I've fantasized about seeing you naked? How often when we were teens I would think about you and yank my own dick? Sitting near you in math class is why I almost failed."

"You never almost failed a class in your life." Ty was far smarter than he let on. Sometimes she thought he discounted himself. He could have gone to med school, but he'd wanted to be back here with her. He could have gone to a big city and found a good-paying job, but he'd left it behind for her, and she believed him now. She'd put up walls, and he'd been too afraid to knock them down for fear they'd both be caught in the landslide.

"Well, I thought about you far more than geometry," he muttered as he twisted the clasp of her bra and it came off.

Cool air hit her nipples and they tightened and peaked. She looked at Michael, whose eyes were on her chest, taking in every inch of her.

Ty's hands reached around to cup her naked breasts, molding them. She loved the warmth and rasp of his calluses against her skin. She had to remember to breathe as his hands skimmed down her torso to the waistband of her undies. He slipped his fingertips under and eased them down her legs, helping her when she stepped out. He tossed them aside, showing her she wouldn't need them again. Not tonight.

"Yes, that's what I wanted." Michael reached over his shoulders and pulled his own T-shirt off, tossing it aside and sitting back like he was a decadent king on his throne and she was the serving girl brought in for his nightly entertainment.

She might have some kinky scenarios of her own she wanted to play out with these guys.

"She's fucking gorgeous," Ty said, his fingers tracing down the line of her spine to her lower back. "Even better than I imagined."

"I didn't have to imagine most of Ty since he always found a reason to take his shirt off around me." She couldn't help but smile now. She was staring at Michael and admiring that sculpted chest. He proved a man didn't need a gym to stay in shape. Michael's shoulders were broad and strong. His chest had a light dusting of dark hair in a *V* that led down his six-pack abs to disappear into his jeans, but she could imagine where that trail would lead her.

She shivered as Ty lightly bit the nape of her neck.

"I was trying to tempt you to jump me." Ty licked the spot he'd nipped. "I hoped you would take one look at my manly chest and fall at my feet."

A smile lit Michael's features. "And when she didn't the first time? You kept hoping it would have a cumulative effect?"

Ty's hand slipped lower on her back, resting right above the curve of her ass. "I kept working out, hoping someday I would meet her very high standards."

She'd gone out with a former cult leader, so she didn't think she had super-high standards. More like fumble along standards because she couldn't face the fact that she was in love with her best friend and falling for the damaged dude on the mountain. "If you knew how many times you distracted me, you would feel very good about yourself."

"Is he distracting you now?" Ty's lips were right against her ear.

It took all her will power to not lean back against him. "A bit. I think I shouldn't be the only one who's naked. It's lonely."

"I wouldn't want you to be lonely, baby. And I think I can distract you, too," Ty promised.

"Why don't you do that while I make myself more comfortable. I don't want Lucy to be lonely either." Michael stood and kicked out of his boots.

That was the moment Ty's fingers moved lower, and she felt one finger caress the split between her cheeks.

She was caught between the visual feast of watching Michael undress and the dark temptation of that finger getting closer and closer to her asshole. No one had ever played with her there. It was completely new territory and one she'd been almost sure she'd never try.

Michael pushed his jeans and boxers off and stalked toward her. He was muscled everywhere from his shoulders to his strong legs. His cock was hard, jutting out from his body as though trying to get to her as fast as it could.

Her heart raced as Ty skimmed over her asshole, making her squirm and shiver. Michael moved into her space and took her face in his hands before lowering his mouth to hers. He kissed her while Ty teased her, and she couldn't think about anything but how her body felt electric, a live wire waiting to spark.

Michael kissed her over and over before stepping back. "Ty, it's time to get serious. I think we both promised her something and we should deliver."

She felt Ty move away from her as Michael leaned over and picked her up, carrying her as though she didn't weigh a thing. He moved toward the bedroom and laid her out. Before she could wonder what he was doing, he showed her. He gripped her ankles and dragged her down the bed, arranging her feet on the edge.

She was open wide and vulnerable, and for a moment she felt like she was on the edge of more than just the bed. Then she wasn't thinking at all because Michael's mouth was on her pussy. He didn't play around and tease her. He suckled on her clit before parting her labia and spearing her deep with his tongue.

In the meantime, she watched as Ty shucked his clothes before climbing on the bed and lying next to her. His hand found her breast, fingers plucking at her nipples while he leaned over and kissed her. He was kissing her when Michael pressed a finger deep inside her while using his tongue on her clit, and she went careening over the edge.

The orgasm slammed into her and rolled through her system.

Ty pulled back but only a bit. His domineering kiss became softer, sweeter, and he rubbed their noses together. "Is that better, baby?"

"So much," she replied with a sigh.

"Good because now it's my time," he vowed before rolling away.

She got the feeling the night was far from over.

* * * *

Ty rolled off the bed and thought about the fact that it didn't feel weird to be around another dude with his clothes off. It felt oddly right. They'd talked about the fact that they weren't ever going to be like Max and Rye, who seemed to share a soul, but it did feel like destiny to have Michael here.

Although the man was bossy as hell, and now Ty felt like he needed to assert himself a little, too. After all, he had something he wanted to do to Lucy, and why shouldn't he get a show while he was doing it?

"It's your turn, baby. I want to watch you suck Michael's cock while I play with your ass," he commanded.

This wasn't even close to the way he'd always envisioned the night when he made Lucy his. Those dreams had been soft and sweet. He would have taken her to bed and gently made love to her and held her all night, and maybe he would never have shown her the side of him that wanted to fuck her hard and in all kinds of dirty ways. He would have protected her from that side of his personality.

Now he realized she would revel in his bad boy side. They didn't have to hide anything from each other. They could play and explore and fuck to their hearts' content.

Michael made that possible.

Michael sat back on his heels, his lips glistening with Lucy's arousal. Yep. That did not turn him off.

"You taking the reins?" Michael asked in a way that let Ty know he wasn't upset at the thought.

"I am." He'd already gotten what he needed. While Michael was setting Lucy up, Ty had gotten undressed and grabbed the little kit he'd set up this afternoon. Lube and a prepared small plug. The bathroom was only a few steps away when he needed it.

He was ready.

He wanted her to be ready, too.

Michael stood gracefully, extending a hand to help Lucy up. His dick was as hard as Ty's, but he would find some relief first. "We should do what the man says, honey. How about it?"

There was the sweetest grin on Lucy's face. He'd thought she might be nervous about being naked, shy about being around them, but she was confident now, and that made him want her even more. She should be because she was absolutely the most stunning woman he'd ever seen. She had an hourglass figure and perfect breasts, hips he could hold on to, and that ass. Damn he wanted that ass. Even the thought of how she'd shivered when he'd briefly skimmed over the crease of her cheeks made his dick harden painfully.

He was glad Mike had given her an orgasm because he had twenty plus years of wanting her, and there was no way he would last once he was inside her. More than twenty since he was fairly certain he was born loving her.

Lucy let Michael help her up, let him kiss her, their tongues tangling. Ty watched them. They were beautiful together. Lucy's hair plunged down her back like a dark waterfall. Michael matched her, like they were parts of a whole.

But he was absolutely certain he was part of them, too. They needed his positivity. They could both go dark. He and Lucy might have been hesitant to communicate, but Michael had his issues, too, and they would have to deal with them if they had a shot at staying together.

Somehow over the last few days, staying together felt like something Ty wanted. Really wanted.

Michael broke off the kiss and moved back to the bed that was probably going to be a tight fit for the three of them. He settled himself with his back against the headboard. He stroked his own cock with one hand as Lucy knelt between his splayed legs.

That was exactly where he wanted her. "Ass in the air, baby."

She turned to him, a hint of a grin on her face. "You know most people don't start with the perverted stuff."

He had a very good answer for that. "If you didn't want the

perverted stuff, you wouldn't have moved to Bliss. So ass in the air."

"He's right about that. Why don't you bring that hot mouth of yours down here and take care of me while Ty starts to get you ready for us," Michael commanded.

Lucy leaned over, and Ty knew the minute she touched Michael's cock with her tongue because a low groan came from his partner's throat. "Have you done this before? Not you, Ty. I know you have."

She needed to stop that. He hadn't been planning on discipline, but he gave those cheeks a light swat. Nothing that would hurt her because they would have to have another conversation about whether she wanted that, but a light touch to let her know that wasn't okay. "I don't want to get slut shamed any more than you do. I had reasons for the way I behaved, and most of them didn't have to do with wanting to become some player."

Lucy sat back on her heels. "I'm sorry, Ty. I was doing that, wasn't I?"

"Ty doesn't need to be shamed for his experience any more than you and I need to feel bad about our lack of experience." Michael reached for her hand with his free one. "I've only been with a couple of women in my whole life, and I'm ready to explore my sexuality with the two of you. I'm open to all these experiences, and I get the feeling we're both going to benefit from what Ty's learned."

And that was why he felt safe with Michael. Despite his rough exterior, there was a deep streak of kindness in the man. He was tough but he would make himself vulnerable if he thought it would help the people he cared about.

"I'm sorry," Lucy said, her eyes starting to water.

He couldn't have that. He moved in and kissed her cheek. "Forgiven, baby. Now ass in the air. I want to play with you."

She resumed her position, and Michael hissed in pleasure and wound a hand in her hair.

"As to your question, no. I haven't been in a threesome," Michael replied, his jaw clenched. "But I have had anal sex."

Ty reached for the glove he'd set up earlier and tugged it on his hand before grabbing the lube. "And I've done pretty much everything." That sounded bad. "I mean everything consensual and sane."

Michael chuckled. "Like I said, we'll benefit from your experience."

He was grateful for his experience now. If he and Lucy had gotten together back when they were kids, they likely wouldn't have experimented at all. They might not have moved to Bliss. They likely would have stayed close to their parents and already started a family. There was nothing wrong with that, but there also wasn't anything wrong with seeing a bit of the world, learning something of who they were individually before they became a couple.

They definitely wouldn't have become a threesome.

He wouldn't have figured out how much he was looking forward to sharing Lucy with a friend. "You keep doing what you're doing, baby. Don't you mind me."

Michael groaned again, tugging lightly on her hair. "I almost wish I could see what you're doing."

"She needs to wear the plug for a few days." Ty spread her cheeks, and there was a pretty little asshole. She was going to be so tight around him. But after she got used to the plug, not so tight it was uncomfortable for her. "I'll show you how to plug her. And after she's been a very good girl and taken her plug, she'll get a cock, too."

His cock. He would make love to her for the first time. She would be the last woman he ever made love to because no matter what Michael eventually decided, Ty was going to stay with her for the rest of his life.

He dribbled lube right on her asshole and heard her gasp, saw her whole body go tight.

He couldn't have that. "Relax, baby. Don't worry about a thing. You're going to learn to love this."

"I know I love this," Michael declared.

Well, it was obvious that the distraction he was providing was working because Lucy seemed to relax.

He rimmed her asshole, massaging the lube in. A shudder went through her, and he heard Michael groan again as Lucy made a whimpering sound around his dick.

It made Ty's jump at the thought of having her pretty mouth around it, but that was for another day. He wanted to be inside her, looking down into her eyes as they finally came together the way they were always meant to.

He worked one finger in, slowly willing her to open for him, making sure he lubed every inch of that rosebud of hers. Then he picked up the plug. All the while Lucy kept working Michael's cock. As Ty started to press the plug inside, easing it in and out, he could see the way Michael's whole body had tightened.

Lucy started to move in a rhythm that helped him push the plug deeper and deeper. She was fucking the plug, and Ty reacted to the sight. His arousal went through the roof, blood pulsing through him. His dick was going to go off if he didn't get inside her soon.

"It feels weird, but I don't hate it." Lucy had lifted her torso back now that she'd finished Michael off, and she twisted slightly so she could see Ty. Her lips were full and red from the work they'd just done, and she looked a bit like the cat who'd gotten all the cream.

She tilted her hips up and the plug slid home.

Ty stepped back. "Good. I need you to keep that in. I can promise you I'm going to love how that plug feels while I fuck you."

He pulled the glove off his hand and laid it back on the tray, picking up the condoms and rolling one on with shaking hands. He loved her. He was going to make love to the woman he loved, and his heart raced at the thought. He stroked himself, making sure the condom was on properly. He wasn't about to risk anything with her. One day they might talk about kids, but they needed time to themselves, time to build a strong relationship.

He was going to marry her.

When he turned to the bed, Michael had Lucy on her back, kissing her. His big hand was on her breast, but he was covering her. He kissed her for a moment and then moved to the side, allowing Ty to climb on the bed to join them.

Lucy's head came up and she looked at him with those gorgeous eyes of hers, holding a hand out to him.

He took it, lust and love making his brain foggy with desire. He covered her body with his and kissed her. He'd waited all of his life for this moment. Her legs wound around him and he could feel her heat.

"I love you, Lucy," he whispered against her lips.

"I love you, too." She tilted her hips, urging him forward.

Ty couldn't hold back another second. He thrust in. She was so tight, her pussy gripping his cock in silken warmth. The plug dragged

151

against him as he pulled back out before thrusting in again.

It was everything he'd feared it would be. Perfect. Addictive.

He wouldn't ever want another woman again.

He held on to her, thrusting up and trying to find that perfect spot to send her over the edge again. He watched her gorgeous face as she came, her nails digging into the skin of his back. He didn't mind. He would love the little marks. That bite of pain sent him over the edge, too. He felt his balls draw up and then blessed pleasure coursed through his body.

He relaxed down against her, loving the feel of her skin against his.

Home. That was what she felt like.

A long moment passed, Ty's whole soul at peace.

"We should get to bed." Michael stood at the edge of the mattress, a blank expression on his face. "Maybe I should stay in the guest room." Michael stood there like a kid waiting to be invited in, to be told he didn't have to leave. "This bed's pretty small."

Lucy gave him a dreamy smile and held her hand out as Ty rolled off her. "Then we'll have to cuddle. Don't leave us. Stay here. I want to sleep with you."

"We can smoosh her in between us," Ty offered. Michael sleeping apart from them would be a mistake. It was obvious Michael was caught between wanting to be with them and the safety that would come from getting some distance. "Besides, it's going to get cold tonight."

"Do you know how long it's been since I was really warm?" Michael asked the question with a hint of a smile as though the last two years of roughing it was something he could finally joke about. "Scoot over. It's already cold."

Ty rolled off to go deal with the condom and clean up, but he was happy and warm again within minutes. Lucy nestled down between them when he turned out the lights and the room was awash with moonlight.

Outside the snow had started to fall in earnest, but Ty was warm and happy.

Chapter Nine

Lucy opened the door to the Jeep before Ty could get out and open it for her as Ty stopped in front of Trio. She'd sat in the back since they were dropping her off first. Despite Ty trying to get her to sit beside him. It didn't make sense, and now she wanted both men to stay warm and dry until they got to Michael's place.

Ty's eyes narrowed as he rolled the window down, but he didn't turn off the Jeep. "You know if I was Stef, I would spank you for that."

He really was gorgeous, and the sun brought out all the gold in his hair. She leaned in and gave him a kiss. "Then I'm happy you're not Stef. Though I could use a couple million of his cash. Text me when you're back, and be careful on the mountain."

Michael turned and gave her a nod. "You be careful here. I want to know if that guy comes back."

Oh, there was a reason she hadn't talked to him about her encounter with Brock the night before. Sometimes she thought Michael was itching for a fight, and Brock would be an excellent excuse to start one. Michael had been seemingly happy this morning. By seemingly she meant he hadn't growled or frowned much. He'd even hopped in the shower with her while Ty was making breakfast and pressed her against the wall and fucked her until she'd cried out, and then Ty had climbed in and did the same thing. She'd been very dirty/clean by the end of her long shower, and Ty had managed to burn the bacon.

They'd ended up grabbing coffee and muffins in the staff room. Hopefully it would be her staff room at the end of this weekend.

"Zane banned him from the bar," she replied cheerfully. Not that it had stopped the asshole from showing back up, but again, Michael didn't need to know about that, and the lodge was big enough that she should be able to avoid the Foster family altogether since beyond the party this weekend she would mostly be behind a desk.

The siblings would be back in their California palatial estate after Sunday night, and by the time they showed up again, she doubted Brock would even remember who she was. And that was how she would like it.

Of course if one of her boyfriends beat the crap out of him, his memory would probably be better.

"Good." Michael sat back and stared out the front window.

Ty winked her way. "We shouldn't be too long. We're going up the mountain to pick up some of Michael's stuff and then we'll stop by River's to get his car. We'll come back here and have lunch before I go on shift this afternoon. See you soon."

Michael would be taking her back up to the lodge after her shift, and they would all three stay there this weekend. Ty would be on call in case of skiing injuries or any minor medical emergencies among the guests, and Michael had announced that he would be taking a temp security job. He would be monitoring the parties that would take place over the weekend.

The idea that they would all be together made her happier than she could have imagined.

As they drove off, Lucy strode into Trio as the snow fell, but she didn't feel the cold at all. She went in the back, wrapping her apron around her waist. Trio would have just opened for the early lunch crowd. From the glimpse of the county vehicle in the parking lot, it looked like the sheriff was here, too. It wasn't a surprise. Nate Wright was often found in Trio since his partner ran the place, but not usually this early in the day. Nate tended to work early shifts so he could be home with their twins at night.

Still, she didn't think much of his presence as she walked in the

154

door. The smell of coffee hit her and the scent of bread baking.

She was going to miss this place.

If she got the job.

She was almost having to force herself to remember this was all a test run to see if it worked out.

Sort of like her and Michael and Ty.

"Hey, you." Van was in the storage room, a clipboard in his hand. His dark hair was held back in a tie, and he wasn't in the Trio uniform. He wore a dark T-shirt and jogging pants with sneakers.

"I thought Alexei was working days this week." She'd been almost sure the big guy would be here. She'd wanted to subtly ask him a couple of questions about Michael. She'd always wanted to ask, but after the night they'd shared it seemed like she had a right to now.

"He's out front. Micky's out there, too. I think it's the three of you and Zane for lunch today," Van explained. "I'm here on an errand from the lodge. We ran out of tequila, if you can believe it. Zane agreed to let us buy a case from him since we're not getting another shipment until Monday. The bastards went through a whole case, though I'm pretty sure they didn't drink some of it since there were broken bottles all over the place last night."

Whoa. She'd heard a couple of the service staff talking about a private party in one of the villas, but she hadn't heard the whole story. She'd been too interested in staring at her men to listen in, and now that seemed like a mistake. "What happened?"

"To be honest we were already down to what I would call a basic level of tequila because when those fuckers drink, they really drink," Van said, signing off on the clipboard. "But apparently last night was epic. It's not like I can tell them no. They own one of the villas. I'm so glad I have very little contact with them. You know when I first hired on I thought I would have trouble with the lifestyle weekends. Now I live for them because the lifestylers tend to have some discipline. Give me a BDSM group over a bunch of rich dickheads any day of the week."

She got a bad feeling about who might be the perpetrators. "Was it the Foster kids?"

Why she was calling them kids, she had no idea. They were grown-ass people, but she still thought of most of them as children.

"Yeah, they had some friends fly out to join them and pretty much acted like entitled assholes," Van confirmed. "They had the villa staff pulling their hair out. A couple of them quit at two this morning, hence me getting involved. And we had to have security out. If Mr. Roberts had been here, I would bet they wouldn't have a damn villa anymore."

"What happened? I mean I understand drinking too much, but why would they throw bottles around?"

"It was some kind of fight," Van replied. "The brothers really got into it over something. I even took a punch trying to break them up. Naturally the oldest sister smoothed things over. Security didn't call the police after the sister offered a twenty K tip to the whole staff. I wanted to have the jerk hauled off, but if I hadn't agreed everyone would have lost the cash, and one of the maids had been talking to me earlier about how her mom was about to get evicted. So here I am begging for tequila and praying we don't have another night like last night."

She didn't like the sound of any of that. "Is security ready? The staff shouldn't have to be afraid. I don't care that they're in the villas. Someone should talk to Mr. Roberts."

"No one wants to because the dad is a big investment partner with Mr. Roberts' company," Van said with a sigh. "I think it's fine. The brothers had a blowout. One of them took a suite in the main lodge and they're cooling off. He was so drunk I doubt he'll be able to do anything but lie around and moan for a couple of days. We're all taking a deep breath and pocketing some cash."

It was what staff who served the superwealthy tended to do. They had to bite their tongues and hope they got paid well. When a couple million a year was on the line, staff was far more replaceable than guests. It was a sad reality of the world they lived in. Another reason why she was happy to be dealing with the lodge proper and not the superrich. "Well, let me know if I can help in any way. I'm going to be working the party tomorrow night."

Van's lips curled up in a surprisingly sexy grin. "That's right. You start tomorrow. Any chance I can convince you to come up to mine and Hale's room afterward? We're throwing a little after party."

Oh, she knew when someone was hitting on her. "How little? Can I bring my boyfriends?"

Van sighed. "I was hoping we could sneak in before there were boyfriends. So you and Ty finally hooked up? And the scary cop guy?"

"He wasn't a cop. He was a marshal."

"Same thing," Van replied with a careless shrug. "He's got the cop look about him, the one that says he could arrest you at any time. Kind of wish he'd been around last night. And the after party is totally open to both your guys. I'd kind of hoped you'd come alone, but I'm glad you all got your shit together."

"Me, too." She glanced to her left and Nate was standing there, obviously waiting for her to finish. "Hey, Nate."

"Lucy, I was hoping I could have a word with you."

Crap. That didn't sound good. "Of course." She gave Van a wave. "I'm staying out at the lodge this weekend. I'll see you around."

"I look forward to it." Van flashed her a grin and hoisted the box of tequila up. "Tell Zane I appreciate it."

Nate nodded. "Will do. Lucy, why don't we talk in Zane's office."

So this was something serious. She followed him down the hall. "Is everything okay?"

Nate opened the door to Zane's small office and strode in, taking the big seat behind the desk. "Yes, but I wanted you to know what's going on."

This had to be about Brock Foster. He'd mentioned he'd talked to the sheriff the night before. "With the guy from the villas?"

Nate sighed and sat back. "Yeah. Sometimes the tourist dollars aren't worth the pain in my ass."

She often got the feeling Nate would be happy if the town was closed off and hidden from the world. Sometimes she thought that would be nice, too.

"He warned me last night that he'd gone to you and you wouldn't let him press charges." She sat down, and it felt a little like being a kid called into the principal's office.

"He confronted you again?" Nate asked, brows rising.

"Yes. He was waiting out back for me when I took out the trash," she explained.

"Did he try anything?"

"He tried to convince me that the only way he wouldn't ruin my life is if I went out with him so his siblings would stop teasing him." When she thought about it, Brock was really pathetic. "I'm not sure how he plans to ruin my life, but he seemed pretty convinced he could do it. He's probably going to try to go over your head."

"I'm not worried about that. We've got a security camera on the hall to the bathrooms," Nate admitted. "It usually catches Rachel and Max going at it before they sneak into the bathroom. Actually a lot of people sneak into the bathrooms for a quickie. I'm sorry you have to clean up in there."

"Oh, our people are very neat about their quickies." She'd seen some things in her time at Trio. Things she couldn't unsee. "I don't mind cleaning the women's room, but I also won't hate not having to clean."

"I can imagine you won't. Anyway, the camera caught your interaction with Foster. I asked Zane to preserve the footage. It clearly shows he instigated the encounter and you were defending yourself. I'm not worried about him finding some fed to arrest you. He won't be able to do it. But I want you to stay away from that man."

"Oh, I am going to try to," she vowed.

"I think he's dangerous." Nate's voice had gone soft, but there was no doubt he was serious about what he was saying. "I've done this job for a long time now, and I know when someone is making idle threats and when they truly mean to do what they say. You wounded more than his dick. You got his pride, and that's important to him."

She shrugged off the worry. "I think he'll forget I exist the minute he leaves this place."

"I don't," Nate insisted. "I think he's the kind of man who won't let it go until he's punished you. I don't want you to be alone until he's gone. I want to put a bodyguard on you."

She should have known Nate would be overly protective. He was that way about the whole town, but she knew something he didn't. "I think I already have two."

Nate frowned. "Two?" Then he huffed. "Damn it. I knew there was a reason the betting had exploded. Last night?"

She couldn't help the smile that spread over her face. "Yes, and we're all staying at Ty's. When I'm not working the opening weekend party, I'll be with Ty and Michael. Michael's working security this weekend, and it might turn into a permanent gig."

It would be nice to have them all working in the same place. The resort was big enough that they wouldn't be stepping over each other all day but small enough that they could have lunch or take breaks together. She liked the idea of spending the winter exploring their relationship.

She liked the thought that Michael might find something he loved doing here in Bliss.

He'd said he couldn't love her, but that didn't mean their relationship couldn't work out. Michael had been burned, and he was still healing. The way he'd held her the night before had felt an awful lot like caring. He cared about her, was letting her far deeper than he'd allowed anyone in since his fiancée had betrayed him. She needed time to show him it was okay to love again.

And if that person he loved happened to be her and they lived happily ever after in Bliss, then that was fine with her.

"I don't know that I see Michael working security on a permanent basis," Nate said with a frown. "I know they've held his job open. He was a dedicated marshal. I suppose I always expected him to go back to it when he got done punishing himself."

She frowned at the thought. "I've heard that a couple of times now. Ty thinks he's punishing himself, too. Michael didn't do anything wrong. I think he might still be in mourning. They were engaged. She died."

She couldn't imagine how she would feel if something happened to Michael or Ty. She would definitely mourn for a very long time. Michael was just starting to come out of it. It could take him years to truly process a loss like that.

"I don't think that's what he would call it," Nate replied. "I don't think he's mourned her or their relationship at all. I think he's convinced himself that he hates her, but what he truly hates is the fact that he got tricked. He doesn't trust his own instincts anymore. I know how that can feel, and it's a hard place to come back from."

"His instincts?" She wasn't sure what Nate meant. "Like his professional instincts? You think that's why he didn't go back to work?"

"No. I don't think it's about work at all. Michael doesn't have a problem sticking his nose into police business when he thinks he can help. What he's worried about is far worse," Nate corrected. "He doesn't trust his instincts when it comes to who will hurt him. He thinks because Jessie fooled him that he has to have his walls up at all times. He doesn't trust himself to make the right decisions about people. I think it's good that he has you and Ty now. Ty's a good man. Michael can learn to trust him if Ty gives him time. I'm happy that he's coming out of his shell, and I'm happy to put all of this on his lap instead of mine. The truth is we need to hire a couple of new deputies. I was going to see if we could get a professional guard up here, but I trust Michael to keep you safe. Are you sure you need to work at the lodge this weekend? You couldn't put it off for a week or two? I don't like the idea of you being so close to him."

"I know I could run into him at the resort, but I'm planning on staying as far from the villas as I can," she explained. "From what I understand the people who stay in the villas don't normally spend a lot of time in the lodge proper. They have everything brought out to them and they have their own staff, so I think I can easily fly under his radar." She thought Nate was making a little too much of this. "I need to work this weekend to prove I can handle the job. We won't have another big party for a while, and I want to nail this job down as fast as I can. Not that I don't love it here."

She didn't want him to think she was ungrateful for everything his family had done for her.

Nate held up a hand. "No one wants to see you go, Lucy, but we're all happy you're moving on to a bigger, better job. We've enjoyed having you around, and we'll be sad if you don't come back every now and then."

"Of course." She just had to get the job first, and that might mean ducking every time she saw one of the Foster siblings until she had herself firmly established in the role. Once Mr. Roberts knew her better, she would feel more comfortable going to him with the evidence she had against Brock. "We'll need to get away every now and then. And I'll be back lots over the next month or so because I'm helping with Winter Festival."

"Yes, we always have our festivals," Nate said with a grimace. "They usually end up with someone being murdered."

"We haven't had anyone murdered in a while now." It was true that Bliss had a pretty bad murder rate per capita, but it was almost all out of towners.

"I was very happy that Henry chose to kill all his guys down in Mexico."

Nate seemed to be forgetting a big part of that story. "I don't think he chose to. I think he was kidnapped."

"Yes, and his friends killed the whole cartel in a place where I didn't have to do any paperwork. I sent him a fruit basket to thank him. You get through Winter Festival with no deaths and you get a fruit basket, too."

She could use a fruit basket. "I'll make sure it's on our list. No murders."

Nate stood and reached for the Stetson that had been sitting on Zane's desk. "All right. You tell Michael if he has any questions about this guy to call me. He also needs to call me if he shows up again. I know y'all have security up there, but I'm still the sheriff. He needs to let me handle the situation if I can."

She agreed whole heartedly which was why she fully intended to tell Michael about Nate's visit. But maybe soften it up a little, not mention the whole Brock-had-threatened-to-ruin-her-life thing. "Will do, Sheriff."

She joined the rest of the staff and started her day.

* * * *

Michael wished he'd insisted on getting his vehicle before they came up the mountain. He wasn't even sure why he hadn't. Ty had mentioned he would drive him up and he hadn't pushed back.

Probably because he was still thinking about the night before.

I love you, Lucy.

Watching Lucy and Ty together had done something he hadn't thought it would. He'd been prepared to find it distasteful. He'd been prepared for jealousy. He'd been ready to admit that watching two other people got him hot.

He hadn't expected watching them would make him long.

Ty put the Jeep in park and turned his way. "Maybe I should stop by the Trading Post and get some coffee. I know we can go down to

161

the kitchen, but Luce is a badger before she gets some caffeine in her system. You're not far behind her. At least I think that was a need for coffee this morning. It could be your usual morning grump."

"Morning grump?" He knew he shouldn't ask, but Ty often amused him. Well, he wanted to punch Ty less than most people.

Ty nodded. "Yeah, I've noticed you go through a daily series of grumps."

"That's not a word. I mean it is, but not the way you're using it. Grump is a noun. I'm a grump. I can be grumpy. But I can't have a grump."

"Sure you can," Ty insisted. "It's a mood. It's also something you do. Your morning grump seems to be cut off with shower sex, although that was so long ago. Did we slide back into the morning grump or are we pregaming for the afternoon session?"

"You're an asshole." But he was smiling as he got out of the Jeep.

No one joked with him anymore. Probably because for a long time he bit the heads off of people who did. Still, despite the fact that he came down off this mountain more often now, the people around town tended to give him a wide berth. It was kind of nice to have someone call him on his morose shit.

He didn't have grumps. He had…moments of contemplation.

"Hey, Mike." Ty had gotten out of the Jeep, and he nodded toward the side of the cabin. "It looks like you have company."

Michael's hand immediately went for his gun. And then he remembered he wasn't carrying the sucker. He hadn't wanted to scare Lucy, so he'd locked his semiautomatic in his gun case that was hidden in the floor of his cabin, and now that seemed like a bad idea. He held up a hand to ask Ty to go silent.

"You want a fist bump?" Ty asked.

He was going to have to train him better. He suspected Ty's EMT training hadn't included military signals. "Hush. I need to figure out who it is. Get back in the Jeep."

Ty frowned his way. "I think it's someone who rented a car. It's got a sticker on it from the rental place in Alamosa. I'm surprised that sedan made it up the mountain."

"Hey, I'm serious." A whole bunch of scenarios went through Michael's head, the worst being the assholes who'd turned Jessie against everything she'd believed in had come looking for him. She'd had a bank account with seventy thousand in it that he hadn't known about until after she'd died. They might have come looking for their money since she hadn't finished the job. "Get back. We don't know who we're dealing with."

"I think we're dealing with her." Ty pointed. "Hi, lady. Are you planning to murder us or did you just get lost?"

"Hi," a familiar voice said. "I'm looking for the guy who lives here. At least they told me he lives here. His name is Michael Novack. Have you seen him? I'm worried about him. Especially since he lives here."

He gritted his teeth and thought seriously about running. He could sprint through those woods and never come back.

Then he wouldn't have to face Trina Wilson. Jessie's sister.

"Oh, he's right here." Ty ratted him out and pointed his way.

His past had caught up to him.

Fifteen minutes later, he sat down on the couch—if it could be called that—and faced the woman he'd spent two years avoiding.

Trina Wilson was the opposite of her sister in almost every way. She was blonde where Jessie had dark hair, and Trina was one of those women who would go to the grocery store in high heels and full makeup. He'd rarely seen her looking less than perfect, though she wore a worried expression now as she glanced around the place he'd been living in for years.

"I'm sorry. I know you wanted to never see any of us again, but I needed to talk to you." Trina was two years younger than her sister. She'd been engaged when Jessie died, her wedding set for six weeks later.

He glanced down at her hand, expecting to see a wedding ring there. The only jewelry she wore was a watch. "You didn't marry Tommy?"

Her fist closed as though trying to hide the fact that she no longer wore the one-carat diamond she'd been so proud of. "No. Tommy's father was running for DA back in our hometown. He wanted to avoid the scandal that would have come if he married me. At first he told me we should postpone the wedding, and I agreed. I figured out it was completely off when the wedding planner sent me a bill marked final. Apparently even if you don't get married, you still get a bill."

Trina and Tommy had been together for a long time. "I'm sorry to hear that."

He didn't want to be here. There was a reason he'd ignored Trina's calls. He'd finally shut off his phone and gotten a new one.

How many times had he and Jessie been out with Trina and Tommy? Even before they'd gotten together, he'd spent time with Jessie's family. His own parents had split when he was a kid and they'd each moved on, forming new families he didn't feel comfortable in. When he and Jessie had partnered up, she'd invited him back to her place that first Christmas and he'd met the woman in front of him.

"I don't know about that." Trina looked weary for a moment before her jaw went straight, an expression he'd seen a thousand times on her sister's face. Pure Wilson stubborn. "I understand that you find me and my family distasteful."

"I never said that."

"Your actions speak far louder than words, especially since you haven't actually talked to us in years." She shifted on the love seat. The small cabin he'd been living in had a tiny front room that led to an even tinier kitchen and bedroom, if it could be called such. It was more of a cot room since all he had in it was a cot.

He kind of hated this place.

"Well, it turns out Mike has next to nothing in his pantry." Ty walked back in with two cans of soda and a bottle of water. "And by pantry I mean a shelf over a sink that doesn't actually work. I did get the generator on, though, so I can turn that space heater on. Mike might be warmed by the fiery depths of his rage, but the rest of us need some help."

"This won't take long, Ty. We'll be out of here in fifteen minutes or so," he murmured before turning back to Trina.

"Fifteen minutes? That's all you'll give me?" Trina asked.

"I don't want to talk about Jessie. I've made myself clear. That part of my life is over, and I need to move on."

"You moved on five minutes after she died."

"Oh, I couldn't have done that. I was passed out from the drugs

164

she gave me when she died," he shot back. "It was at least ten minutes. She knew how to do it right."

Trina's eyes widened and he knew he'd hurt her, but he couldn't call the words back. If she hadn't wanted to get hurt, she would have honored his wishes and stayed away.

"Okay, maybe I can find something stronger," Ty offered.

He could use it. "There's a bottle of whiskey in the bedroom."

"She drugged you?" Trina asked the question with obvious shock.

Fuck. How could she not know this? "Didn't your father get the police reports? I know he requested them. I know the director gave him as much as he could."

She stared down at her hands. "He did, but I guess Dad didn't tell me everything. I guess he thought it was bad enough that Jess…"

"Betrayed everything she ever said she believed in?" He wanted to be sympathetic but he couldn't find it deep down. Trina had to have known what Jessie was doing. They were close, very close. Trina knew everything about Jessie. Certainly more than the man she'd claimed to love.

Trina blinked back tears. "Before she got so desperate she did something stupid."

"Desperate? She wasn't desperate. She was greedy. I know what she said right before she died. I've read those reports, too. She told everyone she was trying to kill that the government didn't pay enough. She also told them all I was an idiot, so don't expect some grand sympathy from me if that's what you came here for."

"You didn't bother to come to the funeral, so I don't expect that at all. I came here so you could sign the paperwork so I can sell the house," she shot back. "The house that's in both your names."

He and Jessie had bought a little house in the suburbs. He didn't like to think about it, didn't like to think about the fact that he'd never gone back. He'd had a friend ship him some clothes and items he'd needed, but he'd never walked back into that house. Sometimes he dreamed about it, dreamed it was exactly how they'd left it when they'd come to Bliss on assignment. Sometimes she was still waiting there for him.

"What you want is cash then." He should have known. It seemed to be a theme in the Wilson family.

Trina flushed a deep pink. "What I want is to believe in any way that you still care about us. What I want is to think the man my sister loved wouldn't throw her away like she was garbage."

"If the name fits," he said, a chill coming over him. That was exactly how she'd treated him. She'd tossed him away without a thought.

Trina stood up. "You don't care at all, do you? My dad…never mind. I shouldn't have come here. I'll let everything rot. None of it matters, right? It doesn't matter that we took you in and made you part of our family. It doesn't matter that my family missed you almost as much as we miss her. It doesn't matter. You can be happy wherever the fuck this is."

"Bliss," Ty said in a quiet voice. "That's the funny thing. The town is called Bliss, though for a long time I don't think he found any here. I hope that's changing. Let me help you out to your car, ma'am. There's a storm coming. It might be best if you let me drive you down the mountain. Mike can bring the Jeep down."

"I can drive myself." Trina walked to the door. Her heels clomped against the wood floors, and the door slammed as she left.

A blast of cold air had accompanied her exit.

Ty handed him the keys. "It's harder going down than it is coming up, and she doesn't even have snow tires on that thing. I'll get her into town and meet you at Trio, okay?"

"You're not going to yell at me for being mean? Is this another grump stage of mine?" There was a nasty twist in his gut. He wasn't the bad guy here. Jessie was. She always had been, and all Trina wanted was the money from the house.

Ty put a hand on his shoulder. "No. I was there that night, Mike. I remember. You're not ready to deal with her family yet. I think you might have been nicer to her sister, but how about I handle that part and you take the time you need. But hopefully not more than an hour or so because I'm hungry. I'll meet you down at Trio and then we'll get your car before I have to go on my shift. Okay?"

Had he ever had a partner like Ty? He wasn't sure he'd ever had a friend who'd watched out for him the way Ty was today. He'd always had to be the dependable one, the stalwart one, the one who never really felt anything. Ty was giving him space and cover. "You'll make sure she knows where to go if she needs to stay in town?"

"I'll take her out to Gene's myself if I need to." Ty stepped away.

"Thanks." He wasn't sure what else to say, wasn't sure how to put the gratitude he felt into words. For all the harsh emotions seeing Trina had brought up, Ty was easing them all back down.

He wanted to see Lucy. He wanted to hug her and tell her what had happened, and then she and Ty could talk about how he should handle things.

He definitely wasn't sure he liked how vulnerable that made him. He wasn't sure he liked it at all.

Chapter Ten

Ty eased the sedan onto the narrow road that wound down the mountain and would eventually lead them past Hell on Wheels. The sky was a gray that promised coming storms. If it was spring, they would have seen some rain that would wash away in hours. But this was the first storm of winter, and he feared it meant the woman next to him would be seeing a whole lot of Bliss over the next couple of days. He hoped the Movie Motel had some vacancies. "Did you fly into Colorado Springs?"

"Yes, and then I drove from there to here." Trina Wilson sniffled into the tissue she'd pulled out of her purse. "You should know I took a picture of your license plate and texted it to a friend back home in case I go missing."

"Good. That's smart. You should tell her my name is Tyler Davis, and I work for Bliss County," he replied. "And tell her if we die, she should sue the rental car company for not putting snow tires on this hunk of crap."

She bit her bottom lip and sighed. "I didn't know I was going to be driving on mountain roads. Which considering I'm in Colorado seems like I should have. They asked me if I would be doing any off roading. I said no, I was just visiting a friend. I think they thought I wasn't going far. That was a lie, too. Thanks for driving. I was pretty terrified I was going to slide off the road all the way up. What happens if two cars are on the road going opposite directions?"

"It's wider than it looks," he promised. "And mostly you won't see another car. There are only a couple of people who live on this mountain. I happen to know one of them, and he usually rides his bike down."

Sawyer's place was higher up than Mike's and a lot nicer. So much nicer. His grandfather had left the cabin he'd built with his own two hands to Sawyer and his brothers, though Sawyer was the only one who still lived there.

"That's good to know." She dabbed her eyes with the tissue and then slipped it back into her bag. "Is it supposed to keep snowing? I'm afraid I don't know how to drive on snow."

"Yes, ma'am," Ty replied. "We're expecting it to snow all weekend. Are you supposed to fly back home soon?"

"Not until Monday, but I was going to drive back to Colorado Springs tonight. I guess I won't be doing that." She went silent as he made the first of the twisting turns that would take them to the valley.

"I'm sorry about your sister. I was there the night she died. You should know the doc and I both tried to save her." He felt compelled to let her know he'd been there.

"You were the EMT? I'm not sure why the doctor would have tried to help her. She'd tried to kill him."

"Because that's who Caleb Burke is." Ty didn't like to think about that night, but when he did Caleb was always there. Always working to save anyone he could. "It's who I want to be. We took an oath, and we do our jobs no matter who is in need. I just wanted you to know I'm sorry for your loss."

She pulled out another tissue. "Thank you." She sniffled again and stared straight ahead as snow hit the windshield. "Not many people have been sympathetic. That's been one of the hardest parts. They all act like she meant nothing because of what she did, but she was still my sister."

"You'll still feel her loss every day of your life." He needed to become the go between in this situation. Michael couldn't do it. He wasn't ready, but he might be one day, and if Ty could keep open the possibility of a decent relationship, he would. "And I think Mike does, too."

She stiffened, her shoulders straightening. "It's obvious he doesn't."

"No, it's obvious that he hasn't moved on from being angry with her. He's spent quite a bit of time in that stage. So much time that I'm hoping he moves through the rest of the grieving process quicker." Watching how Michael dealt with Trina had let him know he definitely was in a bad place when it came to Jessie. The question was could he move on with Ty and Lucy? Or was he only passing time with them?

A few days ago that would have been Ty's dream scenario—that Michael would get tired of the whole threesome thing and move back to Florida to restart his life. Now he couldn't stand the thought of it. Sometime in the last couple of days, Michael had become necessary. Which was probably why he'd jumped at the chance to help someone who knew him before he came to Bliss.

He didn't want to intrude, but he was curious about who Michael had been before he'd holed himself up on a mountain.

"My dad said the same thing," she said quietly. "He thinks what Michael's doing is a kind of mourning. Not only of his relationship to my sister, but to the man he was before that night. My dad's got a degree in psychology, so he understands guilt. He feels it every day because he didn't see how far she could go. My mom's just sad. She loved Mike like a son. She's the only one who doesn't care why Jessie did what she did. She lets herself mourn."

"I thought Jessie needed money." It was the motive he'd heard, but then he probably shouldn't listen to gossip. He'd never read the police reports or asked Nate what he'd learned.

"She did. She'd gotten in some trouble. Jessie liked to gamble. She hid it from Michael, but even I knew she'd gotten in over her head a couple of times. Look, I loved my sister, but she had some entitlement problems. She thought she was underpaid and she deserved more. So when she was offered a bunch of cash by one of her bookie's contacts, she took it. It solved both of her problems. He forgave the debt and she got seventy thousand dollars, and according to the emails I found all she was supposed to do was tip off the guy as to where Markov was."

"That was still murder."

"I know, but I somehow try to tell myself it's not the same." She leaned her head against the window. "At the end of the day it doesn't matter what she did. I still miss her. Her crimes don't invalidate my sorrow."

"No, they don't. I don't know if Michael has figured that out yet." He made it to the end of the mountain road, the lights of Hell on Wheels marking the place where he would turn to head back into town. "Why did you really come to see him?"

She breathed an obvious sigh of relief as they made it to the highway. "For the reason I said. I need him to agree to sell the house. My dad has cancer, and even with insurance we can't afford the payments for his treatment. Jessie paid half the down payment. She would want our dad to have the money."

"Okay. I'll talk to him about it." He would tell Lucy and they would figure out how to best broach the subject.

"I don't know that it will help. He's not the same man. Michael...even I was half in love with him. My dad was thrilled when Jess brought him home. He was like Superman and Captain America all rolled into one. He thought Michael would be an excellent influence on her, and it seemed like he was," she said, a wistfulness about her. "He fit in with our family. While he and Jessie were together, he was one of us. It's funny because when I think about it, it wasn't such a long time. They kept their relationship on the downlow because they worked together. According to all the records, Jess still lived at home with us. That was the biggest fight they had. Well, up until she tried to murder a guy she was supposed to protect."

"I don't think there was much of an argument. She totally drugged him so he couldn't argue with her." He frowned. "I'm sorry. I shouldn't joke."

But Trina was chuckling. "I don't know about that. Sometimes it seems so absurd I have to laugh. Like what was she thinking? My parents and I, we find it easier to laugh now, to remember the good times. It's probably why I hoped I would come out here and Michael would see me and he would remember that he was part of those good times." She sniffled again. "We miss him. It's like he died, too, because I don't recognize the man I saw today."

"He's better than he was when he first moved up here. He didn't talk much during the first year, just came down for supplies." He didn't want Trina to think Michael hadn't been affected by Jessie's death. "It was at least a year before I heard him talk."

It had been then that he realized how Michael's eyes had watched Lucy's every move. He'd been jealous then.

"Why won't he come home?" The question seemed like a plea from her.

"I don't think Florida is home for him anymore." Ty couldn't help but remember that the option was still on the table. His old job was still open, and Michael could return. He could still walk away from both of them.

"Well, I would appreciate you talking to him for me. My presence seemed to bring out the worst in him."

"Probably because he hasn't faced what he needs to." It was the only reason he could think of because Michael, for all his gruffness, had never seemed cruel before. "I think you reminded him he still has work to do."

She nodded and shifted in her seat. "So you're his friend?"

He had to wonder how long she would be stuck here and how much she would find out. If she mentioned she had a connection to Michael, she would likely get all the gossip she could never want. Still. He had to take into account what Michael would want her to know. "Yes, we're friends. He's actually starting a new job out at the lodge I work at. It's part time and temporary, but he might like it. It's security so it's in his wheelhouse."

Her nose wrinkled up. "Oh, he wasn't security. What Michael did best was track people down. That was what I always found sad about his last assignment. He didn't usually work protective services. Jessie liked those jobs. He liked to find people who didn't want to be found. He was excellent at it. The protective duties always seemed to bore him a bit. It was one of the things they fought about. He wanted to concentrate on fugitive apprehension, and she liked where they were. He switched departments for her. I think Michael thought Jessie would settle down and want to start a family. Well, he thought that because she said she did, but she kept putting him off."

"Do you think she was lying to him?"

"I think eventually she might have wanted to get married, but mostly I think she would have done anything to keep him with her, including embellishing the truth about what she really wanted from life." She sat back again, her eyes trailing to the side, watching the road. "Which was apparently a ton of money and him."

He turned at the river, starting into town. "Well, I think Michael needs some more time, but I promise I'll let him know what we've talked about and the position your family is in. For now I think it's best that I take you to a motel. I don't think you're getting out of Bliss tonight."

"Yeah, I was starting to get that feeling." She frowned as she stared up the road. "Are you taking me to that movie place?"

"Yes, you'll like it. The rooms are comfy, and I think he's running *Back to the Future* this week," he murmured.

"I don't…I can't stay there," she whispered, her eyes wide.

Because that was where her sister had died. Fuck. He hadn't even thought about it.

"Of course you can't." He started to look for a place to turn around. "I've got somewhere I can take you. You'll like it."

The lodge was big enough that it should be okay.

He hoped Michael agreed.

* * * *

Lucy wondered if Michael was going to talk at all as they drove through the snow toward the lodge. He'd been quiet since the moment he'd picked her up. Was he regretting the decision to stay up at Ty's place? Had going back to his cabin made him want to stay there? Alone?

"Maybe we should stop by River's place and get my car." If he was going to change his mind about staying with them, she would rather have the option of her own transportation.

"I don't think you want to drive up to the lodge in your car. It's not meant for mountain driving, and I'm pretty sure it's leaking oil," Michael said, his eyes on the road. "I talked to Jax earlier today, and he's going to check it for me. There's a stain on the parking space you normally use."

Well, she'd known she was leaking oil for a little while, but she didn't have the cash to fix it. She would in a couple of weeks. "I'll let him know he doesn't have to bother. I'll take it to Long-Haired Roger's in a few weeks."

"Or you can use mine or Ty's while you save up some money to get a better car. I'll look around for something safe, something you can afford."

It was the first time he'd talked about doing anything beyond the next few days. "So you're staying?"

He turned into the parking lot of the lodge. The big main building looked warm and homey against the gorgeous winter backdrop. He pulled around to the employee lot that led to the wing the staff lived in. "Why wouldn't I stay?"

Frustration welled. It had been that kind of a day. She was in the midst of a bunch of possibilities, but with that came uncertainty, and she didn't handle that well. She liked to know what was going to happen, what to expect. Much of her life had been spent walking a knife's edge, and now she craved peace and stability. She wasn't sure she could have that with Michael. She might not be able to have it with Ty. Her insecurities had crept back in all day. "I don't know. Neither one of you showed up for lunch, and then you pick me up and you haven't said more than a couple of words to me."

"I explained that something came up," he replied with a huff.

"We have two different definitions of explain," she shot back.

He was quiet for a moment. "I think I might be having a grump."

"What?"

He pulled into a space and put the SUV in park before turning to her. "It's something Ty came up with to describe my brooding nature. I'm sorry, Luce. I ran into a problem today, and I needed some time to think about it."

"A problem?"

His face went stony. "I don't want to talk about it. It doesn't involve you, and I would prefer to keep it that way. I'm sorry about lunch. I really am. I'm sorry I had to bring Ty into it. I would really like to go inside and maybe we can go to the café for dinner. Ty should be back soon. I thought we could have dinner and then maybe watch some TV. I already did all the paperwork for this weekend, and I made sure I'm working the same shifts you're working. So we've got the whole evening free, and I promise not to grump."

She wanted to tell him he could talk to her, that he didn't have to shove down whatever it was he was feeling, but she rather thought what he needed was support more than anything. She believed that he felt bad about missing lunch, and he'd texted her rather than leaving her to sit there wondering or forcing her to get in touch first. She had to give him some grace. "Okay."

He stopped for a moment, staring at her. "Just like that?"

"Just like what?"

"I didn't show up for our date and now I won't tell you why. Shouldn't you be angry with me?"

Put like that it made her sound like a doormat. She wasn't casually excusing everything he did. She'd considered how he'd handled the situation and how what he'd been through could change the way he behaved. Had Ty not wanted to talk about something, she would have poked him until he did because that wasn't who Ty was. But Michael needed a different approach. "Did you skip lunch with me because you found something more fun to do?"

His face fell. "God, no. It sucked. It was a shitty, shitty day. And me not talking is…"

"You're trying to decompress." She knew that feeling well. "It's okay. If you wanted to talk about it, you could talk to me, but I'm also not going to nag you until you do. Something bad happened, and you need to process it. Me forcing you or holding out until you give me what I want wouldn't help the situation. It would make it worse. I care about you so I'm not going to do that."

He stared at her as though trying to figure out what kind of game she was playing. "You're simply going to accept that I didn't skip lunch to hurt you and that I'll talk to you when I'm ready."

It was pretty simple and made her wonder what his other relationships had been like. "Yes. Michael, people who care about each other, they don't withhold time and affection to get what they want. I'm curious about what happened, but I believe you when you tell me it's not about me. I won't hold our evening hostage until you talk about something you really don't want to talk about. So let's go in and have a nice night since we're going to be working all weekend."

She would have a long talk with both he and Ty about what Nate had to say. She would do it over dinner so they knew what to watch out for, and then she would pray nothing happened because Michael had just gotten this job.

He got out of the SUV and before she could follow him, he was already around to her side, opening the door and holding out a hand to help her down.

She slid out and then gasped as Michael leaned over and picked her up. "What are you doing?"

"Processing," he said, kicking the door closed. She heard the beep that let her know he'd locked the car down.

"Shouldn't you grab your bag?"

He walked to the entrance and fumbled to find his key card, finally getting the door open. "I need you more than I need extra clothes. I can get them later."

What had she said to turn him into a hungry beast? She kind of wanted to know because she could use it like a magic word when she needed some stress relief.

Then she stopped thinking that way because this was obviously more than stress relief for him. Something had happened, something she hoped Ty had helped him with, but it had impacted Michael emotionally. He needed her. It didn't matter what it was, he needed her, and she was going to be there for him.

She held on as he got them to Ty's apartment, managed to get the door open. Then she was on her feet as the door slammed closed, and Michael's mouth came down on hers.

His hand twisted lightly in her hair, and he devoured her mouth.

Her whole body went hot as though his kiss had gone straight to her pussy. She could feel the way her body softened in some places and went righteously hard in others. Her nipples tightened almost painfully, and she could feel the way they rasped against the fabric of her bra.

She let her hands go around his waist, tugging at the bottom of his shirt because she was suddenly desperate to feel his warm skin against hers.

Michael's arms came up, allowing her to drag the shirt over his head and toss it to the side before he pulled her close again. "I hated the fact that I didn't think about you all day." He shook his head. "I didn't mean it that way. I meant sometimes all I think about is you. I like those days. I like the days when you're the only thought in my head."

He really could be sweet when he let down all the walls he'd built up around himself. "I did think about you all day. I thought about you and Ty and the fact that I'm supposed to wear that plug again tonight."

His face lit with amusement, and he picked her up again. "Damn straight you are. You're going to wear it so we can take you together. So we can be together the way we're supposed to be. Do you have any idea how hot I get thinking about you wearing that plug so we can fuck your ass? I don't even think about it as me doing it anymore. It's us. Me and Ty. It feels right. I'm crazy about you, Lucy. Sometimes getting to see you was the only thing that kept me going, and now that I've had you I can't think of anywhere else I want to be than in a bed with you, wrapped around you."

He tossed her on the bed, and she watched as he kicked off his boots right before his hands went to the fly of his jeans and shoved them and his boxers off his muscular hips. Those notches made her mouth water almost as much as the sight of his cock.

She knew she should be getting out of her clothes, but he was so gorgeous she couldn't take her eyes off him. She loved the contrast between her men. Where Ty was lean, Michael was broad, one sunny and the other holding all the bad boy sexiness she could handle.

Michael tossed his pants aside and stood over her, completely naked. Every inch of his body was muscular and stunning. She could believe the rumors that he'd been a linebacker during college and had dreamed of having a pro career.

Now she was the one dreaming about a future with him. She prayed it wasn't a futile hope, but she shoved those thoughts aside now. Her insecurities had no place here. She'd promised to live in the now, and she meant to honor that vow. All she needed was him to be here with her, to be open in the moment.

She got to her knees and pulled her T-shirt over her head, eager to be flesh to flesh with him. Michael moved in, looming over her. He watched as she undid her bra and let it drop to the side.

"You are so fucking gorgeous." He palmed a breast, his eyes hot on her. "You're so much more than I dreamed you would be."

And then it was like he couldn't control himself a second more. He wrapped an arm around her waist and dragged her up, balancing her against his strong chest. She was above his head, her hands on his shoulders as he pressed his mouth to her breast and sucked her nipple inside.

She held on as he nipped and sucked and licked her breasts, moving from one to the other. One of his hands went down to cup her ass through her jeans. She was caught against him, completely dependent on him for support, and there was something deliciously decadent about the position.

She looked down, watching as his tongue came out to circle her areola. He nipped her lightly, making her moan as the flicker of pain shot through her, heating her blood and making her want more.

He lowered her to the bed and she stared up at him, his cock jutting out from his body. She'd tasted that cock. She'd licked and sucked the head, gathering the pearly arousal she'd found there. She'd sucked his balls, lavishing affection on each in turn. He'd come in her mouth, and she'd swallowed him down.

He pulled her shoes off and then her socks before tugging her jeans down and off in a powerful move. Her underwear didn't stand a chance against him. They were gone in a second and he was kneeling, spreading her legs wide. He breathed her in, the growl from the back of his throat dismissing any self-consciousness she might have had. She simply laid back and let him touch her with his fingers and his tongue. He licked her with a long swipe and then settled in, eating her pussy with the relish of a half-starved man at a banquet. She clutched the comforter, twisting it to stay in place while he swamped her with pure sensation. A big finger pushed inside her, stroking her as surely as his tongue moved against her clit.

He pushed her to the edge and when she thought she would go screaming over it, he stood.

Before she could complain, he was grabbing a condom from the nightstand, rolling it over his dick. His balls were already drawn up tight against his body. He fell on her, pushing inside her in one long stroke.

He felt so good. He was big and thick, but her pussy was so slick. He kissed her, his tongue sliding against hers. The taste of her own arousal was right there in his kiss, like she'd become an essential part of him, something that changed him on a base level.

She held on as he started to thrust inside her, his hips finding a pulsing rhythm that she matched. She wrapped her legs around his waist and fought for every second of pleasure she could find. This felt primal and raw, a moment he needed from her to wash away the pains of the day, and she needed to give it to him.

Then his cock slid across the perfect spot, his pelvis grinding down on her clit so both buttons were pushed at the same moment, igniting a spectacular fire.

Through her own orgasm, she felt Michael stiffen above her. He held himself hard against her, elongating the pleasure, and then he dropped on top of her, pressing her into the mattress. She held him tight as her blood pounded through her body, the relief a secondary wave of pleasure.

It was almost as sweet as the rush of emotion she got from the way he covered her with his body, his head cuddled against her neck.

"Hey, Mike," a familiar voice said. "You in a good mood now?"

How had they missed Ty coming into the bedroom? He stood at the foot of the bed, a six-pack of beer in his hand. Ty wasn't a big beer fan, so he'd obviously stopped somewhere to pick it up for Michael, who didn't even raise his head.

"I'm in a perfect mood," Michael said with a sigh. If he was bothered that Ty was staring at them and likely had watched them have sex, he didn't show it at all.

Yep. A couple of days before she would have jumped up in pure embarrassment, shocked at anyone witnessing such an intimate moment between her and her boyfriend. But it had only been her other boyfriend, and he seemed pretty cool with it.

"Good because your ex-fiancée's sister is here at the lodge. I brought you beer and your favorite chips, but Lucy seems to have handled it for me." Ty gave her a grin and a thumbs-up. "You did good, baby. Also, you look really pretty tonight."

She snorted as Michael rolled off her. Well, at least she knew what had happened and that Ty hadn't planned to keep it from her.

Ty made his way back to the kitchen.

"I'm still going to need that beer, Ty." Michael propped his head up with his hand and sighed as he looked her in the eyes, a soft expression on his face. "Jessie's sister showed up. She was at my cabin when Ty and I got there, and I'm not sure I handled her well."

"You were awful," Ty yelled from the next room.

Michael groaned and dropped back down, his head against her breast. "Fuck. I was awful."

No wonder he'd been in a mood. He wasn't ready to talk about

Jessie at all, much less face her family. She stroked his hair. "Then maybe it's a good thing you have a second chance to make it right."

Ty strode back in, an opened bottle of beer in his hand. "I have some thoughts on how you can do that."

Michael's lips curled up. "All right. Let me clean up and I'll hear you out."

He rolled off the bed and started for the bathroom. But not before he grabbed his beer.

Ty's eyes lit up. "We have at least three minutes. The Farley brothers tried to make their own fireworks, and I had to do a lot of eye washing. It was a day."

He jumped on the bed while Lucy laughed.

Two men could be a whole lot of work.

Chapter Eleven

The following evening, Michael looked out over the big ballroom and wondered if he would survive the weekend.

This was not the job he wanted. This was a babysitting job, and he pretty much wanted to punch all the babies.

"What do you want, Harper?"

Max Harper had been staring at him for a good five minutes. He knew the man in front of him was Max and not his identical twin Rye because Rye never managed to raise his blood pressure the way Max did. Rye was out on the dance floor with their shared wife. Max didn't seem to know what to do without them.

"Nothing. I was just surprised to see they got you into a tie." Max had a beer in his hand. "Did you fight it?"

"It's part of the uniform, asshole." He rather wished a gun was part of his uniform. Or maybe a taser. Yeah, he could tase Max and spare the world his sarcasm.

"I always thought you would be the last one to sell out to the corporate world. You were the best of us. The lone ranger, out there living your life with no one telling you what to do."

"With no working toilet." He felt the need to point out the drawbacks of his recent lifestyle.

Max plunged ahead. "No one telling you 'no Max, you can't

have five waffles because your cholesterol is high.'"

"I ate shitty canned chili for a year. Do you know what that can do to your digestive tract? And again, no working toilet." It had been a miserable couple of years, and he was starting to believe it had all been one long grump and he was ready to be done with it.

"You were living the dream, man. You could sleep all day and drink all the beer you want. You didn't have to worry about using the wrong blanket because some of them are decorative. No one made you get up early to hit the farmer's market."

Max was forgetting one big point. "Yeah, because no one gave a shit about me."

Max sighed. "So now you've found a woman, and she made you wear a tie. It's like a leash, man. She's going to tug on it and make you do her bidding."

"I'll do her bidding any time she asks. Don't make her sound like some nagging harpy. In fact, don't make any woman sound like that. Women nag because men can be lazy as shit. You lazy, Max?"

Harper pulled his phone and started typing. He looked up when he was done, sliding the phone into his pocket. "Excellent, man. Hey, that suit looks good on you, brother. When you three have some time, come out to our place for supper."

To his surprise he could actually hear the chimes from several of the phones around him going off at the same time. He watched as some of the residents of Bliss who'd come to the opening night party checked their cell phones.

A sigh of collective relief seemed to go through the crowd.

"Stef sent you to see how things are going?"

Max nodded. "Yeah."

"You could have asked."

"Nah, that's boring and people lie. I already thought it was good since Lucy is running around with a smile a mile wide." Max relaxed and came to stand beside him, taking a long drag off his beer. "But there were some rumors running around about you not showing up for lunch and her being in tears over it. Then you didn't come into Trio to pick her up, and some of us were concerned. Now before you tell us to get out of your business, you should know…"

He hadn't been about to give that lecture again. "You care about her and I've been a walking powder keg for the last couple of years. I know, but we're fine. The three of us. We're all good."

"I'm glad to hear this, my friend," a familiar voice said. Alexei Markov wore dark slacks and a black sweater that matched. He was a handsome man in his early thirties. It hit Michael that despite his brooding good looks and tendencies to wear a lot of black, Alexei was the Ty in his relationship. Caleb was the brooder, and Holly the happy woman who brought them all together. "Max, thank you for the update. Could I have a moment with my friend?"

Max nodded. "Sure thing. I got some more of Roberts's free beer to drink. And I spotted some wings. There is no cholesterol this evening."

"I'm going to have Luce send him an astronomical bill and watch his head explode." He felt a smile cross his face. It wouldn't be real, of course, but Max would think it was.

It was good to fuck around with friends.

It was good to have friends.

"You are to be looking good tonight." Alexei's English had gotten better over the years, but he was still Alexei.

"So are you." There had been a year where it had hurt to hear Alexei's name because if they hadn't taken the job, they wouldn't have been there. Somewhere into his second year on the mountain he'd realized that Jessie simply would have found another way to get the money she'd wanted, and without Alexei she might have gotten away with it and hurt someone. Someone besides him.

Tonight was weird because looking at Alexei didn't bring even a second of pain. Tonight he realized that without Alexei he wouldn't have met Lucy. He would never have known Ty.

"This is lie on your lips. I am looking like new father." Alexei chuckled and then yawned behind his hand. "I am looking like man who never sleeps. I fall asleep behind bar at Trio the other day in the middle of happy hour. I was leaning against bar and then I wake up and it is closing time and Zane has decorated me like I am Trio Christmas tree. How he gets those lights around me I will never know."

That sounded like Zane. "Asshole."

Alexei waved him off. "He lets me sleep. Amelia does not let me sleep. Baby girl prefers to be held while she sleeps. I tell Caleb that in Russia babies sleep out in the snow so they become strong, learn to fight off wolves." His lips kicked up. "This is not true, of course. But Caleb is gooey puddle when it comes to our daughter. Anytime she cry he is wanting to put her into MRI and make sure she is not to be dying."

Alexei had a baby girl. It was crazy when he thought about it. When he'd met the man in front of him, Alexei's life had been precarious. He'd been alone and sad and brave. "You know when we started working together I would have never thought you would be the one to have a wife and kids before me. I felt sorry for you."

Alexei snorted. "I feel sorry for me, too. I was named Howard and living in bad motels. If you ask younger me, he would also be surprised about wife and baby. He would be very surprised about Caleb."

"Yeah, I'm sure mine would be shocked by Ty."

"I think it would be good shock. I think perhaps our younger selves did not know how much better world is when we open our hearts and minds to possibilities," Alexei said. "I meet with Jessie's sister today."

Michael's gut tightened. He'd known she was here, but he'd never dreamed she would reach out to Alexei. "What?"

"She calls me. She did not know I was coming to lodge for party. So she asks if she can meet me. I let her know I can come a bit early if she would like to talk."

"What the hell did she want to talk about?" He didn't understand what Trina was doing. He got that she wanted money, but why talk to Alexei?

"She wants to talk about her sister," Alexei explained.

"Her sister who tried to kill you."

Alexei sighed. "There is always something more to story, Michael. Trina and I are strangers, connected by one person. We are both impacted by choices her sister made. I think she is trying to feel not so alone."

He couldn't believe she'd bothered Alexei. "She's being selfish. Jessie caused the problem. She should leave well enough alone."

"I don't think she can. I think she needs to find some peace. She asks my forgiveness. She asks it of me and Holly and Caleb."

It was worse than he'd imagined. "She forced all three of you to talk?"

Alexei's head shook. "She doesn't force. We were willing to meet her, to help her. Tragedy doesn't define us if we don't let it. Tragedy is a storm we live through or choose not to live through. I'm sure I would feel different had Holly or Caleb died, but I would have gone on. I wouldn't have allowed hate to be my fuel. I did that for years, and it is fuel that burns everything around it. Tears everything apart. I didn't forgive Trina because she did something wrong. She did not. I forgive her because she needs to hear words from me. I forgive her because I forgave her sister long ago. I can hate what Jessie did and not hate the woman herself. You see difference?"

"I don't need a therapy session from you, Alexei." He didn't like the antsy feeling threatening to overtake him. He wasn't here to mix and mingle. He was here to make sure no one did something stupid. "I'm working, so I should get back to that."

Alexei frowned. "I think you should talk to Trina. Her heart aches as much as yours does."

He doubted that. Trina hadn't had a choice. She'd been born Jessie's sister. He had. He'd chosen her, and he'd been a moron to believe she'd loved him for a single second. He'd always been her chump, the lap dog she sent to do her bidding. He'd given up everything for her, and she'd fucked him over and ruined his life.

And Lucy and Ty didn't understand. They couldn't understand because they hadn't made those kind of poor choices in their lives. They'd skipped dinner the night before and ordered in and sat up for a while talking about how to handle Trina. They wanted him to be nice to her.

He didn't owe anyone anything. Not her. Not them.

Michael, people who care about each other, they don't withhold time and affection to get what they want.

Didn't he owe something to a woman who knew how to love? Didn't he owe a friend who watched his back some consideration? If dealing with Trina would make Lucy and Ty feel better, didn't he owe them? Couldn't he trust them since neither would lie to him the way Jessie had?

"I'll talk to her." It would be uncomfortable, but he would do it.

"She's here." Alexei gestured to the buffet. "Her flight was canceled, and she will be staying here until storm is passed."

He glanced over and sure enough, there Trina stood, filling her plate. Ty was standing not ten feet away, laughing at something River was saying. She and Jax had come up for the party on a snowmobile, the way many of the Bliss citizens had. With as much snow on the ground, it could be a more convenient method of travel.

He couldn't talk to her. Not tonight. "I'll have breakfast with her."

That seemed civilized. He didn't have to work until tomorrow afternoon, and neither did Ty and Lucy.

"Good. This is good," Alexei replied. "It is good for both of you."

"But I want Lucy and Ty there."

Alexei smiled, a gentle expression. "This is good, too. They are good for you. You could be good for them, too."

He didn't like the *could be*, but Alexei's English wasn't always precise. He *was* good for them. He could be assertive where their natural personalities tended toward the passive. They were already starting to fall into roles that suited them, and he was beginning to get comfortable.

It was good to feel comfortable.

Lucy chose that moment to walk up to him, a tray in her hand. She gave him the sweetest smile and a wink. "Hey, Alexei. Different place, same old job, huh? I'm supposed to be the boss, but here I am serving drinks."

"Sometimes boss must be playing for team," Alexei said with a slight bow.

Michael frowned. "I thought you were supervising."

"I was, but we had a guest spill a drink on another guest's apparently very expensive dress, and we're having to fix their whole table while attempting to stop red wine from staining Gucci." She held up the tray. "Hence, here I am taking this super-expensive glass of Scotch to one of the suites. Can't keep some high roller waiting. Be back soon."

She strode toward the staff elevator, her hips swaying.

He had it so bad for her.

"I will miss her at Trio," Alexei said. "Though I am thinking I will not be here for long either. I tell Zane he must accept two week notices this afternoon."

Alexei didn't actually have to work. Caleb had enough money

for all of them. He had generational wealth that paid for the big cabin they'd built and the medical practice that couldn't possibly bring in much since half the time he didn't take payment. "Wow. So you're going to school full time then?"

"I am starting work with counseling group," Alexei said with a yawn. "It's a kind of internship while I finish degree and before I open own practice. I hope I do not fall asleep on patients."

It would be weird to walk into Trio and not see Alexei and Lucy. Not that he planned to often walk in without her, but it was still change. Good change, though, since both were moving on to bigger and better things.

It also meant a job was open, but he didn't know a damn thing about mixing drinks. Still, it had to be better than standing around waiting for some drunk asshole to throw a punch.

"You won't because Amelia is going to get on a good sleep schedule." Holly moved in behind her husband.

"I don't know. I think we should check in to that sniffle she had." Caleb Burke was frowning but that was nothing new.

Holly sighed and held a hand out to both of them. "She's fine." She looked to Michael. "A couple of us with babies rented a room and hired two babysitters so we could have a nice night out. Well, I'm having a nice night. Nell is protesting in the snow. But Poppy and Amelia are fine, as my husband knows because we went to check on them. Now we're going to dance."

"You will set up meeting?" Alexei asked as his wife started to lead him away.

Michael nodded. It would be better to get it over with. He'd been putting off selling that place for far too long. He'd avoided it, not wanting to think about the life he'd had there. The lie he'd lived there.

It would be good to divest himself of that baggage and move on with his life. He might even look into buying a proper cabin, one with working water and heat. Someplace cozy where they could be together and happy.

The problem was he was starting to miss his job. Being with Ty and Lucy made him realize he missed more than companionship. He missed his job, missed feeling like he was doing something important.

He studied the big ballroom that had been decorated like a winter palace. There were cozy conversation spaces and tables around the bar. A band played in the background, covers of bouncy pop songs intermingled with rock and country favorites. The lodge had tables where guests could learn about all the activities planned for the ski season and the many amenities the Elk Creek Lodge had to offer.

Ty seemed happy here. Lucy was excited about her job.

He didn't want to live here, didn't want to work here.

He wanted to be out in the field, working with local law enforcement, using his skills to hunt down the worst of the worst.

He stood there for a long while, contemplating the fact that by finding something good, he'd also started wanting the one thing that could blow it all up.

He watched as Trina put down her mug and stood, smiling Van's way, but not the way she used to. Trina had been one of those bouncy, happy people who lit up a room when she walked in.

Was he punishing her for not recognizing the lies her sister told?

Like he was punishing himself.

He saw someone move out of the corner of his eye, a quick flash that let him know someone was running away. He turned and saw it was Ty, and Caleb Burke wasn't far behind him. Both men were sprinting like their lives depended on it.

Or rather someone else's.

He tossed aside all of his doubts. It was time to go to work.

* * * *

Lucy glanced over to where Michael stood at the back of the ballroom. He and Max Harper seemed to be having a stare off.

Otherwise, everything seemed to be going all right. Mostly.

"He keeps eating all the shrimp." One of the servers huffed and put her now empty tray on the top of the table where Lucy had been coordinating service. She was set up behind the bar, out of the way of the guests. There was a discreet hallway that led to the kitchens and staff rooms. "I swear I step out on the floor and that one guy sucks up all the shrimp. Like he's a whale and they're whatever whales eat."

"Sorry, that's Long-Haired Roger. He really likes shrimp." He was also a cheapskate who would find the highest value item at any buffet and eat as much as he could. And he'd probably come armed with plastic sandwich baggies to "take some home" to his dog, Princess Two, who also enjoyed high-priced snacks.

"He's bald," the server pointed out.

"Yeah, it's an aspirational nickname." Once Roger's hair had been long and flowing, but she wasn't getting into ancient history. "Why don't you take a break and let him find the specialty cheese on the buffet? He'll focus on that for a while if you let him, and maybe the north side of the ballroom can get some shrimp, too."

The server picked up her tray. "Such a weird place."

Van set three longnecks on a serving tray at the end of the bar. "Don't listen to her. This is an awesome place. I mean, the town is. I'm not sure how much I love lodge life, but I do love the town."

Something about his tone made her wonder what he meant. "You're not thinking of leaving, are you?"

He shook his head. "Not at all, though I'm wondering if this is the right job for me. I'm thinking about asking Zane for a full-time job if one comes up. I know the housing here is nice, but it's also seasonal for most of us. And Hale was not meant for a high-level service job, if you know what I mean. He does not suffer assholery in silence."

She'd met his best friend. He was a big man with a grim handsomeness about him.

"Then I would get to see you because I spend a lot of time at Trio," she admitted. "Even when I'm not working."

"I would enjoy that." Van continued mixing drinks as he talked. "I think we'll fit in better in town than we do here. If we can find jobs, there are a couple of cabins to rent in the valley we might be able to afford. It would be good to put down roots. I spent the entirety of my childhood on the road."

She knew his parents had been somewhat bohemian. "On the road?"

"Yeah. I grew up in an RV," he explained. "My mom and dad decided they didn't like the idea of being part of the rat race, so we pretty much drove from place to place and stayed as long as my dad's attention could be held. He would find some seasonal work for a while and we would have a couple of months in one place, but then the festival season would start up and he would decide we should all

189

make crafts to sell. I saw a lot of the country. I met a lot of interesting people, but I'm like my older brother. I need some permanency in my life."

"I can understand that. I had a rough childhood when it came to financial stability, but I had friends to rely on." She glanced over to where River and Jax were dancing to a slow ballad. River grinned up at her husband, and there was such joy on her friend's face that it filled Lucy's heart. "Friends are important. Sometimes they're more important than family."

She loved her siblings, but she wasn't close to them anymore. Her brothers were living their lives, and her younger sisters had each other. River and Ty and Sawyer had been her lifelines.

And now they were all back in Bliss where they belonged, and their little family could get a wee bit bigger with the additions of Michael and Jax. Someday Sawyer would find a blow-up doll he truly loved and they would all be complete.

"Don't I know it," Van replied. "My blood family scattered to the four winds, but Hale is still here with me."

She had to ask the question. "So…are you thinking about it?"

She had to wonder if they were curious about the lifestyle here in Bliss.

Van's lips curled up, and he didn't pretend to misunderstand. "Hell, yeah, we're thinking about it. If you hadn't gone and gotten a couple of boyfriends, you would have known exactly how hard I've been thinking about it."

She had to chuckle. "Well, I will be on the lookout for the right woman. I'm feeling like matchmaking."

Van's hands came up. "Nope. We can totally do that ourselves. Thanks."

She kind of liked the look of fear in his eyes, and she immediately started making a list in her head. She knew some fun ladies.

"Hey, what the hell, Sonya?" A feminine shout could be heard over the dance music.

She turned and sighed because the Fosters were sitting at a table in the back, champagne and wine bottles all around them. She'd been surprised they had come to the party. Well, three of them were. Sonya, Kendall, and Chet had taken the table and ordered bottle service. There was a cheese plate that hadn't been touched in the middle of the table, and they'd spent most of the night staring down at their phones.

"Damn, that is going to stain, but at least you can try." Van opened a bottle of club soda and offered it to her with one of the clean towels. "Tell her to dab not scrub."

Kendall Foster was standing up, pointing to the large stain on her gray and black jumpsuit. It fit her slim form to perfection and was likely from some celebrity designer.

Lucy grabbed the club soda and towel and started to make her way over. Sonya was setting her now half-filled glass of Pinot Noir on the tablecloth, that had also taken some damage.

The laundry team would love that.

"Could you watch what you're doing?" Kendall asked. "Do you know how much this cost?"

Sonya had already grabbed a napkin off the table and approached her sister. "I'm sorry. It slipped out of my hand. And of course I know. Who do you think pays your credit card bills?"

Kendall set her own glass down. "Don't make it sound like you pay for me. You just do the paperwork."

"Because you're too irresponsible to do it," Sonya shot back.

"I brought some club soda." Lucy didn't want to get in the middle of this, but she also didn't want the sisters to start a fight. At least Chet seemed deeply uninterested in anything except his phone screen.

Hailey, one of the servers working the rotating hors d'oeuvres, strode up. "Don't use club soda. We need hydrogen peroxide and dishwashing soap for that material. We've got both down in the laundry."

Kendall groaned. "Fine. I was planning on wearing this to a party next week."

"Go. Let the professionals help you," Sonya urged. "I'll deal with this."

Kendall's eyes rolled. "Fine. But I'm going back to the villa. This is all lame."

She walked away with Hailey.

"Sorry. She's not in a great mood." Sonya started picking up the bottles as a couple of the staff members began the process of cleaning up the table. "This is all very nice. She's just still upset about what happened the other night. We had a little incident."

"That fucked up party was all Brock's fault." Chet didn't miss a beat. He picked up his glass as they were moving the soiled tablecloth out. "And I say that bartender over there is a fucking hero."

Sonya sighed. "Again, sorry. The gathering we were having got out of hand. The bartender took a couple of punches meant for Chet. They were drunk and he got in between them. He was really mad. I thought for a moment he was going to kill Brock."

That seemed overly dramatic. Van hadn't mentioned it had gotten so heated. He'd made it sound like he'd simply taken an accidental hit. "I assure you our staff is always professional. Here, let me take those and we'll bring out some new food for you."

Sonya waved her off. "Don't worry about it. I think I'll head back, too. It was so nice to meet you. Chet, let's go. We can get more wine back at the villa. I want to ski before we have to leave. You know Dad said we should all enjoy our last weekend here. We have a big meeting when we get back home."

"Yeah, sure. Like I need to be there." Chet yawned and stood up anyway. "You know big brother will shoot down any suggestion I have. I don't know why any of us go to those things. Brock is going to get everything after Dad croaks, and he's going to hold it over our heads forever."

She was so glad she wasn't a member of that particular wealthy clan. They couldn't pay her enough to deal with that shit.

"Hey, Lucy," Van called out. "I've got a problem, and you might be the one to solve it."

Well, she'd known the evening wouldn't go off without a hitch. She made sure the table was being properly reset before turning back to the bar. In the distance, she could see that Alexei had found Michael and they seemed to be talking.

"What's up?" It looked like the servers were all circulating. Well, all but the server with shrimp, but sure enough Long-Haired Roger had taken up a space at the fancy cheese section and was even now slipping some cave-aged Gruyère into a sandwich bag.

"Whoever stocked this bar for me mistakenly brought over this Scotch." He patted the super-expensive bottle. It was the kind of Scotch that could easily vote, a single malt. "It's a private bottle for one of the suite guests. I could send it back to the main bar…"

She immediately saw the problem. "And then it would take twenty to thirty minutes to get up to the guest who's paying for good service."

"And good service is quick service," Van summed up. He poured out three fingers of the amber liquid. "I don't know why it's being stocked down here, but there it is. Suite 210. Can you have someone run it up there?"

It wasn't the largest of the suites, but it had a nice view. She picked up the tray. "I just sent one on break and another to help save a jumpsuit. I'll run it up myself. It's not far. I can be back ten minutes tops. When Charlene comes off the floor, ask her to switch to the canapés. We need to keep a vegetarian tray circulating."

Bliss had several non-meat eaters. She liked to make sure they had some snacks, too.

Lucy balanced the small tray that held the glass and strode around the dance floor.

She definitely wasn't going to let this opportunity pass her by, though. Ty wasn't anywhere close, and she'd barely seen him all night long. But Michael was right there, and he looked deliciously masculine in the classic suit the security guys wore to these kinds of events. She winked his way and gave Alexei a grin. "Hey, Alexei. Different place, same old job, huh? I'm supposed to be the boss, but here I am serving drinks."

Alexei bowed her way. "Sometimes boss must be playing for team."

A frown crossed her boyfriend's face as he took in the sight of the tray in her hand. "I thought you were supervising."

"I was, but we had a guest spill a drink on another guest's apparently very expensive dress, and we're having to fix their whole table while attempting to stop red wine from staining Gucci. Hence, here I am taking this super-expensive glass of Scotch to one of the suites. Can't keep some high roller waiting. Be back soon." She hustled because she needed to get back in place to ensure the food kept flowing.

Luckily the ballroom wasn't far from the elevator the staff used. She caught a glimpse of Nell and Henry, who were currently protesting right outside the big lobby doors. Technically they were supposed to stay off the actual property, but Nell was a close friend of the owner, who pretty much told anyone who didn't like it that Nell was part of the daily entertainment and to get used to it. Cole Roberts often sent them hot chocolate when it was cold and let them chant and sing next to the big outdoor patio heaters.

And yes, they often protested those too for their overuse of propane.

Nell seemed to be singing something about killing trees and using them cruelly. She sounded pretty good, and the dancing she was doing would totally keep her warm.

She went up to the second floor and down the hall to the suite at the end, knocking on the door. "Room service."

The door came open, and she caught sight of a dark-haired man with a towel around his waist turning away from her. "Put it on the table. I'll be right back."

Rude, but she walked through the door, flipping the in-room lock out so the door wouldn't close. She probably wouldn't have done that if the guest had been a woman, but there it was. She moved into the room, following the elegant foyer to the sitting area of the suite. There was a dining table and she moved there, setting the glass down.

"Your Scotch, Mr…" She opened the bill. Though the guest had already bought the bottle, there was a small fee for storage and service. She didn't expect much of a tip, and then she saw the name and really didn't expect one. "Foster."

Damn it. Now she knew where they'd stashed Brock after his fight with Chet. Could she run before he saw her?

A derisive snort let her know she wouldn't be getting away so easily. "Damn. You actually work here. Wow. I guess you're one of those hard-working rural girls I always hear about. Need two or three jobs to support all those kids you had at seventeen."

He moved to the table and took a long swig of the Scotch.

As long as she was here. "I need your signature, sir."

His disdain meant nothing to her. She could come back with all the ways he was a stereotypical douche nozzle spending Daddy's cash and probably always on the lookout for his next woman to sexually harass.

He took another sip and opened the receipt book. "And what if I don't give it to you, sweetheart?"

"Then I'll walk away without it and explain that you didn't want to sign," she said simply. She was going to put a note in his guest portfolio that only men were allowed to come into his room. She wasn't going to send her female servers into the predator's den. She reached for the book.

He snatched it away with the hand that wasn't holding the Scotch glass. His eyes lit with malicious glee as he downed half the glass. "I think not. I think you need to go get the rest of this bottle. My sister is an asshole. She thinks if it's left at the bar, I won't drink so much. So you have a choice. Go get my bottle or I'll simply order a glass every fifteen minutes and you can bring it to me all night long."

She couldn't care less if he drank himself to death. It sounded like a great idea to her. "Not a problem. I'll have it up here as soon as possible, sir."

She started to turn, but he reached out and gripped her wrist.

"Hey, I didn't tell you..." Brock began and then dropped her hand. "I...what the fuck? What did you do?"

She backed up because his skin had gone a sickly white right before her eyes. "Nothing. What's wrong? Should I call someone?"

He put a hand to his stomach, his eyes going to the glass in his hand. "You fucking bitch."

He raised his hand and tossed the glass her way. She sidestepped it, glass exploding against the wall and sending Scotch everywhere. It smelled odd—not like she was used to Scotch smelling—but she was too upset to identify the scent. It was all over her blouse. She wasn't sure she hadn't gotten cut up from the glass shattering.

She pulled the walkie from her belt and started to call security.

That was when blood poured from his mouth. He hit his knees and his whole body convulsed.

Lucy put her hand over her mouth to stop the scream that was building. She had to do something, and it wasn't run away. She pushed the button on her walkie and called the only person who could help her right now.

"This is Tyler," a steady voice said.

"Ty? Ty, I need you. I'm in 210. I think he's dying. Please hurry."

She let the walkie drop and prayed he made it in time.

Chapter Twelve

Ty's walkie squawked for the first time that night, the sound surprising him. For a couple of minutes he'd forgotten he was working. It was easy because this particular party felt an awful lot like a town party, although with lots of people walking around with platters of fancy food.

Jax chewed on a stuffed pepper as Ty pulled his walkie out.

"These are delicious," River said with a grin, offering her husband another.

They should get a room.

Of course that thought reminded him that he had a room and all he had to do was maneuver Lucy up to it and he could get into her pretty panties.

He still had hours to go before he could do that. With a sigh he pushed the button to talk. "This is Tyler."

He hoped it was minor. He wasn't sure he could handle a major injury that would require him to drive through a snowstorm all the way to the nearest hospital. The slopes were closed but that didn't mean he wouldn't have to deal with a broken bone.

"Ty? Ty, I need you. I'm in 210. I think he's dying. Please hurry."

His whole body went cold because that was Lucy, and she

sounded terrified.

"Everything okay?" River's eyes were wide.

"I need to find Caleb." She'd said someone was dying. He could do CPR, but Caleb could do far more if he needed to. He glanced around the ballroom, looking for the doc.

Jax pointed toward the dance floor. "He's right there. You need backup?"

He wasn't sure what was going on, but he should figure it out before he brought in a crowd. "No, but you could go and tell the bartender that Lucy might be gone for a while. He'll let her staff know."

He made a beeline for Caleb, waving a hand to get his attention. The doc took one look at his face and broke away from the group he'd been awkwardly dancing with.

"What's up?" Caleb asked.

"We've got a medical emergency in 210." Ty started to run for the door.

Caleb jogged beside him. "Do we know what we're going into?"

"No idea." He passed through the ballroom doors and then saw the staff elevator was open and made a sprint before it could close again. He turned as he held the door open for Caleb and saw Michael was following them.

"What's going on?" Michael wasn't out of breath despite the fact that he'd sprinted to catch up to them. He stood beside Caleb as Ty hit the button for the second floor.

The doors closed and started to ascend. A sense of relief washed over Ty. Michael was a reassuring presence. "Lucy said someone's dying in 210. Probably a heart attack or stroke. She sounded shook."

Michael nodded before turning to Caleb. "How much have you had to drink?"

If Caleb took offense, it didn't show. He merely nodded as though he'd expected the question. "Absolutely nothing. I drove my daughter up here, and I have to drive her home if the storm allows us to leave."

"And I've been working. I would never drink on the job," Ty added.

Michael turned his way. "I wasn't worried about you at all, but the doc isn't on the clock, and that's a big party going on down there.

I only wanted to make sure everything is good."

The doors opened and Ty led the way, jogging down the hall. The door to 210 was slightly ajar, allowing Ty to open it easily.

And then he stopped because Lucy was on the floor beside a body. Her face was pale; her hair had come out of its neat bun. The man on the floor had one of the lodge's thick robes wrapped around his body, the front covered in what looked like a combination of blood and puss. She looked up. "I didn't know what to do. He started...there was blood and white stuff, and I don't think he could breathe."

Fuck. He was almost one hundred percent certain there was nothing he could do and worse, he shouldn't touch that body. This wasn't a case of some guy vomiting from food poisoning.

This was poisoning of another kind.

"Don't touch the body," Ty said, pulling a pair of gloves out of his pack and putting them on. "Did he convulse before he passed out? Michael, help her up but be careful. Consider this a crime scene. We're going to need Nate out here."

"Crime scene?" Michael moved around the body and held a hand out to Lucy.

"Yeah, Nate, you're going to need to come up to the lodge. I know the weather is bad, but we can't wait." Caleb had his cell pressed to his ear. "Call Cam and Gemma in, too. You're going to need forensics on this one." Caleb winced. "Yeah. I'm pretty sure. Ty's looking him over and he's taking precautions. See you soon."

Ty felt the man's wrist. No pulse. He hadn't expected one.

"Shouldn't you put on a mask?" Michael asked. "He could be contagious."

"He's not contagious. This wasn't a virus." Ty unfortunately knew a poisoning victim when he saw one. And he was fairly certain about which poison. He glanced back at Caleb. "He's dead, and I believe CPR would be useless. I can smell almonds."

"Fuck." Caleb slid his cell back in his pocket. He breathed in. "Yeah, you're right. I can smell it from here. CPR wouldn't work. Cyanide stops the body from being able to use oxygen."

"Cyanide?" Michael whistled. "Someone poisoned him? No one touch anything. This whole room needs to be preserved for Nate." He turned to Lucy, whose hands were still shaking. "Baby, was this the room you were bringing the drink to? You need to tell me what happened."

"I think she should talk to Gemma first," Caleb said quietly. "It's why I asked Nate to pick her up and bring her with him."

"Why would she talk to Gemma?" Ty got to his feet. The victim's face was bloated. He didn't recognize the guy.

"Because Gemma is a lawyer," Lucy answered.

"Who made the drink?" Michael asked, his voice going hard.

"Michael, wait for Nate." Ty eased around the body. They needed to get Lucy calmed down. "I know you've been trained, but Nate has jurisdiction here."

"And he would absolutely want me to make sure none of our potential suspects manages to slip out before he can question them," Michael countered.

Lucy shook her head. "It wasn't Van. He just poured the drink. It came from a bottle. It wasn't mixed or anything. I watched him pour it. He wouldn't hurt someone."

Michael was on his walkie, talking to the head of security and requesting that he secure the bottle and the bartender.

"We should get Lucy out of here." Ty was worried about how pale she was.

"Lucy, what's on your shirt?" Caleb asked.

Michael looked down, and then he was going pale, too. "Did it get on you? Did he spill that drink on you?"

Holy shit. Panic threatened to overtake him. "Did you get any of it in your mouth or on your hands?"

"Ty, she's okay." Caleb eased around the body. "If she'd ingested cyanide, she would already feel it."

"I feel fine." Lucy didn't sound fine. Her voice trembled. "He threw the glass at me, and it smashed against the wall over there. Some of it got on me but not close to my face, and not on my hands."

"Let's wash them just to be sure." Ty wasn't letting anything happen to her. "And we can change your clothes while we wait for Nate."

"No." Michael had stepped back, and his expression had gone dark.

"We've got plenty of time." It would take Nate at least twenty minutes to get up here. Maybe longer if he had to pick up Gemma and Cam. "I'll take her to our room and make sure we clean it all off her. I don't want to take the chance that she might touch it and then get it in her mouth or eyes."

"She can't clean up, Ty. A man was murdered, and she was the last person to have contact with him," Michael explained, his tone grim. "She can go sit at the table or we can set up a room for her, but she can't change or clean herself up because she's a walking piece of evidence."

"She's our girlfriend." Ty couldn't understand what Michael was doing. "She's not a piece of evidence. She's gone through something traumatic. We need to take care of her."

"Ty, do you know who's lying on that floor dead from a drink Lucy brought him? Do you recognize him? Because I do," Michael said quietly.

He wasn't sure why the poor dude on the floor was important. Lucy certainly hadn't killed the man, and he worried the poison might get into her system. "I don't care who he is."

"It was Brock Foster." Lucy had taken a step back. "I didn't know he was in the room. I didn't look down at the receipt."

"Brock Foster is the guy who threatened her," Michael clarified. "The man who tried to attack her the other day. He's wealthy as hell and has a family who will demand answers. If we give them any rope, they will hang her with it. We have to be high and tight on this investigation or they'll go after her. That means she cooperates with everything. Everything, Lucy."

Ty's stomach took a deep dive.

"And that's why I called in Gemma." Caleb didn't seem bothered by the dead guy in the room. If anything, he seemed curious. "Lucy will be a suspect. She needs a lawyer with her."

"She doesn't." Michael's jaw had gone tight. "She only needs to tell us the truth and everything will be fine. Unless there's something she needs to tell me. Is there a reason you would need a lawyer, Lucy?"

What the hell was happening? "She doesn't need a lawyer because she didn't do anything."

"She does," Caleb insisted. "I'm not joking and I'm not overreacting. I know how families like the Fosters work, and they will focus right in on her, and that means law enforcement will focus on her. She needs a lawyer, and Gemma is the only one in town who's qualified. When we can bring in a criminal defense lawyer, we will. Until then you don't say anything without Gemma by your side. Nate has to keep a record. I'm not saying Nate would do anything to hurt you, but he has obligations to the law."

Ty felt his gut twist. "Let's all calm down. Luce, baby, it's going to be okay."

"She doesn't need a lawyer if she didn't do anything wrong," Michael insisted.

"That's naïve," Caleb countered. "I trust Nate, but there's the distinct possibility that Nate won't be able to stay in control of this investigation and then anything and everything she's told him can be twisted by whoever they bring in. The Foster family has the money and influence to get the CBI involved."

Colorado Bureau of Investigations. His mind was reeling. How had everything changed in a heartbeat? They were supposed to be counting down the minutes to getting off work so they could get home and be together. He took a long breath. They had to stay calm. Lucy had done nothing but her job.

Michael had stepped away, and he was talking on his walkie. Ty didn't hear a word, but Lucy had gasped.

"I told you. Van wouldn't have done this," Lucy insisted.

"Then he can tell Nate that. I've already had Van Dean secured so he can talk to Nate." Michael had that lawman look in his eyes, the one Ty kind of hoped he didn't see again. "Nate is going to need to talk to anyone who came in contact with that drink."

"How can we know it was the drink?" Lucy asked. "It could have been something else. He could have eaten something. I'm pretty sure he's been doing drugs. There's a powder on that table. I don't think it's baby powder."

"Cyanide has a very specific smell." He needed to let Lucy know what had happened and what she could possibly be accused of. God, he couldn't even believe this was happening. "It's almonds. I can smell it in here. Cyanide works very quickly."

"It could have been as few as five minutes," Caleb agreed.

"What were you doing in here for five minutes?" Michael asked. "Why would it take you that long to deliver a drink?"

"I needed him to sign the receipt. I didn't realize who it was when he let me in. He turned his back, and I didn't see his face. It looked like he'd taken a shower. He was in a towel, and he said he was going to grab a robe. He walked back in and immediately started drinking."

"You should have left the minute you realized who he was," Michael said.

"I'm supposed to get the receipt signed." Lucy stared at the wall.

He wasn't sure what Michael was thinking. He'd worked with a lot of cops over the years, and sometimes they went into a professional mode when in crisis. Michael seemed to have shut down emotionally.

"We're going to the hall right now." It was time to take charge. Normally he would let Michael handle this, but it had been a while since he worked. He seemed to have forgotten how to be both cop and boyfriend.

"That's a good idea." Caleb backed up and started for the hall. "The less time we spend in this space, the better I'll feel. Did I mention how much I hate autopsies?"

Ty reached out for Lucy. "Come on, baby. Let's wait for Nate outside."

Michael's hand came out, settling on Lucy's shoulders. "I'm sorry. I'm not handling this well. It's not how I expected the evening to go. Are you okay?"

She sniffled and looked up at Michael. "No. I don't even understand what happened. One minute he was here and then…"

Michael wrapped his arms around her and drew her close. "It's going to be okay." He looked over her shoulder at Ty. "I'm sorry."

Ty nodded, accepting the apology. "We're all in shock. Let's go outside and talk about this."

There was a knock on the door and then a feminine voice called out. "Brock? Hello?"

Ty watched as a young woman walked in. He'd seen her around the lodge but hadn't interacted with her. She was staying in the villas. Her eyes widened with horror as she saw the body on the floor. Her hand came out to cover her mouth, but not before a scream split the air.

"Brock!" She started toward the body, beginning to get to her knees.

Caleb caught her. "You can't touch him."

"Sonya." Tears streaked down Lucy's face. "I'm so sorry. I don't know what happened."

The woman named Sonya looked her way. "How? Why? He needs a doctor. We need to get a doctor. My brother needs help."

"I'm a doctor." Caleb was a calm presence. "He was dead when we got here. I'm very sorry for your loss, but we need to wait for the police."

Sonya's expression changed, turning angry, and she pointed Lucy's way. "You. You killed him. You killed my brother."

Sonya started screaming, and Ty realized his day had gone to complete hell.

* * * *

An hour later, Lucy was still shaking. She couldn't forget the look in Sonya's eyes as she'd accused her of killing Brock. She sat in one of the conference rooms, the very one where she would have met with her staff had she gotten the job.

Since she seemed to be involved in the murder of one of the guests, that offer was probably off the table now.

"Is there any way it was a mistake?" She looked to where Michael and Ty sat. They'd both joined her in this room after the Sonya incident. Michael had brought one of the security guards to secure the crime scene for Nate while Caleb tried to deal with Sonya.

Sonya. The poor woman. She'd been coming to see her brother and found a dead body.

How the hell had any of this happened?

"Are you asking me if someone accidently put cyanide in Brock Foster's drink?" Michael paced the floor, his gaze trailing to the door as though he was waiting for it to open.

Ty frowned his way. "I think she's asking if I made a mistake identifying the poison."

She didn't like the way her men seemed to be squaring off. Michael had apologized for being a little cold. She knew what had happened. He'd gone into cop mode for a second, and she couldn't blame him for that.

After all, he'd been betrayed once. He hadn't seen the capacity for murder in the woman he'd loved.

She was pretty sure she was more scared of losing Michael than she was of going to jail. She'd done nothing wrong, and there was no way Nate Wright allowed her to be railroaded no matter what Caleb said. Caleb's own paranoia was coming to the surface in this case.

But the idea that Michael might believe she was capable of committing murder was a real possibility.

And despite the fact that she knew why he might think that way, she wasn't sure how they could move forward if he turned his back on her.

Ty had shifted in his seat and reached for her hands, covering them with his own. "I don't think so. I don't think this was a mistake. I don't think it was an accident. I can't be completely sure until the toxicology report comes back, but I'm certain someone killed that man."

"That man who harassed Lucy," Michael pointed out.

Having Ty hold her hand made her feel far steadier than before. He wouldn't turn away from her. He probably wouldn't even if he thought she'd done it. "I'm fairly certain he's harassed a lot of people."

"But only one of them was in his room when he died," Michael replied, his tone grim.

"Michael, I didn't do this." She got the feeling she would have to assure him more than once.

Her calm refutation seemed to make him stop. His blank expression fled, and he looked down at where Ty's hands covered hers. "I know that. I'm mentally going over scenarios of how this plays out. I want to think ahead. Nate's going to ask you a lot of questions."

"And I'll answer them." She would talk to Gemma, but she didn't agree with Caleb about not talking to Nate at all. If she could clear this up quickly, that would be best.

"I'm not sure you should do that." Michael was back to pacing.

"You're the one who told me I didn't need a lawyer," she pointed out.

"I think the sister freaking out made Michael change his mind," Ty replied.

"She immediately accused you." Michael huffed, putting both

hands on the conference table. "She didn't even ask why you were there. She looked down at the body and said you did it. There were other people in the room, but you were the only one she mentioned."

She was also the one Sonya would have recognized. "I was the only one who had fought with Brock. Well, the only one in the room. Apparently he got into a huge fight with his brother."

Michael nodded. "Yes, I heard some of the security guys talking about something happening in the villas the night before last. I didn't listen too closely, but it sounded like a party that went wrong. Is that why Brock was here instead of the villa his family owns?"

"I suppose so. It would also explain why the Scotch was moved. He wouldn't have had access to it in the villas. Though it makes me wonder why he wouldn't simply move it to his room." It was time to start asking some questions of her own. "If he wanted it served to him, it should have been kept in the main bar."

"Do people usually have reserved bottles?" Michael asked.

"Sometimes." She'd studied up on the lodge's practices. "The villas keep stocked bars, but sometimes the liquor requires different storage. Like an expensive red needs to be kept in a cellar. We've got a part of our wine cellar reserved for villa guests to store their wine. Sometimes a guest will bring an expensive bottle but prefers to not keep it in their room. Maybe they have other guests in the room they don't want to share with or they're worried they'll drink too much. Then we'll store it at the bar and have a room service attendant bring them one or two glasses. There's a small fee for that, and they're expected to tip. We're required to get a signature in case the guest later on claims we didn't provide the service."

It happened. There were plenty of guests who sought to take advantage of the "customer is always right" attitude most resorts held. It usually cost the worker their job.

"So at some point in time, Brock would have packed his stuff and sent his precious Scotch down to the bar," Michael mused. "The question is how did it get from the main bar to the one set up for the party. Who would have been involved in setting up? Was Van Dean in charge of that?"

She didn't think Van had anything to do with Brock's death. Though he had mentioned he'd taken a couple of punches at the party gone wrong. "Yes, but that doesn't mean he moved every bottle. It was kind of chaotic today. I'm sure we can find a list of who was working the day shift."

"And there are cameras in and out of the ballroom." Ty sat back, seemingly more comfortable now. "There are a few inside the ballroom."

Michael nodded. "Yeah, I'll ask the security head to lock down that footage. We need to go over it and see if we can find who brought that bottle in."

"It could have been a mistake." It would have been easy to pick it up and put it with the rest of the bottles. "It had to have been marked or they wouldn't have realized it was gone and found it. If we hadn't been so swarmed, I would have sent the bottle back to the main bar and had them handle it."

She wished she had, wished she hadn't worried about being late with the delivery. If she'd been a little less concerned, she wouldn't be in this position.

And then someone else would be.

Of course that someone else probably wouldn't have had a complicated relationship with the deceased.

"Did he say anything to you before he took that drink?" Ty asked.

"He made a bunch of comments about how pathetic small-town people are, me in particular, but I would bet he would say the same things about anyone who doesn't have a billionaire father, so I didn't take too much offense." She had never cared what a guy like Brock Foster thought about her. He didn't matter to her life, so she would never have gone out of her way to change his mind. "Then he refused to sign the bill until I…" She'd totally forgotten about what he'd said. The last hour and a half seemed like a blur, but now she remembered something important. "Until I brought the bottle up. He promised he would call down every fifteen minutes for a new glass unless I brought him the bottle."

"So he didn't ask for the Scotch to be kept downstairs?" Michael stared at her like this was an interrogation. And she supposed it was. It was definitely a preview of what would happen when Nate questioned her.

It was coming back to her. For a while all she'd been able to think about was how the man had died, the blank look in his eyes and how he'd convulsed and then gone still. Now she was calmer and could recall what had happened before. "He said his sister thought he would drink less if the bottle wasn't in his room."

"The sister who thinks you killed him?" Ty pushed his chair back.

"I would bet it was Sonya. He has two sisters, but I don't think Kendall would care how much he drank." She didn't know a lot about their family dynamics, but she was certain Sonya was the caretaker of the group.

"I'm going to go make sure Nate knows where we are." Ty started for the door but it opened before he could reach for the handle.

Nate Wright strode in followed by a lovely blonde in her early thirties. Gemma Wells had moved to Bliss from New York to be with her mom. Like many who walked into Bliss, she'd quickly found two hotties to love and settled down. She ran the sheriff's department, but in true Blissian fashion, also did some legal work on the side. Sometimes against the sheriff's department.

Nate walked to the head of the table and pointed her way. "No fruit basket for you."

Damn. "I'm sorry."

Gemma's blue eyes went wide. "She did not mean that in connection to the deceased. She's apologizing for something else."

Nate huffed. "Come on, Gemma. She doesn't need a lawyer."

"I've got a check from Caleb Burke that says she does." Gemma moved to sit next to her. "And I'm serious about this job, Nate. Mama needs a new bag. I've been drooling over the Pradas that came out this season. Hi, Lucy. Long time, no see. Don't incriminate yourself. That's my advice."

"Nate, what's happening?" Michael got straight down to business. He sat next to Ty. "Are you taking Lucy back to the station? You need to understand she's not going anywhere without me or Ty."

"You couldn't have had this happen before you got yourself two overly protective men?" Nate asked wistfully. He sighed and turned Michael's way. "Even if I wanted to take this to the station, I couldn't. I just ordered the pass closed. The storm's picking up, and it's too dangerous to go back down for a while. We're stuck here probably until tomorrow afternoon when they can get the plows out. But I brought Cam with me, and I pulled in Alexei and Max and Rye. They're going to help me secure everything I need to. Henry's here, too. I've got him sitting in with Cam. He's talking to the Foster siblings who aren't currently dead or sedated."

"Sedated?" Lucy asked.

Nate nodded. "Yeah, Caleb agreed to let Sonya Foster take her anti-anxiety meds, and now she's sleeping it off. He said she had some strong meds, but the prescriptions were all legit."

"At least she's not running around accusing Lucy," Michael muttered under his breath.

"So this young woman openly accused Lucy of being the one who poisoned Mr. Foster?" Nate asked.

"She was out of it," Ty countered. "She was overwhelmed with grief. She walked in and found her brother lying there on the floor. She didn't know what she was saying."

"She might be the one who put the bottle in the bar," Michael said quietly.

A brow rose over Nate's eyes. "Do we have confirmation of that? I've got the bottle locked down, and the bartender is waiting in another room. I'm going to say, though, that he seemed genuinely shocked. I'm pretty good at reading reactions."

"It wasn't Van," Lucy insisted.

Nate looked down at his notes. "According to my talk with the head of security, Van got in the middle of an argument between the Foster brothers. Brock took a couple of shots at him."

"That doesn't mean he would kill the man," Lucy replied. "Also, where would he get cyanide? I've heard of it, but I wouldn't know how to get my hands on it."

"The better response is what is cyanide?" Gemma had a notepad out, too. "My client doesn't know what poison is. Also, make your eyes big and wide."

Nate's eyes rolled. "I don't think it's Lucy. I've known Lucy for years. She's not capable of killing someone."

"Caleb is worried you're going to lose control of this investigation." Michael's fingers drummed over the table until he seemed to realize what he was doing and moved his hand to his lap. "After the way the sister reacted, I'm starting to agree with him. And anything she says now you'll have to reveal to the CBI."

"Come on, Mike. You used to be a fed. I used to be a fed. Local law can make things easy or hard on a federal or state investigation." Nate set his pen down. "I assure you I'm not going to let Lucy incriminate herself. She's right about the poison, though. You can't go to the store and buy it. I need to do some research."

"I do all my shopping at the Trading Post," Lucy admitted. "I really do. One time Teeny found out I bought socks at Walmart and she cried and asked me what she did wrong, and I never shopped anywhere else again."

"I told Teeny that the day she starts stocking Chanel is the day she has all my business, and she cannot pass off Channel handbags," Gemma added. "If Marie wants to make knockoffs, she should at least learn how to spell, and sadly how to sew because that stitchwork was not up to snuff."

"I think that was a practical joke," Nate said with a chuckle. "And Teeny is a little weepy since Logan moved to New York. But I'm fairly certain that the Trading Post doesn't carry cyanide. If they did, I assure you Nell would protest."

"I want to know how that man didn't realize his drink smelled off." Ty directed the statement the sheriff's way. "It's a very distinct odor. I only know it because I took a class on poison control. I've never directly dealt with cyanide, but I've never forgotten the smell. It was all over the room."

"I'm surprised the bartender didn't smell it," Michael offered.

"He's surrounded by booze." She understood what Michael was trying to do, but she didn't want him to throw Van under a bus. "And my staff was coming out of the kitchens. You can get overwhelmed with smells."

"I can tell you why Brock Foster didn't smell the poison," Nate offered. "He was doing a shit ton of cocaine. From the lines of white powder on his dresser, you interrupted his hit. It looked like he'd already done a line and was ready for number two. That would have screwed him in numerous ways. We need to wait for toxicology and Caleb's autopsy."

"Could it have been in the coke?" Michael's expression brightened at the thought.

"I smelled it in the drink," Ty insisted.

"Caleb seems to think it was in the drink," Nate replied. "But we're early in this. We need to be patient. Lucy, tell me what happened this evening. How did you end up in his room?"

Gemma held a hand up. "I would like a moment to confer with my client in private."

"I don't think we need to do that. It's simple." Lucy decided to plunge ahead. "The room service line got a call from Mr. Foster's suite, and he requested a glass of Scotch. That should be in the record. They would send the request to the main bar. The main bar couldn't find the bottle and called to the ballroom, where it had been mistakenly stored. Van poured the drink and printed out the receipt. Normally I would have sent someone to take it up, but we were short staffed at the moment, and I did it myself. I didn't realize it was Brock Foster until I was inside the room and I needed him to sign the receipt. He was drinking and said some nasty things and then he died. I called Ty and he brought Michael and Caleb."

"Did you touch the body?" Nate asked.

She shook her head. "No, and I feel bad about that, but I wasn't sure what to do. I didn't try CPR or anything."

Ty put a hand on her knee. "You couldn't have helped him. You only would have exposed yourself. You did everything you could."

She hated how useless she'd felt in that moment. "I did nothing."

"I believe that's Ty's point," Nate replied and pushed his chair back. "All right. That's all I need for now. Lucy, I'm going to ask for your blouse since it's got some of the drink on it. Other than that, get some rest. I'm going to interview the bartender and the part of Foster's family that's still awake."

Gemma stood up with a sigh. "Well, you're going to be a terrible client."

"I hope I won't be a client for long," she admitted. She wanted this whole thing cleared up.

Nate shook his head as he got to his feet. "I told her to stay the hell away from him, and she didn't listen to me either. After what happened earlier this week, I thought she should wait until the Fosters checked out to start her job."

"I wasn't going to let him get her in a bad position." Michael stared down at the table. "This is my fault. I should have escorted her."

"You can't follow me around. You had your own work to do. If I'd known he was in that suite, I would have sent a male server," she replied.

"You know if they ask, I'm going to have to give up that tape, Lucy," Nate explained.

"The tape?" Ty was on his feet.

"The security tapes at Trio." Gemma stuffed her notepad into the sleek bag she carried. "I heard some of what the sister was saying before she went nighty-night. She was talking about how this was reprisal for what happened at Trio. We should talk about that."

"It was nothing. He tried to make a move on me. I took care of it," she explained.

"I was there," Michael said. "I can promise you she didn't do anything but protect herself. Any security tape will prove that. It's a good thing."

"Maybe the first encounter, but I'm worried she might have said something in the second encounter," Nate began. "If I can't solve this thing before the feds are called in, I'll have to tell Zane to turn it over. If it was actual video tape, he could erase it or tape over it, but it's in the cloud. There's a footprint. There's no sound on that tape, but Lucy's face is clearly visible. They'll bring in someone who can read lips. Did you say anything they can use against you?"

The room seemed to go cold.

She hadn't told them. She'd promised Nate and then she'd kept the incident to herself because she didn't want to disrupt the harmony they'd found.

"What do you mean second tape?" Michael's voice had gone low.

"The one from the other night." Nate's eyes narrowed. "She did tell you that he waited for her outside Trio, right? I talked to her the next morning because he was trying to start trouble with her. He came into the station and wanted me to arrest her for assault. When I wouldn't, he confronted her and threatened her. She promised me she would tell you. It's the only reason I didn't recommend putting a bodyguard on her."

There was pure shock in Ty's gaze when he looked her way. "Luce? What is he talking about?"

"It was nothing." She hated the fact that Ty looked like she'd

211

betrayed him. "He wanted me to go out with him to prove to everyone that he could have any woman he wanted. I turned him down. That's all."

"He promised to wreck her life." Nate seemed determined to get her in more trouble with her men. "That's what she told me. I thought he was a potential sociopath who could actually hurt her. The only reason I didn't have a discussion with the two of you was that she promised she would talk to you."

"It was the day of our first real date. I went to the back looking for you and you came inside." Michael managed to make the words an accusation. "You slammed the door quickly, and I asked if something was wrong. You said no. You lied to me. You lied to both of us."

"I didn't lie." Her gut took a deep dive. She'd wanted to keep Michael out of it, but she hadn't thought of it as lying to him. Of course at the time there hadn't been a dead body to deal with, one he'd literally found her standing over.

Like his last girlfriend. Who had lied to him. Who had betrayed him.

What had she said to Brock? Something about taking him apart if he came after her. She certainly hadn't meant she would kill him.

Michael walked out of the room.

Ty stared at her like he didn't know her. "Maybe you should talk to Gemma."

"Finally someone makes sense," Gemma said with a sigh. "Nate, can I have a minute with Lucy? I'd like to take some notes."

Yeah. She might need a lawyer after all.

Chapter Thirteen

Michael could barely see the hall in front of him. He was moving out of sheer necessity.

"Michael."

He heard Nate talking behind him, and he didn't want to stop. He wanted to walk out to the parking lot, get in his SUV, and go right back to his mountain. He would hole up and not come down again for a long time. Maybe never.

"Michael."

He wouldn't try again. It was bullshit to try. He'd had his shot and proven that he wasn't capable of telling the real people from the liars of the world.

He made it to the end of the hall, to the room where he'd found Lucy with her pale face and wide eyes looking like the world was ending as she stood over a dead body.

He stopped and stared at the door for a moment. Someone had blocked it off with yellow police tape.

"Cam's in there along with a forensic tech who came in from Pagosa Springs. She just made it in before I closed the pass." Nate had stopped behind him, and his voice had gone low. "Rye Harper's helping them process the scene."

Rye Harper had been the sheriff of Bliss for years before Nate had taken over the department. He would know what to do. "Good. Have you moved the body?"

"Not yet. Caleb is downstairs making sure we've got a way to store it over the weekend."

The thought made his stomach turn.

Michael heard the elevator doors open and the chattering of guests as they started to make their way back to their rooms. Luckily they turned down the opposite hall.

Nate's jaw tightened, and he was quiet until the guests were gone. "Come on. We need to get out of the hallway."

That was fine with Michael. He had some things he needed to pick up anyway.

He wasn't sure he could spend the night in that room, in the place where he'd briefly been happy.

He walked to the elevator and pushed the button for the lobby.

What the fuck was he doing? The impulse was there to go back and talk to them. "Why did Lucy stay behind?"

"Ty convinced her to talk to Gemma." Nate stood beside him. "It doesn't mean she's guilty."

It did mean she was taking this seriously. It was a good thing since it appeared she'd had a reason to hurt Brock Foster. "Good. Can we really not get off this mountain?"

"I wouldn't take a car down the pass," Nate said as they made their way to the lobby. "If you know what you're doing, you can get down on a snowmobile, but I think even Stef is planning on spending the night. Max is going to take Rach back home when he can because their kids are with a sitter. But he's made that run a thousand times. Alexei, Holly, and Caleb are staying. I got a room for Henry and Nell and their baby. Under protest, of course."

He huffed out a laugh, surprised he could find any humor at all in the situation, but the idea of Nell staying in the same place she'd recently protested against was amusing.

It was so very Bliss.

He didn't want to leave this place. He didn't want to leave Lucy and Ty.

The doors opened and Nate exited first. Michael followed. There was one thing he needed to do. "I need to see that tape."

Nate let out a long sigh as he found a quiet corner. The lobby bar was to the left, and there were still a few guests milling around. To the right, it looked like the ballroom was dark and closed up. "Do you honestly believe Lucy is capable of killing a man?"

Insidious thoughts crept around in his brain, tickling all those nasty places he didn't want to go to. "She already has. She helped Hope kill Hope's ex-husband."

"That was self-defense."

"Maybe she thought this was, too." He had to consider all the possibilities. "Brock tried to hurt her. I was there. I thought I would have to intervene, but she took care of him herself. Apparently he threatened her again. You said you thought he was a sociopath."

Nate looked around as though trying to make sure they weren't being listened in on. "He was a piece of work. He was definitely determined to get some payback. She hurt his pride, and that was something he couldn't overlook. But I have a hard time believing Lucy could coldheartedly poison someone. And if you trust my instincts on Foster, you should trust them when it comes to Lucy, too. You know what it's like. You're not so far from the US marshals that you don't remember how to size someone up."

Ah, Nate was wrong about that. "Yeah, there's a reason I left. My instincts are shit."

Nate sighed. "Come on, Mike. That's not true. You've helped me more than once over the last couple of years, and you've been damn good. You got tricked once. It doesn't mean it's going to happen again. It doesn't mean Lucy is anything like Jessie."

He'd thought he would never let it happen again, but here he was. In that moment, he couldn't truly see the difference between the two. He needed more information. "I want to see the tape. I want to see what happened between them, what she's covering up."

"I don't know that she meant to cover up anything."

"Then why wouldn't she tell me?" He didn't understand at all. He'd asked her if something had happened. He'd offered to help. He'd wanted to protect her. "You said you had a long talk with her. She didn't mention that conversation at all."

"I was only trying to make sure she took him seriously. She's been a waitress for a while, and she's had to deal with asshole tourists before," Nate explained. "I wanted her to know this guy was different. Have you thought about the fact that if Brock Foster was willing to treat a perfect stranger like that, what he must put some of his family members through?"

Michael forced himself to be still for a moment, to actually think about something beyond his own bruised heart. Nate was right about one thing. He wasn't thinking like a cop at all. "Their father is elderly."

"Yep." Nate leaned in. "That was my first thought. I don't know much about the family, but I do know they're wealthy and the father is very old, and sometimes the fight over the inheritance starts early. I'm going to do everything I can to figure this out before Monday because I assure you someone is already on the phone with CBI, and they will show up. Depending on what buttons get pushed and who's pushing them, Lucy might look like an easy way out for the Fosters."

He didn't like the sound of that, but he wasn't so naïve that he didn't know sometimes corners were cut to protect the wealthy.

Why the fuck had she lied to him?

"I'm setting up in Cole's apartment," Nate offered. "I've already called him, and he's agreed to let security help us with anything we need. Why don't you come up there with me and help me do some research? I know it's late, but the Internet is always open. We can at least get a grasp on the company the family runs. The dad has already been notified, and he's coming back once he can get through the storm. I'd like to have some questions for him. Unless you want to go back and talk to Lucy. She might have a perfectly reasonable explanation."

"I asked her flat out if anything had happened." It had been the day after their crappy first date. "She was mad we hadn't texted her back. That was why she did it. She withheld information because she was angry with me."

"That doesn't sound like Lucy." Nate settled the bag he was carrying over his shoulder. "Look, I can't let you back on the crime scene. You're too close to this, but you can do some research. If you don't want to research the company, you can figure out where the nearest place a person could buy cyanide from would be."

"The Dark Web is where I would go."

"Lucy doesn't own a computer. I don't think she would know how to access the Dark Web even if she did."

"It could all be an act. She could know far more than she's saying, and she could find a computer to use." Michael felt stupid pointing these things out. They sounded ridiculous even to his own ears, but he also knew he would have felt the same way if he'd said them about Jessie at the time.

"We could check the new library branch." Nate was obviously placating him. "It opened last month, and they have three whole computers anyone can use and the best Internet access in the valley."

"I'm just saying, if a person wants it badly enough, they can make it happen." He wasn't wrong about that. He'd seen it time and time again. "I don't know much about cyanide. I can take a look into it and write up a report."

"I would appreciate that. I don't know much about it either. I worked for the DEA for years, but that wasn't the kind of drug we dealt with," Nate admitted.

A familiar figure caught Michael's eye. Nell Flanders walked toward the elevator, Henry beside her. Nell had a bundle in her arms.

He'd spent time with Nell Flanders. He'd known she was an author before most of Bliss had. He also knew she was a walking encyclopedia of weird knowledge. Nell had written twenty plus romance novels, many of them romantic suspense with surprisingly gruesome murders for the hero and heroine to solve.

She would likely be on several FBI watch lists if her husband wasn't so good at getting around the Internet without leaving a footprint.

"Nell," he called out.

She turned, her gaze going straight to him. Her expression immediately softened, and she strode over. "Michael, I'm so sorry poor Lucy got caught up in all of this. How is she?"

"Please let her know we're here for her," Henry said before turning to Nate. "I finished the initial interview with Sylvan Dean. He was very helpful and concerned for Lucy. I wrote up the report. It contains all my thoughts, but I can tell you I don't think he did it."

"Have you talked to Lucy?" Michael asked. Henry's CIA training made him an excellent interrogator.

Henry snorted while Nell full out laughed.

Then they both seemed to realize Michael wasn't joking, and Henry cleared his throat. "Uhm, no. I don't have to talk to Lucy to know she's not capable of this kind of premeditated action. She could protect herself, but she couldn't coldly plan a murder."

Nell smiled up at her husband. "It was nice to watch Henry work.

He's very good at getting people to talk."

She had that glowy look he'd wanted to see on Lucy's face. She bounced her baby slightly. Poppy Flanders was six months old, and apparently her parents took her everywhere. Including interrogations.

"Nell, what do you know about cyanide?"

Nell's eyes widened. "Is that what was used on that poor man? And by poor I mean it's sad when anyone dies, but his corporation is a blight on the planet. I haven't personally looked into Foster Incorporated, but I know they've been cited for environmental concerns in several countries."

"Caleb believes it was very likely cyanide," Nate assured her.

Nell held her baby closer. "That's a terrible way to go, though at least it's quick."

"You know about cyanide?" Nate pointed Henry's way. "I would expect him to know, not you."

Henry's hands came up. "I never used poison. Only guns and knives. And my hands. One time a spatula and five toothpicks."

Nell's glowy smile was back. "He was clever at using whatever was around him. When you think about it, he was very earth friendly. But he doesn't do that anymore. And of course I know. I'm starting a new series of mysteries. It's about a former spy who falls in love with a romance author, and they travel the world solving the mysterious deaths of the people who are murdered around them."

"Okay, that sounds weird," Nate said with a frown. "Why would people be murdered around them?"

Henry shrugged. "*Murder, She Wrote* ran for twelve seasons. Every person Angela Lansbury ran into dropped dead, and not once did anyone accuse her of being a serial killer."

"Henry thinks Jessica Fletcher committed all the murders herself." Nell sent her husband the stink eye. "It's a very misogynistic view."

Henry held his hands up. "I'm just saying it was a lot of murder around one seemingly harmless woman. And also, it would have been a great twist. They could have had a final episode that revealed how she did all the killings and covered them up by proving someone else did it."

Nell shrugged. "Yes, it would have been a surprise. Anyway, in answer to Michael's question, I've recently learned a lot about cyanide. The first victim in the new series is poisoned by his business partner with cyanide."

This was unconventional research, but research all the same. Nell actually knew a lot of odd facts that she'd picked up over years of writing her novels. "Where would you get cyanide? Can you buy it?"

"Of course. It's used in many different and terrible ways," Nell began.

"And some helpful ways," Henry countered. "It can absolutely be found in nature."

"And it can be used to strip the earth of its resources." The baby in Nell's arms shifted as though the words disturbed her. "It's primarily used in gold and silver mining. They manufacture cyanide and then use a process that separates the precious metal from the rock around it. But it's also used by poachers. They poison watering holes to kill elephants for their tusks."

"It's also used in medical equipment." Henry resettled the blanket around his daughter's feet.

"It can be found in pest control," Nell continued. "Though we know who the real pests are. It's been used to control the coyote populations. In New Zealand cyanide became a popular way to attempt to get rid of possums. They're not native to the country. They can spread tuberculosis in bovine herds."

"Oh, fun fact, potassium ferrocyanide is used in sculpting to bring about a blue cast to bronze sculptures," Henry offered. "It's also used in jewelry making. Photography, specifically in sepia toning. See, lots of practical uses."

"So it's pretty common?" Michael asked. So far he didn't see a way Lucy could have gotten her hands on cyanide. She didn't make jewelry. Her only photos were on her phone, and she wasn't an artist. The only artists she knew were painters.

Nell shook her head. "I wouldn't say common, and even if it has practical purposes, it's not easily obtained. It's not like arsenic, which can be used in rat poison. You can buy that fairly easily, but it's far less lethal. Arsenic poisoning takes place over time where cyanide kills quickly. This was ingested and not inhaled?"

"We believe it was placed in a glass of Scotch," Nate supplied.

"It would be easier to get the compound than the gas," Nell mused. "You can make cyanide, you know."

He didn't like the sound of that. "How would you make cyanide?"

"*Make* isn't the word to use. More like you can obtain it organically. Like Henry said, it can be found in nature. It occurs naturally in some fruits and seeds. Peaches, apples, apricots. There's naturally occurring cyanide in their pits or seeds. Also cassava," Nell continued.

"Almonds," Henry added. "I mean if you want to risk your own life you could potentially acquire a small amount by crushing enough seeds of a plant that contains cyanide. The liquid left would potentially be poisonous depending on the plant and how it was raised. There are a lot of factors at play."

"So if someone crushed enough apple seeds, they might be able to get enough to poison a single drink?" Michael hated the way his gut knotted. All he could remember was the basket of apples on River's bar.

I'm experimenting. It takes a lot of apples to make the perfect pie, you know.

Lucy had said she was experimenting. Had she lied about what she'd been trying to make?

What the fuck was wrong with him? She was Lucy. She was the sweetest woman he'd ever known. She was the kind of person who took care of the people around her.

She wasn't Jessie.

And still the suspicion played through him. It curled around him until it was a scream he couldn't ignore.

"I suppose so," Nell allowed.

"If you like I can share our notes with you. We did some pretty extensive research. Nell likes to keep things believable. Well, for fiction." Henry looked down at his daughter. "But we need to get up to our room. Our Poppy is starting to root around, and she can be a bear when she's hungry."

"I would appreciate anything you can give me," Nate replied before turning to Michael. "I'm heading down to see how Caleb is faring in the kitchen. We need to get that body cold as soon as we can. Do you want to come with me? Or you can go up to the room we're going to use. Like I said, it's Cole's suite and it's got several bedrooms. You can pick one if you like."

"I need to make a stop first." He didn't want to do it, but he needed to go back to Ty's room if only for a few moments. "But I'll probably be up later."

Nate stared at him for a moment. "All right, but Michael, if you're going to talk to Lucy, maybe you should think about what you're going to say. Maybe you should take the night to think about it. I would hate for you to say something you can't take back."

Nate nodded and walked away. Michael turned back to the elevators. Nate's advice had been sound, but he wasn't going to take it. He couldn't wait all night to find out if another woman he loved had betrayed him.

The elevator doors opened, and he acknowledged that stupid word. Love. He'd vowed he wouldn't have anything to do with it again, but here he was in love with Lucy. In…whatever he wanted to call it with Ty.

And he was about to lose them both.

* * * *

Lucy felt every minute of the day weighing her down as she walked toward the room she was sharing with Ty and Michael.

Only she was fairly certain she wasn't still sharing it with Michael. "Where do you think he went?"

"I think he's probably helping Nate. I heard the sheriff's office is working out of the big boss's suite." Ty squeezed her hand. He'd barely let it go the whole time she'd talked to Gemma. She and the lawyer had gone over everything that had happened in the last few days. Well, everything that had to do with Brock Foster. She hadn't talked about the important things like falling madly in love with a man who hadn't been able to look her in the eyes.

She forced her feet to move, to take her closer to the door. "Yeah, I know they called him. I would bet that I will no longer be considered for this job."

It was almost impossible to think about what she'd lost in a single day.

"Don't worry about that now." But Ty didn't correct her.

He was right. She had so many other things to worry about. She had to worry about going to jail, and not the nice little cell Nate sometimes put Max in when he couldn't take his sarcasm anymore. The minute the CBI got involved, Nate couldn't protect her anymore. "I don't know that I can pay Gemma."

"Don't worry about it." Ty seemed to be saying that a lot tonight.

"I can't let Caleb pay her." It could be expensive, and Gemma had even told her she wasn't a criminal attorney. If this went on longer, Gemma had explained that she would find a defense attorney for her. She couldn't imagine how much that would cost.

"Yes, you can. Caleb has more money than he knows what to do with. He won't even miss it, but he will feel bad if you don't have a lawyer." Ty stopped in front of the door, pulling out his key card. "I want you to relax. We're going to take a shower and I'm going to take care of you. I'm going to make sure you can sleep tonight, and we'll deal with all of this in the morning."

When she would likely be right back in that conference room, talking to Nate again. He would prepare her to talk to the state investigators, who would almost certainly come. Gemma had told her that the rest of the Foster family had been informed, and they were already moving to make sure this wasn't handled at a local level.

"I'm not sure relaxing is possible."

Ty moved in and gave her a swift kiss. "I'm going to try my best. Luce, you have to know one thing. I'm going to be here for you. I'm never going to leave your side. I love you."

Tears sprang to her eyes, and she hugged him tight. "I won't ever leave you."

He kissed her forehead. "I know."

He opened the door, allowing her to walk through first.

"I could really use a glass of wine." She moved through the little hall into the living room where she stopped because they weren't alone.

Michael sat on the love seat, his eyes steady on her.

"Hey, Mike." Ty joined her, his hand going to her waist, every word seemingly careful. "I'm surprised you're here. I thought you were working with Nate on the case."

On her case. It might mean something if she thought he was working to ensure he caught the person who'd done it. Perhaps he was actually doing that, but he thought the person who'd done it was her.

That was the moment she saw the small bag to the side of the love seat. It was the same bag he'd brought when they'd decided to stay here together. It was supposed to be in the closet.

"I needed to talk to Lucy before I go upstairs." Michael hadn't taken his eyes off her. He stared at her as though he could see through her, see down to her soul.

"Why don't you stay here and we can all talk." Ty didn't seem to understand that Michael had already made up his mind. Ty had always been the most positive thinker of all their friends.

She was afraid Michael had made up his mind the minute he'd seen her in that room. His past had come back and had probably cost them their future. Her heart sank as Michael stood, his shoulders going straight.

"I don't think that's a good idea. But I do have a couple of questions for Lucy."

"She's answered questions all night. She's been at this for hours." Ty moved to stand between them. "She needs some rest, and she needs us. Both of us."

"I don't think there's anything you can say that will make him stay." She was fairly certain she understood what was going through Michael's head. "He thinks I did it. He thinks I've lied to him and used him."

"Why would you do that?" Ty asked, seeming to be genuinely confused by everything about the night.

She looked to Michael. "Because he thinks that's what happens to him. He thinks the people he cares about are bound to betray him." Her heart sank because he didn't correct her. "Michael, do you believe I targeted you because you could help me cover up a murder?"

His eyes rolled. "No. Of course not. You didn't even know Brock Foster when we first met."

At least he admitted that much. "So you were merely useful."

He ignored the comment. "Why didn't you tell me what happened in the parking lot?"

"I thought you would go after him. I didn't want any trouble, and I thought I had handled it," she replied as calmly as she could. She wanted to yell at him, to fight with him, wanted anything but this cold calm between them. But she knew if she pushed him, he would leave. This was something she had to hope she could logic her way through. "Michael, I've had to handle men like Brock all my life. Every woman does. If we sicced our boyfriends on every man who behaved poorly, nothing would get done in the world."

"He threatened you according to Nate."

She was going to be totally honest with him. "Yes, and I threatened him back. I don't remember exactly what I said but it was something like if he was going to ruin my life, then I could ruin his, too. He was a bully. I've found the way to deal with bullies is to let them know you won't be an easy target. It's how I've handled them for a long time. I was worried things could escalate if I got you involved and frankly, I wanted to concentrate on how good our relationship could be, not how much trouble it could be."

"You know who I am, Lucy. Protecting people is what I do. What I did," he replied. "For a long time it was my job. Why would you think I wouldn't want to protect you?"

"I knew you would. There was no question in my mind that you wouldn't protect me. I was so sure of it I didn't want to put you in a position where Brock caused trouble for you. He was supposed to leave in a few days," she explained. "I didn't want to cause a fuss over someone who was going to be gone very soon."

"His family owns a villa," Michael countered. "He could have been back any day."

"And he would have moved on." She'd gone over the situation in her head a hundred times. "He would have barely remembered me the next time he came out here."

"That is not what Nate thinks." Michael held his ground.

This was the one place he had her. She'd promised Nate she would talk to them both, and she'd used every excuse to put it off. "I meant to tell you what Nate said. I truly did."

Michael nodded as though she'd made his point. "But then we didn't meet you for lunch."

Ty huffed. "She wouldn't keep that from you because she was upset with us. She's not like that. I upset her all the time, and she doesn't stop talking to me."

Michael turned his attention Ty's way. "Are you fucking kidding me? She won't even let you feed her when she's hungry. You had to lie and say your mom made too much. You have to go behind her back to make sure she's okay because she won't let you take care of her."

"That's because she's too proud," Ty answered. "That wasn't about punishing me."

"It was because I didn't want to lean on him when I thought he could be gone any second." It was funny how it had only been a few days, but she already couldn't imagine her life without Ty as her boyfriend. Maybe that was what she'd always been afraid of, the fact that she couldn't dream about a future without him. And then Michael had come along, and it had been right for the first time. "I wanted to be independent. I wanted to be some kind of superhero who didn't need anyone. I think I was afraid of needing anyone. I'm supposed to be the strong one."

"You are strong." For the first time since she'd walked in the door, there was real emotion in Michael's voice. "You take care of the people around you. It's why when you had a problem with Brock, I wish you'd come to me. We wouldn't be in this situation."

"You can't know that. I could have told you and I still would have worked the party tonight. I still would have helped out and taken that drink up to the suites." She had to find a way to make him understand he didn't have to worry about her betraying him. She wouldn't ever do it.

"Or I could have taken care of the problem," Michael replied, his gaze going hard.

"I think that look right there is what she was afraid of." Ty backed her up. "I know I would have kicked that guy's ass, and then we both would have been in trouble."

"Or we could have called Mr. Roberts and explained that one of his villa residents was harassing his employees, including finding them outside the lodge and attempting to assault them. I wouldn't have lost my shit. I would have taken care of the situation and made very certain that man can't harm you or anyone here at the resort," Michael replied. "I wouldn't have put you at more risk by beating the man up."

"We can't put that on Mr. Roberts," she argued. "He's busy."

"He is not so busy that he can't protect his employees. I assure you of that. I haven't met the man, but I asked around. He is not a man who allows any person who works for him to be taken advantage of by his guests." Michael sounded so sure.

She had another argument to make. "I haven't been hired yet. I'm not his employee, so he might have decided I wasn't worth the trouble."

"Then he isn't a man I want you to work for," Michael shot back.

"I agree." Ty's jaw went tight. "Mr. Roberts is a good man, and he doesn't suffer fools. The money wouldn't have mattered to him. I should have done the same thing. I should have called him and told him what was happening."

"You didn't know." Michael softened slightly. "She didn't tell you either, so you didn't have a chance."

"I wouldn't have thought of it." Ty's expression had turned grim. "I would have done exactly what she was afraid of."

Michael reached out and wrapped his hand around Ty's neck, a gesture that held such intimacy it nearly made her melt. "It's okay, Ty. That's what I'm supposed to do. I'm supposed to…"

He seemed to realize he wasn't doing what he'd set out to do. Michael shook his head and took a step back.

"Mike, come on, man. Let's sit down and talk," Ty implored. "She didn't do this and you know it."

"Why did you have all those apples, Luce?" Michael's voice was toneless again, his eyes cutting through her.

"What?" Why did he want to know about apples?

"You had a big basket of apples while you were staying at River's. It had to be at least twenty. They were sitting on the bar in her kitchen." There was no way to miss the accusation in the words.

"I told you. Nell got a bunch of apples and she asked if I wanted some." It had been incredibly handy because it meant she could try to get her pie right. It kept coming out soupy.

"You said you were experimenting. Did you know apple seeds contain cyanide?" Michael kept up his questioning.

"What?" She felt herself flush because Michael was staring at her, and she realized why. He wanted to gauge her response, to see if he could learn anything from how she reacted to his words.

He truly thought she could be guilty. He'd made love to her, held her, promised to care about her, but he'd meant the other promise, too. He'd meant it when he'd said he couldn't, wouldn't love her. He would never love her. He would never trust her.

"Cyanide can be made through the seeds of certain fruits that naturally contain the poison in their seeds or pits." Michael's tone had gone academic, and she knew she'd lost him. "You mentioned you were experimenting."

"I think you should go, Mike." Ty's hand found hers again.

"I think I'd like an answer to my question," Michael replied.

Ty shook his head. "She doesn't have to answer any of your questions, and I'd like you to leave now. I thought we might be able to get through this. I thought you were angry that she didn't tell us what had happened between her and Brock, but if you really think she's capable of coldly poisoning another human being, then there's no hope for us. Go back to your mountain. You weren't ready to come down."

"I'd like an answer to my question. I haven't told them about the apples yet. They don't know you kept a basket full of them at River's." Michael dangled the possibility that he could go right up and tell Nate everything he knew.

It made her heart ache. Had he felt anything for her?

"She's been trying to make apple pie because it's my favorite dessert," Ty replied flatly. "I've had to eat five of the damn things in the last couple of weeks. They weren't great, hence the need to try again."

"We have a bake sale at Winter Festival. I'm not good at baking, but I wanted to make something someone would want to eat." She wiped at her eyes. It was time to be away from him. It was time to take stock of what had happened and start to look at a way to move forward. Without Michael.

She'd thought she could heal him, but she wasn't the right woman for him. Or maybe no person could truly heal another. Especially if they didn't want to be healed.

He'd gone silent, his body tense again as though he was getting ready to go another round.

Weariness swamped her. She couldn't do it, couldn't wrestle with his past tonight. She had to pull away from him and protect herself. It was time to let him go.

"You have to know how this looks," Michael insisted.

"I honestly don't care. Good night, Michael." She walked away and didn't look back.

Chapter Fourteen

Ty squared off against Michael when he realized the other man might actually go after Lucy. "Absolutely not. You've done enough damage for one night."

Kicking Michael out was the last thing he'd expected to do today. Even when he'd realized Lucy was going to be seen as a suspect, he'd been able to stay calm because he'd known Michael would take care of them. Michael would help them navigate this insane place they found themselves in. Michael would make things better, and they could laugh about it all someday.

He hadn't thought for a second that Michael could become the enemy.

"It is not my intention to do damage, Ty." Michael took a step back, and the threat of a physical fight deflated.

But there were other ways to fight. "Then what was your intention? Why bother waiting for us? You could have left."

Michael ran a hand through his hair. "I don't know. I wanted to see if she was okay."

"How the fuck can she be okay after what she's been through? Watching that man die was bad enough, but now she's facing down a real fight. She's being accused of something unthinkable, and I would bet that wasn't the worst part of her day. The worst part of her day was realizing that one of the men she loves thinks she's capable of murder."

"I think everyone is capable of it given the right circumstances," Michael countered. "And there's real evidence against her that she's going to have to account for. She did fight with him. There's a tape that shows her threatening him. She delivered the drink. And it doesn't matter that she was using the apples to make pies. It still looks bad."

He didn't want to have this conversation, but he did need to make a few points. Michael, for all his law enforcement experience, wasn't thinking this through. "Think about the timeline for two seconds. Do you believe she was cooking up cyanide just in case she might have to poison someone? Because the first time you caught her with a bunch of apples was the night I fucked up. It was the night we were supposed to have our first date, and it was also the night Brock tried to assault her. So she would have gotten the apples before he'd even tried something."

Michael's head dropped. "And then she basically moved in with us the next night."

At least he could admit some truths. "Do you think she stayed up all that night and crushed up apple seeds to poison a man she'd already taken care of? She wasn't alone, you know. Maybe River helped her. Jax has some interesting skills. He's worked as a mercenary before. We should bring him in, too."

Michael sighed, and his eyes were tired when he looked back up. "Damn it, Ty. It seems suspicious."

"No. It doesn't. Not to me." This was where they definitely differed. "I could walk in and she could have been holding a knife and I would ask her what happened. I wouldn't for a second think she'd done it."

"I can't be that guy."

Yes, Ty finally had to accept that fact. He'd gotten so close to Michael, and he didn't want to believe he was a lost cause, but he had to pick Lucy. She needed him. She needed to be surrounded by people who believed in her.

Nate believed in her. Gemma and Caleb did, too. Why couldn't Michael see who she was?

"All right. You should go. I'll take care of her."

229

Michael hesitated. "You have to understand the position I'm in."

"No." He was resolute in this. "I don't. You got hurt. I do get that, but I don't understand what that has to do with Lucy."

"And how am I supposed to know that? Am I supposed to trust this feeling I have about her? About you?"

It seemed simple to Ty. "Yes. You are. How do you live and find any kind of happiness if you can't trust anyone? Are you going to break from every person who gets into the slightest amount of trouble?"

"It's murder." The words came out on a low growl. "It's not like she's been accused of shoplifting."

"No one's accusing her except you and the person who probably did it herself," Ty shot back.

"You can't know that."

"I know it makes a hell of a lot more sense than suggesting Lucy did it. I would look at all three of them. I would take a big old look at Daddy's will and find out where that money was going to go." He'd thought about this the whole time they'd been sitting with Gemma. "Lucy gets nothing but trouble from this. And quite frankly, I'm offended you think she's this dumb."

"I never said she was dumb."

"No, but you believe she would grind up a bunch of apple seeds to get cyanide and then take the damn drink to him herself."

Michael had paled. "She lied to us."

Ty rolled his eyes. "She's explained that. She was trying to avoid confrontation. It's a thing she's done since she was a kid. You know you're not the only one who has trouble trusting people. You act like you're the only person in the world who ever got hurt. She grew up rough. She watched every mother figure she ever had walk away or die on her while her good for nothing dad sat in a lawn chair and drank his life away. I left her behind because I was too insecure to let her know how I felt. She struggles every day to feel like she's worth something. It's hard for her to trust you, too, but she did it and you bailed on her."

He expected Michael to explode, to rage against him, but instead he sighed and his shoulders slumped. "I'm sorry. I told you I couldn't love her."

"Bullshit. You already love her. I think you've loved her for a long time." He didn't understand where Michael was coming from. "I know what happened with your fiancée fucked you up, but are you really going to let it screw over the rest of your life?"

Michael picked up his bag. "I don't know. I would have told you I'm still angry, but honest to god, all I feel right now is tired. I'm tired of having this empty place inside me. The last couple of days, I didn't feel it, but it's there again. It never really went away."

"We can't fix you." If there was one thing he'd learned from life to this point it was this. "No one can fix you. You have to fix yourself, and sitting on a mountain isn't going to do it. There is nothing I want to do more than sit down and talk to you, try to convince you that you belong with us, but I can't. I can't because she needs me. This is her time to be surrounded by love and support, and I'm pissed as hell at you for making this about you and not her."

"I am not trying to be selfish. Do you think I like feeling this way?"

"I think you're doing nothing to stop feeling this way," Ty replied. "When was the last time you talked to someone? You wouldn't even talk to her sister, who's done nothing wrong. You are holding on to this like you'll die if you let it go."

"I'm not fucking holding…" Michael stopped, his expression clearing. His hand tightened around the bag. "I'm going to go."

Michael wasn't ready. Not in any way. He wasn't ready to move on or be part of a family. Ty's heart ached because they could have had something amazing.

Michael stopped at the door, not looking back. "You're a good man. You can be enough for her."

He wasn't sure about that. He'd needed Michael, too. He let Michael leave, the door closing quietly behind him.

And he was alone. Alone with the weight of protecting Lucy.

He had to be stronger than he'd ever been, better than he'd thought he could be.

"Is he going to be okay?"

Ty took a long breath to try to blow out the anxiety that threatened to explode through him. He needed to be calm for her. He needed to be her rock. He turned to her, praying his expression was as soft as he wanted it to be. "He doesn't matter now."

Lucy walked up to him, her hands going to his cheeks, eyes

taking him in. "Of course he does. You do, too, my love. You'll miss him as much as I will, and that's okay. It's okay to miss him. It's okay to be disappointed."

"I want to be mad."

She shook her head. "That's a useless emotion in this case. Michael proves that. All he's let himself feel is anger, and he can't move past it. We can't force him to. He knows deep down I didn't do this, but he can't let himself believe in another woman, and oddly enough that's not about me either. What he can't believe in is that he can be happy."

Ty felt tears pool in his eyes. He didn't want to fucking cry, but she was his safe place. She'd always been his safe place. "Can I be enough for you?"

"You have always been enough for me," she vowed, tears of her own falling. "You are enough, Tyler Davis. I love you and I wish he could be here with us, but we're going to be okay. We're going to be together, and we're going to get through this."

He was doing exactly what he'd accused Michael of. He was turning this around and making it all about him. "Yes, we are, and now it's time to get you to bed. I think I promised you some relaxation."

She went on her toes and pressed her lips to his. He let his hands find her waist, bringing her close to him, and wondered how he'd survived without this intimacy. Kissing Lucy was like breathing, a necessary thing for him to live.

He didn't have to question how he felt about Lucy. He'd been afraid of losing her, afraid he wouldn't be enough for her, but he'd never once doubted that he loved her, that she was the woman for him. He'd never had to. He'd never had the foundation of his life ripped from under him, so it was easy to kiss her and believe the world was going to be okay because for the most part, it always had been for Tyler Davis.

"I don't want to give up on him," he whispered.

"I don't either, but we have to let him come to us. I wanted to be angry, too. When he asked about the apples, I had a dark moment where I thought I would have to write him off. How could he possibly love me if he could think I could kill someone? Five minutes later and I've already justified it in my head. He doesn't honestly think I did it. Otherwise, he wouldn't have come here. He's in a dark place and looking for a way out. I think there's a little part of him that wishes I'd confessed because then he wouldn't have to try. Trying is scary. I know all about that. So now we have to figure out what we want. We have to be patient, even if it means he never comes back at all," she said as tears caressed her cheeks. "He has to make the choice, but we can't be bitter with him. This isn't him rejecting me or you."

He let his forehead rest against hers. "He's rejecting himself, not allowing himself to be happy. I don't understand it."

"You don't have to. You just have to know that he's not doing this to hurt either one of us." She sniffled, and her hands tightened around his waist. "But, Ty, someone is definitely trying to hurt me."

"Yeah, I think Nate's right and when the state takes over, they'll zero in on you." He couldn't stand the thought.

Lucy stepped back and bit her bottom lip. "They'll have no choice but to do that."

"Of course they have a choice. They can follow the money." He was smart enough to know that this was about money. Women didn't murder the men who harassed them. There would be a whole lot less men if they did.

"They won't. They'll come straight to me, and they won't have to investigate further. Ty, I looked through the bathroom cabinets for some tissues." She'd paled again. "I found a baggie of white powder tucked away behind your extra toilet paper." She laughed, a nervous sound. "I don't suppose it's cocaine."

It was sad that he wished it was.

Someone was setting up his girl, and now he had to prove it.

* * * *

Michael meant to go up to the suite where Nate had told him he could work. Work. That was what would get him through this. Avoiding work was where he'd gone wrong. He would call on Monday and take the job he'd been offered. He would work alone, and he would concentrate on the job, on hunting down people who needed to be found. He would start by helping Nate and Cam and Gemma prove Lucy had nothing to do with Brock Foster's death. Then he would move on and dedicate his life to work.

He wouldn't think about the two people he needed more than anything.

He wouldn't think about the people he'd lost and would never find again.

And yet he found himself going down instead of up. Cole Roberts lived in the penthouse when he was in residence. He and his wife and husband cuddled up in a glorious suite of rooms.

He didn't need that. He'd been happy in Ty's little room. He would have been even happier living with them in the valley, where they would have had a community they loved around them. Where he could have his coffee on the front porch before heading to work.

Where they could have started a family.

Ty would take care of her.

He got to the lobby and realized he was walking for the doors. The lobby was quiet now, and he could practically hear his heart beating, feel a tightening in his chest. He couldn't stay here. The road might be closed but he could get through.

The big glass doors whooshed open, and a blast of air shook him. It was frigid outside, the conditions harsh and brutal. Any sensible human being was hunkering down and keeping warm.

He had snow tires and he could go slow, and did it really matter if he careened out of control and didn't make it?

Had he had that thought? Fuck. Ty was right, and he was fucked up and he wasn't even trying.

He had no idea how to start trying.

"Michael? Michael, you should come inside. It's freezing out here, and you don't have a coat on."

How long had he been standing there stuck between the hard reality of the world outside and the warmth behind him? He turned and Trina stood in the doorway, holding her sweater around her body. She shivered but didn't move back into the warmth of the building.

A strong wind swept by, threatening to knock him back, the cold slamming over his skin.

"Please come inside," Trina implored. "I can't go back without you."

He didn't understand why. He hadn't been kind to her. He hadn't called or checked to make sure she was okay. He hadn't cared if she was okay, and suddenly that seemed like such a crime.

How stubborn was he going to be? Was he going to let them both freeze because he wasn't willing to let go?

We can't fix you.

Ty's words whispered along his brain. He hadn't said them unkindly. They'd been a spoken truth, one that had been between them the whole time.

They couldn't fix him.

He was worried he couldn't be fixed. He hadn't even bothered to ask the question. Did he want to be fixed?

He stepped back into the lobby and the doors closed behind him, locking out the frigid wind, though the cold had settled into his bones.

"Come over here." Trina gestured to one of the many seating spaces across the big, homey lobby. She seemed to have settled in front of the big fireplace, looking out of the floor-to-ceiling glass windows. It was a cozy place to sit and read and enjoy the warmth while watching the beauty of the winter storm. Sanctuary. "I ordered a pot of tea. They brought two cups. I don't think they realized I was alone. Come on. It'll warm you up."

He should walk away. He should get back on the elevator and do what he'd intended to do, but when she sat down, he found himself sitting across from her, allowing her to pour him tea. He sat back in the comfort of the sofa, allowing the glow from the fireplace to start to dispel the chill in his bones.

"It's Earl Grey. I gave up coffee a while back," she said quietly as she offered him the mug. No delicate teacups for the Elk Creek Lodge. "Right around the time I gave up alcohol and all the other stuff."

"You didn't drink much. Not that I remember." His voice sounded weird to him. Like he'd forgotten how to talk in the brief time since he'd walked away from Ty. Like any conversation was surreal.

She smiled, but it was a tight expression. "Well, I made up for it. In the last two years I drank enough and did enough drugs to put me in a hospital. You don't know you've hit rock bottom until you wake up in a hospital and your dad is on his knees begging God not to take another daughter. My mom had to be sedated. I gave her a nervous breakdown."

"God didn't…" He had to stop that.

"He knows," she replied, picking up her own mug. "My dad, that is. He knows Jessie did it to herself, but he finds comfort in religion, and I don't see the harm in it. He wants to believe there's a higher power who has enough grace to forgive us so we don't spend an eternity being punished. The point is I now indulge in tea because I can't do that to them. No matter how much my addict brain wants to."

"I have a hard time seeing you as an addict."

"Me, too. But I spiraled after Tommy left me. I felt like I'd lost everything, like Jessie cost me the rest of my life with her selfish choices. I took some pills one night at a club and I felt good for the first time in months. And then I chased that feeling until it almost killed me. Now I wonder if I would have ever unleashed that beast had Jessie not died. I worry it would have come up at some point down the line. Some tragedy would have happened, and I wouldn't have known how to handle it. It's funny. I've figured out that the result of having an awesome, pain-free childhood is an adult who doesn't understand how to really process pain. I'm not saying I wish I'd had a tragic childhood. I'm simply recognizing that I wasn't ready for this, and it's hard to acknowledge that my grief caused my parents more pain."

"I'm sorry to hear that, Trina." He couldn't imagine the sweet, happy young woman he'd known turning to drugs and alcohol. She'd been a bright light to Jessie's sometimes darkness.

"I'm glad to know you didn't end up like me," she said. "I worried about it. I thought you might find the bottom of a bottle and not come out of it. That's good."

"No. I found something else to get addicted to." He'd stayed in Bliss because he hadn't been able to face going home. He'd bought the place on the mountain because he'd convinced himself that what he'd needed was time alone. "My rage."

Her eyes widened, and she set down her mug. "I was angry with her, too."

She didn't understand. "I was…am angry with me."

"Why?"

He couldn't seem to make anyone understand. "I should have

known who she was. I should have seen it. I asked her to marry me. I was ready to spend my life with her, have children with her, and all along she was someone completely different."

Trina leaned in, her skin warmed by the glow of the fire. "But she wasn't. I mean I never thought she could turn her back on her badge like that, but she wasn't merely one moment in time, Michael. You're viewing her whole life through that one incident, and I think that's where you're missing the point."

"I would love for you to tell me the point."

She stiffened, and he realized those words had come out harsh. They'd been yet another accusation, a way to put up walls so he didn't have to be vulnerable again. Like the way he'd leapt on any slight possibility that the sweetest woman he'd ever met could have killed someone.

"I'm sorry." He softened his tone and leaned in. "I really would love for you to tell me the point because I can't find one. I meant what I said. I've been addicted to my anger. I've let it lead me, let it make all my choices. I don't know how to let go of it."

She was quiet for a moment. "Is it still anger? I was angry in the beginning, but I think it was because it was easier to be mad than to mourn."

"I shouldn't have to mourn."

Her face softened, and she reached out to him, holding her palm up. "None of us should, but you have to mourn or you can't heal. Even if what you mourn is the love you gave her, you have to see that nothing she did invalidated how you felt. You loved her. You have to mourn the life you could have had. Even if it wasn't real. It was real to you. My life with her was real to me. The rest of the world can shrug and say she deserved it, but we have to acknowledge that she's gone and it affects us. It makes us sad. It leaves a hole. Anger has a place, but so does our sorrow."

He didn't want that sorrow. It struck him suddenly that he didn't want what could be a wave of pain to hit him. He didn't want to mourn the years of his life he'd enjoyed. It had been the first time he'd thought he could have something good, and she'd ruined it.

The anger rose again, a loyal companion that always protected him.

Protected him from unwanted emotion.

Protected him from being vulnerable.

Protected him from any kind of happiness he might find if he could only be fucking brave enough to confront what had really happened, what he really felt.

"I'm ashamed I loved her."

Trina gasped and tears pooled in her eyes, and for a moment he thought she would walk away from him. She stood but instead of walking away, she moved to his side and slid her arm around his. "I'm so sorry you feel that way. I wish you could see there was good in it, too. I felt that way and it nearly killed me."

"I can't remember the good."

"Do you want to?" She asked the question simply, as though she would easily accept any answer he gave her.

"I don't know." He turned slightly, not breaking contact with her. "Why are you being so nice to me? You were angry with me."

"I talked to my dad, and he reminded me that I was here, too. Where you are. But I had him and Mom to hold on to. I wasn't alone in my grief. He reminded me that anger can lead to regret, but kindness is never wasted. My sister didn't take that lesson to heart, and I won't make the same mistakes. So I'm sorry that I was harsh the other day. I guess seeing you again brought back some of my own pain, and I had a lapse when it came to dealing with it."

"You don't have to apologize to me. I was an asshole."

"I've found that giving myself grace makes it easier to offer it to others. I thought seeing you would be different. I thought I would see that you had moved on and come to the real recognition that you didn't really love her or us and I would be able to move on, too. But that's not what I see. It was okay to love her. It's okay to feel betrayed by her. It was okay to be angry. And it will be okay if you let go of that anger and feel some affection for that part of your life." She leaned against him. "I missed you. You were like a big brother, and I missed you."

Sitting here with her…felt good, felt right. For the first time in years he felt some piece of himself slide back into place, the piece that was open, the piece that could care.

The piece he wanted to share with Lucy and Ty.

"I missed you guys, too. I couldn't…I couldn't face you. I thought maybe you would think I was in on it, and I got away with it.

I couldn't explain that I loved her and lived with her and slept with her and I didn't see what she was capable of."

"Don't you think we felt the same way? And no, we never thought you were in on it. We thought if anyone could have saved her it would have been you." She let go of his arm and sat back, simply sharing the space with him. "You should know I told her flat out that you were too good for her."

He had to chuckle at the thought. "I'm sure that went over well."

Trina grinned. "Oh, so not well. She was such a bitch to me that whole weekend. It was when we went to the coast for Mom's sixty-fifth."

He remembered that trip well. "When she jumped in that freaking freezing pool and tried to convince you it was fine."

"Her lips turned blue," Trina said with a laugh.

"Yeah, but she was committed," he replied, a hundred memories flooding into his brain. "When she pulled a prank, it was spectacular."

"Did I ever tell you how she convinced me I was being stalked by a Barbie doll?" Trina's eyes lit up.

"No. I haven't heard that one." He was shocked to find out that he wanted to hear that story.

Michael sat back and listened.

Hours later, Michael sat in the backyard, in one of the chairs he'd bought when they'd moved in together.

Somewhere in the recesses of his mind, he knew this was a dream. It had to be because he hadn't been back to Florida in two years. He'd paid someone to cover the furniture and close down the house. There was a security system to keep the place safe, but otherwise it was empty. There certainly wasn't a warm fire glowing in the fire pit.

The long talk he'd had with Trina had led him here. Hours spent laughing and joking and acknowledging that his relationship with Jessie hadn't been all bad had brought him to this. It was odd to know he was really in a suite in Colorado. He'd sat up with Trina for a long while and when it had been time to go to bed, he'd taken himself up to the suite where Nate had shown him to a small room and he'd actually fallen asleep quickly for once. There had been peace in knowing he was in the same building where Lucy and Ty were.

"Hey, you need a beer?"

That was a familiar voice, one that had called to him once. One that now could speak to him from beyond the grave.

Yeah. He was dreaming, and he thought he'd had enough for one day. "I don't want you here. I've already dealt with this today."

"Well, tell your subconscious that, buddy." She wore the black and tan wrap she'd bought at a flea market they'd visited. "Because you're kind of the only reason I'm here. Talking to my sister must have opened something up."

Jessie sat down across from him, her pale skin warmed by the glow of the firelight.

"Then my subconscious brain can go fuck itself. I want to sleep."

Her nose wrinkled. "I think that's the point. It's already fucking you over. I'm still in your head, Michael. You tried to pull me out by the root, like I'm a weed that will grow back if you don't get all of me out."

"So you're saying I'll never be rid of you."

She shrugged in that nonchalant way of hers. "Not entirely. We were together for years. We were in love."

"You weren't capable of love."

"Wasn't I? Maybe not the way you were, but the love I did have I gave to you. I was harsh at the end, but there was love in there somewhere." She settled back, a contemplative look on her face. She wore her hair up like she usually did when they weren't working, and she wore the fluffy house shoes her mother had gotten her for her birthday.

"I think it was more a case of me loving you and you using me." Talking to Trina had opened him up to the idea that he could still care for Jessie's family, but it hadn't convinced him anything about her.

"Ah, so we're going the victim route," she mused.

"What else would you call me?" It didn't seem like he was going to be able to wake himself up. Maybe he should engage. Maybe he should get some answers.

"A man who didn't want to see that the woman he loved was out of control. I was in a bad position, and I didn't know how to get out."

There was one problem with that. "You could have told me."

"Yes, I could have," she replied. "Have you thought about that? Why do you think I wouldn't tell you?"

"Because you were afraid I would turn you in." It always killed him to think that she hadn't trusted him.

Her brows rose. "You wouldn't have turned me in."

"You couldn't have known that." He'd asked himself the same question a million times, gone over it in his head as he lay awake every night. What would he have done?

"Of course I could. You did lots of things to cover for my failings. I knew damn well I could talk to you and you would have either helped me get out of the situation or simply backed me up."

"I wouldn't have gone after Alexei. I wouldn't have helped you hurt him." He'd been their charge, and somewhere during those months of protecting him, he'd become their friend.

"I didn't want to go after Markov either. That wasn't supposed to be the job, but I was already in too deep," she admitted. "I couldn't walk away. They wouldn't let me. I was supposed to facilitate the damn assassin. Not become the assassin. However, when it all went wrong, I knew I couldn't go to jail. I had to follow through on the assignment. Then Holly and the doctor showed up with him, and it became this massive clusterfuck. But none of that explains why I drugged you that night."

That seemed clear to him. "You didn't want me to stop you."

"If I'd wanted to do that, I would have knocked you out some other way. Do you remember anything about those five or ten minutes before you passed out?" Jessie asked.

"No."

"Think, Michael." She leaned forward. "It's all in there. You do remember. Sometimes you dream about it at night. You remember how we were both drinking and you told me that something was wrong, and I said I felt it too. I tried to help you to the bed, and I told you someone must have drugged our drinks."

He did remember that. She'd fallen to the floor once he was on the bed, and she'd promised she was getting her cell phone. She was going to call for help. "Why would you do that?"

"Why do you think?"

"You were trying to give yourself a way out. You knew you had to help the assassin that night, but you didn't know how it would go," he mused. "You thought you might be able to get back to the room and pretend it was the assassin who'd drugged us both so he could take Alexei out. You must have been disappointed when you realized you would have to use your gun."

She wouldn't have been able to hide that. After that kind of an incident, someone would have checked her weapon simply out of protocol, and she would have had questions to answer.

"I must have been disappointed because I would have to do the one thing I didn't want to do. The one thing I'd worked so hard to avoid." She leaned forward, the glow of the fire casting shadows on her face. "It would have been easier to tell you. The truth of the matter is you would have moved heaven and earth to help me. So why wouldn't I use that against you? Why wouldn't I drag you in and make you fix things for me? You always fixed things for me."

"You didn't want me to know." That truth hit him. She'd been willing to risk a lot so he didn't find out. He didn't know whether or not he would have turned her in. Almost certainly not immediately. He would have stopped her from harming anyone, but he would have tried to save her.

"Why wouldn't I want you to know?" He could have sworn there were tears in her eyes. They shone right on her lashes.

The answer played at the edge of his brain. "I don't know."

"Yes, you do, and you have to accept it. Not accepting it is what's keeping you here. You might have left the house we lived in behind, but you didn't leave me. I'm still here haunting you every day, and that's gotten old," she insisted. "You might have needed it at first, but there's this part of you that wants out. You want to move on. You bring me into every decision you make. I'm the reason you can't move on. Do you honestly believe that woman could kill a man?"

Yes, he was obviously having a weird fucking therapy session with himself. "No."

"Then why are you pulling away from her?"

"She lied to me." Stubborn. Even the words were stubborn.

"She didn't want to cause a scene," Jessie shot back. "If she'd told you what that prick had said to her in the alley, what would you have done?"

He wanted to lie, but it would be stupid since he wouldn't be lying to Jessie. She wasn't really here. He would be lying to himself, and maybe he'd done enough of that. "I would have confronted him."

"And she was trying to avoid that. She thought she'd taken care of the situation. She told his ass off and then walked away because she truly believed he wasn't going to physically attack her again. She handled the situation, and bringing you into it would have made everything worse."

"Because I would have lost my temper. Because I'm always looking for an excuse to lose my temper these days."

"But she helps you be calm. He does, too." Jessie's eyes lit with mirth. "I was surprised by that. I wouldn't have put you on that end of the Kinsey scale."

"Yeah, I kind of held back on the kink with you. You weren't interested in anything but pretty straightforward sex."

"Was I? Or did we just never talk about it? Were we in our comfortable corners? Unwilling to do anything to screw up our status quo?"

"I think betraying your oath was going to screw up the status quo."

She nodded. "And we're right back to where we need to be. We're right back to why I would have done anything to keep things the way they were. Anything but tell you the truth. Why? I need to hear you say it."

He went stubbornly silent.

"You need to say it, Michael. You need to say it so you can forgive me."

"I don't want to forgive you."

It was strange to see tears in her eyes. She never cried. Except she had that night. When she'd helped him to bed, there had been the glossy sheen of tears in her eyes.

Was he making that up? Was he misremembering? Trying to make the moment softer than it had truly been?

Did it fucking matter?

"No, baby, you don't forgive yourself for not seeing who I was," she said, quietly. "But it's more complicated than the one-sided evil I appeared to be at the end. A human being is complex, and so is a relationship. You've spent two years punishing yourself for not seeing how I used you. Two years of telling yourself our relationship was predicated on a lie, and therefore you can't trust any other

243

relationship that came after because I never loved you. So why would I put everything at risk for the tiniest shot at you not finding out what I'd done?"

"I don't know," he insisted quietly, fighting the truth.

"Because I loved you. Because I wanted a life with you, a life that wouldn't have worked because I was lying to you about who I was. I loved you. It might not have been the best love, but it was what I was capable of giving you. It was love. It just wasn't enough. That doesn't mean you can't find a woman who can give you what you need, who needs what you can give."

"How can I trust myself to know?" He asked the question without a shred of the anger he'd felt mere hours before. He'd said his rage had kept him warm, but that had been bullshit. His rage had kept him locked in ice. His rage had squashed any warmth he'd had in his soul, and only Lucy had been able to find a tiny ember.

Then Ty had helped her nurse the tiny bit of warmth.

"Because I did love you," she said with certainty. "Because deep down you know I loved you. I made a mistake and it cost us. Are you going to let it wreck the rest of your life? That's not the man you want to be."

"How would you know the man I want to be?"

"Because I'm not me." She chuckled softly. "You're arguing with yourself. I'm a ghost. I don't exist anymore. Not here. Not with you. I'm that piece of Jessie you're holding on to. Maybe I'm the part of you who wants so badly to forgive."

"Why should I forgive you?"

She stared at him for a second, a deep sympathy in her eyes.

He took a long breath. "Why should I forgive me?"

"That's the right question. And you know the answer. You're not all knowing. You are arrogant, and it's costing you."

"I don't feel arrogant." He felt weary.

"If a friend came to you in similar circumstances, how would you react? Would you tell your friend that he was responsible for someone else's actions? Would you tell your friend that he obviously shouldn't allow himself an ounce of happiness because he hadn't seen what his girlfriend was doing?"

"Jessie, you died."

She nodded. "I did and that wasn't your fault, and until you recognize what you are truly feeling, you won't be able to move on."

"I think I know…" He stopped because he did know. He'd known all along and he hadn't wanted to face it, couldn't handle what he'd really felt. So he'd allowed the emotion to become one he could handle, one he could hold up high.

He'd taken the agony of his sorrow and shaped it into rage. Instead of embracing the grief of losing her, he'd turned it all into hate so he wouldn't have to feel the shame of being tricked.

Shame. It was a useless, hateful thing. It did no good, robbed him of the chance to move forward.

It robbed him of his humanity, his grace and goodness. It made him hate, and he'd turned it inward. It froze him in place and allowed no sunshine in his life.

It took away his faith.

But he could take it back.

He stood up, something infinitely warm washing over him. "I'm sorry, Jessie."

She sighed and stood, keeping a careful distance between them. "Me, too." Her lips curled up slightly, a bittersweet expression. "You won't see me again. I won't whisper in your head anymore, but you have work to do."

He nodded. "I know." He moved to her and held his arms open. "Thank you for the good times we had. Thank you for leading me here because I think I'm going to stay."

"I think you're home." She hugged him, squeezing him tight. "Good-bye."

Michael woke up, the sun filtering through the curtains.

And knew what he had to do.

Chapter Fifteen

Lucy sat in the gloriously beautiful suite that Nate had taken over as his base of operations and wondered where Michael had spent the night. She prayed he hadn't tried to get back to his place. The snow was still falling this morning, and she couldn't stand the thought of him getting hurt.

"You found it in Ty's bathroom?" Nate held up the container. He'd bagged it before examining it.

"Yes, she found it when she went looking for tissues." Ty frowned. "I don't actually have any of those. I use toilet paper when I need to sneeze."

"I was crying," she reminded him. "I don't suppose you do a ton of crying, so you can be forgiven."

"Was it in a closet you use often?" Gemma had her notepad out again, and there was a serious look on her face that let Lucy know she would pull her away at any given moment.

"Closet?" Ty snorted. "You've spent too much time in this suite. I don't have a closet in my bathroom. I have a shower, a toilet, and a sink. She looked under the sink. I keep a few rolls of TP and cleaning supplies under there."

"I moved some stuff around," Lucy admitted. "I found that in the back. Obviously it's got my prints on it."

"I've already taken her prints. But I'll need to process the bag." Cam Briggs was still in his pajama bottoms and a T-shirt, a mug of coffee in his hand. When they'd walked in, he'd been on the phone talking to his wife about how he was stuck up here.

Because someone was trying to frame her for murder. It was completely surreal. Ty had moved the cyanide the night before and talked her into sleeping on what to do about it. She'd let him since it was clear it had been left for the state investigators to find, and there was no way they could get to the lodge before morning. Ty had needed time to be comfortable going to Nate. She'd always known they would be here this morning. She wasn't about to fall into the trap of trying to cover up the cover-up.

"We'll see if we can find any others," Nate promised. "Ty, you're sure this isn't some cleaning product you use?"

"No," Ty replied with surety. "We can check with the cleaning staff, but I know they wouldn't store any cleaning product like that. It would go against protocols. Everything has to be labeled. Is there any way it's not what we think it is?"

Cam shook his head. "I wouldn't bet my life on it. It's either cyanide or something like coke. The cocaine would be to give you a reason to have killed Brock."

"Why would I kill Brock over cocaine?" Lucy wasn't sure she followed Cam's line of reasoning.

"Brock had cocaine in his room," Nate replied. "They could claim you supplied him with the coke and killed him when he wouldn't pay. I would bet whoever's behind this has figured out the connection between Ty and Sawyer."

"Sawyer doesn't deal drugs," Ty said, his voice going hard.

Nate held a hand up as though holding off the argument. "I know that. Sawyer and I have come a long way. We're good, he and I. But he's got a reputation, and if I was going to set Lucy up, he would be part of the narrative. Whoever this is obviously knows a lot about the two of you. Enough to know she's staying with you."

"Apparently lots of people know that since there's a betting book at the Trading Post," she pointed out. "But why would anyone want to set me up for this?"

"Because someone knows you fought with Brock." Cam put down his mug and glanced around. "Shouldn't Michael be here?

Anyone wake him up? It's getting late."

"He took off about an hour ago," Nate informed the room. "He said he had something to do, and he would be back later."

"Then he was here?" She couldn't believe the amount of relief that flooded her system. "He stayed here last night?"

"Yes," Nate replied. "He did."

"And he was totally worse for the wear," Gemma added. "Like he'd been doing some serious thinking. Not drinking, but he was weird. He talked to Nate and asked what was going on in the investigation and if he could help. Politely. Something was wrong with him."

"He was fine," Nate assured her.

"I saw him sitting with a woman in the lobby last night," Cam admitted. "They were close."

"He was doing what?" Ty asked, his voice going tight.

"They were sitting together, and she had her arm in his and was leaning on him," Cam replied. "It was weird because she reminded me a little of his ex."

Another pulse of relief. She sniffled at the thought because when they'd left things, she'd expected him to do what he did—run and isolate himself. Not reconnect with someone from the very past that had torn them apart. "Do you think it was Trina?"

Ty's hand found hers, and she could feel his relief, too. "Yeah. I think it was. I had a bad moment there, but I don't think Michael would go from walking away from you to another woman's bed. He's not like that. I was worried he would try to leave and get himself killed. I hoped he would talk to her while she was here." He turned Cam's way. "Did they seem okay?"

"I think they were having a good talk. Nothing bad," Cam explained. "I was worried because they seemed pretty cozy. Who is she?"

"Jessie Wilson's sister. He hasn't talked to her since Jessie died. He was close to her family, and he cut them out when he went to live on the mountain," Lucy explained.

"She showed up earlier this week." Ty sat back. "She came to talk about selling the house he owned with Jessie, but I think she wanted more than that. She wanted to see how he was doing. She cared about him. He was like a big brother to her, and she lost him when she lost Jessie. I think it was hard on her. If he's talking to her, being affectionate with her, it's a good thing."

Nate's arms crossed over his chest as he regarded Lucy and Ty. "You're not jealous? You find out the man who walked out on you is snuggling with some other woman and you think it's a good thing."

"Like Ty said, Michael didn't walk away because he was bored and wanted someone else to sleep with." Lucy didn't want Nate to think poorly of Michael. "He's scared to feel anything, and he needs some time to deal with what happened. I know he's had two years, but that's what it took for him to start to think about moving on. He was grieving in his own way, and there's no timer on grief."

"He told you that?" Cam's brow had risen, giving him a quizzical expression.

"He didn't have to. Lucy pointed it out, and I agree with her," Ty replied. "And you're both staring at us because you didn't think we were this smart, but we are."

"We learned from all the dumbass stuff you guys did. By you guys I mean most of the town," Lucy pointed out. "There's always one person in the threesome who's all wounded and freaked out at the thought of a relationship with one person, much less two."

Gemma held a hand up. "Cade. It was totally Cade for me. Childhood trauma."

"Rafe." Cam nodded. "Dumbass thought we would move to Miami and I would like live in the garage or something."

Then every eye was on Nate, and the sheriff went the slightest pink and shrugged. "We all know it was me."

She had to smile because it really had been him. Zane had known he would stay in Bliss long before Nate had committed. "All I'm saying is Michael is our Nate."

"Or Michael is your Rafe," Nate countered. "Look, it doesn't matter who he most closely resembles. I'm glad that you two learned from our mistakes. Did he say anything he shouldn't have? Because that can happen, too."

Oh, she'd heard all of Callie's stories. At least Michael hadn't left them with nothing but a note and disappeared for years. Yet. "Beyond being worried I might have killed Brock Foster? Not really. He was mostly sad and confused. He hasn't figured out how to let go yet. We have to hope he doesn't take forever to come back to us."

Nate's expression softened. "If he's smart, he won't take too long."

"But until then, we need to deal with the problem at hand," Cam said. "The weather is supposed to break this afternoon. Our suspects will likely leave as soon as they can. We have today to figure out what we can about them. I have interviews with all three siblings set up this morning, and we should be getting our initial reports on each sometime today."

"I'm working on that," Gemma offered. "I can tell you that the younger sister's socials are full of really good bags and absolutely no intellect at all. She's serious about being an influencer, but I'm not sure she knows what the word means. The surviving brother is a frat-boy nightmare just waiting for a sexual harassment complaint. Sonya is the only serious one. She heads one of the divisions of the company. From what I can tell she travels a lot. Her socials are full of pictures from different sites she's visited. She was recently in South Africa. No significant others for any of them, though Kendall seems to be working her way through all the minor European royalty she can get her hands on."

"Sonya's the one I've talked to the most." She liked the other woman, which was why it had hurt to have Sonya point the finger her way. "She's stable. She seems to take care of the group. From what I overheard, they all have jobs with the company, but she and Brock were higher up than the others."

Was Michael downstairs having breakfast with Trina? Was he talking to her and realizing it wasn't so bad to reconnect with the people he'd known?

Was he still in love with the woman he'd asked to marry him?

"I have to think this is about money." Nate stared at the bag of white powder. "I'm going to have to take this to the lab."

"And you have to tell them where you got it." She wasn't going to put Nate in a bad position.

"Or he could flush it down the toilet and it will be like it never happened," Ty countered.

This was why they hadn't immediately come here the night before. Ty had wanted her to think about what they did, had hoped sleeping on it would change her mind about turning the substance in.

She'd always known they would do the right thing. "It might tell

Nate something important."

"Absolutely," Nate replied. "It could tell us a lot about where they bought it or stole it from. I know Gemma's worried that the CBI is going to zero in on Lucy and not look anywhere else, but I disagree. I would be far more worried about local law enforcement being lazy than the CBI. They're good investigators, and they're used to dealing with complex cases."

"They'll also listen to Nate," Cam added. "And me. We've got experience with federal law enforcement, and we both have contacts in the bureau. I agree with Nate. It's not the best-case scenario, but we can work with CBI agents. And they will see that the timeline is problematic. Lucy would have to have had this on hand when she met Brock. She's got no priors and no history of violence. Why would she have this hanging around? I'm afraid whoever did this overplayed their hand here."

"Yeah, it's better to leave things open when you're trying to get away with murder." Gemma had her blonde hair up in a bun. "It's better to make things confusing than to try to make a direct line to the person you're trying to set up because that means you're leaving clues. Clues like who could have put that in Ty's bathroom. Clues that lead to people we can talk to. Like the maid who cleaned Ty's apartment yesterday morning. The one I have on camera going in at eleven a.m., eight hours before Brock Foster died, but after the rumors about Lucy moving in would have made the rounds."

"My service isn't until today." Ty moved forward in his seat. "The staff apartments are cleaned in rotation every two weeks. Mine is today. She would have been working the odd numbered apartments yesterday. Evens are today."

"Then she was confused." Gemma turned her laptop so everyone could see it. Sure enough, there was a young woman pushing a cart down a familiar hallway. The cameras covered both ends of the hallway. Ty's apartment was close to the elevator, so it was easy to watch the door come open. Michael exited first, holding it for her. His lips curled up in an intimate smile as she came through the doorway, followed by Ty.

They hadn't even noticed the woman with the cleaning cart.

Ty reached for Lucy's hand as they'd turned toward the elevator on their way to their respective work shifts. He'd brought her hand up to his lips, and Michael had taken the other hand in his.

Michael didn't look like a man who would leave them within twenty-four hours. He looked happy and relaxed.

They moved out of frame, and the woman looked up and down the hall.

The dark-haired woman turned the cart back, going straight to Ty's room. She slid her key card in and entered.

"Damn it." Ty's hands fisted. "She's not supposed to go in unless asked or for a scheduled cleaning."

"Do you recognize her?" Nate asked.

Ty was quiet for long enough to let suspicion flow. "Her name is Ashley."

"Would she have any reason to help someone hurt you?" Gemma asked.

Lucy couldn't help it. Her eyes rolled because she knew. "He slept with her and didn't call."

Ty's jaw turned mulishly stubborn. "I never said I would call. I never told anyone I would call except Lucy, who I called all the time without even sleeping with her for years."

Oh, his poor damaged soul. "And even then most of the time you text." She turned back to Nate. "It's safe to say Ashley wouldn't mind getting some revenge on Ty, but there's no cameras inside the room. She can easily explain that she was confused."

"Well, she didn't actually clean," Ty admitted. "I can tell when housekeeping comes."

"She spends very little time in your room, and if you'll notice she doesn't even take the cart in." Gemma pointed to the screen. The door had been propped open, as was protocol whenever housekeeping entered a room. Usually it was left open by sliding the inside lock outside, but this time she used her cart. Ashley picked up two rolls of toilet paper from the top of her stack and entered the apartment. "I believe she's got the bag stashed inside the roll, and if anyone asks she simply restocked Ty's room. Did you call for toilet paper?"

"No. Like I said today is the day I get cleaned and restocked." Ty stared at the screen like he could fix something. "Why would she do this? I wasn't nasty to her. I was honest about what I wanted and could give. Hell, I'm pretty sure I talked to her about Lucy the whole time. She was the last person I slept with before I decided I couldn't do it anymore."

She reached over and covered his hand with hers. She'd let go of this anger a long time ago. They'd dealt with their insecurities in their own ways. He was solid now, and she wasn't going to punish him for something he'd done when she wasn't ready to be with him. "As a woman who has slept with you, I can promise she's still thinking about you. You make an impression, babe. But she was also probably paid. However, I don't know why she would ever admit to it. She's going to say she got confused about who put in a request for restock, and that will be that."

Nate's lips had lifted in a distinctly predatory grin. "Not after I get through with her she won't. Cam and I are pretty good at bad and worse cop, and if it doesn't work, we'll send Gemma in."

Gemma snorted. "Yeah, because this one will be hard to break. We'll tell her we've got her on tape, and she'll give it all up as soon as possible. She's not exactly a hardened criminal." She closed her laptop. "I feel bad for our killer. They thought they were in some small town and could railroad a local, and they forgot they're in Bliss and we do murder investigations all the time. We're like the *Murder, She Wrote* of small towns."

"Do not say that to Henry," Nate said with a shake of his head. "He's got some crazy theories about that show. I'm going to call them in on this. I'd like to know a little about the corporation the Fosters run before my interviews with them this afternoon. I'm curious about the cyanide. It's not easy to obtain."

She huffed. "Michael told me I could make my own by crushing apple seeds."

Nate sighed. "Mike has some hang-ups about the women in his life going nut-bag crazy and trying to murder people. If it helps at all, I think he can get over it. Especially given the fact that you two are human beings who don't hold a man to an unreasonable standard."

"Six years," Gemma interjected with wide eyes. "You brooded for six years. Sorry, I have to say that because your wife isn't here. She does the same for me when it comes to Cade. Can't have you men forgetting what you put us through."

Ty frowned. "I don't want to wait for six years. I was kind of hoping he would figure this out quickly because there's a cabin in the valley I happen to know is going on the market soon, and I don't want it to go to another freaking Texan. That friend of Henry's asked Marie to let him know if anything went for sale."

"You want to buy a cabin?" Her chest felt tight because that had always been her dream. She liked his apartment and it was close to work, but she longed to live in the valley surrounded by happy families.

"Yeah." A soft smile creased his lips. "I've always seen us there. We can still have a place here when we work longer hours, but I definitely want to spend summers down in Bliss. But, baby, I don't have the cash. I was kind of counting on convincing Mike to make the down payment and we could handle the mortgage."

"You do realize we've only been together for a few days," she pointed out.

He shrugged. "When it's right you know it's right. And Mike doesn't like the sarcastic Texans any more than I do."

"Be patient with him," Nate said. "And be a little patient with me. Even if I can't solve this today, I'll work with whoever the CBI sends and we'll get this all settled. Thank you for bringing this to me. It would have been easy for you to flush it down the toilet and pretend it never existed, but it's a good clue."

She stood. It was time to get going. She had a meeting in an hour to conduct about this evening's activities. After all, everyone was stuck in the lodge, so it was important to keep everyone entertained. "Let me know if you need anything else from me. Ty and I are going to grab some breakfast and then I'll be in meetings most of the day, but I'll have my cell on me."

"Keep a low profile today," Nate advised. "And I don't want you to be alone."

"I'm on call, but I should be able to stick close to her," Ty promised.

They said their good-byes and walked to the private elevator. The Roberts' suite was at the top of the employee wing but came with its own private elevator and private entryway. They would have to walk down the long corridor to get to the kitchens and the break room. She was feeling hungrier than she'd been before, a bit more hopeful. The fact that Michael had talked to Trina had to mean something. It had to mean that he was willing to give a little.

"Sorry I didn't tell you about the cabin. I kind of wanted to talk to Mike before we had a discussion," Ty said as the elevator descended.

"I would love to buy a cabin with you. But I think it's pretty early to ask Michael to put a bunch of money down on a place. We should talk about taking out a loan." She wasn't going to let go of the best idea she'd heard since the whole let's-stop-fighting-and-love-Lucy-together thing.

"I have to because I am not a man with a ton of disposable income," Ty pointed out. "Though I'm hoping that can change with River back and Mountain Adventures up and running full time this spring. You have to face facts, baby. I'm never going to be white collar. I'm kind of happier with no collar at all." His eyebrows waggled. "But I'm more than happy to serve management. You boss me around all you like, and I'll take it out on your sweet ass at night."

"Well, I think you'll be doing that here for at least the winter." She hoped Michael would stay in Bliss and give them a chance, but she got the feeling he would need some space. "Do you think he'll go back to that cabin of his?"

Ty sobered. "I don't know. I hope not, but I also hope he doesn't leave Bliss. I hope we get a chance to talk to him before he makes a decision."

The elevator doors opened and they stepped out.

"We have to be patient with him," Lucy said and then realized they weren't alone.

Chet Foster was standing in the hallway, waiting.

And he had a gun.

* * * *

Michael stood in front of the resort room door and wondered if he was going to have the courage to knock. If he knocked on that door, it meant he was moving forward. It meant he was ready to really love Lucy.

And Ty. It meant he was ready to be a partner to Ty.

It was funny to think that way because this morning he'd already made arrangements with a real estate agent to put his house on the market and to give Trina and her family half of the proceeds. He'd talked to Jessie's mom and dad for the first time in years and found an odd comfort in hearing their voices, in knowing he could help ease the financial burden of what they were going through. He'd even promised to visit them when he came to sign the paperwork and close up his storage unit.

Because he was coming home. Coming back to Bliss. Coming back to them.

If they would have him. He knew what he wanted. It was time to stop procrastinating and start living again.

Michael knocked on the door, all hesitation fleeing at the thought. He knew what he wanted, and now he had to make sure he was worthy of them.

The door came open and Caleb Burke stood there, a baby in his arms. Amelia Burke had dark curls on the top of her head and wore footie pajamas. She clung to the father who looked nothing like her, but who obviously adored her. The doctor frowned. "If Nate found another body, tell him I quit."

Still, Caleb stepped back to let him in.

"No. There's only the one body I'm aware of. I'm here to see Alexei." His stomach was tight at the thought of what he was about to do.

Caleb's brows came up, but he turned and walked into the big suite. "Hey, you've got a visitor."

Michael followed him, and Holly and Alexei were sitting together at the small breakfast table, the whole thing laid out with coffee and croissants and danishes.

He'd interrupted an intimate family morning, one they might not get often since they were all busy. "I'm sorry. I can come back later."

Alexei pushed back his chair. "Not at all. I assume you've come to see me. Or did you wish to speak with Holly?"

"You, of course. I had something to talk to you about, but it can wait." He didn't want to wait. He wanted to get this over with so his real life—his second chance—could start.

If they would have him. If he hadn't fucked everything up completely. That fear was what had kept him from rushing to Ty's apartment this morning. He needed to be able to show them he was willing to change. He needed to do this for Lucy and Ty.

And he needed to do this for himself.

Holly stood. She had one of the lodge's robes wrapped around her, her hair up in a bun. She held her hands out to Caleb. "Please come in, Michael. You're not interrupting at all. I was about to get this little one ready for her playdate. Henry is bringing Poppy by. He and Nell are helping Nate out this morning. They're going to be supersleuths or something. Nell is very excited about it. She's even forgoing her preplanned protest of the Lodge's overuse of laundry soap."

"I get to make sure a corpse is secure so I can perform an autopsy tomorrow." Caleb stared at him like he'd done the deed.

Caleb could be intense.

"Sorry about that," Michael muttered.

"Did you run out on Lucy because your dumbass thinks she's guilty?" Caleb also never minced words.

"Caleb." Holly settled her baby on her hip and sent her grouchiest husband a death stare.

"That was kind of why I wanted to talk to Alexei," he admitted.

Caleb's expression softened. "Well, then one good thing came out of this. I'm going to take a shower so I can check on my corpse."

Holly smiled her husband's way. "You do that." She looked to Michael. "Don't mind him. He really hates autopsies. Why don't you and Alexei take the office?"

"There's an office?" The suite was huge.

"Yes, Caleb rushed to get the biggest suite he could find when snow keeps us all here," Alexei admitted. "Luckily we keep to-be-going bags in car for emergencies. Sometimes Caleb must go on emergency runs, and we end up spending nights in places. So pj's and extra clothes for everyone. I have learned to be very prepared out here in the country."

He wondered if Ty did the same. He'd seen a gym bag in the back of Ty's Jeep, but there wasn't a handy gym to work out in here in Bliss. Likely it was a go-bag with extra clothes and protein bars and stuff he might need in an emergency.

He would have to keep one soon since his job would likely take him interesting places.

He followed Alexei and sure enough, there was a small office with a desk and a couple of wingback chairs. The curtains were drawn back, and the big windows offered a stunning view of the winter wonderland Bliss had become overnight. He stared for a moment, taking in how crisp and pristine the world looked. Brilliant white snow covered the messy earth beneath. It was beautiful and seemingly perfect, but it was the mess beneath that sustained life.

He'd lived in the cold for so long that warmth had scared him. He hadn't trusted it.

Alexei sat in one of the chairs and simply waited. He said not a thing, and Michael realized he had no idea how long he'd been standing there keeping the man waiting. He turned back. "I'm sorry. I was just thinking about a few things."

"Thinking is good." Alexei was the model of calm perfection, so far from the man he'd been once. Alexei had changed, had opened himself and embraced the possibilities life had offered him.

Michael sat down across from Alexei. "I thought that was what I was doing this whole time, but I was wrong. There's a difference between thinking and brooding."

"Yes. One is constructive. The other is necessary, too, at times, but perhaps you are ready to move on," Alexei said. "Grief is a process. It is nothing to be ashamed of and it is nothing to hurry along. I believe the problem you have is that you do not understand that you are grieving at all. You think she does not deserve grief. You believe the love you have is wrong because she was not woman you think she is." Alexei frowned. "I am sorry. I do not ask what you wish to talk about. That was presumptuous of me. I've been thinking about this for a long time, but that does not mean I should push my ideas on you. Forgive me. I have taken too many classes and now think I should be everyone's therapist."

He shook his head. "No. I mean there's nothing to forgive. I did come here to talk about...how to move on. I know you can't be the person I talk to. You're too close to the situation."

"We're friends. I cannot be your therapist, but I know a good one in Del Norte. I can set up an appointment for you. You'll like him. Good man. He used to practice in Denver. He came down here to enjoy rural life and discovered we need help, too, from time to time," Alexei explained. "We will be opening small office together in a few months."

"Good. I think it would be good for me to talk this out."

It was awkward, but it was also right. It felt like a weight was starting to lift.

"You are ready then?" Alexei leaned forward. "I cannot be your permanent therapist, but we can sit here and talk about things if you would like. It can be good to talk when you are ready to accept the truth of a situation."

"Yeah. I'd like that." He wanted to get some stuff off his chest before he went to talk to Lucy and Ty. It would be good to feel like he'd started. It would be proof that he was willing to do the work he needed to do. Hopefully it would be enough to keep the doors open between the three of them.

"Excellent," Alexei said. "Tell me what you are ready to accept. I've found it is helpful to say things aloud."

He wasn't sure exactly what Alexei wanted from him. "I'm ready to accept that I need to move on."

Alexei's dark head shook. "No, this is not what I think we need to acknowledge. Let me tell you what I believe you need. And I say this as your friend. Your therapist will merely be a guide to help you find your healing, but I am a friend so I get to say more. Michael, are you ready to accept that your pain was valid? That your love was valid?"

Fuck. The world went a little watery because Alexei was cutting to the heart of the problem. It should be easy. He would tell anyone that what they felt was valid. It was harder to accept for himself. "Yes."

"Are you ready to accept that you are worthy? Worthy of happiness and love?"

God, he hoped so. He was ready for his ice to melt, to deal with the complexities that lay beneath. He was ready to risk it all again. They were worth the risk.

He was worth the risk.

"Yes."

Alexei sat back. "Good. Then we can begin."

Two hours later Michael walked across the lobby and into the hallway that led to the employee wing. He felt lighter than he'd been before.

He'd told himself that he didn't need to talk, didn't need to work through anything. He'd told himself he was strong enough to handle anything.

But sometimes there was strength in asking for help.

The hallway that led to the elevators was quiet at this time of the day. Everyone was either at work, or the late shifts were in their rooms, enjoying their down time. If he'd had a brain in his head, he would be up in the apartment, cuddling with Lucy and contemplating what they would have for lunch. None of them were due at work until four p.m. Lucy was overseeing the evening's events.

Were they still having events?

Between the winter storm and the murder, he wasn't sure. It was odd how normal the lodge seemed. Things were still running like nothing had happened. The restaurant had been busy when he'd walked by it. The same with the coffee stand.

Life moved on. He'd forgotten that. It was all right to grieve, to process, but life didn't stop, and there was something comforting in that. The world hadn't ended because he'd gone through something terrible. Bliss had moved forward. Alexei had spent those years at the local college, learning the art of listening. He'd been ready when Michael was. Lucy and Ty had been working all this time, growing so they were ready when it was time to start their little family.

He wasn't going to look at the last two years as wasted time. It had been necessary time. No one could tell him how to grieve—and now he realized that was what he'd been doing. He could tell himself he'd been angry, but that was his pure stubbornness. He'd grieved the loss of something important, and now he was ready to begin something even more important. Now he was ready to reclaim parts of himself he'd thought lost forever. The parts that could love, the patient part of himself, the one who could be a husband and a friend.

Behind him he heard a door open and slam shut. He glanced back. Sylvan Dean walked down the hall, a grim look on his face. He stopped when he saw Michael, and his expression went blank.

It was definitely time to reclaim the part of himself that could feel compassion. Lucy thought a lot of this young man. "Hey, you doing okay?"

The younger man blinked. "Is that a real question or part of the interrogation, Marshal?"

That kid had obviously had a rough night. "I'm not working, Van. I'm really asking. Are you okay?"

Van's gaze softened. "I don't know, man. All I can think about is the fact that I poured that damn drink. I should have…I don't know. Shouldn't I have known? Doesn't that poison have a strong smell?"

"Yes, but there's also a portion of people who can't smell it at all. It's a genetic thing." He'd done some research before going to sleep. It had made him feel like he was helping Lucy. "Also, you were surrounded by booze last night. I'm going to assume you don't smell every drink you pour."

"No. Of course not. I know it wasn't my fault, but it's hard to not think about the fact that I had a hand in that guy's death." His shoulders squared. "The same way Lucy did, which is to say, neither one of us killed him. She wouldn't do that."

Did everyone know what an ass he'd made of himself? "I know that. Look, I know we're supposed to evaluate all the evidence and take time to really build a case, but I'm not technically working on this sucker, so I can tell you the truth. It's one of his siblings, most likely. No one poisons a dude for throwing a punch or making an unwanted move. This was planned, and I suspect whoever did it waited patiently until they could make their move. The killer likely wanted multiple suspects, and he or she found that here. I know you have to answer some questions, but you should understand that Nate is a pro. He's not going to be fooled."

Van let out a long breath and seemed to relax a bit. "Okay. I'll be patient then. I'll be honest. I was thinking about calling my brother. He's kind of a big deal in the investigative world. He's a missing persons specialist now, but he used to do PI and security work. I didn't want to because he already thinks I'm a fuck-up. I didn't want to add potential murderer to the list of ways his baby bro is a dumbass. Not that he would really think I was a killer. I'm afraid my brother wouldn't think I could be organized enough to kill someone."

It sounded like those brothers needed some bonding time. "Well, you should know I don't suspect you. I had a bad reaction to Lucy being involved at all. I'm seeing things much more clearly today. I've got some questions I want to ask, and the first one is about how the father's will is structured and who benefits from Brock dying."

"Anyone who ever had to serve him." Van grimaced. "See, that's where my brother would smack the back of my head and call me a dumbass because I said that out loud."

"I was thinking more in a financial sense. Like I said, if this had been about anger, I would bet on a different method of murder." This hadn't been a crime of passion. This was a cold, calculated kill. It likely hadn't hurt that the out of towners would view Bliss as some sleepy place where the local law enforcement wouldn't have much pull with the state investigators. A person with wealth and privilege often thought those things would protect them from the responsibility of their actions. He'd met plenty of people who believed they were far smarter than they actually were. "I know it's stressful, but I truly believe this is going to be okay. Give us a little time and be careful around the Fosters. Are you working today?"

"No, it's my day off. I'm planning on going back upstairs and hiding for the rest of the day," Van admitted. "I only came down to sign off on some paperwork. I actually saw one of the fuckers coming down the hall and ducked into the break room."

"One of the siblings? Why would they be here in the employee wing?"

Van shrugged. "No idea. It was the younger dude. He must have swiped a key card from someone. Not that it's a hard thing to do, but I don't know why he would come over here unless he wanted to start some shit. You don't think he's going to confront me, do you? Or Lucy... Ty's with her, right?"

Ty wouldn't let Lucy out of his sight. But Ty also wouldn't know how to deal with an angry confrontation. He might lose his shit, and then he would be in trouble, too. "Which way did he go?"

Van gestured toward the west end of the hall. "He was going that way. He could get to the stairs. The key card would make the east elevators work, but you have to use it with an employee code, and he wouldn't be able to steal one of those. The stairs only require the card."

So he was trying to get into the employee housing units. Michael didn't like the sound of that. He pulled his cell out and quickly dialed Ty's number.

It went to voicemail.

He started down the hallway, dialing Lucy. She didn't answer either.

"Should I call security?" Van followed behind him.

"Yes," Michael replied. "Tell them we have a potential problem and then stay in the break room."

He jogged down the hallway, trying to pull up Nate Wright's number on his phone.

"Hey, we don't want any trouble."

Michael stopped before he turned the corner because that was Ty's voice.

He went still for a moment, his blood chilling as Chet replied.

"If you didn't want any trouble, then maybe that bitch shouldn't have killed my brother."

Michael's heart rate tripled as the endless, awful possibilities ran through his head.

"I didn't kill anyone, Mr. Foster." Lucy sounded calm and cool. "It wasn't me."

"No one else would have wanted him dead. We talked about it all last night. He was my brother, and it's my duty to avenge him." Chet was anything but calm and cool. His voice shook.

Michael eased around the corner and got lucky. Chet was facing away from him. It looked like Lucy and Ty had come off the private elevator that led to the Roberts' suite. Chet was roughly thirty feet away, and he was holding a gun. Michael couldn't get a good look at it from this angle.

He had to be careful. He didn't want that gun to go off and possibly hit either one of them.

"You don't need revenge on me." Lucy was behind Ty, who'd obviously placed his body between her and the gun.

"That's not what my sister says. I'm the man of the family now, and I have to fix this problem." Chet's whole body was trembling. "My father can't do it, so it's up to me."

Michael caught the moment Lucy saw him. Her eyes went wide, but she didn't draw attention. Ty had backed her against the wall. He'd run out of space, and Michael could practically feel his partner's fear. He wouldn't be afraid for himself. Ty would be terrified of losing Lucy.

"You don't have to do anything at all," Lucy said.

"I can't leave it. I can't. He was my brother." Chet sounded tortured. "He was a Foster. We're not like the rest of you. Brock taught me that. We're kings. We were born that way, and someone has to teach the peasants how to behave."

His arm raised, and that was when Michael leaped. He launched himself onto Chet as the gun went off, the sound shocking in the small hallway. Michael tackled the man, landing his full weight on him and bringing them both to the floor.

"Get the gun," Michael commanded.

Ty picked it up as the elevator doors opened and Nate came out, gun drawn and ready, Cam at his back.

Nate quickly holstered his weapon in exchange for a pair of cuffs. "Damn it. What the hell is going on? Security called. They said they caught someone trying to assault a couple of employees outside this elevator."

Chet's body bucked. "Get off me. What the hell are you doing?"

Nate knelt down and had the man in cuffs. "Arresting you, though I don't have a place to put you until we can get off the mountain. Cam, let's strap this fucker to the back of a snowmobile and take him to jail."

"You didn't bother to arrest the woman who killed my brother." Chet's eyes were red enough that Michael wondered if he was on something.

Michael got to his feet and looked over to where Ty was still standing in front of Lucy, obviously not sure the threat had passed.

Or he was trying to protect her from more than Chet. Michael's heart clenched at the thought that Ty might be trying to protect her from him.

"No, I haven't." Nate helped Cam haul Chet to his feet. "But I do think you're right. I think a woman might have done this. Now it's all about proving it. But you don't worry about a thing. You've got your own problems."

"I'm going to sue this place for everything it's worth. I mean it. I will not be treated this way," Chet vowed.

"And yet you are," Cam assured him. "Hope you've got a good coat. It's going to be a long trip down this mountain."

Cam started to haul the man off. Nate turned Michael's way. "I'm going to need a report. I take it he came looking for revenge."

"We're okay." Lucy moved to Ty's side. "Michael was here. He saved us."

"You made it easy, baby. You both did. You stayed calm." He needed them to know how proud he was.

Ty's shoulders shrugged. "There are a couple of things you learn to do as a citizen of Bliss. Don't fuck with the beekeeper who supplies Stella's creamed honey. Aliens like to probe you so eat your beets. And stay calm when someone pulls a gun because someone always pulls a gun."

"And trust your partner," Lucy said quietly. "Because your real partner always has your back."

"Always. Even when he's the dumbest ass in the world," Michael replied.

Nate huffed. "I'm not getting my report now, am I?"

Lucy stepped up. "We'll come by later, but for now, we need to talk."

Michael took her hand and prayed this talk of hers would change his life forever.

Chapter Sixteen

Ty opened the door to his apartment, a deep sense of caution in his veins. His hands were still shaking from what had almost happened in that hallway. He could have lost her. Now he was almost sure he could lose Michael, and he didn't know how she would handle it.

He wasn't sure how he would handle it.

It had been such a short period of time, but he'd come to rely on Michael Novack. He'd settled into his place in this relationship, and he didn't want it to change. He'd been shocked at the surety that had come over him when he'd realized Michael was behind Chet. He'd gone from utter terror to a deep belief that Michael would get them out of the situation. He wouldn't let them down. Ty had known in that moment that he could have that certainty for the rest of his life.

Or Michael could take it all away in the next few moments.

This was why the relationships of this town worked. It wasn't merely about sex. It was about support. It was about a firm foundation of love and friendship that they could all build a life on.

He wanted that life. He wanted what the Harpers had, what Alexei and Holly and Caleb had found.

"First off, I want to apologize for how I acted yesterday." Michael sat down on the love seat, leaving Ty to sit next to Lucy.

Was Michael placing a careful space between them? Ty reached for Lucy's hand, needing the comfort of her warmth.

He wasn't sure what he would do if Michael had changed his mind. Oh, he knew exactly what he would do if Michael left them. He would surround Lucy with love. He would do everything he could to make up for the loss of their whole—because he was almost certain they couldn't be complete without him.

But there was the darker scenario—the one where Michael asked Lucy to leave with him. The one where he got left behind.

"Okay," Lucy said. "Why don't you tell me how you think you acted?"

"Like a massive jackass," Michael replied flatly.

It was good to know at least Michael was being honest. "You did."

Lucy frowned his way. "I thought we were going to be understanding about this."

"Well, I'm not sure what *this* is, so I can't possibly understand," Ty shot back. They'd talked about some of the things Michael had been through and how those experiences would affect him, but they couldn't go through this every time Michael was worried. There had to be ways for them to deal with it beyond walking out. "What I do know is Michael broke trust with us yesterday."

When Lucy started to counter his words, Michael stopped her. "Ty's right. I did exactly what he's saying. I broke trust when I walked away and didn't try to talk this through with you. Lucy, you have to know that I don't think you're a killer. I never believed it deep down."

"That's not what you said last night." He knew he was annoying Lucy, who simply wanted to forgive Michael for everything, but they needed to sort through the rubble before they started to rebuild.

"No, it's not. I said a lot of things that I thought were said in anger, but they were truly all about my fear." Michael looked a bit weary. "I didn't want to admit how afraid and sad I've been. Anger feels more familiar to me. But I have come to realize that I have a lot of work to do."

And there it was. Ty's gut twisted. This was when Michael told them he was leaving. He would be kind about it, but he would go back to his real life. "Back with the US marshals?"

Michael nodded. "That's certainly part of it, but it's not the most important part. I have work to do on me. Not physical work, but work. I want you to know that I've talked to Alexei and I'm going to be seeing a therapist who can help me figure out why I struggle to share myself with the people I love. I don't want to carry around this anger anymore. I want to be open. I need to move past this time so I can get on with a life I think I'm going to love."

There weren't any therapists in Bliss, which given the damn fact that half the town was nuts and the other half was even crazier seemed like an oversight. Alexei was in school studying psychology, but he wouldn't be setting up a practice in the next few weeks.

So Michael was leaving.

How had it only been a few days before that this would have been the best news he'd ever heard?

"I think that is a wonderful idea, Michael." Lucy leaned over and put a hand on Michael's. "It doesn't hurt to ask for help. I saw a therapist in Alamosa for a year after what happened with Hope's ex-husband. It did me a world of good. And I'm glad you talked to Alexei instead of someone else. I asked Cassidy because I thought of all the people who might know a therapist, Cassidy would be the one. She sent me to Irene, who turns out to believe she can purge bad spirits with the proper Blizzard blending. She worked at the Dairy Queen. That should have been my tip-off that all was not right. I got such a brain freeze."

How was Lucy so calm?

Michael's eyes had lit up. "I think I should try that, too. I think the right amount of cookie dough in my ice cream would definitely make me less angry."

"It would, but alas, Irene had to close her practice when she went to jail," Lucy replied. "Money laundering. She was a crappy therapist but turned out to be a half-good money launderer. Except for getting caught, of course."

"See, this is one of the many reasons I love this place." Michael brought her hand to his lips.

"Then why would you leave it?" The question was out of Ty's mouth before he could think to keep it bottled up so Michael wouldn't see how vulnerable he was.

Michael's brows rose. "Leave? I never said I was leaving. I

mean, I have to in order to get the paperwork on the house back in Florida done. There are a lot of things I need to take care of before I can truly settle in here. I was kind of hoping you guys could come with me. It should only take a couple of days, and I'm willing to work around your schedules. But I'm getting ahead of myself. I don't have the right to make plans for you. I broke trust, and I have to earn it back by showing you I'm willing to work hard to be a better man, to be the best partner I can be."

Lucy had turned Ty's way, a quizzical look on her face. "What are you worried about, babe?"

It was apparently not the same thing Lucy was worried about. "I thought he was going to tell us he was going to Florida. I thought the talk with Trina had convinced him he could go home and get back to his job."

"My home is here in Bliss," Michael said resolutely. "No matter what happens between the three of us, you should understand that I'm not planning on leaving. If you can't bring yourself to forgive me, then we'll find a way to be polite and get along, but I'm not leaving."

"But you said you were going back to the marshals." Ty's head was reeling.

"Yes. I've been talking to my old boss, and they need someone who can specialize in locating fugitives in rugged terrain. She offered me my old job back, but I told her I want to be here. I'll work with local law enforcement when someone goes on the run. I would pretty much be the one to do anything that needed to be done in this part of the country. They've agreed to let me work solo, though I'm technically under the Durango office, but I'd likely work for the Santa Fe District Office as well. I'd be a specialist, and I might have to work all over the western states if this goes the way they want. I was actually hoping to get you to help me hone my skills, Ty. I've spent the last two years learning how to survive in the mountains, but you're the real expert. I thought between you and River, there's not a lot you don't know about these mountains. Maybe we could even bring you on as a consultant from time to time."

Michael wanted to work with him? He'd started out just happy Michael tolerated him, and now he was talking about trusting him to watch his back in the wilderness. While they hunted dangerous fugitives. "That sounds awesome."

"It sounds like a couple of guys leaving their girl behind so they can have fun running around the woods," Lucy said with a pout that made Ty's dick swell. "And also dangerous. Ty needs more training if you two are going to be taking out bad guys. Though you both did great today."

"I promise I'll make sure he's safe." Michael's eyes had warmed.

"I'm confused. I thought you were leaving." He was still wrapping his head around the idea that he might get everything he wanted, everything he needed.

Lucy grinned his way. "I don't think that's what's happening, babe. I told you we had to be patient with him and he would find his way back. He's a quick learner. We didn't have to wait years like Callie and Nell. Just a night. We picked a smart one."

Michael sat back. "Wait a minute, Lucy. I want to talk to you about how we move forward. Like I said, I broke trust, and I have to earn it back. I'm going to work on myself, and normally I would say I need some space to figure things out."

"Normally?" Ty wasn't sure any of this felt normal, but then maybe that was a word he'd put too much value in.

Michael nodded. "Yeah. I talked through this whole process with Alexei. He said he would tell a person in my position that it might be good to take a step back from outside relationships so I can truly figure out what I want for myself. But I don't need that. I know I want a life with the two of you. But I'm also willing to wait. If you want to take some time to make sure I'm willing to do the work I need to do, then I'll deal with it. I'll look for a cabin in the valley, and I can stay there while we work through what we need to. I only ask that before you move on without me, give me a chance to plead my case."

That wasn't going to happen. He didn't need a couple of months to figure out if Michael was going to be solid. He was willing to take the risk. He believed Michael when he said he would do the work, had faith that he'd made his breakthrough and wouldn't leave. Sometimes a relationship required a leap of faith.

He was ready to take it.

He looked to Lucy, who simply squeezed his hand, and he knew they were on the same page. It had been years since they'd been so in synch, years since he'd felt like there was a person in the world who truly understood him. Not since they'd had their break.

Michael had brought them back together, and there was no way they lost him now.

It was time to show Michael how welcome he was.

There was zero reason for them to wait. "Should we show him how uninterested we are in being apart?"

Lucy leaned forward and brushed her lips against his, sending sparks through his system. "I definitely think that's the way we should go. I've had a rough couple of days, and I could use some time with my men."

Michael stood, his whole body going tight with obvious anticipation. "Be sure, you two. Be absolutely certain because this is what I want for the rest of my life. This isn't some rebound relationship. It's the most important one of my life. I want you two to be my family, and I promise I won't ever let fear control me again. I promise I'll never leave you again."

Ty stood and helped Lucy to her feet. Given the situation they'd been in earlier today, the manager of the lodge had found people to work their shifts. They had the whole rest of the day, and Ty knew how he wanted to spend it.

With Lucy in between them.

"Then let's make things plain, Mike. I want this life, too. I want to live with Lucy and you. I want to share her and the life we can have together with you." He was speaking to his partner, but his eyes were on Lucy. He let his hands find the buttons of her blouse. She wore her uniform, a white professional-looking blouse with dark slacks, her hair up in a bun that had been tidy before she'd nearly been shot.

He wasn't going to think about that right now. He would have nightmares about it for years, but not today.

He undid the buttons of her shirt, exposing inch after inch of beautiful, warm skin.

"I promise. Never again, Ty. I want to be the best partner to the two of you," Michael vowed. "We'll always work things out. Always."

He knew there were people who would think he was naïve, but Ty believed him. Michael wasn't a man who made vows without thought. He'd been open and honest about his feelings even when it could have hurt his chances at getting in bed with Lucy. He was being the same now. Michael was allowing himself to be vulnerable, and Ty wasn't going to punish him for it. He was going to do the same thing Michael had promised—be the best partner he could be. Today that included showing off and sharing the most gorgeous woman in the world.

He shifted so he was behind Lucy, easing the shirt off her shoulders. "Good, because I'm tired of waiting for my life to start. Lucy and I have wasted years, and I don't want to wait another single day."

Lucy's hair fell around her shoulders as he undid the tie that held it in its bun. "No. We didn't spend those years wasting time. We spent them waiting. I love you, Ty, but I don't think we work without Michael. This is what we waited for. For you and me and Michael."

He kissed the nape of her neck and went to work on her bra. Lucy was right. Things had worked out the way they should have, and he wasn't going to be bitter about it. He was going to honor their past and find joy in their future. "You're so right. This is what we waited for. I know it's early, but it's also not. It really has been years we've waited to be complete, and we finally are. I want a life with the two of you."

"That's everything I want," Michael replied.

Ty got her bra off and let his hands cup the warm flesh of her breasts. She was perfect in every way, the mere touch of her calming his fears, easing his anxieties.

Everything was going to be okay. He felt it. Lucy was going to be all right. They would figure out who had killed Brock Foster. Between Nate and Michael, he could relax because they were smart and knew what they were doing.

His whole body suddenly felt electric. This was happening here and now, and it would cement the love between the three of them. All three of them. He and Michael might never touch in a sexual way, but there would be love between them. And then again, who knew? He wasn't saying no to anything. The three of them had all the time in the world to experiment. All the trust in the world to be open to possibilities.

But today they were going to be all about the girl.

"She is so gorgeous," Michael said, moving in and getting Lucy in between their big bodies. "Tell me you took care of her last night. The only thing that gave me comfort was the thought of you being with her."

Ty felt a smile slide over his face as he continued to lay sweet kisses over her neck and shoulders. The night before had been emotional and hard, but there had been good parts. "I made sure she couldn't do anything but sleep last night. I promise I tired her out. I fucked her at least three times before I let her sleep."

"And he made me wear the dumb plug," Lucy complained.

"Even though I wasn't there?" Michael looked up from his study of Lucy's breasts.

Ty nodded. "I knew you would come back. Deep down. Or maybe I just hoped, and I wanted us to be ready."

"I think we both pretended you were there with us," Lucy admitted.

He'd been able to feel the drag of the plug in her ass as he'd fucked her pussy. And yes, he'd thought about the fact that it would be better with Michael on the other side, better with the three of them being together.

"No more pretending," Michael vowed before lowering his mouth to hers.

Ty rolled her nipples between his thumbs and forefingers even as Michael took her mouth in a long, luxurious kiss. Ty let one hand slide down Lucy's body, delving under her slacks and teasing inside her undies until he could feel the mound of her pussy. He slipped a finger over her clit and found her already wet. "Oh, baby, do you feel that?"

She gasped and pressed her pelvis against his hand.

"She responds so quickly," Michael said in a low tone that let Ty know he was definitely affected by Lucy writhing against him. She was pressing her pussy against Ty's hand, and that pressed his hand against Michael's erection. His partner was hard as a rock, but then so was he. Ty's cock swelled against her backside—as though it knew it was going to be inside there very soon.

"Only to you two," Lucy admitted. "Nothing ever worked for me until I found the two of you."

"Good, because that's how it's going to stay." Ty was ready to move on. "No other men for you. Don't worry, though. I get the

273

feeling we're going to keep you busy."

"So busy," Michael promised. "Starting now."

Ty got the feeling Michael was about to take charge, and he was fine with that.

It was time to find their places, to start their lives.

* * * *

Arousal was rapidly overtaking relief as the most important feeling Michael had ever had.

He'd walked into the room ready to take whatever judgment they meted out. He'd hurt them both, and he'd been willing to work his way back into their lives, to rebuild trust between them. He'd been prepared for anger and recrimination, and he would have taken everything they needed to send his way.

They'd welcomed him with open arms, as though they'd understood what he'd gone through and that there wasn't a place for anger between them.

There wasn't. There was kindness and love and trust. He could screw up and as long as he made things right, there would be a place for him.

This was his family, the ones he would build a life with. Right here in Bliss.

He'd found the one good thing that had come from Jessie's betrayal. He'd found a real home, the place he would live and love in.

Ty pulled back, stepping slightly away. He tugged his shirt over his head and tossed it to the side.

Lucy was still wearing far too many clothes. Her breasts were naked, nipples pink and peaked from Ty playing with them. Michael ran a hand down from her neck to her waist, loving the feel of silky skin under his palm.

He undid the button on her slacks. "I want these off. I want you naked. Go into the bedroom and wait for us. We won't be long."

Her mouth turned down in a frown. "You're not coming with me?"

There were things to discuss. "We have to game plan."

"Game plan?" she asked.

"He means we have to decide who's fucking your pussy and

274

who's fucking your ass, baby." Ty had a grin on his face and not an ounce of tact in his words.

Lucy flushed a vibrant pink, and her nose wrinkled. "Well, I'll leave you to it, then." She started to walk toward the bedroom. "But you two are carrying me around tomorrow if I'm sore. Think about that."

Oh, she should get used to it. She was going to spend a lot of time between them from now on.

He looked to Ty. "I think it should be you. I don't have the experience you have, and don't get self-conscious. In this case, your experience will likely save her that soreness she's worried about. Are you ready for this?"

"I'm afraid I spent a couple of years of my life getting ready for this." Ty kicked off his boots. "I'll be careful with her. I've had a lot of anal sex."

And Michael had a fairly staid past. He understood the mechanics and had done it a couple of times, but he wasn't an expert. All of that ended now. When he thought about it, it had truly ended when he'd stayed in Bliss. "I'm going to follow your lead when it comes to this, but I'm in charge the rest of the time."

"I can handle that," Ty promised.

"I think you'll like what I have planned." He pulled his shirt over his head and soon his boots had joined Ty's. He walked into the bedroom, Ty right behind him.

Lucy had done as he'd commanded. She'd shed the rest of her clothes and sat with her knees folded on top of the too small for all of them bed. Her dark hair tumbled around her shoulders, almost caressing those gorgeous breasts of hers. Her eyes were lit with desire, and she bit her bottom lip, the sight going straight to his dick.

"Lucy, spread your knees. I can't see your pussy the way you're sitting. You're so fucking pretty I want to see every part of you," Michael commanded. He wanted to study every inch of her and know she was his. His and Ty's.

He definitely wanted to watch her take Ty's big cock in that hot mouth of hers right before she moved on to suck his own. He wanted her on her knees in front of both of them, taking what they had to give her.

Lucy's knees spread on the comforter, her pussy coming into

view, and Michael could already see she was coated with arousal. Her pussy was ripe and ready, but he had a couple of games to play before they got to the main event.

This was what he'd wanted all along—intimacy with people he trusted with his soul.

He moved to the edge of the bed, close enough to touch her, to let his hand find her core. She leaned back slightly, as though offering herself up to him. He would never refuse her. Never again. He was done with the punishment phase of his life and ready to get on with the joyful part. He slid a finger over her clitoris and was rewarded with a breathy gasp.

Ty had been right. She was responding to them beautifully. She'd shoved aside what had to have been anger or disappointment in him and was offering him nothing but love now.

He was going to offer her everything he had, all of his heart and soul. The rest of his life.

And tonight he would offer her his body and all the pleasure she could handle.

But first he wanted to offer something to his partner. "I want you to wrap those gorgeous lips around our cocks. Did you suck him off last night? I spent the whole night thinking about you and Ty. Some of it was hoping you two were holding each other, but there was a part of me that also wondered how hard he was fucking you, how many times he made you scream out his name."

"I didn't scream. I was very ladylike." Lucy's hips moved, pressing her clit against his fingers in a not so ladylike manner. Or maybe it was since he didn't see anything wrong with a lady enjoying sex.

"She was a little emotional last night." Ty moved in. He'd taken the rest of his clothes off. Ty was a Greek god of a man, his every muscle sculpted and perfect.

He would have to keep up. He would have to ramp up his workouts. "Did she suck you off last night? Or did you concentrate completely on her?"

"Besides playing with her ass, we were pretty vanilla last night and pretty missionary position," Ty admitted. "I think we wanted to wait for you. I think even though we were worried, we knew you would come back. Well, she did."

They would always be faithful to him. He intended to make sure he deserved their devotion.

"I want you to suck our cocks until we can't take a second more and we have to fuck you. I want you to swallow us both down deep." Michael could already see it in his head, and it got his dick pulsing. "On your hands and knees, and keep those legs apart. Think about the fact that you're going to be full of cock very soon. We're going to both be deep inside you, fucking your pussy and your ass until you forget anything about being a lady and can only remember that you belong to me and Ty."

He undid the fly of his jeans and shoved them down in his haste to feel her mouth on him again. He hadn't lasted long the first time and wasn't planning on doing anything more than letting her tease him today, but he wanted the feel.

He held his cock in his hand, pumping it a couple of times. Ty came to his side, not an ounce of self-consciousness apparent. He followed Michael's example, stroking himself, all the while staring at Lucy as she watched them.

She licked her lips and looked like the most tempting woman in the world. She was more than enough woman for two men, and it would take both of them to love her properly, to give her everything she could need.

She leaned forward and swiped her tongue over Michael's cock, eliciting a long hiss of pure pleasure. She then turned her head slightly and did the same to Ty, who came closer, his hip bumping against Michael's, warm flesh brushing.

Yep. That did something for him. He wasn't sure they would ever have full-on sex, but he wasn't going to let anything stop him from enjoying every minute of being with the two of them. It made it easier for Lucy to move from cock to cock when they were intimately close, and there was something sexy about the three of them touching.

Lucy moved between them, licking his and then Ty's cock. He watched as she sucked the head of his cock inside her mouth, and then lapped at the arousal that seeped from Ty's dick and groaned as she took it down. Ty's hand went to pet Lucy's hair as she worked her mouth over his cock.

The sight of Ty's dick being swallowed deep sent a jolt through

Michael, and he knew there was no way he would last under the lash of her tongue. He stepped back and shoved his jeans and boxers off. He watched as Ty fed Lucy that big cock before moving around the bed so he could access her pussy.

The globes of her ass were in the air, her pussy peeking out, and he could see the cream of her arousal. He got on his knees behind her, a steadying hand on the small of her back as he let his free hand find her pussy.

A shiver went down her spine as he dipped into her wet pussy and stroked her clit before delving back in. Her pussy was warm and wet, like soft silk against his fingers.

"Don't stop. You suck his cock," Michael commanded.

"She won't have to do it for long," Ty promised. "Her mouth feels so fucking good."

"Her ass is going to feel good, too. Maybe you should take the edge off." He had zero doubt Ty could get that monster up again and quickly, but it might be easier on both of them if he'd come once. She'd been wearing the plug, but he wanted to make it as easy on her as possible.

He wanted her to love being with them both, to be addicted to it because he was pretty sure he was already there.

Lucy settled in, and Michael watched as Ty's jaw went tight. It wouldn't be long before she'd coaxed him to come in her mouth.

He wanted for her to not be far behind.

He slid another finger inside her, searching for her G-spot as he rotated another finger on her clit, building and building the tension. Her pelvis started to move, finding a rhythm that matched his hand and connected the three of them in harmony.

Ty's whole body stiffened and he groaned, a low, sexy sound.

Lucy came off Ty's dick and started to fuck Michael's hand in earnest. A gasp escaped her throat, and he felt her clench around his fingers, cream flowing freely as she came.

Michael moved his hand back as Lucy collapsed to the bed. He brought his fingers to his mouth and licked them clean, enjoying the taste of her arousal. Tangy and yet somehow as sweet as the woman it had come from.

His love. His life.

His cock was hard, the slit weeping with arousal of his own.

He flipped Lucy over. She was the perfect picture of a satisfied woman.

But he wasn't satisfied. Not yet. Not until he'd had her the way he wanted.

He leaned over and kissed her.

It was his turn, and he was going to make the most of it.

Chapter Seventeen

Lucy's whole body felt languid, the little orgasm she'd had flowing through her.

But she knew there was more waiting for her. Michael's gorgeous face stared down, his eyes hungry. She could hear Ty moving around the bed, likely going to get the things he would need to move on to the next phase.

The one where they would all be together.

Michael lowered his mouth to hers, covering her and letting his tongue delve deep. She kissed him back, her hands finding the strong muscles of his back. It didn't escape her that she could taste herself on his tongue, and he would be able to taste Ty on hers. She'd swallowed Ty's cock down, milking him for all she could. She'd loved the way he'd groaned and filled her mouth.

Now she loved how Michael's body moved against hers as they kissed, like they were in synch.

One big palm covered her breast, and she could feel need start to hum through her again. His fingers hadn't been enough. She had to have more.

She needed them both.

Michael moved down her body so he could get his mouth on her breast. He sucked her nipple into his mouth, and she let her hands find the dark silk of his hair. He sucked and nipped at her, stoking the ember of arousal right back to life.

"I don't ever want to spend another night like last night," he murmured against her skin. "I hated sleeping away from you. But we need a bigger bed."

"Oh, we so need a bigger bed," Ty said with a chuckle. "I was smooshed against the wall when we all slept together."

She'd been smooshed between them, and it had felt like heaven. Like she felt now with Ty looking down at her, a warm smile on his face. Her best friend and now one of the loves of her life.

"We'll find something that's perfect for us," Michael promised right before he wrapped his arms around her. Suddenly she was moving as he flipped them over so she was on top.

"That's where I want you," he growled. His hands cupped her ass, pulling her cheeks apart. "I want you on top of me so I can offer up your ass to Ty. He's going to fuck you there, baby. He's going to ease his cock inside, and I'll be able to feel him move inside you."

The thought sent a thrill through her system. She would be able to feel them both. She would be so full.

"He's right. We'll be able to feel each other. It's going to be so fucking good." Ty was at her feet, moving on the bed. She felt another hand on her backside. "But first we need to get you ready. You stay still."

She gasped as she felt something cold tease at her asshole. Lube. She'd gotten used to the feeling. Ty seemed neverendingly fascinated with her ass. She relaxed because Ty had never done anything but bring her pleasure.

"That's right, baby. Don't even try to keep me out. I'm getting in here tonight. I'm going to slide my cock in, and it's going to be the best feeling in the world." Ty pressed the lube around, massaging it over her skin.

The sensation wasn't unpleasant. It was weird at first, and then the cold gave way to the heat of anticipation. Michael's hands moved across her skin, and he held his torso up so he could kiss her. His cock was between her legs, brushing against her labia, rubbing close to her clit.

It wouldn't take much to get that big cock inside her, but she held still so Ty could do his work.

She held on to Michael as Ty pressed a finger inside, easing past the ring of muscles and rotating.

Michael kissed her over and over, tangling their tongues together and swamping her in pure sensation. Her skin was covered in warmth, and she could feel arousal pulsing through her blood, a siren call she couldn't resist. Didn't ever want to resist.

This was where she always wanted to be.

Ty's fingers stretched her, easing her open. He pressed a finger inside and then rotated, making sure the lube got where it needed to be. She started to push back against his finger, wanting more of him. He pulled his hand away, and she groaned her frustration.

"She ready?" Michael asked.

Oh, she was so ready. She was ready for everything life had to offer. Her life felt like it was starting. Finally starting.

"Yes," Ty said, his voice deep. "I'll be right back."

Ty made his way to the bathroom.

Michael palmed her breast again. "Do you remember when I said I couldn't love you?"

Yeah, such a dumbass. "Yes."

"I lied."

She smiled down at him. "I know. I love you, too."

"And I love everyone." Ty was back with a box of condoms. "Love later, fuck now."

He could be a bit single-minded. "I can love and fuck at the same time."

"You are excellent at multitasking," Ty said with a grin as he leaned in and kissed her. "Baby, I need you to ride Michael's cock."

She could do that. She shifted up to her knees and looked down at the magnificent man under her. Michael was gorgeous, his muscular chest covered in a light dusting of hair. It tickled her breasts when she lay on top of him and made her feel so soft and feminine. She put one hand on his chest and let the other find his cock. She stroked him, watching as his jaw went tight. Ty handed her a condom and she rolled it on, smoothing it over him.

"Fuck, that feels good. Putting on a damn condom shouldn't feel like heaven," Michael groaned. "You're going to have to hurry, Ty."

"Nah, you're going to have to exercise a whole lot of self-control," Ty replied with a chuckle. "Because I'm going to enjoy the hell out of this."

She barely heard him because she was lowering herself onto Michael's dick. She went slowly, letting the sensation flow over her as she watched Michael's whole body go tight. Inch by inch he filled her up and she leaned down, bringing their chests together. "You feel so good."

His lips curled in the sexiest smile. "You're the one who feels good, baby. You fit me like a fucking glove. But watch out. We're not done yet."

She kissed him even as she felt Ty part her cheeks again. Michael's hands went to her hips, holding her in place as Ty fitted his cock against her.

He worked his way in, thrusting lightly and pulling back out, allowing her to get used to the feel of having that big cock breach her.

"You okay?" Michael stared up at her.

She nodded. "It's weird, but I think I like it. I didn't mind the plug. This is a little different."

It was warmer. Far more intimate. Michael's hands moved on her hips, brushing up her body and soothing her. She could feel Ty's hand on the small of her back, steadying her as he started to thrust inside.

He was so big. That cock of his forced her asshole open, and she had to fight to breathe as he filled her up.

She was so tight, so full, caught between the two loves of her life.

Ty pulled out, and she felt herself clench around him, trying to keep him inside.

Michael pressed up and slid over some spot deep inside her pussy.

Then she stopped thinking about anything but pleasure. She moved between them, riding the wave.

She found the rhythm between them, each thrust bringing her closer to the edge.

One more shift from Ty and she went over it, the orgasm rocketing through her even as she heard her men call out.

She slumped down, the three of them in a warm, happy pile.

Their arms were around her, and she knew this was forever.

And they would definitely need a bigger bed.

* * * *

The next morning, Michael felt magnificent as he walked toward the east elevator back in the employees' wing. The sun was shining, and the world felt different than it had the day before. Today it was filled with possibilities.

And bacon. The three of them had chosen to go to the restaurant for breakfast this morning and taken in the glorious views of the mountains while they'd eaten bacon and eggs and pancakes and talked about what to do this winter.

The night before had been one of the best of his life. Everything he'd been through had led him to last night. To the man who would become his best friend and partner, and the woman who would be the center of their world. He'd let go of the past. Oh, he was certain it was still lurking around, but that was what therapy was for.

It was odd because he was even looking forward to that. He was looking forward to doing the work because Alexei's words from the day before had sunk in. Lucy and Ty were worth him doing the work, but he was worth it, too. He was valuable. It had taken these two to prove it to him.

"Do you think this will take long?" Lucy sounded less nervous than he'd expected. "Because I have a meeting with the service heads this afternoon, and then I'm supposed to sit in on a call with a couple of vendors for Winter Festival."

He loved how confident and competent she sounded.

Between bouts of making love, the three of them had talked—really talked—about what they wanted for their future.

If she wasn't arrested by the CBI.

"Hey, you need to let Gemma lead you through this." Ty was on Lucy's right.

"Yes, you need to do everything Gemma tells you." Michael had completely changed his stance on lawyers. "I don't like the fact that the CBI is here so quickly. Nate's about to lose control of this case, and that's going to make things much harder for all of us. I'm also worried about your friend."

They'd gotten a call from Nate this morning that the CBI had managed to make it to the lodge. The storm had broken yesterday afternoon and the snowplows had gone to work. A helicopter had brought in the two agents from Lakewood along with a ton of forensic equipment the Bliss County Sheriff's Office simply didn't have.

Michael wanted to believe these investigators would do their job and find the real killer, but he was glad to have Gemma sitting in.

"Gemma talked to Van last night," Lucy assured him. "She's going to sit in on any interviews either of us might have."

"Is Chet still in jail?" Ty asked. "He wasn't able to buy his way out, was he?"

"Hell, no. He's finding out that small-town jails don't work the way he thinks they should," Michael replied. "The judge won't be back until Monday. He's sitting his butt at the station house. I hope he enjoys Stella's burgers because that's all he'll be having for a while."

"Stella's burgers are awesome. He doesn't deserve them," Ty complained.

"I don't understand why he went off like that. I know he was obnoxious, but he didn't seem like the kind of man who would turn violent," Lucy mused. "If anything, I didn't think he cared for his brother much."

"I suspect he was on something," Michael explained.

Ty nodded. "That was my thought, too. I would say he was on some kind of upper. He was shaking and his eyes were red. Since his brother had all that coke in his suite, that would be my suspicion. Paranoia is a real side effect, especially if the person using is already under duress."

"So he took drugs to make himself feel better and it made him worse?" Lucy asked.

"That happens a lot," Michael replied. "I should know. Not the drugs, exactly. Self-loathing and anger were my drug of choice. Isolation. In a lot of ways, it's just as destructive. But I think it was more. He said something about his sister, didn't he? I don't remember exactly because I was mostly trying to be as quiet as I could be."

"Yes." Lucy's lips pursed. "He said his sister told him he had to do something about it. Why would she say that?"

"And when did she say it?" Ty asked. "Because Sonya was

sedated the night of the murder."

Lucy seemed to consider the problem. "I have a hard time seeing Kendall being so emotional."

"You don't know any of them well enough to let your guard down around them." The last thing he wanted was one of the Foster siblings getting Lucy's sympathy.

"Oh, I don't intend to be in a room with anyone named Foster ever again," Lucy vowed.

"I don't think that's going to be a problem." Ty pressed the button for the elevator. "I got a text from one of the managers I'm friends with about the fact that he's been in touch with the big boss and he's not happy. It's exactly how we thought Mr. Roberts would react. He's taking his employees' side. The Fosters aren't happy either. They're having all their stuff moved out of the villa and are preparing to sue."

Lucy had pulled out her phone, looking down at the screen. "Oh. I got a text from Mr. Roberts himself. He says he wants me to know I'll be safe if I take the job." She looked up, her eyes shining with unshed tears. "He says he'll make sure I have any representation I need. He's going to protect Van and me. He's not making us go through this alone."

Relief flooded Michael as the elevator dinged and opened. It was good to know Lucy was going to get her chance. This job was important to her, and he couldn't stand the thought that it would be over before she'd been able to show how good she would be at it. "I'm glad to know that. Another reason for you to listen to Gemma. If she says it's okay to answer a question, then it is."

They entered and the doors closed again. "I thought Nate could share the interview he did that night. How many times will I have to answer the same questions?"

"Hopefully only once more." Michael didn't want to tell her it could be a hundred times if the investigators decided to zero in on her. He intended to make sure that didn't happen. "I want to know more about where the Foster siblings were the day of the party."

"It was weird that they were there," Lucy admitted. "I didn't think that was the kind of party they would be interested in. They were the only villa guests who attended. In fact, there were several private parties going on at the other villas."

"I don't know how popular they are with the other guests." Ty wrapped an arm around her waist. "I suspect no one wanted Brock around."

Michael shook his head. "That's not the way that world works. Brock had power, and that means no one in his world would refuse him. How do you think he ended up being such a dick bag?"

"I agree with Michael," Lucy said. "Men like that go where they want. And the whole family has connections. It doesn't make sense they would come and hang with a bunch of locals and regular guests."

"Unless they wanted to make sure their plan was working," Ty said with a huff.

"How could they make sure by going to the party?" Lucy asked.

Michael had been thinking about this all morning. The Fosters had taken a table in the back and hadn't mingled with the other guests. He'd checked up on them because he'd wanted to make damn sure their older brother didn't join them. "If I was the killer, I would want to make sure no one else used that bottle of Scotch. The killer needed it in a place where he or she could reliably expect that it would make it up to Brock when he called for it. But I think whoever did this specifically wanted Lucy to be the one to take it. That's why he or she moved it from the main bar."

The doors opened directly into the Roberts' suite, and they could smell coffee and hear the hum of people talking.

Nate wore his full uniform and stood in the elegant entryway talking to a dark-haired man in a crisply pressed suit. Nate turned their way and nodded. "Ah, here she is. Agent Slate, this is Lucy Carson and her…"

Nate hesitated as if trying to figure out how to handle the out-of-towner.

"Boyfriends? Or are you husbands?" Slate's lips curved up. "I've been in Bliss before, Sheriff, though I worked with Rye Harper when he was in office. You're not going to shock me, though it was a fun conversation with my partner. She's new."

A woman with honey blonde hair stepped into the entryway. She was also in a suit, though hers was feminine. She looked to be in her late twenties and wore her hair in a stylish bob. "I'm learning a lot today. And, girl, good for you. They do threesomes right in this town.

Good morning. I'm Agent Joy Wallace. Thank you for coming in on such short notice."

"Well, it wasn't like we were going anywhere," Lucy said, shaking the woman's hand. "I'm surprised you made it in so quickly."

"Me, too. It was not what I planned on doing this weekend. We came in via helicopter. It was the single most frightening twenty minutes of my life," Agent Wallace said with a frown.

"It was safe," Agent Slate argued. "I wouldn't have let you on that chopper if it hadn't been. But it was very windy. I personally would have waited until Monday, but they're holding our feet to the fire with this one. Hence, we're grateful for you being willing to talk."

"Not without me, she won't." Gemma looked peppy this morning. She had a notebook in hand. "I've been doing some research with Nell, but I can take a break to make sure Lucy doesn't do anything that might make this tougher on her."

"I don't think she's going to need you." Slate led them into the big living space. "Though you're absolutely welcome to stay. You've got an interesting team set up here, Sheriff. I heard you have some mystery writer and her husband doing background work for you?"

Nate nodded, standing behind one of the big wingback chairs. "Yes, Nell and Henry Flanders. Don't underestimate how helpful they can be."

"Or annoying," Ty supplied helpfully. "If you don't do your job, they will protest you, and now they have a baby and she can cry forever."

Michael shot Ty a stare to let him know he was not amused.

Ty shrugged. "Well, she can. She has a real high pitch. Gets some dogs howling, too, and then everyone just wants to do whatever Nell asks. That baby is her secret weapon."

"Don't worry about Poppy. She's with Holly," Nate assured them. "Nell says she's found something interesting. They'll be by when they're ready. You know anything about it?"

That last question had been directed Gemma's way. "Not really. I know she was looking into the Foster Corporation and its many branches. It's huge and covers the whole damn globe. But I think what set her wheels in motion was what I found on some of the siblings' social media, so in a way I'm going to have solved this whole thing."

Nate snorted. "You are not getting a raise."

"Shoes don't buy themselves, Sheriff," Gemma pointed out.

Joy Wallace chuckled but turned Lucy's way. "We're going to talk to you here because the office is occupied right now. The deputy is in there. Don't think of this so much as a formal interview as a way to exchange some information."

"I still think this is a mistake," Nate said.

Slate shrugged. "I want to see how it goes."

"How what goes?" Lucy asked.

Michael went on full alert.

There was a tension to Nate's stance that made him think something was about to go down.

Lucy settled on the couch and Michael sat beside her, Ty taking the opposite side.

So she would know they were with her always, protecting her.

"I'd like to start with how you met Brock Foster." Agent Slate settled in.

But Michael noted that Agent Wallace didn't sit at all.

Before Lucy could say a thing, another voice was heard, this one coming from the hall.

"I can't thank you enough, Deputy," Sonya was saying as she walked into the space. Her attention was on Cam, and she dabbed a tissue at her eyes. "It seems like my whole family is falling apart. My father will be here soon."

"Daddy will take care of everything." Kendall followed behind them. She was dressed to the nines for her police interview, wearing a skin-tight dress, sky-high heels, and sunglasses even though they were inside. "And honestly, it's better this way. Now that Brock's dead, Sonya gets his job, and she's way nicer. My brother was an asshole. I don't hate that chick for...oh, hey, girl! How are you?"

Kendall smiled brightly Lucy's way.

Sonya's face went a pasty white.

"Sorry Chet got all crazy," Kendall said, her phone in hand. "I think it's the weather or something."

"What is she doing here?" Sonya's eyes narrowed as she stared at Lucy.

Slate sat back, his attention going to Sonya and Kendall. "Ms. Carson is here for our initial interview. Like you were."

An elegant brow arched over Sonya's eyes. "I was here to help you find out who killed my brother. She's here because she's the one who killed my brother. It's not hard. I understand that my brother was awful, but he didn't deserve to die."

Ty huffed and moved closer to Lucy.

Lucy had stiffened beside him. "I did…"

Michael put a hand on her thigh, and Lucy stopped, her eyes going wide.

He leaned in so he could whisper her way. "They want to see how she reacts. Maybe how you react, so don't say anything at all. Let her do the talking."

And likely the accusing. Sometimes a person could get tripped up this way.

"Ms. Foster, let me show you to the elevator," Cam began.

Sonya turned to Agent Slate. "I understand that she's got a relationship with the local sheriff, and he's not very good at his job. But I thought things would change when you got here. Is there a reason you haven't arrested her yet?"

"Absolutely," Slate replied. "I just got here, and I don't typically arrest people before I've even talked to them."

"Do you arrest them when they're caught standing over a dead body, the murder weapon in hand?" Sonya countered.

"She was caught standing over the body because she called for help." Nate stood back, but he was watching the Fosters.

"Yeah, that's weird." Kendall was typing on her phone as she spoke. "She probably shouldn't have…" Kendall looked up. "Why would you call in your own murder?"

"She's covering, Ken," Sonya said. "Of course she called for help. She had to cover her tracks. People would ask questions if she didn't try."

"Or she could walk away and let us find him," Kendall continued. "Like who would know? I mean you would have because you had to talk to him."

"She had to talk to him about what?" Slate asked.

Kendall shrugged. "No idea. I was trying to get the red wine out of my jumpsuit that she spilled on me. And then she suddenly needed to talk to Brock when she hates Brock."

"Kendall," Sonya hissed.

"Well, we all do," Kendall insisted. "Which is why I don't understand why Chet went crazy. Chet hated Brock more than the rest of us."

"We're leaving now." Sonya started for the elevator.

Slate stood. "I think I'd like to talk to you, Ms. Foster. Both of you, actually. I'd like to interview you separately."

Michael bet he did. Kendall obviously had no freaking idea what she should or shouldn't say. She was an investigator's dream.

"I don't think that's a good idea." Sonya settled her bag over her shoulder. "I'm going to call my father. I don't think you're the right investigators for this case."

"Sheriff," a feminine voice called out.

All heads turned as Nell strode into the room. There was an unmistakable air of excitement about her. Henry followed behind her, though at a more sedate pace.

"I thought you were going to call," Nate said. "And how did you get here? I turned the code back on after Lucy and her men came up."

Henry lingered near the hallway. "I don't need a code, Sheriff. One of the fun things about having my past out in the open is I don't have to pretend anymore. I can use all my skills out in the open. As to why we didn't call, Nell wanted to tell you in person."

"We'll leave you to it then." Sonya gestured to her sister. "Let's go. We need to call Dad."

Nell gasped. "Are you Sonya Foster?"

The blonde's head came up, a superior expression on her face. "Yes, I am. And I've been through too much to have to deal with a second more of this town's nonsense."

Nell pointed at Sonya. *"J'accuse, mademoiselle. J'accuse."*

Michael stood. Nell knew something, and he trusted her. This was the moment when things could get dangerous. He moved in front of Lucy and Ty, placing his body in the line of fire just in case. Ty stood beside him. His first instinct was to tell Ty to sit back down, but Ty would want to be with him, both of them protecting Lucy.

"What is this about?" Sonya asked. "And who the hell is this woman?"

"My name is Nell Flanders, and I protest you and all your earth-killing businesses," Nell announced.

Behind him he felt Lucy stand. She went on her toes, her hands against his back for balance. She was trying to watch the shitshow that was absolutely about to go down.

Michael glanced over at Henry, who was relaxed and watching his wife with a lazy indulgence.

He trusted Henry's instincts and relaxed a bit.

"I am not about to stand here and listen to the ravings of a lunatic," Sonya began.

"I will," Slate said.

"I will, too," Agent Wallace agreed. "What have you discovered, Mrs. Flanders?"

Nell paced like she was the detective in an Agatha Christie novel. "The question is how did the killer get the poison in the first place. Lucy rarely leaves Bliss, and she doesn't have a lot of contact with anyone who would know about poison. The Foster Corporation is known primarily for sporting goods, but that's not really true, is it?"

"We have lots of companies." Kendall looked around like she'd finally figured out something was happening. "I'm going to be a buyer for our new fashion line. We're calling it Kendall 4Eva. Get it? Because that's my name. My first name is Kendall and my middle name is Eva."

Nell ignored her entirely. "But when you look deeper at the corporate infrastructure, you find out a lot of the money is made in minerals and gas and oil."

"I don't see what our corporate infrastructure has to do with the fact that a waitress killed my brother," Sonya insisted. "Has anybody even checked her room? She has to have kept the poison somewhere. We've all been stuck in this building. She couldn't have taken it too far to dump it."

Oh, she'd planned this carefully. How long had she had that poison? She traveled in private jets. It would have been fairly easy to transport. Security was different on private airlines, and if she'd stored it as a powder, she wouldn't even have been questioned if she'd hidden it properly. She could have disguised it as a beauty product, and no one would call her out on it.

"Lucy turned over a bag of a white substance she found in the bathroom of the room she's staying in," Nate admitted. "It's waiting to be tested."

Lucy's arm wrapped around Michael's waist, and he could feel her tension.

"See." Sonya pointed toward Lucy. "You should arrest her."

"But why would she turn it in if she did it?" Even Kendall seemed to see the problem. "That doesn't make sense. She's not a very good murderer."

Nate kept his eyes firmly on Sonya. "We also talked to one of the maids who admitted putting it there. Now, she got the baggie from a man who paid her two hundred cash to stash it. She was a might bit miffed that Ty didn't call her after they…well, did what Ty does."

"Used to do," Ty argued. "I only sleep with one person now. Well, one person and Mike."

They were going to have to work on how to talk about their relationship in public. "Still a person, Ty. But we understand. You're a changed man and this Ashley isn't happy about the change. It was smart to put a couple of layers between the person who wanted that poison in your room and the one who actually put it there. That took planning."

"It won't matter," Nate acknowledged. "Ashley claims she doesn't remember the man's name, but I can find him. I wonder who would have paid for that extra service."

Kendall took off her glasses. "Holy shit. You think it was us? Huh. It wasn't me. I don't have cash. I lost a thousand dollars in a Starbucks and Daddy said I can't have cash anymore."

"Oh, it certainly wasn't you." Nell continued to pace. "You aren't the one who recently spent time in Johannesburg."

Kendall's nose wrinkled in obvious distaste. "Eww. Why would I go there?" She frowned. "Where is that?"

A low huff came from Sonya, but she ignored her sister instead, turning toward Nell. "No. I did. I was there on business. I go to a lot of places. What does that have to do with it? And I don't like being accused of this."

"I'm sure you don't. You've been very careful," Nell said. "I suspect you've had this plan in mind for two years."

"Why two years?" He was interested in watching Nell work. He had to wonder if Nate was allowing her to control the conversation out of sheer amusement. He was giving the novelist her Sherlock Holmes moment.

"Because the new will of one Bob Foster was filed then," Nell announced with a nod of her head. "Now, that will is not in the public record, but Gemma found some old social media posts from Brock Foster. He says shortly after the will was filed that he just became a king."

"I can get the will," Slate promised.

Kendall made a vomiting sound. "He's such a prick. He thinks he's a king because Daddy was putting him in charge of every…"

"Kendall," Sonya barked.

Kendall stopped and stared for a moment. "But that's what happened. It's okay to talk about because we didn't do this." Her lips pursed and then there was a sheen of tears to her eyes. "You didn't do this. You can't have done this. He was our brother."

"Of course I didn't," Sonya insisted.

"You were the one who went to Harvard." Nell's tone had gone sympathetic. "You got the grades. You did the work. But your father thought a man should be at the head of the table. I'll be honest, I am against murder, but I am also against misogyny."

"Nell, focus, please," Michael warned. He'd spent enough time with Nell to know exactly where this could go. He wasn't going to listen to an hour-long lecture on the history of women in business. "You were telling us why you *j'accused* her. That was a nice touch. Very international."

Nell frowned but continued. "Like I was saying, two years ago Sonya Foster realized that everything she'd worked for was going to be handed to her brother. That was when she started trying to find a way out. Agents, did you know that Brock Foster has been involved in two strange accidents in the last eighteen months?"

"That is interesting," Agent Wallace allowed. "What happened?"

"He was taken to the hospital when the horse he was riding bolted and nearly killed him," Nell explained.

"That was stupid hunters," Kendall argued. "He said it himself. Someone was shooting and his favorite horse was known for being jumpy. It was an accident."

"And then he was also nearly killed when the brakes in his brand-new vehicle went out," Nell continued.

"The dealership admitted they didn't do a proper check on the car." Sonya's voice had gone toneless. "None of this explains how someone got poison into his drink. The only one who could is Lucy or the bartender."

"Not at all." Nell seemed to relish her role. "On the night of the party your brother gave in the family villa, you helped him move into the suite after he and Chet fought. We've got security camera footage of you walking him to the suites. You were the one to convince him to move, not Chet."

"Chet had already passed out," Sonya replied. "I would have to have carried him."

Nell continued on. "You were also the one who ordered one of the maids to take the Scotch to the main bar. The next morning you went to the main bar and slipped the bartender a hundred. We have that on security camera, too. Unfortunately the bartender went off shift early in order to get down the mountain before the storm hit, and we haven't been able to get in touch with him. He was the one who gave the order to move the Scotch."

"We'll contact him," Nate advised. "It's only a matter of time."

Sonya's head shook. "Of course I asked him to move it. I was hoping that Brock would join us at the party. I tipped him well because I didn't want him to forget. I was trying to force my brothers to make up before we went home. My father doesn't like it when they fight, and he always takes Brock's side. I was watching out for Chet. That's all."

"Maybe that's why you did it," Lucy said, her voice going soft. "You couldn't make your dad see who the real Brock was, and you had to protect your siblings. I know how that feels. I understand. I would have done almost anything to save mine."

Sonya's jaw went tight. "All of this is ridiculous. Where would I get cyanide?"

"Who said anything about cyanide?" Michael was sure Nate wouldn't have said a word to Sonya Foster until he'd gotten the toxicology report back.

The room seemed to go still, and for a moment Sonya didn't move a muscle. Then she seemed to decide on how to handle her flub. "I'm not stupid. Like you said, I'm Harvard educated. What other poison works as quickly? I read, you know. I'm afraid the fact

295

that I'm educated doesn't make me a killer."

"No, but access might," Nell continued. "What work were you doing in Johannesburg?"

Sonya ran a hand over her hair. "I was visiting one of our companies. I take a hands-on approach. Unlike some executives, I want to know how things work."

"And what company were you visiting?" Nell asked quietly.

Sonya stopped, seeming to realize she was caught in a trap.

Kendall frowned her sister's way. "Was it the gold mine one? I don't remember the name, but you went down into that mine and they taught you how they get the gold and then you talked about it incessantly."

Sonya's eyes closed. "You are such a moron, Ken." She opened them, a grim resignation coming over her face. "I'd like to speak with my lawyer before this goes any further."

Slate stood, his hands on his hips. "Ms. Flanders, I'm afraid you're going to have to illuminate me on why the fact that she was in a gold mine makes Ms. Foster our prime suspect."

"Cyanide is how they separate the gold from the rock around it." Nell took a deep breath as though she'd found the entire experience satisfying. "And the precise chemical mixture can likely be traced right back to South Africa. I don't believe Lucy has been out of the state lately, much less to South Africa."

"Ms. Foster, I believe we're going to have to talk further," Agent Wallace said. "You should call your lawyer, and we're going to need for you to not leave the resort for the moment."

"I'd like to see you try to stop me." There was no mistaking the righteous anger in Sonya's eyes.

"Is this why you told Chet he should hurt the waitress chick?" Kendall had started crying.

"Shut up, Kendall," Sonya growled.

"Did you give him the gun?" Kendall wasn't listening. "Because I couldn't figure out how he got that gun. He doesn't know how to use a gun. Were you going to use me, too?"

"I have done everything I've done to protect you. I did it all for you and Chet," Sonya practically roared. She shook her head and grabbed her sister's hand before pointing Agent Slate's way. "This is not over."

But it felt like it was. She stormed out, dragging Kendall with her.

"And that is why you shouldn't talk to the cops without a lawyer around," Gemma said triumphantly. "Like I kind of wish we'd recorded that whole thing so I could use it as a teaching point."

"Who said we didn't?" Henry asked with a predatory grin. He pointed to the chandelier hanging in the middle of the room. "I wired it myself. Colorado is a one-party consent state, and Nell consented. We can use that in court."

"I don't think we'll have to." Agent Slate shook his head as though trying to process what had happened. "I think forensics and eyewitness testimony are going to be key here. She had means, motive, and opportunity. Once we talk to the bartender, we'll be able to arrest her."

Lucy wiggled her way in between him and Ty. "Does this mean I shouldn't be worried about going to jail for a crime I didn't commit?"

Agent Wallace flashed her a smile. "I think we'll be turning our attention another way. But you should know the attorney she hires will use you as possible reasonable doubt."

Michael let his hand wrap around Lucy's, giving her a squeeze. "Don't worry about that. We'll handle it if it comes up. There's nothing we can't get through."

"As long as we're together," Lucy replied with a squeeze of her own.

"I just wish she'd confessed fully and we'd gotten a *I would have gotten away with it if not for those meddling kids* from her," Cam mused. "I'm going to go to security and make sure we've always got eyes on her. She's not going to be able to slip away."

"And I'm going to take this lady detective back to our room because we've got a good hour before we pick up Poppy." Henry strode over to his wife and lifted her against his chest. He smiled down at her. "Did you have fun, love?"

There was that dreamy look Nell got when she stared at her husband. "It was magnificent, Henry. Maybe we should start a detective agency."

Nate groaned. "Please, no."

"I think we should stick to our books. But we can certainly play." Henry started for the elevator. "This time, though, I'll be the one

297

interrogating you, naughty girl."

"Such a weird fucking place." Agent Slate sighed. "We're going to go and update our office."

It was time to take his little family home, too. "We'll be at our place if you need us."

Ty frowned at Nate. "Try not to need us."

Michael noted that Ty had taken Lucy's other hand. They were all connected. As they should be.

When he glanced down, Lucy was looking up at him. Ty was, too. They were both staring at him like he was the sun in the sky, the one they could count on.

The one they would love the rest of their lives.

He would never let them down.

Epilogue

Lucy looked around the festival grounds with a deep sense of satisfaction. Winter Festival officially opened this evening with a message from the mayor and a couple of local bands playing, but there were already tons of people milling around, sampling the treats offered and admiring the work of the artisans who had taken booths.

"Hey, you." River walked up, Buster at her side. "I've barely seen you this week. Is the rumor true?"

Lucy fell in step beside her bestie. "Which rumor? I'm sure there are several. Is it the one about me no longer being even a person of interest in the Brock Foster case? Because that is true. They finally arrested Sonya Foster. I've heard she's trying to negotiate a plea deal because her father cut her off and now Chet and Kendall are taking over the business. Well, after Chet finishes his rehab and probation."

"So I should sell my stock," River said with a nod. Not that River had stock, but it was probably something a smart investor would do.

Lucy actually felt some sympathy for Sonya. She did understand what it meant to love her siblings. Luckily hers were doing great, and they adored their new almost brothers-in-law. Ty and Michael had taken to accompanying her to visit her family, and her sisters thought they were the best. They even managed to not punch her dad.

But what she loved was how Ty's parents had embraced Michael. They hadn't batted an eye when the three of them had shown up for Sunday dinner, welcoming them warmly and becoming the support they all needed.

"But that's not the rumor," River continued.

"Okay, is it the one about me taking management courses?" There had been so many positive changes in the last six weeks. "I talked to Mr. Roberts and the lodge is helping with tuition costs and working with my schedule. He wants to be able to promote from within. Right now I'm the head of entertainment and food service, but the head of all service is planning to retire in five years. I want to be ready to take over."

"I'm thrilled to hear that." River waved at Jax, who was manning the Mountain Adventures booth along with a familiar face.

Ty looked adorable wrapped in his coat, a cap on his head. He winked her way before turning back to the pair of women he'd been talking to.

They were giggling like schoolgirls over the two big, gorgeous men.

"If only they knew what a goofball he is, they would run," River said with a shake of her head.

She never felt any jealousy when it came to her men. It was funny because she'd been so jealous of Ty before, but now she knew he was with her. Michael had brought them all together in his odd way, and there was no chance either of her men betrayed the love they'd found. "Is it weird that I'm okay with making a bunch of money off women who objectify our men?"

River grinned. "Girl, I am more than happy to do it. I told Jax when summer comes we're getting him shorts that show off his legs. We need to upgrade the cabin. I want to add on at least one more room."

"You're adding on?" Something brushed by her side.

"Sorry!" A girl in a pink coat ran through the snow, her brown braids bouncing as she laughed and raced toward Stella's booth.

"Paige!" Max came jogging up behind his oldest. He gave Lucy an apologetic wave. "Sorry. She's excited about hot chocolate."

"Me, too," Lucy proclaimed. And then she realized why River might add on to her cabin. She stopped and turned to her friend. "Are

300

you?"

River flushed and shook her head. "No. I'm not pregnant." A smile crossed her face. "Not yet, but we're going to try. He's going to be the best dad."

And River would be an amazing mom.

But the fact that she wasn't pregnant and they were close to the Trio booth gave Lucy an idea. "Come on. I'm in the mood for hot chocolate, too, but the adult kind. Now let me guess which rumor again. It's weird that there are so many."

River followed her, waving to friends as they passed. "This place runs on rumors, but they're not really bad rumors. It's just people talking about the other people they care about. We're one big old family, and that means everyone is in everyone else's business. So guess the next rumor."

"Well, Michael drove to Durango last night to meet with his new boss. He starts Monday, and I'm a little nervous." It was the first time they'd been apart. When Michael had gone to Florida to clean up all his affairs, they'd gone with him. The three of them had met with Jessie's parents, and she believed it had been a genuinely healing time for all involved. He still talked to Jessie's family every few weeks.

"He talked to me about this new job of his," River said as they approached the little bar Trio had set up. Van was in the booth that had three stools in front of it and five stand-up tables. He was talking to a woman who nodded his way and picked up her mug before walking away.

Van stared, completely ignoring the dude who was trying to order. He was staring at the woman like he'd seen something amazing.

Well, someone had caught his eye.

"I'm excited to give him some backup," River was saying. "When it gets warm again, Ty and I are going to test some of your man's skills. It's going to be fun. I'm all for being the hunter instead of the hunted. And that is not the rumor. I will put you out of your misery. Did you really buy the cabin across from Callie's?"

She gasped. "Michael said he had a surprise for me when he got back."

River winced. "Pretend I didn't say anything."

"I promise to be so surprised." They moved in as Van finally shook his head and poured out a couple of beers. "I'm not sure how Michael thought he would be able to keep that under wraps. Marie is the realtor, and she's bad at keeping a secret. Oh, River, I'm so excited. I can't believe I'm here. I'm in Bliss and I'm in love and I'm…I'm just good, you know."

River wrapped her arms around her. "You were always good, but now you're home. I'm home, and it's so good."

She squeezed her bestie and turned to Van. "We need champagne. I thought I wanted hot chocolate with Bailey's, but we're celebrating."

"What are we celebrating?" a deep voice asked.

She turned and Michael was walking up.

Lucy ran to join him, throwing herself into his arms. "I thought you wouldn't be back until tomorrow."

He hugged her close, and the world felt infinitely warmer. "My meetings ended early. I thought I would come out and lend a hand."

He'd wanted to be home.

"I'm so glad." She kissed him and her feet found the ground again.

"You're back!" Ty ran across the festival ground and then her men were hugging in that back pounding masculine way.

River passed her a glass as the men started talking about Michael's trip. "Hey, I talked to Van. I asked about that woman he was so obviously into, and I have gossip. Such good gossip."

Lucy took the champagne. "What?"

"She's staying at the Movie Motel," River said, her own glass in hand. "She introduced herself as a lieutenant, so she must be military, and she asked about finding someone."

"Who?"

"She's looking for her father," River explained.

"Huh." She didn't know anyone in town who had a kid she hadn't met. Or at least heard about. The woman had looked to be in her late twenties. Maybe early thirties. "Does she not know her dad's address?"

"Apparently this is a first meeting, daddy-doesn't-know kind of thing. And yes, she went to his place, but he wasn't home. There was a note on the door she didn't understand. Something about taking to a bunker," River said, her eyes wide.

Holy shit. "She's looking for Mel?"

River nodded. "Mel has a daughter he doesn't know about and she's military, and I'm super excited about what happens next. It's so freaking good to be back in Bliss."

Lucy held up her glass. "It is."

After all, there was no place like home.

Mel gets a big surprise when the whole Bliss crew returns in *Unexpected Bliss*, coming in 2022.

Author's Note

I'm often asked by generous readers how they can help get the word out about a book they enjoyed. There are so many ways to help an author you like. Leave a review. If your e-reader allows you to lend a book to a friend, please share it. Go to Goodreads and connect with others. Recommend the books you love because stories are meant to be shared. Thank you so much for reading this book and for supporting all the authors you love!

The Man from Sanctum
Masters and Mercenaries: Reloaded, Book 3
By Lexi Blake
Coming March 8, 2022

A painful past

Deke Murphy and Maddie Hall should never have worked as a couple in high school. She was the class valedictorian and he the jock who took nothing seriously…except her. Together they formed an amazing team, and young love blossomed into something that strengthened them both. Until tragedy struck and Deke made a sacrifice that split them up forever.

An unexpected reunion

Seventeen years later, Maddie is living her dream working for a brilliant tech guru in the beauty of Southern California. She's made a life for herself and it's first class all the way. She rarely thinks of the jock who dumped her all those years ago. But when Maddie realizes her boss might be part of an international conspiracy, she can't deny Deke might be her best bet to solve the mystery. Her one-time sweetheart works for one of the world's premiere security and investigative firms. She'll hire him and prove to herself their relationship could never have worked.

A dangerous future

As Maddie and Deke begin to uncover her boss's secrets, they can't deny the chemistry that has reignited. But before they can explore the connection growing between them, they must survive the deadly forces hunting them down.

About Lexi Blake

New York Times bestselling author Lexi Blake lives in North Texas with her husband and three kids. Since starting her publishing journey in 2010, she's sold over three million copies of her books. She began writing at a young age, concentrating on plays and journalism. It wasn't until she started writing romance that she found success. She likes to find humor in the strangest places and believes in happy endings.

Connect with Lexi online:

Facebook: Lexi Blake
Twitter: authorlexiblake
Website: www.LexiBlake.net
Instagram: www.instagram.com

Sign up for Lexi's free newsletter!

Made in the USA
Coppell, TX
15 February 2022

73622838R00184